D0909378

Laramie: Journey to the White Clouds

Laramie: Journey to the White Clouds

Wallace J. Swenson

FIVE STAR
A part of Gale, Cengage Learning

GALE
CENGAGE Learning

Farmington Hills, Mich • San Francisco • New York • Waterville, Maine
Meriden, Conn • Mason, Ohio • Chicago

LIBRARY OF CONGRESS CATALOGING-IN-PUBLICATION DATA

Names: Swenson, Wallace J. author.
Title: Laramie : journey to the white clouds / Wallace J. Swenson.
Description: First edition. | Waterville, Maine : Five Star, 2016.
Identifiers: LCCN 2016024394 | ISBN 9781432832537 (hardcover) | ISBN 1432832530 (hardcover) ISBN 9781432832483 (ebook) | ISBN 1432832484 (ebook) | ISBN 9781432833442 (ebook) | ISBN 1432833448 (ebook)
Subjects: LCSH: Frontier and pioneer life—Nebraska—Fiction. | GSAFD: Western stories.
Classification: LCC PS3619.W4557 L37 2016 | DDC 813/.6—dc23
LC record available at https://lccn.loc.gov/2016024394

First Edition. First Printing: December 2016
Find us on Facebook– https://www.facebook.com/FiveStarCengage
Visit our website– http://www.gale.cengage.com/fivestar/
Contact Five Star™ Publishing at FiveStar@cengage.com

Printed in the United States of America
1 2 3 4 5 6 7 20 19 18 17 16

To fellow travelers who know the journey can never end,
until it does.

ACKNOWLEDGMENTS

A wholehearted thanks to Tiffany Schofield at Five Star who took another chance on a new writer. Thanks also to Rod Miller and J. D. Boggs who encouraged me to submit my work to Tiffany, and to Alice Duncan who edited the work, liked what she saw, and said so. I am grateful for the group of people I write with: men and women of the West, writers of all stripes, and readers who've told me what they want to see in a book. I thank God for my gift and His continued support. I am humbly grateful.

Chapter 1

Resolute, Simon Steele focused his attention on the western horizon, still purple-black in the early morning. Since ghosting out of Carlisle with Buell Mace, his best friend, the ties that bound him to the small Nebraska prairie town pulled harder and harder. With each step his horse took, the nagging urge to look back grew stronger, until, lowering his head in resignation, he reined his mount around and stopped. Buell did the same, and then they stood, side by side, looking at the town that had rejected them, Simon for thievery, and Buell for . . . well, Buell for being Buell.

A light flickered in the newspaper office, dark when they had ridden past it fifteen minutes before. Several slender columns of chimney smoke rose vertically in the dead calm air as kitchen stoves were lit for breakfast. The eastern horizon glowed yellow-orange as rays of light, like tethers tugging the sun out of bed, reached into the morning sky.

"How'd yer folks take it?" Buell asked.

"Ma got pretty upset last night. Pa still can't see the sense in our leaving, but he's willing to let me try. How about you?"

"Pa surprised me. I felt like he'd expected this. Found out he came to Carlisle at nineteen, same age as us. He jist asked that I keep in touch."

They sat and watched as the town slowly woke up.

"Gonna miss it?"

"Huh?" Simon answered, startled.

"Are ya gonna miss it?"

"Some of it. My family, John, Fred Luger and Jake, your pa."

The question was already floating around in Simon's mind when Buell asked. He'd been falsely accused of stealing from Swartz's Mercantile where he'd worked. Sheriff Staker had no choice but to go with the evidence that showed Simon did it. The sheriff suspected what Swartz knew: the truth; but nothing could hold the tongues of the jealous and the mean-spirited. For them, Simon had been proven a thief and was treated as such.

And Sarah, his Sarah from childhood, suddenly rejected him, no reason given to him or anyone else. Yeah, he'd miss some of them, but all the things he'd been taught, like honesty, tenacity, faith, and loyalty, had let him down. He no longer knew what to believe. He had to find something he could live with or by. And that something wasn't in Carlisle.

"I'll miss Pa and Jake but that's about it," Buell said. He surveyed the scene, from the Platte River north of town, to the South Road, still hidden in shadow but familiar in his mind. Just to the west of where he now sat, that road swung north and joined this one, the Kendrick Road, the one he'd been on only days ago.

There, he'd waited in the moonlight for a talk with David Steele, Simon's cousin. Buell had wanted to talk, to warn him of the consequences if he continued to abuse people, especially the people Buell cared for. But the talk turned to violence, and Buell shot David, right through his mocking mouth, his face untouched, killing his brain even as it remembered Sarah's rape. The sheriff ruled it an execution by a bushwhacking back shooter, and with David's money belt gone, robbery seemed the motive.

With David's death, Buell remained the only person besides Sarah who knew the horrible truth of her rape and the shame she claimed for herself. Shame so great she denied the one thing that could make her happy: Simon.

Simon picked up the slack in his reins. "Ready?"

"Guess so."

"One last thing. Don't mention her name. Ever." Simon touched his reins to the horse's neck and turned toward the west. He hoped Buell couldn't see his face in the early-morning light. The low bushes shimmered, and Simon turned his head as tears coursed down his cheeks.

A few minutes later Buell stopped in the road. "Hold up for a minute. I gotta run over there." He nodded his head toward the river, half a mile away.

"Okay. Nature?"

"Somethin' like that." Buell turned and urged his horse toward the distant trees.

Simon watched him ride away, a little puzzled by the distance he went. He freed a foot from a stirrup, moved his rump off center in the saddle and relaxed.

The sun cracked the horizon as he watched. The blood-orange slice of solar fire flashed into view and grew thicker by the second. Soon a quarter, then a half and finally, sitting huge on the river bluffs, sat the mother of the universe in all her glory. The crispness in the morning air rapidly lost the lopsided battle with the sun, and its warmth crept through his coat. Buell appeared, centered in the flaming disk. As he loped toward Simon, the dazzling light jerked him around as though a crazed puppeteer held him on strings.

"Get 'er dropped off?" Simon squinted as Buell rode clear of the bright light.

"Shithead," Buell said, a grin breaking across his swarthy face.

"Took ya long enough, and you sure got private all of a sudden."

"Picked up a bonus." Buell reached into his coat pocket and pulled out something flat and square. He handed it to Simon. "This is yours."

Simon looked at a folded stack of bills, then at Buell. "What's this?" He unfolded the money and counted it. "There's two hundred twenty-five dollars here." The source of the money dawned on him. "Buell, what in hell have you done?"

"Ol' Swartz cheated ya outta that. You know it, I know it, and so does he. I expect in 'bout an hour he'll find out he didn't get away with it." He offered Simon an impish grin.

"But this isn't right. You stole it from him. Damn, Buell." Opposing sets of ethics, one old, and one just being learned, crafted the confusion Simon felt.

"And he stole it from you."

"Yeah, but two wrongs don't make a right." Simon stared at the sheaf of money.

"Does this time. You was always right, and I just got it back for ya. He's still wrong for cheatin' ya, only now it's a little more even. One right, one wrong, and another might-be wrong, dependin' on who ya ask."

Is this what Avery Singer called ad hoc justice? Simon recalled the crooked town banker. It's my money. And I didn't steal it—it came to me by proxy.

"But it was stolen," his conscience shouted.

"It's stupid to look a gift horse in the mouth," he argued with himself, shaking his head sharply. "It's mine, legally. It's simply been reappropriated."

"No, it was stolen. Please, reconsider," Conscience said, weaker now.

"Swartz will know how it feels. Serves him right."

"Please," the voice said, now barely audible.

Simon smiled. "Damn right. Let's get going." He leaned forward and his horse responded, moving ahead at a fast walk.

Buell felt the weight of David Steele's money belt around his middle and chuckled. He clicked to his horse and caught up.

A couple of hours later they spotted the small town of Kendrick, about a mile away. "Might be a good idea if we rode a little wide of the town," Buell said, and angled his horse south.

"What you got to worry about in Kendrick?"

"I expect by now Swartz will have told Sheriff Staker somebody robbed the store. And knowin' Staker, he's gonna put two and two together and ask the law in Kendrick to keep an eye out fer us."

"Now you know why I got a little upset about you taking it. We haven't been gone a day, and we're already dodging like a couple of criminals." Simon scowled at Buell.

"How long's it gonna take you to learn that if you lie down, you're gonna get stepped on? You want to go back and let 'em give ya another dose of fairness and honesty? I don't!"

"I'll give you that point, but I still wish we could've just ridden out, never mind the gettin' even."

"You amaze me, Simon. What did turnin' the other cheek get ya? Slapped again, that's what." Buell puffed out a cheek full of air and kicked his horse forward.

The morning disagreement simmered throughout the day as they skirted two more small settlements. Three other riders had appeared near the last one, but had been some distance away. Simon watched the landscape now with an eye for a campsite since they'd decided not to stay in a town even if one was convenient. Riding closer to the river, it wasn't long before Simon spied a good stand of trees. "What say we stop for the day? My butt's about to join my shoulders."

Buell shrugged. "Suits me."

They turned their horses toward the trees.

The reason for the trees became apparent when they rode into them; a seep fed the tiny stream that ran off to the river. They weren't the first to take advantage of the spot. A clutter of cans, their tops peeled back like rusty petals, surrounded a well-established rock fire ring. Abundant grass allowed Simon and Buell to unsaddle the horses and turn them loose with nothing but rope hobbles to keep them close.

"Guess we better sort out right now who's gonna do the cookin'," Buell said. "And it probably better not be me."

"And why not?" Simon hadn't thought about it.

"Cuz you'll starve. I can't cook a thing. Pa always did it at home, and I wasn't much fer watchin' Randall when we was herdin' with the Texans. I'd be hopeless." Buell smiled, obviously pleased with the way he'd stated his case.

"So I get done for being the one who paid attention?" Simon felt a little irritated.

"Looks that way. Sorry. I'd do it, you know I would, but I just don't know how." He looked almost contrite. "I'll do what I can." Buell shrugged, then offered a cheeky grin.

"Can you make coffee?"

Buell hesitated. "Yeah."

"Then this is how we'll do it. I cook, but you have to make the coffee first thing in the morning."

"But, that means I have to—"

"And . . . you get the wood and make the fire. That about evens things up." Simon smiled at Buell's confusion.

"But. You . . . I . . . shit!" Buell shook his head and stormed off into the trees.

Simon's mother had packed his saddlebags tight with supplies, and she knew how to conserve space. The cornmeal had been salted with a little soda mixed in. All he had to do was pour in the water and stir it up. She'd sliced the bacon and cut off the rind. The ground coffee and sugar rode in the pan used to brew the drink, and the skillet had almost no sides. Simon was sitting on a chunk of deadfall wood, forming corn cakes, when Buell struggled into camp dragging a fifteen-foot maple tree branch.

"They've burnt up everything for half a mile," he groused, "and I shoulda worn m' damn gloves." He inspected the several bloody spots on his hands. Unbuttoning his shirtsleeve, he further inspected a fiery-looking scratch that ran up his arm. "So what we havin'? I'm hungry."

Simon looked up from his work. "Nothin' till you get a fire going. Then fritters, bacon and coffee."

Buell licked at one of the larger bloody spots on his hand, wiped it on his pants leg and kicked the maple branch.

Simon stood. "C'mon, you big boob. I'll help you bust that up."

The meal hit the spot, a whole lot better than either had expected. Simon had cooked the corn cakes in the quarter inch of grease formed when he crisped the bacon. The pot made nearly two quarts of coffee and they'd drank most of it. They had enough cakes left over to make getting breakfast an easy chore.

Buell took out his tobacco and papers and rolled a smoke. "That was real good, Simon. I think maybe I got the best of the deal." He poked a twig into the fire and then lit his smoke.

"You'll talk different in the morning. I'm not getting up till you have the fire going." Simon put the paper-wrapped bacon in the skillet and stuffed it into an oilskin bag. He pointed at the pan by the fire pit. "You want to save that coffee for morning, or do you want to make fresh?"

Buell shrugged. "I suppose if I'm gonna make a fire, I can make coffee too."

"We can have a cold breakfast. Up to you. You're the man in charge of the fire." Simon chuckled.

Buell flicked the charred twig at him. "So, where we headed?"

"I've dreamed of seeing the Rocky Mountains. Ever since Miss Everett read to us about them in school, I've wanted to go there. Just where exactly, I don't know."

Buell took a drag on his smoke. "You mentioned Fort Laramie once. What d'ya know about there?"

"When Ma sold chickens to the trail folks, I heard them talk about Fort Laramie. She said folks stopped there just like in Carlisle, the last place to adjust wagonloads and buy stuff for the trip over the mountains. Sounds big enough to support a couple guys looking for work."

"Got any idea how far it is?"

"About three hundred miles. But it's not rough or steep. Mostly like it is here, so I'm told. That being the case, it'll take us about two weeks to get there." Simon reached over his saddle, dragged his saddlebag around to the front, and opened one side. "I got a map." He pulled out a folded piece of paper and flattened it out. "Next fair size town is Platte City. I figure to stop there and get some more corn meal. Maybe buy a few cans of fruit and vegetables. Eating just corn meal and bacon is gonna stay with ya, if you know what I mean."

"That's only about fifty miles from Carlisle. I think we still wanna be careful. I don't expect we'd get rousted, but ain't no sense takin' a chance. One of us can go in."

"Still hate to think we're hiding. But that two hundred dollars does come in handy. I only had eighty-seven saved up. Wished I felt better about it." Simon's conscience stirred again. "How much have you got?"

"More than that. I kinda run onto a little bonus." Buell poked at the fire.

"How much more?" Buell always seemed to have money, but other than helping his father run the livery stable and feed supply store, he'd never worked at a paying job. Simon had always found that curious.

"Plenty." Buell didn't look up.

Simon knew from countless past conversations that Buell had said all he intended to say. He put the map away and got up to drop another chunk of the hard-won wood on the fire.

Darkness still claimed the sky when Simon awoke the next morning. Lying flat on his back, he wondered if he had moved the entire night. Shifting to his side, he got his answer; he felt stiff as a fence post. Groaning, he rolled over and could just barely make out Buell's sleeping shape about ten feet away. Rolling back, he pulled an arm from under the cover and laid his hand on cold dewy ground. His mind drifted to Sarah, his efforts to push her back as futile as punching at smoke. Her face lingered at the edges of his consciousness as he drifted back to sleep.

All his brothers and sister sat around the table, Axel and Abe squabbling over table territory as they did every morning. The door to the sod house opened, and Simon hunched his shoulders, hugging his chest against the blast of cold air coming through the door. His father, Paul, walked in carrying a milk bucket that he set on a counter by the stove. Ana, his mother, scooped oatmeal porridge into bowls for the children. She looked tired. The winter had been hard on everyone; most of their chickens had frozen to death in a blizzard, costing them the little money they got for their eggs.

Simon hurried his meager meal, wanting to get to Sarah's

house for their walk to school. Sarah with her fair skin, and a lilting laugh that made the mockingbirds jealous. His father sat down and Ana poured him a cup of coffee. "That's the last," she said sadly, and then she put her hand on Simon's shoulder and squeezed. "You better get going, Sarah will leave you." She prodded him on the shoulder. "Hurry." She prodded him again, harder.

Simon awoke with a start, looked around for his family, and found Buell standing over him.

"Wake up, ya slug." Buell nudged Simon on the shoulder with his boot. "Coffee's ready." He offered a cup. "Here."

Simon sat up and took it. "Thanks. Dreamt I was back in the old sod house. Trying to hurry through breakfast like I used to. Wanted to see Sar—" His mouth snapped shut and his brow furrowed. "Cold this morning." He took a couple sips of the scalding brew, then put the cup on the ground and folded back the canvas cover of his bedroll. He dragged his boots out of the bottom and put them on. Standing, he grabbed the jacket he'd used for a pillow and shrugged into it. Then, cup in hand, he moved closer to the fire.

"Still had some hot coals, twern't no problem gettin' a fire goin'." Buell blew steam off his cup and sipped it gently.

"Want me to fry some bacon?" Simon turned his back to the fire and rubbed the heat into his butt.

"Naw, I already ate three or four of yer corn cakes. I'm ready to go."

"Where're the horses?" Simon looked into the trees.

"Right down on the riverbank. You eat what ya want. I'll go get 'em." Buell set his cup on a flat fire-ring rock, and headed for the river.

Simon picked up two cakes, warm from the fire, and with alternating sips of coffee and bites of fritter, had breakfast eaten in a matter of minutes. He had his bed rolled and was ready to saddle up before Buell got back.

Platte City appeared bigger than Carlisle, a lot bigger. The Union Pacific Railroad had made it a center for maintenance and supplies, bringing hundreds of people to the area. They'd also built a big hotel, and Main Street featured several two-story buildings. Simon rode down the center of the street looking at all the businesses. A boardwalk ran down either side, and even at this early hour, the place bustled with traffic. He found a mercantile sign and tied his horse out front.

Inside, the familiar smell, still very fresh in his memory, swept him back to Carlisle for a moment, back to Swartz's store. He'd worked there for nearly three years, clerking, filling orders, stocking, ordering, and even changing the way inventory was tracked and paid for. The nostalgia also brought back the anger of being falsely accused of stealing, and being barred from the store.

"Can I help you, sir?" A young man in his mid twenties stood behind the counter.

"Uh, yes, thank you. I need four pounds of corn meal, two cans each of plums, peaches, and pears, six cans of beans, some sugar and four pounds of bacon. And an old beanbag, or something like that to carry it in. I'm on horseback."

"No problem." The clerk finished writing on his pad. "That'll take just a few minutes. Anything else?"

"Do you have a newspaper?"

"Local or out of town?" asked the young man, pride in his voice. "We have both."

"Lincoln County if you have it."

"We do, sir. Should I put it with the order or do you want to have it now?"

It surprised Simon that he could get a hometown paper, and

it must have showed.

"With the railroad, we get all manner of things from the East we never dreamed of only five years ago." The storekeeper waited for Simon to answer.

Simon's desire to have news of home and the need to make a clean break fought for control. "Never mind."

"Very well." The clerk hustled off.

Back on the street, Simon picked out a gunsmith's shop two doors down. Buell had asked him to look for one and get some more primer caps for his pistol. Simon went in. "I need a tin of number-ten caps."

"Right here," the gunsmith said as he reached under the counter. "Anything else?"

"Yeah, I need a rifle. My partner and I are going to Fort Laramie, and I'd feel a little safer if we had something along besides a pistol." Simon scanned the rack behind the counter.

"You looking for a percussion rifle or something a little more up-to-date?" the smith asked, glancing at the primers.

"Well, all I've ever shot is percussion, so I don't know."

"Let me show you something." Anticipation lit the man's face. "You'll like this." He stepped into his back room and returned with a long, lever-action rifle. He handed it to Simon.

"I've seen one of these one time. It's a new Winchester isn't it?" Simon ran his hand over the smooth walnut stock.

"You're right, Model eighteen sixty-six King Improved. Load it on Sunday and shoot it all week. That's what the Rebs said about it." He leaned back against the rear counter as Simon admired the gun.

"Is this one new?"

"Nope, bought it from a soldier 'bout a month ago. He bought it new though, and then mustered out. I've checked it over, and if it's been fired more'n twenty times I'll eat that tin o' primers. Make ya a good deal on it."

"How much?" Simon gritted his teeth and watched the gunsmith's face.

"Fifty dollars." The smith didn't bat an eye.

"I worked a long time for fifty dollars. I don't think so." He offered the gun to the smith, who made no move to accept it. Simon's heart started to race. He'd been on the other side of the counter not that long ago.

"Back East, that gun cost fifty-six dollars new a little over a year ago. And like I said, it ain't been fired enough to even count. Couldn't let it go for a dime less than forty-four." He folded his arms across his chest.

"I'll give you thirty dollars for it." Simon reached into his pocket.

The smith put up his hand. "Don't even bother diggin' it out. Got too much in it for that. Gimme forty and you can ride safe to Wyoming Territory." He shook his head as though resigned.

"Thirty-five."

"Can't do it."

Simon laid the rifle on the counter. "How much for the primers?"

"A dollar sixty."

Simon dug in his pocket, and took out the correct amount. Laying it on the counter, he picked up the tin of primers, stroked the rifle's stock once more, and turned to leave.

"I'm not making a nickel on that rifle at thirty-five," the smith grumbled.

Simon waited until he had control of his smile, then turned around. "I'll need some cartridges, too, and a scabbard," he said as he unbuttoned his shirt pocket.

★ ★ ★ ★ ★

Buell caressed the stock of the new rifle. "And just four years ago you were in big trouble for just shooting my pistol. Now look." He pushed the lever down, and the action made the ominous mechanical sound of weaponry being readied. He levered the action shut, the imposing hammer remaining at full cock.

"Load it," Simon said. "I got three boxes of cartridges." He groped around in the bean sack and found one. Busting the top loose, he handed Buell a fistful of shells.

Buell fed them into the side of the rifle. "You go first. It's yours." He handed the Winchester to Simon. "Let me go set something up."

Running to the river, he found a charred piece of old campfire wood. Propping it up between two rocks, he paced the sixty yards from where Simon stood.

Simon levered a shell into the chamber and raised the rifle to his shoulder. Squinting across the open "V" of the rear sight, he lined up the silver front sight with the black target and squeezed the trigger. The chunk of wood went skidding across the dirt. He turned to Buell. "Hits right where you aim it. It's a little heavy in the barrel, but it sure feels good." He handed it to Buell.

Buell fired and split the piece of wood in two. Jacking in another round, he hit the larger piece, worked the lever again, and barely missed the small chunk. "Boy, that's fast. How many will it hold?" He turned the rifle in his hands admiring it.

"Sixteen, if you put one in the chamber." Simon reached for the gun. "Let me try it again."

They burned up a box of cartridges chasing the increasingly smaller pieces of wood around the riverbank. Simon knew he was going to like his new rifle.

CHAPTER 2

The country had turned to a landscape of long rolling hills. Simon pushed his horse closer to Buell's. "Have you noticed there are a couple of riders going the same way we are?" He glanced back as he spoke.

"Nope." Buell turned in his saddle and looked to the rear.

"Well, I think I have. Let's stop just over this next rise and take a leak. I'd like to see if they're still back there."

They climbed off their horses a few minutes later and peed on a couple of weeds, then walked back a little and peered over the ridgeline at their back trail. Ten minutes passed, and a lazily circling hawk was the only thing to break the monotony of the view.

"How long's it been since ya spotted 'em?" Buell asked.

"I thought I spied 'em early this morning and started watching. At that time, they were right behind us. A couple of hours later, I saw them for sure, only this time they were more south of us than behind. And then about two hours ago, I thought I saw 'em again."

"That map you got show any towns they might be headin' for?"

Simon took the map out of his coat pocket and unfolded it.

"Nothing between here and Fort Laramie except campsites. They could be heading for the South Platte, but you'd think they'd have rode that trail right out of Platte City." Simon handed the map to Buell.

"Don't make no sense. Let's ride closer to the river. If they're headed for Fort Laramie, we'll let 'em get in front of us. I don't like 'em behind." Buell folded up the paper and handed it back. "Let's sit here a while, and see if we can spot 'em. Maybe we're just a little skitterish."

They sat for over an hour, then got back on the horses and headed west again, angling closer to the river. Both men kept an eye on the horizon, but didn't see another person the rest of the day. They passed two obvious wagon train campsites, the areas well worn and littered with trash and dozens of fire beds. Neither had any firewood within a mile, so they passed on, but decided to leave the prairie and ride closer to the river. There they found untrampled ground, inaccessible to wagons because of the uneven bluffs and draws. Simon spotted a two-acre cottonwood grove and they headed for it. Seventy-five yards or so from the river and near the center, they found a clearing. Travel weary only four days out of Carlisle, they reined their mounts to one side of it and climbed off.

Once free of their saddles, the hobbled horses wandered into the trees to browse. Buell started gathering wood from under a lone maple tree. Simon unpacked the food and rolled out his bed before going to the river for a pan of water. When he returned, the fire, sparking and crackling, had a fair start, and Buell hunkered over his bedroll, getting it laid out. "That is one muddy stretch of water," Simon said as he set the pan carefully on the ground.

"So I noticed." Buell stood, arched his back and came over to the fire, now picking up size and spirit. He dropped a few larger branches on it and stepped away. Simon settled down on the ground and leaned back against his saddle to join in Buell's vigil. Three even larger pieces of wood went on the fire, and Buell folded his long legs to join Simon on the ground.

The sun dropped below the bluffs and the air cooled rapidly

as they watched the fire in silence. When the flames reduced the maple wood to a bed of red-yellow coals, Simon laid two fairly straight pieces of wood side by side across the fiery heat. He placed the coffee pan on top. In a few minutes, steam wafted off the water as Simon busied himself making corn batter. Buell napped.

Fried corn cakes, beans with bacon, and coffee made a satisfying meal, and Simon proved himself quite adept at camp cooking. In the gathering darkness, he walked to the river with two forks, a pair of tin plates, and the skillet. He soon lost to the trees the reassuring glow of the fire, and deepening shadows hurried his return trip.

"Dark as the inside of a crow," Buell said when Simon walked into the firelight. "I could hear where ya were, but I couldn't see ya."

"Yeah. I didn't used to be uneasy about the dark, but something about being out here, completely alone, gives me the jitters." Simon put the dishes by the saddlebags and sat down cross-legged next to the fire. "I think seeing those riders got me going."

"Steep as it is here, we'd hear 'em comin'. But yer right, it is dark. I'm gonna have a smoke and go to bed." Buell started building a cigarette.

"Good idea. I don't remember getting this tired herding cows with Nathan Greene and the guys."

"That's cuz we sat still most of the time. We've covered about eighty miles the last four days and that means a lot of hangin' on with our legs." The flare of the flaming twig he drew back from the fire amplified Buell's steady gaze. Blowing a cloud of smoke skyward, he stood and turned his back to the heat. "I think it might get cold."

"Feels like it." Simon stood. "Let's drag something big over here and lay it across the fire for tonight."

They found a punky deadfall branch on the fringes of the campfire light. It soon started to burn, the heavy bark and damp decaying wood keeping the flame low. Settling down in his bed, Simon struggled out of his boots, folded up his coat for a pillow, and pulled his covers over his chest. He looked up to find Cassiopeia—the familiar "W" put him at ease. How many times had he and Sarah . . . he took a deep breath and let it out slowly before peering across the smoky campfire. "See ya in the mornin'." Buell didn't answer.

Buell sat with his back against the maple tree. He could see the fire glow, but the smoldering cottonwood branch cast scant light over the camp. He'd seen the riders before Simon had, two of them, and they'd been there since Platte City, always about a mile back. They'd appeared one last time just before he and Simon descended to the river. Certain they'd come into camp and try to steal the horses, he'd decided to watch and wait.

Through the treetops, he scanned the sky until he made out the Big Dipper—well after midnight. The air lay so still he could hear the slow-moving river a hundred yards away. Doubt crept in as his back stiffened up with the cold, and he considered going to the fire to absorb some heat.

The snap of a breaking branch rippled his scalp and sped his heart. Deer? He breathed softly through his mouth and peered into the woods, keeping his eyes away from the dim firelight. The darkness threw the silence back at him. Fully five minutes later, another sound, almost too soft to be heard—someone breathing. Buell lowered his head to hide his white face. The nasal sound passed a few feet to his right. It amazed him that someone could walk through the trees without making any ground noise. The breathing sound, definitely moving towards the fire, passed out of range before Buell looked up. He could just make out the immobile shape of a man, who appeared to be facing the fire.

A charge scampered up his spine when he caught movement on the other side of the camp. Another man, barely visible in the starlight, stood motionless directly opposite the first. As Buell stared, the dark shape moved closer to the smoldering fire, angling away from the river in Simon's direction. As he advanced, the long gun he held chest high became apparent. The nearer man, the Breather, moved the opposite way and toward Buell's bedroll. He knew then they were not looking for horses.

The farther man, now more visible in the low firelight, raised his rifle, the dull reflection of firelight on metal winking across the space. It pointed at Simon! Buell raised his pistol, cocked hours ago, and sighted across the camp, trying to line up on something more precise than a dark shadow. Then came the unmistakable crackle of a pistol being cocked—the Breather—followed instantly by the double click of a rifle hammer being drawn back. Buell pulled the trigger.

"Oh!" The grunt came from the far side. Buell, already moving left, saw the Breather turn his way. He fired at the shape, something thudded to the ground, and the form disappeared. Buell stopped behind a tree and listened intently.

"Buell! Bueeellll!" Simon's terrorized voice split the silence.

Rocks rattled—someone scrambling up the slope to his right. And then came a splintering of wood and a gasp of pain from across the camp, followed by the sound of someone tearing through underbrush and hanging branches. Buell remained pressed against the tree and listened, as both sounds became fainter.

A minute or two passed, then he heard horses being spurred urgently, and as they sped out of earshot, he peeked around the tree at the camp. Nothing moved. He crept up on Simon's form, looking for the Winchester. He spotted it, angled over a saddle that lay off to one side. He let out his breath when he'd moved close enough to make out Simon's form, head covered and knees drawn up tight to his chest.

"Simon? You okay?"

Slowly the scrunched form started to straighten out. "Buell?" Simon whispered. "That you?"

"Yeah. I think our visitors are gone. You all right?"

Simon pushed the canvas cover off and sat up. "Yeah. Scared shitless, but I'm okay. What the hell happened?"

"Those two fellas followin' us. I thought they might try to get our horses so I waited up for 'em. Looked like they wanted more'n the horses. One of 'em had his rifle pointed right at you. When he cocked it, I shot at him."

"Did ya hit him?" Simon stood.

"I think so. Heard him grunt, and he took off. The other fella ran up the hill. I got a shot at him, too, but I don't think I hit 'im. Nothing to shoot at but a shadow. Heard somethin' hit the ground, or else he kicked somethin'. Anyhow, he took off. You hear the horses?"

"Yeah, they left in a hurry. Think they'll be back?" Simon peered in the direction of the bluffs.

"No idea."

"Well, I'm not going back to bed, I'll tell ya that."

"Me either. Let's get away from the campfire and wait for daylight. Can't be long till sunup."

"What time is it?" Simon asked.

Buell looked up. "About two thirty or three, near as I can guess."

"Two thirty! You waited out there in the dark for six hours?" Simon stared at Buell and swallowed hard.

"Nothin' new to me. I can't count the times I sat out in the prairie at home. More nights than not." He walked over and grabbed his canvas bedcover. "Let's go."

Simon went to his saddle and picked up his rifle.

Night's tenacity punished them, giving way slowly to the first dim hint of morning. Both men had dozed fitfully, the simple act of nodding off snapping shots of adrenaline into their blood. They walked into camp as soon as they could make out their saddles and beds. The flames had gone out, but Buell tossed some small wood pieces on the ashes and they immediately began to smoke. In a couple of minutes, flames rose to cast a welcome light.

"I'm going to climb up and see if I can spot where their horses were tied up," Buell said.

"It's still too dark." Simon looked around at the deep shadows.

"Not up on top, out of these trees. I won't be long." Buell strode into the woods, and a minute later rocks clattered down the side of the hill.

On top he found where the horses had stood, tied to a low shrub about fifty yards from the lip of the bluff. Out of the trees, he had more light, just as he'd thought. The deep prints of a hard-spurred horse led straight south. Buell knelt for a closer look and found blood on the ground by the bush, lots of it. He walked back to the bluff and slid down stiff-legged, knocking dirt and rock loose as he descended. Simon sat hunkered by the fire, his rifle across his knees.

"What'd ya see?" Simon asked glumly.

"I can see where the horses were tied. Quite a ways back. They took off in a hurry. The one I hit is losin' a lot of blood." Buell squatted down by the fire.

"You think they're gone, then?"

"I ain't got no doubt. They're gone." He picked up the coffee pan and sniffed it. Grimacing, he dumped the wet grounds at the edge of the fire.

"Well, I'm glad for that," Simon said. "I was afraid something like this might happen, but I didn't think it really would. We could have been killed in our sleep." Simon squinted across the fire at Buell. Concern crumpled his face.

"And weren't. Shit, Simon, look at the bright side. Want some coffee?"

"How in hell can you be so calm? We coulda been killed!" Simon stood.

"Sometimes I can't believe you." Buell grabbed the coffee pan and stomped off toward the river.

"Can't you wait till it's light?" Simon took a tentative step in Buell's direction.

"Humph." Buell snorted his disdain and disappeared.

Both of them stared at the pan of water as it absorbed the heat and started to boil. Buell shook a heaping handful of coffee from the bag and dumped it in the roiling water. Instantly, foam rose and overflowed the sides. He put on a glove and pulled the pan back to the fire's edge, and they watched it roll the coffee grounds around for a couple of minutes. Then he lifted the pan out of the coals and dumped in the cup of cold water he'd saved. A minute later they both held cups of hot coffee.

The light in the eastern sky finally lit the camp completely. Buell put his empty cup down, and walked to the maple tree where he'd spent most of the night. Positioning himself, he estimated where the Breather had stood and went there. He found footprints in the dirt, not boot prints—footprints. Then he saw the blood, about four feet up the trunk of a tree. The splatter of dark crimson speckled the bark, and drops of it marked the bush behind. He walked closer to inspect the ground and nearly stepped on the gun. He picked up a gleaming blue-black pistol with carved ivory or bone grips—it was cocked. A Remington just like his .36, but bigger and heavier. Pat Lacey, a Texas herder back home, had taught Buell to shoot with a pistol just like it, only not so fancy. He lowered the hammer, and a glance at the front end of the cylinder showed six loaded chambers.

"Buellll! Hurry!" Simon shouted, nearly screaming.

Tearing out of the trees, he charged into an empty camp with his pistol drawn, the new gun stuffed in his belt. "Simon?"

"Over here."

Buell moved toward Simon's voice until he found him just inside the trees, looking down at a rifle and a large black patch of blood.

"There's more over there," Simon said, pointing further into the trees.

Buell followed the blood trail, advancing carefully. When he stopped, Simon bumped into his back. "Hey, you," he shouted, "get up!"

A skinny man in ragged clothes sat with his back against a tree, legs outstretched. His head hung, slightly cocked, on his chest, and he held his hands folded in his lap. He looked quite comfortable.

"Get up!" Buell shouted, his pistol leveled at the sleeping man. The man didn't move.

"Look at his leg," Simon whispered. A black blotch stained the man's crotch and thigh. "He's all bloody."

Buell advanced slowly, his pistol trained on the man's chest. He kicked the bottom of the man's foot. "Hey!"

When the man didn't respond, Buell reached out and pushed on a shoulder with the muzzle of his gun. The man toppled sideways, his body stiff.

"He's deader'n Moses, Simon." Buell peered down at the man. "Look at all that blood under his butt. He bled to death. Wonder where I hit 'im." Buell poked at the bloody leg.

"Leave him alone. He's dead." Simon curled his lip and wrinkled his nose.

Buell stooped for a closer look. The man's filthy hair lay in a matted tangle, his partly open mouth full of rotten teeth, and his pasty face a disaster of pockmarks. "He don't know nothin'." Buell felt the man's pants pockets, and then the shirt pockets.

"What're you doing?" Simon protested, but he made no move to get closer.

"Lookin' for his money." Buell unbuckled the leather strap holding a pouch slung around the man's neck. He pulled it loose and undid the catch on the flap. He inspected the contents, grinned, and closed it again. "I can see why they wanted more'n our horses. This fella ain't got a dime, but he's got plenty of patched-bullet cartridges. Must be fifty shots in here, and primers too."

Buell triumphantly hoisted the pouch, and when Simon just looked at him, he shoved past him to charge through the brush and into camp. By the fire, he picked up the short rifle lying in the sparse grass and took it over to his bedroll. Pulling his newly found pistol out of his waistband, he laid it on the canvas rain cover, and then sat down by the fire. Tipping the carbine muzzle down, he carefully lowered the hammer, then pushed down on the under lever of the Sharps. As soon as he saw the gleam of brass in the breech, he closed it again and laid the gun across his knees. He looked up as Simon walked out of the trees.

Simon seemed dazed. "What are we doin', Buell? You just robbed a dead man," he murmured, his speech low and monotone.

"Don't start. I could be buryin' my partner." Buell's voice rose slightly.

"I know that. I know that for sure. I'm sick to my stomach knowing it." Simon shook his head. "But to take a man's stuff when he's dead. That can't be right." He now looked absolutely dismal.

"And what the hell's he gonna do with it?" Buell glared at his friend. "It'd be stupid to leave this here." He slapped the Sharps's butt stock. "Have some Indian come along, and shoot you with it later."

Simon did not reply.

"Them bastards figgered to kill us both. Hadn't been for me, you'd be wrapped in that bedroll right now, cold as that feller out there." He scrambled to his feet and faced Simon. "I'm glad we found him dead. Now I know I hit 'em both, cuz that blood up on top sure can't be his. And I think the one that rode off is an Indian. The footprints over there ain't from boots. Now, where do ya think an Indian got a pistol like that?" He pointed at the gleaming Remington lying on his bed. "Expect he went to Swartz's and paid cash money for it? Not likely. Some poor sumbitch lost his life over that gun, and that stinkin' Indian probably had somethin' to do with it." He glared at Simon. "So I don't want to hear ya mewlin' about no damn dead man."

"But I still don—"

Buell yanked back the hammer on the Sharps and pulled the trigger. The deafening report slapped the air, and sparks, ash, and coffee grounds erupted out of the campfire, the coffee pan kicked, spinning into the treetops. Simon staggered back and fell full length on the ground. In one stride Buell stood over him. "Ya little shit. Ya wanna go back to momma, you go right ahead. Ya wanna go with me, ya better grow some goddamn bark. Your choice." He threw the carbine down beside Simon, and stomped out of camp.

Simon Steele suffered a lot of mental anguish over the next few days. Everything he had been taught as a young man had been assaulted, the very basis of his morals challenged. And he didn't have answers to the questions his righteous self screamed at him. His hardworking parents had told him that you earned what you got. You didn't steal it, borrow it, or find it. His adopted uncle, John Lindstrom, wealthy but disillusioned Eastern lawyer, turned town drunk, turned family benefactor, had told him a man lives by his word. And now, doubts about the man who'd just saved his life crept in—the same man, who, as a boy, had saved it before. Buell had not uttered a single word since storming out of camp. They had saddled the horses, and over Simon's protests—visions of birds and coyotes ravaging the body—left the dead man lying where he fell.

Simon's mind thrashed in turmoil. Can you label a man a murderer if he simply attempted it? He looked at the back of the man riding in front of him. Was it murder to lie in wait for those men to come into camp? Am I glad Buell was out there, ready to shoot? If I am, am I also glad the man's dead? He shook his head to stop the voice inside. Do I wish I were dead? That can't be. I have a right to live, to protect myself. He searched his soul for support, and his memory for guidance. You are who your company is. Sarah's declaration rang clear in his mind, as did his response. I like Buell for who he is, not what he is.

Is Buell right? Am I best suited to stand around in a store somewhere, counting money and selling stuff? His horse's right ear rotated back, listening, and he realized he was mumbling. Do I care what people think anymore? Who said, "A contempt for a good reputation is impudent"? It was in one of those dusty old books I read in Judge Kingsley's library. But another one said, "A man cannot step in the same river twice." And I think he's right.

Simon kicked his horse to a trot and caught up with Buell. "Thanks," he said as he pulled alongside.

"Don't mention it."

They were now eight days out of Carlisle, about halfway to Fort Laramie.

★ ★ ★ ★ ★

The solitary finger sticking into the sky made them want to hurry up the next rise to see the hand it must surely be attached to. But on arriving, the finger stood alone, set against the rolling prairie, mocking. Could it be that far away? They rode the rolling hills all that day, and some of the next before they started to make out the base of Chimney Rock. They were back on the Oregon Trail now, the ruts deep and many. The bones and carcasses of oxen, cattle, horses and mules, worked to death by uninitiated pilgrims, fouled the prairie. The progress of man littered the landscape: farm implements, beds, heavy furniture, even a piano, all the droppings of constipated wagons that had been stuffed with wants instead of needs. The more human toll lay buried and hidden by the wagon tracks, the graves deliberately pounded beyond recognition by the inexorable churning wheels. They set up camp near the river, the towering formation a couple miles to the north.

"Looks like we eat cold again tonight," Buell complained. "Those wagon folks burned everything. I haven't seen a stick of wood for forty miles. Even the buffalo dung is gone."

Buell took his duties seriously, and was somewhat put out when he couldn't find something to make a fire with. They had burned clothes closets, trunks, tables, chairs, even a coffin once. Here, nothing could be found.

"I don't mind," Simon said. "We got a couple of cans of beans left, and some fruit. From the looks of the country to the west, we might get into some rougher riding. Shows here that a place called Scott's Bluff is near. I hope bluff means something more than riverside like we been seeing since Carlisle." He studied the map.

"So, how many more days to Fort Laramie?" Buell asked. "I'm gettin' tired of sleeping damp, and it's starting to get cold."

"Another day to Scott's Bluff and then about sixty miles

more. Figger four days." Simon folded the map and put it away. "I'd say we've been real lucky not to get snowed on."

The country didn't change as much as Simon had anticipated. It got a little higher on either side of the river valley, but the bluffs were farther away. They didn't know it, when, on September 27, 1868, they passed out of Nebraska and into Wyoming Territory. To them another Sunday had arrived, and tomorrow they would ride some more.

CHAPTER 3

Fort Laramie proved a disappointment. Set in the same rolling hills they had been riding across for seventeen days, it contained a spread-out conglomeration of buildings of various sizes and conditions. A two-story structure on the far side of the fort stood out above the rest. An American flag flew from a pole a little left of the center of the place. People, some on foot, some mounted, and some in wagons, all seemed to be moving aimlessly. Near the flag and facing the two-story building, a group of soldiers stood in some sort of formation. Brass buttons flashed in the sun as they turned and moved, the commands too far away to be heard by Simon or Buell. The small river they looked across forked around sandbar.

"Not a very purdy place," Buell observed.

"Doesn't look like Fort Hartwell at all." Simon brought the image of the fort near Carlisle back to his mind. "Where are the walls? You could run a herd of cows through the place and never scrape a hide."

"And if I ain't mistaken, them's Indians going into that building over there." Buell pointed off to the right.

"And civilians. Bet that's the sutler's store," Simon said. "Probably as good a place as any to ask a few questions." He kicked his horse into motion, and they splashed across the two branches of water and skirted the military part of the settlement.

★ ★ ★ ★ ★

The interior of the trading post welcomed them with its familiarity. Tall shelves of bare wood held cans, packages, sacks, and boxes of every description. Where there wasn't a shelf, a barrel or a bin stood. A counter filled the left end of the store, and behind it stood a medium-tall man with the wildest face full of hair Simon had ever seen. He even had hair growing out of his ears. He held a packet of tobacco firmly to the counter with his hand, also hair covered, and faced a half-naked Indian. The native pointed to the package, then held up three fingers. The hairy sutler held up both his hands, all his fingers extended. The Indian put his right hand palm-down in front of his chest, moved it quickly out and away, showing his palm, and brought it back again. Then he held up four fingers. The sutler held up eight.

"They're hagglin'."

Simon started at the voice. He turned to see a grinning short man. He looked old, except for his eyes—gray, with an intensity that demanded attention. Short whisker stubble frosted his tan, weathered skin. A dingy union suit peeked through the worn elbows of his shirt. But it was the hat that claimed Simon's attention. It defied description—animal fur and felt, it looked like some sort of . . . nest.

"See'd ya watchin' and knew ya might be a wonderin'. The quick move of his right hand means no. You kin guess what the fingers mean."

His eyes sparkled, and the creases around them could only be caused by the present condition of his face, a full-fledged, genuine and friendly smile. The expression looked as natural as breathing.

"Guess I was," Simon said. "How much can they say with their hands like that?"

"Prit'near anything they want. I know up'erds of two hunert

signs. Name's Prescott, Taylor Prescott, folks call me Tay. I'm a trapper, miner, scout, or whatever pays." His eyebrows arched in anticipation as he stuck out a calloused hand.

Simon reached for it. Tay's flesh felt like a piece of weathered wood, hard, dry, and unyielding. He mentally braced himself for a crushing squeeze, but received a surprisingly gentle grasp—firm, but gentle. He met the old man's smile. "I'm Simon Steele, late of Nebraska, and looking for work. This is my friend, Buell Mace."

"Please to meetcha both." Tay held his hand out until Buell took it.

The Indian had said no twice more, and they had agreed on sixty cents for the package of tobacco. The Indian turned and walked past them like they didn't exist.

"Howdy gents. What can I do for ya?" the sutler asked, black eyes peering from beneath bushy eyebrows.

Momentarily transfixed, Simon simply looked at him.

"These fellers is lookin' fer work, T. P.," the trapper, miner, scout said.

"Well, that shouldn't be too hard. Plenty of work to do and mostly the army to pay for it. Whatcha got in mind?"

He seemed to be smiling under all the hair, but Simon couldn't be sure. He smiled back just in case. "I got a lot of experience working in the mercantile trade. A store a lot like this."

"Ya might be in luck. The roadhouse just west of here is lookin' for someone to help 'em. Ain't exactly a tradin' post, more like a saloon and rowdy house if ya get my meanin'. If ya ain't particular, you could look there. In here, I purdy much keep up with it by myself. Figger if they cain't wait a minute they really don't need it."

"I appreciate that. I'll go ask. About how far west?"

"Five miles, north side o' the river. Get ya anything while

you're here?" He looked at Buell.

"I need some leather. A holster and a scabbard."

"Ain't got that here, but we do have a gunsmith. He's got a place in the rear of the blacksmith. Ya passed it on your left coming in from the east."

"How'd ya know we came from the east?" Buell met the sutler's black eyes with a suspicious frown.

"Nebraska was over there last time I heard. And ya told Tay you was from Nebraska. Touchy young feller, ain't ya?"

"C'mon, boys, I was jist headin' that way m'self. Be glad to point it out." Tay Prescott nodded at the door. "See ya, T. P. And ya stuck that buck fer the 'baccy too. Sixty cents, ya oughta be ashamed." He chuckled as he headed for the door.

"Are the Indians all that tame?" Buell asked. "I thought they were raising hell out here."

"Jist barely signed a new treaty. As of August twenty-five, we ain't gonna mess with them, nor they with us. Damn, that'll feel good, not havin' ta be lookin' over my shoulder all the time when I'm huntin' and such. They still give me the bumps, though."

Tay Prescott moved over the slightly uneven ground like cream over warm pie—he flowed. His feet seemed to never quite leave the ground, his gait a sort of shuffle. Simon expected him to stumble or trip with every step, but quickened his stride to keep up. He caught himself slightly imitating the old man.

They pushed open the door to the livery and walked in. The smell stopped both young men in mid stride. The scent of hay, horse sweat and dung, liniment, dust, and the unique odor of old wood, connected with boyhood memories of Buell's father's blacksmith and livery. They looked at each other and grinned.

"Looks like Rawlins ain't here right now," Tay said after a look around the livery. "C'mon back and we'll see if Kent's in."

He shuffled across the floor to a door in back, and pushed it open. "Hey, Berggren, ya in here?"

"Yeah, come on in."

Tay stepped back, and motioned Simon and Buell into a spacious room.

"Gents." A big-boned man stood at a bench to the left, a leather apron covering his chest and legs. He held a six-foot-long flintlock rifle. He stuck out his hand: "Name's Kent Berggren."

Simon thrilled at the soft rounded cadence of a Swedish accent.

"Kent, this'er young fella is lookin' fer a holster and scabbard. Name's Mace, Buell Mace." He indicated Buell. "And this's Simon Steele." Simon shook his hand.

"Another Swede," Berggren said, and smiled. "Always pleased. Now, my business. Lookin' to replace that one?" He pointed to the rig Buell had strapped to his right hip.

"Nope. I need something for this." He unbuttoned his coat, and pulled the shiny Remington out of his belt.

"Oh, shit." The gunsmith stared at the shiny pistol. "Can I look at that?"

"Sure." Buell handed him the butt.

The smith turned the pistol end for end and peered closely at the pale yellow grips. His fingers traced the outline of the perched eagle carved in the ivory. "Beautiful. Where'd ya get this one?"

"It's mine, fair and square. Does it matter where I got it?"

"Not really. It's . . . a . . . I know another fella had one like it. Matter of fact, I put his grips on. Carved his initials 'KB' on the inside." He handed the pistol back to Buell. His hand trembled slightly, but it didn't escape Simon.

"You sayin' this is the gun?" Buell's voice had a flat challenging edge to it.

"I'm sayin' I saw one like it. Belongs to my brother."

"He went to Omaha the first of the month, didn't he?" Prescott asked.

"Yeah, and we ain't heard a word from him. It's not been that long, but—"

"I didn't get it from no white man," Buell said.

Panic suggested itself to Simon. He blinked rapidly as he studied Buell.

The gunsmith's face turned ashen, and he slumped back against his bench.

"We were attacked in the night. These—" Simon started to explain.

"Keep yer mouth shut." Buell cut him off. "Ain't nobody's business but ours." He looked back at the gunsmith, who now stood studying the floor.

"Mind if an old fart says somethin'?" Tay asked Buell.

Buell looked at him for a second, and then nodded.

"I got a feelin' about you fellers. Call it sure learnin' from survivin' forty years in the hills. Anyhow, when Mister Mace here says he come by it fair and straight, I figger he's got 'nuff sand to make it stick. So, let's hear how ya come by it, and maybe we kin clear this up."

Buell frowned. "About ten or twelve days ago, a coupla roosters jumped us at night. They figgered to sneak up on us, but we saw 'em followin'. They was cocked and ready to shoot. I blasted one in the leg, and hit the other one somewhere else. The leg-shot feller run off a bit and bled till he died. The other man got to the horses and rode south. I know he was shot cuz he left plenty of blood where they tied up. He dropped this pistol when I hit 'im." Buell released a pent-up sigh. It could have been either relief or resignation, Simon couldn't tell which.

"Ya say it was 'bout ten days ago?" Tay shot a glance at Berggren.

"Somethin' like that," Buell said.

"Was the one ya kilt real skinny, face that looks like scrambled eggs, all pockmarked?" Berggren asked. "Had a mouth full of rot that'd back up a skunk."

"Yep. And dirty, I mean real dirty. He's the dead one," Buell said.

The gunsmith sucked in a sharp breath, and his hand went to his clenched jaw. He shook his head, then lowered it as his eyes glazed over.

"The feller what's dead is named Skinner," Tay said. "Him and another feller has been stealin' and killin' on the trail for years. Ya did us all a favor." He walked over to the silent gunsmith. "I'm plumb sorry, Kent. Damned if I ain't." He put his hand on Kent's shoulder.

"I told ya," Buell said emphatically, "he weren't no white man."

Tay's eyebrows shot up.

Buell continued: "He didn't wear boots. I saw his tracks, and in the woods, he walked as close to me as you are. If I hadn't heard him breathin', I probably wouldn't be here."

"Ain't got no way a knowin' fer sure," Tay said, "but the other'n could have been Injun. Nasty bastard named Knife."

"He rode through here two days ago," Berggren said. "Had the army doc take a look at a hole in his hand. Bet ya it was a . . ." He paused and glanced at the gun in Buell's holster. "A thirty-six-caliber ball. Dirty bastard. Murderin' son of a bitch." He shook his head from side to side. "Can I look at the grips?"

Buell handed him the gun, and Berggren backed the screw out of the ivory. He looked at the underside of the right grip. Tears sprang from his eyes and he grabbed the bench for support. "Oh, Karl. Oh, God."

"I'm sorry, mister," Buell said. "I owe that bastard, and I pay off."

The four men stood silent for a while, unable to find words. Slowly the smith regained control of his emotions and put the pistol back together. Finished, he carefully laid it on the bench. Neither he nor Buell took their eyes off it.

"I'll make ya a deal, Mister Mace. I want you to keep the pistol, and I want you use it when you find him. I want you to shoot him once for each of Carl's three children and three times for his wife."

"Are you sure?" Buell asked. "It rightly belongs to you, or his wife."

"No, I've decided. But promise me you'll do as I asked. And if not with that gun, then with some other. I'd be in your debt."

After caressing the grips again, he handed the pistol to Buell, then turned and opened a drawer. He offered Buell a tooled, mahogany-colored leather holster and belt with a silver buckle. "I was going to give him this for Christmas. They go together."

The look of sadness on his face made Simon's throat sore, and he swallowed hard to make the knot go away.

"Like I said, I kin judge a man better'n most, and I reckon Mister Mace will do as he says." Tay shook his head sadly and touched the gunsmith on the arm again.

Berggren took a deep breath and shrugged his shoulders, letting his breath out in a long sigh. It seemed to signal his resolve to accept for now what had happened.

"You needed a rifle scabbard too. What do you shoot?"

"Sharps carbine."

"Skinner's? I'm sorry . . . doesn't matter. Got one here—matter of fact, several." He reached under the bench and brought out the short scabbard. Straps were attached at the big end. "Four dollars."

Buell paid him.

As they left the shop, Simon noticed the smith sag onto a stool and bury his face in his hands.

Once back in the livery barn, Tay turned and stopped. "Damn, I hate to see that. Kent's a good man. Doc took that Injun's thumb off." Prescott shook his head and looked at the closed door for a moment. "Where ya fellas figgerin' on stayin' tonight?"

"Hadn't really thought about it particularly," Simon said. "Figgered we could sleep rough another night if we had to."

"Well, you can stay in half a dozen places here, or they's two roadhouses within six miles, one down river and the other up. Either will do. Else ya kin stay with me. Yer more'n welcome. Got a little dugout, 'bout a mile out."

"Don't want to put you out, Mister Prescott. We can find something." Simon looked at Buell.

"Ain't nobody puttin' nobody out. Be glad to have the company and catch up on some news. And call me Tay. Mister makes me nervous." His face lit up again in an all-consuming smile.

Buell nodded.

"Thanks for the offer," Simon said. "We'll take you up on it. I'd like to stop by the store again, and buy a few things. And then send a telegraph."

"Be ready ta git scalped. Ya saw what he did to that Indian? You ain't gonna fare much better. Ol' T. P. Triffet treats everybody more or less the same—puts the screw to all of 'em." Tay chuckled. "I'll gather up m' horse and meet ya over there. Won't be long."

The dugout Tay had alluded to turned out to be exactly that. The sharp slope had been dug into, and the front and sides of the dwelling constructed of stacked rough-hewn logs. A ridgepole ran back into the hillside, and a shallow-pitched roof of sod-covered rough boards, run off to each side. The door hung on three leather hinges. A twenty-foot square pole corral backed into a lean-to covering six or eight neatly stacked cords of wood. Tay rode up to the corral and dismounted. "Unload yerself, and put yer horses in the corral, or loose hobble 'em and let 'em go. The grass down by the creek'll keep 'em happy." He uncinched his saddle, took it off his horse and threw the blanket and saddle over the corral rail. The bridle followed a minute later. He slapped his horse on the rump, and it meandered off toward the creek.

"Won't he take off without hobbles?" Buell asked.

"Nope. He'll be there in the mornin'. Indians have tried to steal him three times, and ain't got 'er done yet. Hobble 'im, and they will fer sure."

"Then what about ours?" Simon asked.

"Haven't had any horse thievin' fer quite a spell. Reckon ya got to do what ya think is best. It were me, I'd hobble 'em." He winked and headed for the dugout door.

Simon and Buell unsaddled the horses and turned them loose, with hobbles. When they entered the home, they found Tay busy building a fire in a black iron stove. The whole dwelling only measured about sixteen feet square. Once inside, Simon saw that the dugout was, in fact, a squat, square log house set in the hillside. The rear end contained the stove and wall-to-wall shelves from the ceiling to the floor. On the left side a four-legged rawhide bed stood, with more shelves above it. A table and bench stood at the foot of the bed. The right side had a matching bed, and at the foot of it stood a squat ten-gallon pickle barrel. Simon had seen dozens just like it. A ladle hanging above on the wall suggested it might be the water supply. Traps, skins, rolled up hides and several leather packing bags hung from the ceiling in various places. A long flintlock rifle leaned against the wall just inside the door.

"Make yerself at home. I'll get a fire goin' and rustle up some grub." He added some larger pieces of wood to the small fire struggling for life in the stove.

Buell looked at the single bed and then at Simon. "Flip ya for it." He dug into his pants pocket for a coin.

Simon had never enjoyed a meal like it. Hunger, the good company, and the simple fact they didn't face another day of riding tomorrow helped a lot. Fried spuds, boiled carrots, steak, bakery bread and plum jam with butter, fresh tomatoes, and milk, tucked away until he could hardly breathe. "I hadn't counted on eating like this out here." He leaned back against the rough log wall.

"Why'd ya think that? There's upwards to a thousand people in and around Fort Laramie. We got most things ya have back East; they just cost more here and sometimes ya gotta wait a bit. A few of them shabby-lookin' houses near the fort has got some of the finest furniture and stuff you kin imagine. Lot of it jist picked up by the trail as the folks passin' through discovered they had too much to carry and threw it off."

"But, tomatoes?" Buell asked. "And spuds?"

"Sure. Folks gotta eat, so folks raise what's needed. I reckon if the damned railroad hadn't decided to run south of here, we could have grown into a big town. Now, looks like we'll start to fade along with the trail."

"Wasn't there one that runs into Montana Territory?" Simon asked.

"There was, the Bozeman. The Sioux shut 'er down, and the treaty we just signed says we ain't gonna use it no more, another reason we ain't gonna last."

"So, you think we might want to consider going on?" To Simon the idea didn't have a lot of appeal.

"Not really. I've been pokin' 'round some in the hills northeast of here. Found some interesting country. Ain't 'sposed ta be in there, but I reckon one lonely prospector ain't gonna disturb much." He seemed to enjoy dangling just enough of a story to draw more questions. They came instantly.

Buell leaned forward and rested his elbows on the table. "Whatcha mean, interesting?" His eyes reflected one of the kerosene lamps burning overhead. "Ya mean gold, don'tcha?"

"Ain't found enough to make me stay any place long. The Indians consider that country sacred, and they take it serious. But I've seen enough to know I'd like to have a free hand to nose around."

"How can you get in and out without them spottin' ya?" Simon asked.

"That's big country, boys. Contrary to what ya might've heard, Indians ain't no smarter or bigger than any other man. They do have the advantage of being growed up right there, but once a man has moved about some in those hills, that advantage is gone. I ain't afraid of 'em, but I do respect 'em."

"So, exactly where you finding this interesting country?" Buell asked.

"Cuz yer a little new here I'll overlook that, Buell. But fer yer own good, I'll tell ya that ain't a question ya ask of a prospector. I've had more'n one feller try to follow me inta the hills. Couple of 'em are still there." He lowered his head slightly and looked at Buell under a beaded brow. His meaning could not be mistaken.

Chapter 4

The McCaffrey roadhouse west of Fort Laramie consisted of a motley group of buildings set right on the road. The main building boasted two stories with a porch and a hitching rail out front. On either side of the building, a pair of nearly identical structures leaned into the big one, either for support or to hold it up; it was hard to tell which. A livery and blacksmith shop took up space across and down the road a little, with two large corrals that contained a dozen or so horses. Three more small buildings finished the scene. Simon and Buell reined up at the rail and tied their horses amongst a dozen others. Standing outside, they could hear the noise from within, but when they opened the door, the cacophony that greeted them made Simon blink with astonishment. They walked across the room to the bar.

"Where can I find the owner?" Simon asked the bartender, a tall, skinny man with oily hair.

The barkeep cupped his ear with one hand and raised his eyebrows.

"I'm looking for the owner." Simon glanced down, embarrassed for shouting.

"That'd be Amos McCaffrey." He pointed towards a table at the foot of some stairs that led to the upper story. "He's that fella in the brown coat and the derby hat."

Simon leaned closer. "Do you think he might be looking for help?"

"You what?" The bartender leaned over the bar with his head cocked sideways.

"How's my chances of getting a job?"

"You want to work here? What the hell for?" The bartender grinned at a customer standing next to Simon. "Amos is always hiring somebody. Maybe you can have my job." He turned and headed down the bar.

Simon and Buell walked half the length of the room to the table the barkeep had pointed out where six men sat playing cards. Simon waited until Amos McCaffrey caught his eye and nodded.

"Excuse me, sir," Simon said.

Amos nodded again.

"A Mister Triffet referred me to you about possible employment."

"Referred?" Amos grinned at the other card players. "Mister Triffet? You mean T. P., the sutler at the post?"

"Yes, sir."

"Gawdamn, he talks pretty don't he fellas? And respectful too. Now why can't you hard-asses treat me that way?" He held his hand up. "Don't answer that." He turned his chair and looked up at Simon and Buell. "So, just what can ya do?"

"I'm a skilled bookkeeper. I know how to order and inventory supplies, and I know how to work with the public. I worked in the mercantile trade for over three years."

McCaffrey directed his attention at Buell. "And what about you? You lookin' too?"

"I can shoe horses, do some vettin', drive a wagon team, and I've herded cows. And I can shoot."

Amos's gaze went to the ivory-handled pistol strapped to Buell's right hip. His eyes narrowed. "Nice-looking piece. Ya say you can use it?"

"I can, and have."

"Don't talk near as pretty as yer partner." He turned back to the players at the table. "Ain't near as respectful either." And then back to Simon and Buell. "Where you boys from?"

"Nebraska," Buell said quickly and glanced at Simon. "Near Fort Kearney."

"The law after you?" Amos held up his hand as Buell started to speak. "You answer," he said to Simon.

"No, sir. We left of our own accord, peacefully."

"Your own accord. Peacefully." He chuckled. "Don't ya love the way he talks, boys?" He grinned at his fellow players. "Well, matter of fact, I could use a man who can cipher and write. Talkin' like ya do, I don't have much doubt you can do both quite well. And I have need of someone to keep the lid on this place at times. So, here's what I'll do. You, what's your name?" He looked at Simon.

"Simon Steele."

"And you?"

"Buell Lacey."

Simon's eyebrows shot up and he looked at Buell.

"Okay, Simon. I want you to come back tomorrow, and I'll show you how I've managed to keep track of some of this place. Buell. I might want you to start right away. We'll go outside, and you can show me how well that pistol talks for you. But first I gotta try to skin a couple more cats right here. You two go and get yourself a beer or a whiskey, on me." He raised his hand over his head. "Twiggs!" he bellowed across the saloon. The bartender's head snapped around. "On me," he shouted, held up one finger and then pointed at Simon and Buell. He winked at Simon, turned his chair around, and picked up his hand of cards.

Twiggs waited for them at the far end of the bar. "Little quieter down here. What can I get ya?"

"I'll have a whiskey," Buell said. "Something with a label on it."

Twiggs smiled. "And you?" he asked Simon.

"I'll have a beer, thank you."

Twiggs pulled Simon's beer and set it in front of him and then reached under the bar for a bottle. "This one do?" He hoisted it.

Buell nodded.

Twiggs filled the shot glass and stepped back, the smile still on his face.

"Well, here's to a new place and a fresh start." Buell raised his glass.

"New place, fresh start." Simon touched his to Buell's and took a sip of beer. Warm, it tasted flat. He scowled at it for a moment, and then looked at Buell.

Eyes squinted shut and his face screwed up in a grimace, Buell had a hold of the bar, shaking his head: "Gawdamn, that's nasty shit." He gathered his spit and unloaded in a spittoon before glaring at Twiggs, who was now chuckling, his eyes asparkle.

"Thought the label meant something, didn't ya?"

"Well, it usually does."

"Not here. Pick any bottle in sight, and the contents came from the same barrel. Only difference is, some's watered and some's not, and even I can't tell which is which."

"How do you get away with that? At home we'd go to another saloon," Simon said.

"And you can here. There's one five miles east of the fort and another three miles west of here. They all serve the same stuff. So go ahead."

"You mean you don't have anything except that rotgut?" Buell asked.

"Sure." Twiggs smiled. "You just can't see it." He turned and sauntered down the bar.

"Don't know why you drink that stuff anyway, Buell. I know ya don't like it."

"Yeah, and I see you're really enjoying that beer."

They turned around and surveyed the saloon that Simon figured to be about seventy feet wide and thirty feet deep. On the left, a stairway angled from the front of the room, up to the second floor and over a door built into the staircase. A piano stood at the base of the steps, but against the street-side wall and just past where Amos McCaffrey played cards. Two four-by-six windows bracketed a set of double doors that opened to the street. Black sheet-iron stoves stood at either ends of the room. The bar itself ran the length of the back of the room except for about four or five feet on each end. Three dingy mirrors reflected the stacks of glasses and bottles lining the counter behind the bar. Coal-oil lamps, with polished reflectors, hung from the ceiling, placed to light the fifteen or so tables set up around the room. More lamps clung to the pair of evenly spaced, floor-to-ceiling pillars supporting the upper floor. Soldiers made up about half the people in the place, most of the rest roughly dressed beer drinkers. Simon counted four women. Everybody seemed to be shouting.

"Get you another?" Twiggs was back.

"If it's not the same stuff," Buell said.

Twiggs winked at him. "What'd Amos say about a job?"

"Looks like we're hired. I'm Simon Steele and this is Buell . . . Lacey." Simon extended his hand.

"Maxwell Twiggs. Call me Max. And seeing as how you're now members of the staff, I can get you a decent drink." He reached under the bar and retrieved a bottle, then looked at Simon. "You still drinking beer?"

"Yeah, I don't like whiskey much. I'll get along with what I have here."

Twiggs poured Buell's glass full.

"That's two dollars. Amos is watching." Twiggs chuckled again. "Amos is always watching."

"Two dollars! For a shot of whiskey?" Buell stared at the amber drink.

"For that, yes. Oh, never mind, it's on me. And don't just toss it back. Sip it."

Buell looked at him sideways and then eyed Simon. "Sip it?"

Simon shrugged.

Buell's face lit up and he grinned. "Simon, you ought to try that." He slid the glass toward him. "Try it."

Simon wrinkled his nose. "I really don't like it."

"C'mon."

Simon picked up the glass and took a small taste. And then another.

Buell took the glass away from him as he started to tip it again. "Hey, I said try it."

Simon looked at the bartender. "That's wonderful. What is it?"

"Napoleon Brandy. French. Good, isn't it?"

Amos McCaffrey laid his hand on Simon's shoulder. "I see Twiggs give ya a taste of my good stuff."

"Yes'ir. I've never tasted anything like that."

"One of the privileges that comes with ownin' the place." He turned to Buell. "Ready to show me what you can do with that fancy gun?"

"Anytime."

A shooting exhibition always draws a crowd, and the open space behind the saloon soon filled with over forty people. Several boxes, standing at increasing distances toward the river, suggested this wasn't an unusual event.

"Daggett!" Amos shouted at a short, filthy man standing

outside the back door of the saloon. "Grab three or four targets, and set 'em up on the boxes."

Daggett sauntered over to a barrel and retrieved three bottles. As he walked past and headed towards the target stands, Simon thought he could taste what the man smelled like.

"So, ya say you can and have," Amos said. "Are you quick?"

Buell drew his pistol part way out of the holster and let it drop back. "Quick enough so far."

"Quick enough. So far?" Amos looked at his cronies, chuckled and shook his head. "No respect at all."

Daggett set the first bottle on a box about fifty feet away and walked unsteadily toward them. He set the second bottle at about thirty feet.

"I guess we'll see." Amos glanced at Buell.

Daggett came to the closest box and reached out to set the bottle down. About a foot above the box, it exploded with an ear-shattering blast. A split second later the second bottle splattered. Daggett slumped to his knees and covered his head.

"Su'um bitch!" someone in the crowd said.

Amos turned to Buell, working his jaws and digging his finger in his left ear. "You don't mess around. Let me see you hit the last one." He stepped behind Buell while Daggett scrambled to his feet and hurried for the edge of the crowd.

Almost too fast to see, the Remington flashed out of the holster and went off. Wood splintered a couple inches to the left of the last brown target, followed almost instantly by a second shot. The top of the bottle vanished. Buell dropped the pistol into its holster.

Amos nodded his head slowly, his thumb scratching the stubble on his chin. "Yep, you kin shoot. Let me buy ya another drink—the good stuff."

★ ★ ★ ★ ★

Simon held his cup out as Tay Prescott poured it full of steaming coffee. The old man put the pot back on the stove, then sat at the table.

"Not surprised ya landed jobs right off," Tay said. "Ol' Amos is a sharp operator, but he's actually fairly honest. Not sayin' he won't take advantage of a good deal when he sees it, but he'll do what he says and keep his end on a bargain. Some o' the rest of them ain't so sweet, and I'll leave it at that. You'll sniff 'em out."

"What about the other place, the one you said was east of here?"

"B'longs to a feller named Evans. Crooked as hell, and he don't care if ya know it. Never been one ta in'erfere, but if ya ever figger to buy me a drink, I'd 'preciate it if ya didn't expect ta meet me there."

"What about the sutler?"

Tay leaned both elbows on the table, coffee cup held between cupped hands. "Drives a hard bargain, but he's honest. Gotta be, else the army'll send 'im packin'. I like ol' T. P. Acts kinda crusty, but I think his heart's well placed."

"How 'bout the army?" Buell asked. "I get the feelin' they pretty much run things around here."

"And you'd be right. Both those roadhouses are jist a twitch over five miles from the fort. Ain't no coincidence. Any closer and the army has control of who runs it and what kind of place they are. T. P. Triffet is granted full rights to all tradin' business within five miles of the fort. He has an agreement with Clay Rawlins about the stable and feed store. And Kent Berggren—he's married Clay's daughter—has a deal to sell guns and stuff like that. Everything else is T. P.'s business. Ya wanna buy some lumber, you buy it from T. P., even if it's sawed right here."

"Do you have any law?" Buell asked.

"Army law if it has anything to do with the soldiers or the forts and the roads that run between 'em. Or if Indians are involved. Course, they can stick their noses in anywhere they want to and do. Then there's a fed'ral marshal that comes up from Cheyenne once in a while. Mostly we settle our differences any way we can. I suspect that's what Amos hired you for, Buell."

The image of Judge Kingsley at home came to Simon's mind. "Don't you have a judge or a court?"

"Not as such. The military has the provost and the commander—Colonel Maynadier? I think he's still here—they change a lot, and I ain't got no reason to keep up anymore. The US marshal comes by when he's called, and we have a judge come through once a month fer a two-day stay."

"So if a person has a legal complaint, they wait until someone shows up to help them with it?" Simon shook his head. "That seems a little capricious."

"Cap, caprish . . . ca what? Damn youngin', d'ya always talk like that?"

"Yeah . . . he does. Irritatin' as hell, ain't it?" Buell chuckled.

"I mean, it's kinda hit and miss," Simon explained.

" 'Tis that. We've had three or four citizen groups git together and even had a couple town constables, but they soon turn to scrappin' with each other and fall apart. Things git real serious, they'll form a posse of sorts, and jist hang a feller, or run 'im outta the country. The army settles a lotta stuff ya might not think is any of their business, but they's not many will argue with a troop of soldiers. Seems to work so far."

"You mean a posse will hang a person without benefit of a trial, or some formal defense with a judge deciding?" Simon said.

"Yep. 'Cept there is a trial and there is a judge. The posse does both. Like I said, seems to work. I kin honestly say I don't know of a single person handed that kinda justice that didn't deserve it, and then some."

"Hmm. Lot different than what we're used to seeing. We had a sheriff at home who knew everything that went on in town. He took care of enforcing the law, and if any justice was dealt, he dealt it. Right, Buell?"

Buell stared at his cup, apparently lost in thought.

"Right, Buell?" Simon persisted.

"Wh—what?" Buell looked at Simon.

"I was saying Sheriff Staker didn't allow anyone but himself to lay down the law."

"Oh, yeah. Right. He was the law." Buell mumbled almost absently. "We better get goin'. I ain't sure when we're 'sposed ta be there, but I expect we should git."

"Don't figger you'll see anybody before about nine. They run that place till three or four in the mornin' sometimes."

"No, Buell's right. We'll show up just in case. We appreciate you putting us up again. We'll find a place to stay today."

"No problem. Been a real pleasure havin' ya. Don't talk to many, and I find you two real easy to git along with. Yer welcome anytime."

Tay followed them out and stood in the doorway as they went for the horses. Tay had been right—the animals grazed within a hundred feet of where they'd been left the night before.

Chapter 5

They arrived at McCaffrey's to find empty hitching rails and not a soul in sight. They tied up their mounts and tried the door to the saloon. It opened.

"Good morning, gentlemen," hailed Twiggs from one of the tables.

"We were beginning to wonder if anybody was here." Simon closed the door and headed for the bartender.

"Oh, they're here all right, just not conscious yet. Can I get you a cup of coffee or something?"

"Not for me. We had breakfast." Simon looked at Buell, who'd gone over to a tall stool by the stairs.

"Me either," Buell said.

"If you don't mind me asking, where you staying?" Twiggs asked Simon.

"We met a fella first day we were here who offered us a bed. We stayed there last night."

"We have rooms here," Twiggs said. "Unless you really want to stay at the fort."

"It's not at the fort exactly. His place is a little dugout north of the river, right on a small meadow. Got a corral and everything."

Twiggs's eyebrows arched. "You're staying with Tay Prescott?"

"Yeah. You seem surprised."

"Tay Prescott is not the friendliest person I've had the pleasure of meeting. Matter of fact, I find him downright unpleasant."

"And now *I'm* surprised," Simon replied. "I've enjoyed his company. He's told us a lot about the fort and how things run around here. What do you think Buell?"

"Hasn't been uncomfortable a bit, just the opposite. And he's a good cook."

"Well, I'm amazed. He has two friends around here that I know of, the gunsmith at the blacksmith's place, and strange as it may seem, an old Indian who lives east of the fort. Huh. Be that as it may, I know Amos can make you a deal for some rooms here. There are two buildings adjacent to this one with space in the back, and he has a small—can't call it a house—guess you'd call it a cabin, over by the stables. He'll be down in an hour or so, and we can talk to him."

"Well, if we have an hour, I think I'll take you up on the coffee. I can get it if you'll tell me where it's at."

Twiggs jerked his thumb toward a door at the right end of the bar. "Through there and on the left. You'll see it."

"Buell?"

"Yeah, might as well."

Simon returned with two enamel cups. They sat and jawed for a while.

The man clumping down the stairs didn't look anything like the person they'd talked to the night before. Hair disheveled, he wore a long robe that badly needed washing. He paused halfway down and studied the three men at the bar for several seconds, scratching his butt.

"So, ya did decide to take me up on the job? I'm a bit surprised." He continued down the stairs and came over to the table. "That coffee?"

"I'll get you a cup. Sit down." Twiggs left and returned with a large cup that he set in front of Amos.

"Got a little rowdy in here last night, so I didn't sleep too good." Amos took a hissing sip of the scalding brew. "Oooff, that tastes good. So, Simon, tell me a little about yourself."

"Not a lot to tell. I went to school until I was almost eighteen. Worked in a trading store for over three years. I've helped several people with new businesses set up their accounting books and inventory controls. Saved our mercantile store a lot of money by adding a few simple cross-checks. I can do sums, including fractions, and even some algebra and geometry. And I've read more books than I can count. I had a real good teacher who arranged for me to visit our local judge and read his books too."

"How about you Buell? I saw last night what you can do. Anything else?"

"My pa run the livery, so I know some about horses. I ain't afraid of work."

"Uh-huh," Amos grunted. "So, where ya plannin' on stayin'?"

"Mister Twiggs said you might have a place, or we can get something near the fort." Simon glanced at Buell, who shook his head. "I think we'd prefer to stay out here."

"Ain't no sense in you stayin' anyplace else. I'm gonna charge ya rent same as anyone, but maybe you'll get a break with me. Then again, maybe not," Amos added with a mischievous grin.

"And if you want to sleep, I'd suggest you negotiate for the little house over by the stable." Twiggs raised his eyebrows toward the ceiling. "The girls live upstairs and in the buildings either side. And they can get boisterous."

"I saw it," Buell said. "Is there room for both of us?"

"Easy," Amos said. "There's two rooms. Couple of beds in the one, and the other has a stove for heatin' and cookin' plus a sofa, a soft chair, and a table for eating on. Built it for myself, but found I wasn't spendin' a lot of time there, so I moved upstairs."

"How much?" Buell asked.

"How 'bout twenty dollars a month each? And I'll keep the woodpile supplied."

Simon thought about it a second. "That's about a dollar thirty a day, between us. I'm in." He glanced at Buell. "How about you?"

"You're the money man. I'll go along with whatever you decide."

"That's done, then," Amos said and rubbed his hands together. "Now, let's talk about what I need. I make my money by providing services the fort commander won't allow. Now, that don't mean we ain't got no rules—we do, and we enforce 'em. No whippin' up on the ladies. No knife fightin'. I hate knives. No sleepin' in the saloon. You rent a room, go with one of the girls and pay the fare, or you sleep outside. No credit, n-o-n-e, none. That's about it. Questions?" Amos leaned back in his chair and took a sip of coffee.

"Two. I can see where Buell fits, but I'm having a harder time seeing what you want from me. Bartending?"

"Yours is easy. You make me more money. You said you saved that storekeeper back home a lot by findin' better ways to do things. Do the same for me. Bartendin' is Twiggs's job."

"Might I work the same financial arrangement as I had at home with Mister Swartz? As an incentive bonus, I get a percentage of any increase in income realized because of my innovation?"

"Realized income? Ya leave me speechless, Simon." Amos chuckled and winked at Twiggs. "And who determines what's . . . realized?"

"You do."

"In that case, yeah. When I see the difference, we'll talk, and I'll cut ya a piece. Ya said two. What's the other one?"

"How much are we to be paid?"

"Five a day for each of you."

Simon nodded.

Amos looked at Buell. "Now, for you. After your little demonstration, there wasn't a man in here that didn't have something to say about it. Most were as impressed as I was, and you gained a lot of respect, the fearful kind. But—and there's always a but—there were one or two who see you as some parvenu shooter who needs to be taken down a peg or two. And they're gonna push ya soon's they get a chance." Amos studied Buell's face, which showed no emotion. "You hear what I'm sayin'?"

"Yup."

"Well, ya don't act like it. Ain't ya worried about someone looking to put a ball in yer gut?"

"Not much."

"Damn boy, ya got brass. So, I'll add this to give ya something to think about. I don't want no killin' if ya can help it. Dead yahoo can't buy a thing, and that makes killin' one bad for business. Understand?"

Buell looked at his cup for a time, and then nonchalantly picked it up. Peering over the rim, he gave Amos a fleeting half smile, then slugged off the cool coffee. "Makes it a little harder to be sure of the end result."

Amos huffed and shook his head. "All right then, you're now working for me." He stood and offered his hand to Simon. "Only contract I need, and the only one you're gonna get." Simon shook it. He then turned to Buell and did the same before heading for the stairs. "I'm gonna go back to bed for an hour."

Simon watched Amos to the top of the stairs, then leaned his elbows on the tabletop, and studied Twiggs. "Any ideas?" He grinned.

"Sounds to me like he's given you free hand. I've never really thought about how to make more money. I get three dollars a day and six percent of everything I sell at the bar. That can get substantial during the winter."

"I didn't see anyone eating in here last night, yet you have a full kitchen. Back home, the saloon we went to was famous for the food."

"Had a cook for a time, but he poisoned us twice, and Amos sent him packing. Nobody complained about the loss, and I don't think Amos has really been looking."

"So you make your money in the drinks alone?"

"Damn near. Amos gets a cut of the ladies, but they don't last long. Most take a look at the place and leave for Cheyenne or Denver. We only got four presently."

"I noticed last night that Buell didn't think much of the whiskey." Simon punched Buell on the arm. "The brandy was good, but the other—what was it?"

"Pure grain alcohol, molasses, water and cayenne pepper. Maybe Buell got a shot of some stuff that had a little too much pepper."

Buell's eyes squinted. "You mean it ain't real whiskey?"

"Nope. Costs too much to ship. We get a barrel of the two-hundred-proof stuff, cut it half with water, flavor it, and pour it in bottles. Doesn't taste that good, but that isn't why they're drinking it."

"How much do you charge for a drink?"

"Two bits a jigger, or five for a dollar, or eight dollars a bottle, and they pour their own."

"How many drinks in a bottle?"

"About fifty; the bottles vary a bit."

"Do you sell much of the French stuff?"

"Maybe two bottles a week. Mostly on paydays, and usually when they're so drunk they don't know the difference anyway." Twiggs smiled. "Pay's the same for me."

"Do you have something I could write on?"

"Sure. I can see the wheels turning already." Twiggs got up and went to the bar.

Buell sighed and slumped back in his chair as Twiggs handed Simon a notebook. Simon asked, and Twiggs answered, questions for the next hour, Simon diligently making notes. Buell sat quietly and watched.

Simon had just come back from a visit to the privy when the front door banged open and the man who had set up the bottles for Buell's shooting the day before shuffled into the room.

"Morning, Plato," Twiggs said.

"Mister Twiggs," he replied and looked at Simon and Buell. "Mister Lacey, Mister Steele," he said with a nod.

He scowled through a month's growth of scraggly beard, his hair sleep-plastered to one side of his head. Simon smelled him long before he got to the table.

"Had your breakfast yet?" Twiggs asked.

"Nope. Ain't got three cents on me, so I figgered I could get some o' my jobs done first and then eat." He swallowed as his mouth reacted to talk of food.

"You can eat first if you want, Plato. Hell, no sense waiting. I know you're good for it."

"Nope, don't wanna ride if I can't pay the ticket."

He walked to the end of the bar, and picked up a couple of the spittoons arrayed along the front. He carried them through the kitchen door, and then another one slammed shut. Pretty soon, he was back, and gathered up all of the fifteen or so brass and copper pots, two or three at a time, and carried them out.

When Daggett didn't come back, Buell looked at Twiggs. "That's his job? Cleaning out spittoons?"

"Somebody has to do it. And it's a rare morning when he doesn't show up for work."

"Damn. I'm not sure I could do that."

"Probably not his choice either, but he has a problem with whiskey. A morning job is about all he can handle. By afternoon I wouldn't trust him to hold the door open. He's his own Nemesis."

"So Amos lets him clean spittoons in exchange for something to drink?" Simon asked. "That seems like . . . I don't know, taking advantage—exploiting."

"Would it be better to let him go hungry as well as dry? It's damned if you do and same if you don't." Twiggs huffed. "And spittoons isn't all he does."

Sometime later, Daggett clanked through the door with the last of the pots and set them on a table. Retrieving a broom from the kitchen, he went to work on the floor, starting at the stairwell end. Simon noticed he never made eye contact as he swept the floor around them. Twiggs continued to chat idly with Simon and Buell. When Daggett finished, he took a seat at the far end of the room.

Twiggs said, "I'm going to get him something to eat now before the rest come down and take over the kitchen. I'll see you guys later." He pushed out of his chair and went into the back.

Simon leaned over the table, closer to Buell. "He reminds me of John Lindstrom." He nodded in Daggett's direction.

"A little I guess, but John never looked like that."

"Not that. The drinking. I heard Ma and Pa talk about him back home. Always so drunk by afternoon someone had to lead him to wherever he was staying."

"I remember that. He slept in our livery a lot."

"Wonder if Daggett might ever get away from it like John did?"

"I wouldn't think so. Look at 'im. He's squirmin' like a fishin' worm, and it ain't eight o'clock yet."

"I feel sorry for him."

"You would. It's his hole, leave him in it."

"I suppose. Still, wished there was something we could do." Simon glanced at Daggett again, who was now head down on the table.

"Doesn't look like a lot happens around here in the mornin'," Buell said, leaning back in his chair. "Hell, we coulda slept another couple hours."

"Yeah, and listen to Tay stew around that little place of his. I'd just as soon be up and around. You want some more coffee?"

"No. My guts are sloshin'. Let's go out and see some more of this place, and I'd like to take a look at our new home." Buell got up and stretched.

"Good idea."

They left the saloon and stood for a minute or so, looking up and down the street. The porch they stood on, made of two-inch-thick planks, stood about a foot and a half above the street. The street was dusty now, and Simon imagined what it looked like in April, when the frost starts to leave the ground and everything turns to muck. Several chairs leaned against the front of building. They went down the two steps in front, and headed left for the cabin, just past the stables.

Simon pushed the door open and waved Buell in. The little house was exactly as described. "Looks real nice, but I didn't expect curtains and tablecloths."

Buell walked over to one of the easy chairs and sat. He lightly punched both arms with his fist and tilted his head back until it touched the upholstery. "This one's mine."

Simon stepped past the stove and through an open door to the back room. "Just as nice in here. The beds have feather ticks on 'em. Bet we sleep warmer tonight than we did last night." He came back into the living-room-kitchen.

"This is gonna be good," Buell said. "Feels kinda strange having a place of my own, though. Is there a back door in there?" He nodded toward the bedroom.

"Yup."

"Some place we can put the stuff from our saddlebags?" Buell looked around the room.

"Yeah, two wardrobes in the bedroom, and a dresser."

Buell stood and went outside, returning with their bags.

"Here's yours." He passed a bulging pair to Simon and continued on into the bedroom. "I'm gonna take the one on the left. Any problem?"

"Nope," Simon said as he set his bag on the table. He opened the bottom door on the cupboard. "We got pots and pans and everything in here." He opened the rest of the doors and examined the interiors. "Dishes, knives and forks. We won't have to buy much for this place."

"Are ya a little suspicious about this deal?" Buell asked from the bedroom.

"I could be, but the Daggett thing makes me feel a little easier, and Tay said Amos was fair and honest."

"He said fairly honest, if I remember, not fair and honest. There's a difference."

"Ma used to say, the proof's in the pudding. We'll just have to wait and see."

He continued his inventory of the cabinets.

"Simon? You still out there?" Buell asked from bedroom.

"Yeah." Simon stared at the black skillet in his hand. "Just thinkin' for a minute."

"Went real quiet." Buell stepped into the room. "Yeah, I know. I thought about Pa last night. Sometimes I really miss Carlisle."

"Me too." Simon put the skillet on the stove. "But we're here now, and we have things to do. Got your shit squirreled away?"

"Yup. I'm gonna go see what the stable looks like. Want me to take your horse?"

"Yeah. I'll be along in a few minutes."

Buell picked his hat off the floor and went outside.

Chapter 6

Simon stepped through the door under the stairs, leaving the small room that served as his office. The early-evening air in the saloon pounced on him like a sweaty, over-warm pillow. Amos had told them Saturday night would be their first real taste of what the packed roadhouse could be like. Even with his admonition, the noise, smoke and heat came as a stifling surprise.

Every table had at least six men crowded around it, and some had as many as ten. People stood two deep the entire length of the bar. Twiggs, a permanent smile affixed, poured drink after drink of the rotgut for the men standing. A tall woman in a long, sleeveless dress, cut low in front, helped him deliver drinks to those seated. Another woman stood by a table enduring the hand of a soldier groping around under her dress. Amos sat in his usual place, playing cards with four others. Nearby, at the base of the stairs, Buell sat perched on a three-foot-high chair. His Sharps rifle stood butt down on the bottom step and leaned against the banister post. He had an unobstructed view of the whole saloon, and every patron could see him.

Simon made his way over. "Luger's place back home was never this wild, even on New Year's Eve."

Buell leaned down. "And I think it's just gettin' started."

"Any trouble that you can see?"

Buell nodded at the woman Simon had noticed before. "That young trooper there is about to find out it costs money to stick his fingers in the candy jar. Petula has give me a couple of looks, and I think she's about had enough of him."

"Nothin' new there. From what I've seen the last three nights, the soldiers will take what they can for free for as long as they can. I'll talk to you later."

Simon headed toward the bar. "Can I give you a hand, Max?" he asked Twiggs.

"Wouldn't mind a bit. Paydays can be busy, but tonight is unusual. Thanks."

Simon looked down the long counter and saw a hand waving in the air—he headed for it.

Sergeant Adolph Barrschott had endured a lousy day and he needed a whiskey. First, a new recruit had gotten thrown off Stomper, and Stomper, true to his name, had deliberately searched out the rider and stepped on him, snapping the boy's left arm like a dry twig. He threw a saddle on his horse, muttering to himself. "Of course, Lieutenant Fuzznuts blames me for puttin' a raw recruit 'on a rough horse,' as he called it. Rough horse, my ass. Fuzznuts wouldn't know a rough horse if it dumped in his mess kit. Hell, I put all the fresh meat on Stomper. Livens things up. Besides, the little shit coulda got outta the way if he hadn't been all hunkered up like a scared prairie dog."

Then Lieutenant Maupin had taken Barrschott off the escort detail for next week's supply wagon detail. Not only a nice break, a trip to Fort McPherson, it offered other, more important, considerations, and those now looked to be going by the way. And finally, Lieutenant Maupin had made him finish the duty roster for next week.

Barrschott had slapped the stirrup down and climbed onto the animal, still fuming. "Any other time Monday morning is good enough, but Fuzznuts was upset about the horse thing. Shit-ass shavetail."

Arriving at the hitching rail in front of Amos's weathered brown building, he dismounted. Slamming his huge shoulder into a waiting horse's hip, he shoved open a space for his own. Then he stomped up the two steps to the porch and pushed open the door.

Twiggs spotted the dusty, blue hulk as Barrschott intimidated his way in a straight line across the room to the bar. The first sergeant stood six foot seven and weighed nearly three hundred pounds. An extra-wide space opened as the men on either side shrank away from his selected spot.

"Whiskey!" His fist crashed to the bar.

"You needn't shout, Adolph," Twiggs said. "I'm standing right here."

"And a damn good thing. What I don't need is more waitin'."

Twiggs set up a glass and poured it brimming. "Had a bad one?"

"Do beans make ya fart? Where'n hell the army gets these sons'a whores they call officers is beyond my reckonin'. If that gob of mule snot slips me one more notch, I'm gonna pin his big ears back with them shiny gold bars." He carefully picked up the glass, tossed the contents to the back of his throat, and swallowed. Tears glazed his eyes briefly, and he exhaled the breath he'd held in anticipation of the red pepper's bite. "Oh Lord, how kin ya feed that shit to a fellow white man? Pheew. Fill 'er up."

"I gather you're referring to Lieutenant Percival Manwaring Maupin the Third, late of the Hudson Valley School for the Unemployable." Twiggs chuckled.

"That's the sonuvabitch. And ta think the folks that spawned him might have bred some more jist like 'im." The second shot followed the first. He nodded at Twiggs and nudged the glass forward.

Twiggs filled it again.

"Where's Amos tonight?" Barrschott turned around and surveyed the saloon.

"He was over there playing cards at his usual table. He'll be back shortly. Trip to the privy, I expect." Twiggs hustled to three customers down the bar and poured another three drinks.

"Who's that feller sitting in the high chair?" Barrschott asked when Twiggs returned.

"Name's Buell. Amos hired him and that young man at the other end of the bar." He indicated Simon.

"Thought the bar was yours." Barrschott eyed the glass of caramel-colored liquid waiting for him on the bar.

"Still is. He asked to help, and I said I'd appreciate it. I didn't say anything about payment. And that'll be six bits or a dollar for two more." He pointed to the whiskey and winked at the sergeant.

"Ya never miss a one, do ya?" Barrschott laid a dollar on the bar.

"Can't afford to. I've got plans that cost money, and every one of these counts." Twiggs picked up the dollar, dropped it in the cash drawer below the counter, and then headed toward another customer who stood holding an empty glass in the air.

"How are you holding up, Simon?" Twiggs asked as he pulled a mug of beer.

"This is a lot more work than meets the eye. Who's that giant you've been talking to?"

"Name's Barrschott. His bark is a lot worse than his bite. Mind you, it's not a good idea to irritate him, but I actually get along with him quite well."

Twiggs headed back up the bar with the mug of beer, then clinked a dime into the cash drawer as he headed for another customer.

★ ★ ★ ★ ★

Buell eased to the edge of his chair as the corporal who'd been groping one of the girls made another pass at her. She shoved his hand down and tried to turn away. A shout went up from his tablemates as he caught her by the wrist and yanked her to her knees.

"Now yer where ya kin do me some good," the trooper said, sneering.

Buell had already made his way halfway across the room when the woman cried out. "You're hurtin' my arm. Make him let go, please," she pleaded to no one in particular.

"Yer paid to do what I tell ya," the corporal said.

"Let her go, Blue. Now!"

The soldier held onto the woman's wrist, her arm twisted outward, elbow flexed awkwardly. He eyed Buell up and down, his eyes pausing on the uncocked Sharps for a moment. Then he puffed his lips dismissively, and turned his attention to the tearful woman. "Kiss my balls," he said to her.

The butt of the Sharps flashed through the distance to the soldier's jaw in a short arc and connected before his eyes could come back to Buell. Two teeth rattled across the table and fell off onto the floor. They landed at the same time as the trooper and his chair.

Buell helped the young woman to her feet and steadied her until the older woman serving drinks rushed over. She took her across the room to the kitchen door. He turned to find the giant in dusty blue and wearing the three strips and diamond of a cavalry first sergeant between himself and the high chair by the stairs.

"Weren't no need fer that, goddammit," Barrschott's voice boomed.

"She asked him to stop, and so did I. That's enough." Buell gripped the Sharps with both hands.

"She's a whore. That's what she's paid for." The sergeant stepped over and looked down at the unconscious trooper.

"He wasn't payin'. And the rules say no hurtin' the women."

"And what gives you the right ta bust a man's jaw like that?"

"I did," Amos said as he strode across the floor from the rear.

"He weren't hurtin' her much, Amos. Certainly no call for your man to bust 'im up like that."

"His call. It's what I hired him for."

"I've a mind to take some o' the bright offa you." Barrschott took a step towards Buell.

The double clack sound as the Sharps went to full cock stopped him in mid step. Buell pointed the muzzle at the sergeant's throat, and then stared coolly into the man's eyes. Their gazes locked for only a moment, Barrschott's eyes narrowed, and a twitch flicked across his cheek.

Then the tall soldier turned on the seated troopers. "Pick up that shithead, and git him back to the barracks. Doc ain't gonna be happy seein' a skunk-drunk skirt chaser this time of night. Move! Goddammit!" He kicked a chair and dumped the seated trooper sprawling. "And Fuzznut's gonna plug his fuse hole. You bastards have just finished my day for me. Sonsabitches. Now get the hell out of here," he bellowed furiously, and aimed another kick, the target scrambling out of the way.

Simon, mouth agape, watched the huge sergeant shove and drag the five troopers out the door. Barrschott's sulfurous tirade went on for several minutes as he questioned in detail the intellect, gender, and lineage of every one of his men. As the swearing faded, the noise in the saloon returned to its previous volume.

Simon walked over to Twiggs. "I thought we were going to witness a disaster."

"I wasn't so sure myself."

"I was glad to see you had that shotgun ready in case. I'm not so sure Buell would've had time to cock and aim that Sharps if the sergeant hadn't turned to check on the trooper first."

"Shotgun wasn't to protect Buell, Amos, Barrschott, or anyone else."

"Huh? Why then?"

"Couple years ago, we had a full-fledged riot. Barrschott and about twenty troopers went at it hammer and tongs with about the same number of buffalo hunters. Right in the middle of it, someone hit me with a bung starter and knocked me cold as a splitting wedge. Then they took all three cash drawers. Must have gotten away with close to two hundred dollars." Twiggs hefted his shotgun. "I was protecting my investment." Then he put it under the bar. "I got customers, and I better get back at it. Here comes the boss." Twiggs turned away.

Amos and Buell made their way over.

Simon studied his friend for a second. "Damn, Buell, you scare me when you do that."

"I think he did good," Amos said. "I was watchin' too—just went to take a piss at the wrong time. I was wonderin' what yer first problem would be like. This one was perfect. Ya stood toe-to-toe with the biggest the army's got, and didn't blink. Don't know if I coulda done that. Scared?"

"No, but I wouldn't want to try that without something to even things up a bit. That son of a bitch is big."

Amos chuckled. "And strong as a bull. Don't think for a minute that big gut is soft. I saw him take on three buffalo skinners. One hit him smack in the stomach with the butt of a Hawken rifle. Woulda floored anyone else. Just riled Barrschott. They got the best of 'im in the end, but there was a lot of patchin' up to do on several."

"Can we expect that to be the end of it, then?" Simon asked.

"I think so. If Barrschott thought what Buell did was unfair, he'd have had a go, Sharps or not. He's real protective of his men, 'specially the younger ones." Amos looked down at the carbine leaning against the bar. "I'm wonderin', why'd ya use that instead of your pistol?"

"There's somethin' about the big black hole in the end of a carbine barrel that leaves very little doubt. I saw it in that big mule's eyes. You kin never be sure about how fast a man can get to his pistol, but anybody can pull a trigger quicker'n you kin blink. 'Sides that, I can use the pistol if I need to."

"Difference is, most people won't pull the trigger. Would you have?"

"Yup. Wouldn't have pointed it if I wasn't ready to use it."

"But you was glad he backed off? Weren't ya, Buell?" Simon asked hopefully.

"Didn't matter. I know how to take care of myself. And keepin' things under control is what Mister McCaffrey pays me for."

"But I said no killin', remember?"

"That was his choice, not mine. I'm ready to do what I need to." Buell looked at Simon. "Let me see that shotgun Twiggs had."

Simon reached under the bar and handed it over.

"There's more to making good stew than just knowin' how to stir, Buell," Amos said as Buell inspected the gun. "But, good job. Nobody hurt bad, and I think they'll be lookin' at ya before they decide to start something from now on. I'm gonna get back to my card game."

Amos zigzagged across the room to his table, stopping twice to josh with some of the customers.

"What did he mean by that stew thing? I hate it when you guys talk like that," Buell said. He handed the shotgun back to Simon.

"I think he means just your knowing how to shoot isn't all he wants from you. There are other things that make a good saloon peacekeeper."

"Like what?"

"Restraint comes to mind, and tact."

"What the hell do you mean . . . tacked? Gawdammit, Simon, ya know I can't understand those big words, yet ya keep pushin' 'em at me. If ya can't say it in plain talk, quit talkin'. You sons-abitches make me feel like an idiot." Buell grabbed his carbine and strode back to his high chair.

When Simon tried to catch his eye, Buell avoided it.

"I think doing what he does takes a lot more out of him than you think." Twiggs had stepped up beside Simon.

"You heard?"

"Yes. That had nothing to do with you, Simon. He's strung so tight right now, I'm surprised his knees bend."

"I hate it when he's mad at me."

"But it's been like this all your life, hasn't it? Between the two of you?"

"I guess it has. How'd you know that?"

"At one time, it was my job to know things like that about people. Enough to say Buell will be all right in a while. He's full of vinegar now though. I hope nobody else decides to try him."

Chapter 7

Simon spent the winter of 1868–69 learning the intricacies of operating a profitable saloon and gentleman's retreat, and in that six months had come to several conclusions about improving the business's profitability. Buell's single encounter with the brash soldier and subsequent face-off with Sergeant Barrschott had, as Amos predicted, been enough to gain the fearful respect of the regular customers.

Simon rode toward the fort, the April sun well up, but the bright promise of warmth not quite delivered. Since taking the job at Amos's, he had not been back to the fort. Sergeant Barrschott mailed for him the single letter he'd written to his parents, and he'd included a few words in a telegraph Buell had sent to his father. He needed some new clothes, and knew to get it right, he had to get them himself.

"Nice to see you, Mister Steele. Hibernatin' over?" T. P. peered through the mass of hair covering his face. Simon imagined an unseen smile that would match the sparkle in T. P.'s eyes.

He smiled back. "Yes'ir. It's been a busy and interesting winter. First one I haven't spent in school, and I missed that. But I've about worn out the two pairs of pants I had, and, as you can see, the shirts have fared even worse." He tugged at his frayed collar.

"It's all right there." T. P. pointed to a long shelf that carried stacks of folded pants and shirts, bolts of cloth, and a cabinet of sewing materials. "I think you'll find what you need. Underwear and socks are under the counter. Just open those doors and poke around in there."

"Noticed some Indians outside when I came in. They didn't look very friendly."

"They aren't. They're Sioux, and this particular bunch never did cotton to the treaty, but they like comin' here. They have a weakness for tobacco and candy. The tall, ugly one is called Two Strike. They say he killed two Pawnee with one bullet."

As Simon rummaged around looking for some flannel drawers, the door opened, and the tall Sioux T. P. had been talking about strode in. He glided silently to the counter at the far end of the store, and fixed the sutler with a stony stare.

"Tobacco. One." He pointed to the foot-long twists of raw plug behind T. P. and held up a finger.

T. P. got one and laid it on the counter. "One dollar, Two Strike."

"You know name. You know Two Strike chief?"

"Yeah, I know. Still costs one dollar." T. P. kept his hand firmly on the two-inch-wide strip of tobacco.

The Indian stared at him, never looking at the counter. Opening his hand, he let drop a single silver dollar. It rebounded off the counter and onto the floor. T. P. stooped over to retrieve it and when he stood, the Sioux met him with a contemptuous sneer.

"Pick from dirt like squaw." He snatched the twist, and walked silently out the door without closing it.

"Arrogant sonuvabitch." T. P. headed around the end of the counter.

"I'll get it," Simon said. As he closed the door, he glimpsed the Indian gnawing a bite off the twist. Then he finished making his selections at the dry-goods shelves. He put everything on the counter.

"Let's see what ya got here." T. P. sorted through the stack of clothes. "Two pairs of pants, seven dollars, two shirts, eleven, three socks, thirteen seventy, and three drawers comes to sixteen dollars and seventy cents. Anything else?"

"Yeah, I've never seen them before." Simon pointed to a barrel of round red spuds. "They any good?"

"I love 'em." T. P. licked his lips. "Farmer that brought them in says that's the last of 'em. They're best boiled with just butter, salt and pepper on 'em."

Simon thought about it for a moment, then nodded.

"How many?"

"Oh, I don't know, five pounds?"

T. P. went to the barrel and put a few potatoes in a small cloth sack. Hefting it, he said, "That's six, give or take. Fifty cents for five. We'll make it an even seventeen dollars."

Simon left the store and went to his horse. Opening his saddlebags, he stuffed the shirts and pants in one side, and the socks and underwear in the other. As he contemplated putting the dusty sack of spuds in with the socks, he heard a dog yelp. He looked over his horse and at a group of Indians lined up along the store's end. Directly in front of them crouched a puppy, tied to a piece of firewood that must have outweighed it three times. The dog cowered when one of the Indians walked up and aimed a kick at its side. Seeking escape, the pup scampered away crabwise when the rope bit into its scruffy neck. The Indians spit squirts of brown tobacco juice on it as it fled. One stream hit the pup directly in the eyes. It stopped, and whining, pawed frantically at its face. The Indians laughed, and another one stepped out of line toward the dog.

"Hey! What you doing to that dog?" Simon shouted as he headed for it.

Two Strike stepped in front of him. "My dog. You go."

"You can't do that to an animal," Simon said as he tried to walk around the tall Sioux.

Simon was prone on his back before he knew it, his sack of spuds beside him. The Indian stood astraddle him and glared. Looking at the others, he nodded at the dog. The puppy yelped again as a moccasin-covered foot dug into its side. Two Strike smiled down at Simon.

"What's going on here?" T. P. half shouted from the porch.

Two Strike looked at the sutler. "He fight Two Strike."

"About what? Simon?"

Simon scooted back, digging with elbows and heels, and stood. The Indian grinned, then slowly turned his back on him to face his friends. They hollered and laughed.

"They're torturing that dog," Simon shouted. "I can't stand to see that." His voice quaked.

"They see them different than we do," T. P. said. "If they find it amusing, they're likely to do anything. Not much you can do about it. Dog's not worth what that bastard might do if you make a fuss about it."

"I've got to do something. Will he sell it?"

"Two Strike, you trade for dog?" T. P. asked and made a sign.

The Sioux looked at him for a moment, and then a grin spread across his thin lips. "Trade," he said and pointed at the sack on the ground.

"Fine, then." T. P. started to retrieve the potatoes.

"No! Squaw get." He pointed at Simon and then at the sack.

The rest of the Indians watched, sullen and silent, as Simon stooped to pick up the spuds and offer them to the Indian. Two Strike turned his back on him, said something, and nodded at a young Indian, who stepped forward to take them from Simon. The whole group, pointing at Simon, whooped and howled with laughter, spattering tobacco juice everywhere. Two Strike folded his arms across his chest, and launched one final stream at the dog, covering its back with spit. Taking four long steps, he leaped on his horse. Then, kicking it furiously, he led the noisy group south, across the river, and away from the fort.

Simon watched them go, and then went to the cowering dog. He extended the back of his hand as he spoke to it. "Hey, little fella, you look a mess."

The puppy bared his teeth and tucked his tail.

Simon yanked his hand away. "Don't bite me, fella. I'm trying to help."

"That ain't aggression," T. P. said. "The bared teeth and the tucked tail means he knows you're boss. Hell, fer that, I expect he thinks everybody's the boss. Poor mutt. Ain't ya never had a dog?"

"Nope. By the time we could afford to feed one, I guess I'd grown out of the notion."

Simon touched the pup on the head, and it dribbled urine on its leg. Simon drew back his slime-covered finger. "Shit." He looked up at T. P. who now stood with three others watching the play. "Mister Triffet, would you get in my left saddlebag and fetch me a pair of them flannel drawers?"

T. P. got them and handed him the garment. Simon wiped his fingers on one leg and then untied the rope from the wooden anchor. Putting his hand under the puppy's soggy belly, he tucked the scrawny mutt into the open end of the drawers and stood. The puppy's head disappeared from the opening as it snuggled into a ball in his arms.

"Well, ya got yerself a dog," T. P. said smiling. "Whatcha gonna call it?"

"I don't have a clue. My horse is called Horse. I guess I can call him Dog."

"After what you went through? Do you know how close ya come to getting yerself cut? Ya gotta give him a name just cuz he cost ya, if for no other reason."

"Well, he cost me four bits. How about that, Four Bits?"

T. P. and the others, now six of them, all shook their heads and frowned.

"Okay, how about Spuds . . . or Spud. Yeah, Spud."

Everyone nodded and jabbed ribs with elbows. The dog had a name.

Simon didn't miss the fact that Buell wasn't all that happy about living with a dog. At least that was the temper he displayed. Simon taught the puppy to not sleep on his bed, but for the life of him, could not extend that prohibition to Buell's. Spud stayed in the office when Simon worked there, out in front of the saloon when his master worked the bar, and at the front door when they were home.

Daggett catered to the dog, sneaking him tidbits from the kitchen in the morning. Spud spent afternoons on the porch where Daggett sat to sleep off the morning whiskey. Periodically, Spud would go to the door and wait for someone to open it. He'd spy Simon, and then turn back to his spot and lie down again.

Summer blazed by, fall glowed gold for a time, and then the confinement of cold weather settled on them. By spring of 1870, what everyone had predicted about Spud's size was put lie to. He was not the lean, mellow, forty-pound hound as predicted. Instead, he'd grown to eighty pounds of black-and-tan energy. He padded happily alongside Simon's horse as they went to the telegraph office one afternoon to pick up a message.

Standing on the porch in front of the telegraph office, Simon stared at ten words spelled out in bold block letters.

CONFIRM LOCATION STOP REPLY ADDRESS STOP ALL WELL STOP

LINDSTROM

John wants to write, Simon mused. All is well. About what, then? Ma or Pa, one of the kids, Mace? Not Mace. Buell says he's fine and so is Aunt Ruth. What, then? Sarah!

Simon dropped his hand to his side. For the first time in over a year he'd deliberately thought her name, and it made his chest ache. Spud nuzzled his snout under Simon's hand and whined once, softly. Simon knelt in front of his dog. "It's okay. Got a spook that won't leave me alone. It just said hello."

The twin tan spots over the dog's eyes shifted alternately up and down as his brow furrowed into several creases. The liquid eyes beamed faith and support as the white-tipped tail swept the boardwalk clear of dust. Simon grabbed the dog's head and hugged it, then went back into the office. "Telegram to Carlisle, Nebraska, please."

Simon faced Amos across the three-foot-wide desk in his office. "I think we could make a good profit if we started to serve full meals."

"Tried it once, and damn near died from it. Twiggs ever tell ya about that?"

"He did. But from what I can gather, the last cook had more interest in what was just beyond the wall than what was in the kitchen. Our new cook will know how to cook and will not, as a condition of employment, be allowed to drink or be drunk when he's at work."

"Well and good, but where are these happy customers going to eat?"

"Those that want can sit right here in the saloon and—"

"And have some drunk puke in their soup?"

"And,"—Simon sighed—"those who want something a little more private and quiet, can adjourn to our new dining rooms on either end of the saloon."

"What rooms?" Amos cocked his head to one side.

"The rooms we'll convert when we move May, Charlotte, and Beth upstairs with the other ladies."

"Oh, I can hear May right now. Have you said anything to her?"

"Of course not."

"Well, she ain't gonna like it." Amos pursed his lips and shook his head.

"Who owns this place?" Simon waited a moment. "You do."

"Still, she's been here almost ten years and gets something for that. Times weren't always easy, and she stuck with me."

"I can't see how improving our services will hurt her. Surely she'll see that."

"I can see you haven't had much experience with the opposite kind. They know what they want now, and later will take care of itself. And they're contrary."

"Can I talk to her about it?"

"Go ahead. But leave yourself an easy exit." Amos grinned at him. "Now, assuming I agree, and I ain't, how much is this going to cost?"

"Four hundred and seventy-five dollars."

"Holy shit, where am I going to get that kind of money?"

"You forget, Amos, I'm doing your books. I know precisely how much money you make on the saloon. And that's only what I *know* of. God knows how much you have I don't know about. You can afford this easily."

"I don't know." Amos rubbed his chin and scowled. "And when will I see a return?"

"I think, with the right cook, we could see a profit before the end of winter."

Amos snorted. "And there's the hitch, the right cook."

"If you let me take care of it, I can find one."

"All right, Simon. If it wasn't for the whiskey idea, I wouldn't consider this, but shipping in real whiskey and raising the price to forty cents worked. And the new mixed drinks are sellin' good too. I still can't understand why anyone would want to drink that sweet stuff. We took a third of Evans's customers, and he's too cheap to try what you did. How'd you put it, quality wins out? Got to hand it to ya, Simon, you know what you're doing."

Buell walked through the livery to the door in back and opened it.

"Hi, Buell," Kent said.

"Howdy. Tay was out to Amos's place a couple weeks ago and said you wanted to see me."

"Yeah. How's it goin' out there? Haven't seen ya in a couple months." The smith carefully leaned the rifle he was working on against the bench and perched on a stool.

"Been nice and quiet. Usual arguin' drunks, but that deal with the soldier at the very start made my job easy."

"I see him around. Doc didn't do such a good job on his jaw did he?"

"Nope, nothin' lines up. He still comes in a lot, and always makes it a point to catch my eye and scowl. Name's Rankin."

"Someone saw our Indian friend." Kent's brow furrowed.

"Knife? Where?"

"Couple of troopers came in and said they saw him at Scott's Bluff."

"They sure?"

"Positive. A trader there said his name was Knife, and the troopers said he was missing his right thumb." The gunsmith's eyes gleamed.

"That means he's still prowlin' around." Buell unconsciously pushed down on the handle of his pistol. "I wonder if he knows we know?"

"Don't see why he would."

"I'd sure like to get a clean shot at him." Buell's eyes slipped past Kent to go out of focus on the far wall.

"I would too."

"I 'preciate the news. I'll keep my eyes open."

Kent nodded and reached for the rifle. Buell turned and left, his mind filled with the vision of a shadowy figure lurking in the darkness by the river.

Half an hour later Buell tied his horse outside Tay's place and was about to knock on the door.

"C'mon in, Buell. Heard ya comin' half a mile away. Damn boy, you're noisy."

Buell pushed open the door and entered the gloomy dugout.

"I know it's spring, but it ain't that spring—shut the damn door."

Buell stood facing Tay and an Indian, both seated at the table. His eyes scanned the inside of the dimly lit dwelling.

"Don't be lookin' for another'n, t'ain't one." Tay got up and nodded at the Indian. "Buell, like ya to meet Walks Fast."

Buell hesitated, then stepped forward as the man stood and extended his hand. The Indian stood nearly as tall as he did, and were it not for his braided hair, from a distance he would have looked like anyone at the fort. Standing close told a different story, his high cheekbones and mahogany-colored skin labeled him an Indian. He looked older than Tay, but the way he rose from his chair, and moved the two steps belied any sign of old age.

"Taylor says you are a good friend," the tall Indian said as he shook Buell's hand.

"He's been good to me and my friend," Buell muttered. He glanced at Tay.

"You wonder why I speak English?" the Indian said.

"Well, yeah."

"Went to school a long time ago. My father helped William Clark, and he helped me go to school."

"Clark? Like Lewis and Clark, the explorers?" Buell looked at Tay.

"Don't ask me, ask him." Tay grinned at Buell's discomfort.

"Lewis and Clark, yes."

"Simon will be glad to meet you. He read a lot about them."

"Simon is the man with the big dog. The People call him Man With Dog Shadow."

"Yeah," Buell said, "he got it from some Indians last year." He looked back at Tay. "What tribe is he from?"

"I know it's hard gettin' used to, Buell, but for hell sakes, talk to him. He understands ya jist fine."

Walks Fast smiled. "I am from Shoshoni. I live here now, and help the army talk to other tribes."

"Right. You must live in those tepees east of the fort."

The Indian nodded. "Many of us live there."

"Well . . . sit down. I make it a rule to every chance I git." Tay sank onto one of the chairs. Walks Fast sat as well.

"I'm not gonna stay. I just wanted to tell ya Kent said he heard Knife was back in the area. Couple soldiers saw him at Scott's Bluff. Sure like to get up against him again."

"Don't be huntin' trouble, Buell. More'n enough will find ya out natur'ly."

"You say the man is called Knife?" Walks Fast asked. "Does he mean the one who robs people who travel the trail west?"

"Yeah, he's talkin' about Sharp Knife," Tay said. "Skinner and Knife jumped him and his partner at night and Buell kilt Skinner."

"You are the one the People call Shoots Fast." Walks Fast nodded his head slowly. "I hear you killed Skinner. Sharp Knife is a bad man, an Arapaho. He is a half-breed; his mother was white."

"I'm not goin' to go lookin' for him. I just wonder if he knows the fellers he jumped are here at Laramie and itchin' to take a poke at 'im?"

Tay shook his head. "Hard to tell. Some people keep things to themselves, and even if they didn't, Knife don't run with the pack we do. I'd say he doesn't know, but that ain't fer sure. And that reminds me—found out last week that you go by the name Lacey out at McCaffrey's. Don't care if ya do or don't, or why fer that matter, but Amos knows too."

"I was a mite touchy when Simon and I first got here. Lacey is a good friend of mine that I rode herd with for a couple summers. My name is Mace, but I've gotten used to Lacey. I reckon I'll keep it."

"Don't make no never mind ta me. I know ya as friend."

"I'm gonna git. Amos likes me to be there from three or so." Buell moved toward the door as Walks Fast stood. "It was nice to meet ya . . . ah . . . sir?"

"You call me Walks Fast. I'm happy to meet a friend of Taylor's. Maybe we'll talk some more."

"Yeah. Simon would like to talk to you fer sure. He really liked that explorer stuff he was reading. I'll tell him about you." Buell pulled open the door. "I'll see ta later, Tay." He stepped outside and pulled it shut.

The remodeling of the Hog Ranch, as the soldiers called Amos's place, was going very well. The extra wide doors to the new semiprivate dining areas had been created, and the table and chairs, lamps, and carpet had been ordered. L-shaped alcoves were built on the saloon side of the wall to shield the dining customers from both the sight and sound of the main saloon. The doors that led to the street were also enlarged and reframed for a more elegant entrance. The latter work necessitated a new coat of paint for the entire front, and despite

Amos's protests, had been done. Another door to the kitchen had been opened on the left end of the bar and a service bell system installed to announce new customers to the kitchen. The total effect transformed the saloon, giving it an almost genteel appearance.

Simon hadn't yet found a cook. He'd asked T. P. to spread the word, and several candidates had applied, but their experience ran toward logging camp and range cooking, which was not what Simon needed. Worry had not yet turned to panic, but it was impending. In three weeks, everything would be ready, and Amos expected to see some results.

CHAPTER 8

For Lorraine and Zahn Tapola, the journey from Wisconsin had been hot, long, and miserable. Determined to make a better life, they had loaded Zahn's wagon with his tools and their household, and headed for California, knowing an experienced sawyer and woodsman would not be unemployed in the settlements out West. Their marriage—she a Lutheran outsider—had not gone down well with his strict Lithuanian, and Catholic, family. But Zahn was her choice, and she knew in her heart that she would never regret marrying a stubborn, hard-nosed "timber beast," as woodsmen were called in his family.

Knowing they were right, though, did not ease the jolts of the torn-up road. Neither did it clear the clouds of deerflies, mosquitoes and other irritating bugs intent on tormenting man and beast. They had forgone the available railways, determined to bring his trained mule team. Zahn owned the wagon that carried the cumbersome tools of his trade: whipsaws, bow saws, bucksaws, axes, wedges and hones, plus the heavy parts of a pit-sawing machine. The Tapolas' persistence delivered them to Fort Laramie the last week in July.

Zahn hauled the tired mules to a stop in front of the sutler's store. "I think that's the telegraph office just over there." He pointed across the compound. "They're supposed to know where most of the large trains are." He scrambled nimbly down the wheel and hopped to the ground. With a wink at his wife, he turned to go.

"If you think I'm sittin' here for one more minute with this wagon stopped, you're choppin' a punky log, Zahn Tapola," she said. Without waiting, she gathered her skirts and swung a leg over the side.

Zahn reached up and caught her waist, lifting her to the ground as though she weighed nothing. "Guess I wasn't thinking, Lori." He never called her Lorraine. "Let me get the anchors, and I'll tether the mules. You go ahead in, I won't be very long."

Lori didn't see any other customers in the store as she pushed the door shut and peered around, curious. Though slightly built, she strode confidently to the man standing behind a low counter.

"Ma'am. You look like a new face. Welcome to Fort Laramie."

"We are. On our way to California or Oregon. We're from Wisconsin."

"Hmm. Don't see many folks from Wisconsin. Did you drive from there?"

"Yes. It's been a hot-awful trip. We're here to see if we could join a supply train or something goin' west. My husband's just across the way, checking."

"You just missed one by . . . let's see . . . nine days. There's not much pilgrim travel anymore, but plenty of freight and supply trains. I expect there'll be another group along in a week or so."

"Oh, good, I'm pleased to hear that. I'm gonna look around."

"Help yourself." The sutler left the store through the door at the end of the room.

She turned to take a look around and noticed two soldiers, one tall and slim, the other shorter. They grinned at each other and nodded in Lori's direction. She smiled back and went to a counter at the end of the store.

"Howdy, miss. Heard ol' T. P. say you was new."

"Oh!" Lori gasped. "You startled me." She turned from the counter and the bolts of cloth she had been admiring.

"That yer family's wagon settin' outside?" The skinny soldier grinned at her.

She noticed his lower jaw didn't want to line up with the upper. "Why, yes. We just arrived from the East."

"Yer old man let ya go off alone like this reg'lar?" the short man asked. He moved to her right and glanced toward the door where T. P. had gone.

"I'm not alone. He's just outside, and he'll be right in." Lori eyed them coldly.

"Thought I saw someone walk across to the telegraph office. That be him?"

"I'll thank you to leave me alone," she said and attempted to walk between them.

Skinny put out his arm. "Not very friendly."

She backed as far as she could against the counter, looked down at his arm, then up at his face. "I don't mean to be. Let me by."

With his arm still extended, Skinny moved closer and looked directly at her bosom. Instinctively, she folded one arm across it and reached behind her back with the other to grip the counter. Her hand fell on cold steel. Shorty stepped closer, and grabbed her by the waist, roughly pulling her chest against his. The reek from several weeks' accumulation of sweat and spilled whiskey assaulted her nose. He turned to press his face against her neck.

The scissors flashed past Skinny's face, and the points disappeared into the thick muscle of Shorty's back.

"Gawdamn!" he roared as the pain shocked his brain. He stooped over and pawed at the shears that flopped around with his every movement. "Gawdamn, you, bitch. Ow! Get 'em out."

Skinny looked at his partner and then at Lori. His teeth attempted to clench as anger set in; the resulting look was almost pitiful. "Crazy whore," he sputtered as he reached for her arm.

The door crashed open.

"Zahn!"

He crossed the floor in two strides, and his balled fist caught the left side of Skinny's head with a resounding crack. Skinny went to the floor.

"What'n hell's goin' on in here?" shouted T. P. as he charged into the room.

"Get this outta me," Shorty wailed. Hunched over, he headed toward T. P. Just as he got to him, the scissors came out and clattered to the floor. T. P. stared at the blood-soaked tool for a moment, then at Shorty and finally at Lori.

"Did he—"

"He grabbed me and tried to kiss me," she said matter-of-factly, "and I stuck him with the scissors."

"What about him?" He pointed at Skinny, now cowering at Zahn's feet.

"He helped."

"Did they hurt you?"

"No. I'm all right, but the little shit was starting to irritate me." Her hand flew to her mouth.

T. P. stared at her for a minute, eyebrows raised, then looked at Zahn. "Mister?"

"I'm her husband. Just get 'em outta here. You—get up." He prodded Skinny with his boot. "Now!"

Skinny stood and stepped away from Zahn. "We didn't know she was married."

"Get the hell out, ya stupid bastard. Married or not, a man doesn't do that to a woman." Zahn started toward the two of them, and they scurried out the broken door, Shorty whining about his back, and Skinny snarling at him to shut up. Zahn put his arm around Lori's shoulder. She felt small under the plaid-covered arm.

"I'm sorry, ma'am," the sutler said. "Some of the soldiers aren't the best examples. Please accept my apologies."

"It's all right. I didn't feel like I was in danger. I was raised waiting tables in my father's restaurant in Milwaukee. I handled one like that a couple of times a week. I'm just sorry he had to get stuck. I tried to hit where he was solid."

"He got what he deserved. And again, I apologize." T. P. looked at Zahn. "Did you find out what you needed to know, mister? My name's Triffet; folks call me T. P." He stuck out his hand.

"I'm Zahn Tapola and this is my wife Lori. We're from Wisconsin. The telegrapher said he gave the army a message this morning about a group that left Fort Kearney yesterday. Twelve wagons. We should be able to join with them when they get here."

"That's good to hear. It's sure not like it was fifteen years ago. They came through here all summer long—steady stream. What did you do back home?"

"I'm a sawyer."

"Did you say you worked in a restaurant?" T. P. asked Lori.

"Yes. My family owns one. I've cooked, served tables, washed dishes, whatever needed doing, I did it."

"Odd how things like this happen, but there is a . . . well . . . it's almost a restaurant. Young fella showed up year before last and is running a place west of here. It was a . . . uh, a saloon and . . . uh—"

"You're talking about a roadhouse," Zahn said. "We've seen dozens of them."

"Yeah, I guess I am. But Simon, that's the youngster's name, he's changing it into a nicer place. Anyway, what I was gettin' at is, he needs a person that can plan menus and cook. Interested?"

"Not really," Zahn said. "I don't want her workin'. We'll wait around for that group that's comin' and then get on to Oregon. It's what we planned."

"Okay. I told 'em I'd keep my ears open. Now, can I get ya anything while you're in here?"

"Not a lot that we need. Her father runnin' an eating house, we got enough food to last us easily. No, we'll just settle down by the river and wait. Much obliged though."

Skinny and Shorty hurried out the door and scurried to the blacksmith shop just west of the store.

"Take a look and see if it's bad, Rank. It hurts like hell," Shorty whined as he unbuttoned his tunic.

Skinny waited until Shorty had undone his underwear top, and then folded it back, off his shoulder.

"It ain't that bad. Ya got a little fatty-lookin' stuff poochin' out, but it ain't bleedin' much. We'll have Barrschott take a look at it. He'll know if ya have to see the doc. Dirty bitch, she coulda poked ya through the lung."

Shorty, with a wince and a moan, shrugged back into his underwear. "She had no call to do that. Shit, all she had to do was say no."

Skinny turned and looked at the six mules, heads down, patiently awaiting their orders. His eyes moved back to the wagon, then he turned again and looked at the blacksmith's forge. "Let's teach 'em a lesson." He glanced at the sutler's store. "Grab that little nail bucket there and that old horse blanket."

Moments later they hurried across the compound in search of Sergeant Barrschott.

Zahn eased the mules to a stop on a level piece of ground about three hundred feet from the river.

"Looks like we're going to have to skid a stick or two in here for firewood," he said as he surveyed the treeless riverbank. "Sure a nice-lookin' place, though. Doesn't that breeze feel good? Bet that comes all the way from Oregon."

"Just get this thing stopped. I'm ready to sit and look at the same place two days in a row," Lori said and started to get up.

"Whoa, mule." He set the brake and relaxed the reins. "Do you smell something burning?" Zahn sniffed the air. "Don't smell like wood." He stood and looked around.

"I smell it," Lori said and started to climb down the wheel. "Zahn!" she screamed, looking toward the rear. "It's the wagon."

Zahn leaped clear of the driver's box and landed in a heap. Scrambling to his feet, he raced to the end of the wagon box, and clawed at the ropes holding the canvas ends shut. The knots had been altered and pulled tight. He dug his knife from his pocket, the smoke now seeping through small gaps in the canvas. Just as he got the blade open, the right side of the white cover made a soft *wooof* sound and the rear third was burning halfway to the top. Slashing at the ropes, he cut through, and the ends came loose. He threw the canvas back to be met by a roiling cloud of white smoke tinged with flickering yellow. He raced to the front of the wagon and climbed back aboard.

"Get out of the way, Lori," he shouted as he kicked loose the brake. "I'm gonna drive into the river. Git up, mule," he hollered. "Git up! Gee mule, gee. Git around."

Heaving hard on the right reins as the mules responded with a lunge, he swung them around, and they headed straight for the riverbank, now at a gallop. The slope was mercifully gentle, and the six mules crashed into the belly-deep water.

"Whoa," Zahn hollered as the lead pair reached the far side. "Whoa."

He hauled hard on the reins, and tromped the brake with his foot, one action leveraged against the other.

"Gawdammit," he swore when the water only reached the

mule's chests. He scrambled over the front of the wagon. "Easy mule, easy," he crooned. "Now back, back. Whoa. Now easy."

Hanging onto the harness, he walked the two shafts between the mules until he reached the rear of the lead pair. Balanced precariously between the heads of the middle set of animals and murmuring softly to them, he unhooked the leaders. Then he let go the neck yoke on the swing pair. The falling tongue dropped free and one front end sank to the stream bottom. He did the same for the middle pair, working his way back to the wagon where he uncoupled the wheel team. The flames were now intense as the canvas flared in the breeze and he hunkered on the wagon tongue.

Gathering the reins in hand, he hollered. "Git'up mule." Free of the heavy pulling traces, the powerful animals charged up the bank and jerked him off his perch. He fell full length in the water to be pulled facedown toward the shore. When he hit the bank, the drag on the reins stopped the well-trained team. He sat up and looked back across the river. Lori, hands to her face, sat down on the bank, and together, they watched as their wagon burned down to the floor.

Two soldiers on horseback slid to a stop beside Lori. "Is anyone on the wagon?" the sergeant asked.

"No, sir. My husband is over there with the team," Lori said, pointing across the river.

"Trooper, cross over and escort the man to the bridge with his team. I'll take the lady back to the fort."

"Right, Sarge," the man said and plunged his horse into the river and crossed to Zahn.

"Give me your hand, ma'am, and put your foot in the stirrup."

"Will the wagon not float away?" Lori asked. "It has all his tools."

"It'll be all right till I can get a squad out here to tow it back to the bank." He bent over and reached for her. She swung up behind him, straddling the horse.

"How did that happen? Have you been carrying fire?"

"No, we never do. I don't understand it. What are we going to do? Everything we own is on the load."

"Can't say, ma'am. I'll get you back to the sutler. He has at times arranged for folks to stay a bit."

He turned the horse and walked it slowly back to the fort.

Sergeant Barrschott sat at his desk, the two troopers at attention in front of it. Furious, he looked directly at Trooper Pettit.

"I talked to T. P., you little maggot. I know what happened in the store, and you didn't back into no nail. And just based on what I know now, I can guarantee both of ya thirty days in the guardhouse." He turned his attention to the other man. "So, Rankin, I'm gonna ask ya one more time. Did you have anything to do with setting the torch to their wagon?" Barrschott glared at the two troopers.

"I already told ya, no. We was havin' a little fun with her, that's all."

"Yeah, she enjoyed it so much she stabbed Pettit with a pair of shears. Don't feed me no shit about who's the victim here. I've a good notion to let that timberman knock that crooked jaw of yours straight. You're both a disgrace to the uniform. We'll see Lieutenant Fu—Maupin in the morning about your little fete. And I'll have a look at that wagon before he sees ya. God help you, both of you, if I see somethin' that don't add up. Now get the hell out of here and you're confined to barracks. Corporal!"

The two-striper appeared immediately.

"Escort these two pieces of coyote shit to quarters, and see they stay there till mornin'. Get 'em some hardtack for supper."

"Yes, Sergeant. C'mon, you two."

Zahn and Barrschott watched as the soldiers towed the charred hulk to the blacksmith's shop, slipped their ropes, and rode away.

"Looks like you have all the singletrees and the falling tongue in back," Barrschott said as he surveyed the burned wreck. "Guess the wheels were just wet enough to not burn."

"At least I have that," Zahn said. "And my tools look like they made it too." He levered his body onto the charred bed. Reaching down, he caught the end of an enormous two-man saw and lifted it. "The handle's gone but the blade looks just fine. That ax looks good too." He hefted the double-bitted tool. "The handle's nice and brown, but it isn't hurt."

"Not much, but I guess everything counts. Do you see anything unusual?"

"Like what?" Zahn studied the charred mess. "The trunk behind the seat didn't go entirely. And this was the dresser. That looks like . . . that ain't mine." Zahn reached down and picked up a small bucket. "I've never seen this."

"Let me have it," Barrschott said. He walked into the blacksmith shop and came back in less than a minute.

"Dirty little sonsabitches. Hodges says that bucket is his. It's for holding his shoe nails. Always sets by the forge, and it was gone."

"By the forge? You mean they filled it with coals and set it in amongst my goods?"

"Looks like it. Can't say how sorry I am, Mister Tapola. There's not a lot I can do about compensation. They don't make enough in five years to pay off what they ruined for ya. But they will be punished, I promise. Bastards . . . yellow-bellied, pot-lickin' motherless little bastards. I'll let ya know what the lieutenant decides. Did the sutler find ya some place to stay?"

"Only for last night. I'll have to see about something else today. And thanks for helpin'."

Simon and Twiggs sat sharing the morning at one of the tables when Spud raised his head, woofed once, then laid it back down. A minute later the door opened and two people walked in. Surprised at the early arrival of customers, Simon looked the man over closely. Not overly tall, his shoulders were wide, and the loose flannel shirt could not hide his enormous upper arms. His sandy hair refused to stay under the cloth cap that sat slightly crooked on his head. The woman standing beside him wore a simple pale-blue gingham dress and a short coat. Her light-brown hair hung loose. The man looked around the saloon, and finally spotted the two of them by the stove. He snatched off his hat and approached the table.

"Excuse me, I'm looking for Simon Steele."

"That would be me." Simon looked at Spud. "Quiet," he almost whispered, then stood and extended his hand.

The man took it. "My name is Zahn Tapola, and Mister Triffet at the store said you might have a room me and my missus might rent for a while. And maybe some work."

"We're not exactly a hotel you understand? Uh . . . did T. P. . . . er, Mister Triffet tell you what kind of place we, I . . ." Simon glanced across the room at the woman standing just inside the door, and then looked at Twiggs in desperation.

"We are a roadhouse," Twiggs said. "Our rooms are usually only rented by the night, sometimes by the hour. Understand? I'm Maxwell Twiggs." He stood and put his hand out.

"Oh." Zahn's smile disappeared. He fumbled his hat into one hand, and grasped Twiggs's with the other.

"Were it just you, I could see no problem, but I'm afraid your wife could be uncomfortable. Do you see my problem?" Simon asked, his voice again steady.

"Don't be concerned about my sensibilities, sir." Lori walked up to the table and looked Simon directly in the eye. "I was raised to do what had to be done. We lost our wagon yesterday afternoon in a fire, and we need a place to stay till we figger out what we're going to do. I know what an evening lady is. Everybody has to make a living." She folded her arms across her chest and half cocked her head.

Simon started to chuckle, at first a low sound as he struggled to keep it private. Then, its volume rose, and soon he was laughing out loud. He put up his hand in supplication. "Please, I'm not laughing at you, really I'm not." He stifled the laugh, puffing air between his fingers.

Twiggs looked at Simon, his eyebrows raised, his face a full-blown question mark.

"That tilt of your head and the crossed arms," Simon said. "I've seen my mother do that to my father a hundred times, and I saw the same result a hundred times." He started to chuckle again. "I'm sorry, I can't help it. Poor Pa."

"So you know I'm serious," Lori said.

"Oh, no doubt. And we will think of something to accommodate you, Missus Tar . . . poli?"

"Tapola, Lori Tapola."

"And you mentioned work," Simon said looking at Zahn. "What do you do?"

"I'm a lumber sawyer and timberman. I can also handle a square and a hammer if you need something built rough. I'm not a carpenter, but I can build you a corral shed or a barn."

"Hmm. And you, Missus Tapola. Are you interested in working . . . oh, damn, I mean . . . excuse the cuss . . . I mean—" Simon looked at Twiggs again.

Twiggs's brow wrinkled, and he shook his head slowly.

"You're in it, you get out of it."

"Ooof. Of course I didn't mean what you thought I was going . . . aw, I didn't mean you would do what . . ." Simon felt himself slowly dissolving with embarrassment.

"Mister Steele, I'm happily married to a man I love. I understand from Mister Triffet that you're looking for a cook. I worked in my father's restaurant forever. I can prepare single meals, group dinners or run a full eatery. I could also do laundry, scrub floors, even serve drinks at the tables."

"Now wait a minute, Lori, I ain't havin' you working in the saloon. We talked about cookin', that's all." Zahn put his hand on his wife's shoulder.

"We'll do what we need to do." Again the cocked head and crossed arms.

Simon smiled. "We haven't had breakfast yet. Have you?"

"Some rusk and a cup of coffee. Everything else was burned up," Lori said.

"We have a full kitchen right through that door. I want you to go in there and cook breakfast for four. What you make is your choice. Sound fair?"

Lori was already headed for the kitchen, tugging at her coat.

Right then, the front door opened again and Buell stepped in.

"Make that breakfast for six," Simon said. He grinned at his friend. "Your toughest customer just arrived."

Lori glanced at Buell and nodded her head as she pushed through the door.

"Mornin' Buell," Twiggs said.

"Says you," Buell grumped. "I've gotta learn to avoid those late card games with Amos and Rosie." He looked at Zahn.

"Buell, I'd like to introduce Mister Zahn Tapola. Mister Tapola, Buell Ma—Lacey."

"I like to be called Zahn." Zahn extended his hand.

"I gather that's your wagon out front, or what's left of one?" Buell asked as he stepped around the table to an empty chair.

"Yes. Got burned up. Some crazy soldier named Rankin put a bucket of charcoal in amongst our stuff. I managed to get it to the river, or we would have lost it all."

"Rankin, that little bastard. I had a run-in with him some time back. Wouldn't leave the girls alone. Had to bust his chops."

"That explains his mouth being messed up, won't shut straight," Zahn said.

"Yeah, I know. Anyhow, they call me Buell. Last name's Mace, but most know me as Lacey. Started when . . . Oh never mind, don't matter." Buell looked at Simon.

"You started it," Simon said, "so don't give me that nobody-understands-me look." He pushed a chair out with his toe. "Please, sit down, Mister Tapola."

"I was goin' to get us some more coffee. Would you drink a cup, Zahn?" Twiggs asked.

"Thanks, I would."

"You go without asking, Buell. Simon?"

"Why not?"

Twiggs disappeared through the kitchen door, and Buell sat at the table.

"Might have found us a cook," Simon said. "And a solution to something else I've been thinking about."

Buell rolled his eyes. "I don't even wanna guess."

"Mister Tapola, you said you could build a barn?"

"True, and I'm a lot more comfortable with Zahn, Mister Steele."

"All right." He tilted his head to one side to let Twiggs reach past and set four cups of coffee on the table. "Thanks, Max."

"So what do we need a barn for?" Buell asked.

"We don't," Simon said.

"Here we go." Buell slumped in his chair, coffee cup held on his chest with two hands.

"If you can build a barn, you can build a small cabin. All one-inch material except the roof, which we'll shingle. Twelve by twenty feet, two rooms with one door and two windows. I'll hire out the siding and shingles, door and window trim, and the interior finish. Could you do it?" he asked Zahn.

"Yeah, sure. That's all rough work. Set on pillar and beams, I suppose."

"Exactly. I'll also hire the stonework out."

Zahn nodded his head, and Twiggs pursed his lips thoughtfully.

"Now the interesting question. Could you rough saw all the material if I could show you where the trees are?"

"If I had a man to help, yeah, except for the shingles and siding. You need a mill for that."

Simon leaned back and smiled. "I'll give you twenty dollars for a detailed bill of materials for what I described. I've drawn the floor plan. I want eight of them."

"Oh, shit. You're still lookin' to get the girls outta here, ain't ya?" Buell shook his head.

"May is not going to be amused." Twiggs chuckled. "Does Amos know about this yet?"

"Not yet. And I'm not going to be the one to tell him."

"Well, you can bet your suspenders it's not going to be me," Twiggs said.

"Oh, no. None of us. I'm going to depend on a favored customer or two for that. I'll work it out, you'll see."

"When will you need that list of materials?" Zahn asked.

"Soon as you get it put down. Now, how do two men make lumber?"

Zahn explained a little of how a pit saw worked, and what would be required to set up an operation. Buell's eyes glazed over, Twiggs picked at his fingernails with his pocketknife, and

Simon listened intently until the kitchen door opened.

Lori appeared, carrying an enormous tray balanced on one hand and a pitcher of some sort in the other. She swept up to the table and set the ensemble down, pushing coffee cups out of the way with the edge of the tray.

"Gentlemen, let me serve you Lori's breakfast special."

The plate she set in front of each man nearly overflowed with sliced bread smothered in creamy, brown gravy. Settled in the middle were three pepper-flecked, golden orbs with startling white collars. Strands of shredded beef roast peeked invitingly through the sauce.

"Creamed beef on toast with poached, seasoned eggs. One plate with enough food to keep any man going till dinnertime," she announced.

"Boy, that looks good," Buell said as Lori set a knife and fork beside his plate. He scooted his chair closer to the table, and picked up the fork.

"See, Max, there is something else besides eggs with brown crunchy edges and half-done fatback," Simon said.

"And to keep it settled, hot chocolate," Lori said and put fresh cups on the table. She loaded her tray with the empty coffee cups, and went back into the kitchen.

"Chocolate? For breakfast?" Twiggs stared at the squatty brown pitcher, and then at Zahn.

"It's good, 'specially if she's made it like she does for me." Zahn took the handle and poured his mug full. "Anybody else?"

"Oommff," Buell said around a huge forkful of bread and gravy. He held out his cup.

Simon and Twiggs offered over their cups, and Zahn filled them all.

Simon took a swig. "That's incredible." He tipped his cup again and took another.

"It has a faint cinnamon . . . no, it's more nutty . . . no, it's both and it's thick, like it was made of cream, but not heavy like cream," Twiggs said. "Damn, Zahn, how's she do that?"

"Don't ask me. I just drink it and smile. One of the many reasons I married her. Best cook I've ever seen." Zahn smiled proprietarily as he looked at the satisfied expression on Twiggs's face.

"You best be lookin' to yer plates," mumbled Buell, chewing. "Cuz I'm figgerin' on takin' what you don't eat."

The front door opened again and Daggett came in. Spud's tail thumped a greeting.

"And Zahn, here's the man you need. Plato, come meet Zahn Tapola."

Daggett slowly approached the table, and Zahn stood.

"Plato. Pleased to meet ya."

"Likewise," Daggett said, looking a little perplexed.

"Sit, Plato, and I won't take anything else for an answer." Simon rose from his chair and went to the kitchen door. "Lori, would you dress another plate just like the one I had, and hand me a cup. We've got another customer."

"You're gonna love this, Plato. Here, try this first." Simon poured him a cup of the chocolate.

At about the time the third pitcher of chocolate had been finished, Amos came downstairs. Lori treated him to the same meal, and Simon's search for a cook was over.

With only minor finishing touches needed to the interiors of the new dining rooms and a few additional lamps yet undelivered, Simon posted a message in the sutler's store.

McCaffrey's Saloon & Restaurant
Now Open to Serve
New Eastern-trained Chef
Dinner & Supper

T. P. looked at the placard and smiled. "Eastern-trained, eh?"

"Well, she is. And I wouldn't smile too wide until you've tried some of her cooking. I wince when I say it, but she puts my mother to shame," Simon said. "Come on out. I realize Missus Triffet wouldn't be comfortable there, but you really ought to come try it."

T. P. looked skeptical.

"First meal is on me," Simon said. He walked to the door and opened it. "Anytime."

The seated US Army captain stared at Trooper Pettit and Trooper Rankin, who stood at attention in front of his desk, contempt pulling the corners of his mouth down. Sergeant Barrschott stood immediately behind the two.

"Assault and battery, attempted rape, arson, theft, lying under oath, and conduct unbecoming. All serious enough to get you cashiered after your sentence in the guardhouse is complete. It is my inclination to do just that, but Sergeant Barrschott would like to keep you around. I defer to his experience and won't question his motives. Six months in the brig, forfeiture of seventy-five percent of your pay and allowances for one year. I only regret that neither of you have a stripe or two to lose. Sergeant, escort the prisoners to the brig for their confinement."

Buell pushed the office door open and went in. Simon was writing, so he dropped the envelope on Simon's desk, then slumped into one of the two easy chairs. Simon finished his thought on paper and looked up. "Afternoon. Where ya been?"

"Went to see Tay for a while. That Indian Walks Fast was there. You really ought to meet him. He's in'erestin'."

Simon picked up the envelope and turned it over. His eyes went wide. "It's from home," he said.

"I know. I got one too."

Simon cut the top with an opener, and withdrew the two folded sheets of stark white paper. Buell leaned forward and saw the letterhead, "Kingsley & Lindstrom, Law Offices, Carlisle, Nebraska," and below the elegant longhand script of the letter. He leaned back and watched Simon's face in anticipation. His friend's eyebrows went up, and he obviously reread a sentence or two. Then he visibly recoiled, his head jerking back, as he read something farther down the page. He lay down the first sheet, and started on the second. A smile crossed his lips a couple of times, and then he looked at Buell and grinned.

"What?" Buell exclaimed.

"Just a minute," Simon said. He finished the letter and handed the second sheet to Buell. "The first is some family stuff about an inheritance and some money matters. You can read that one."

Buell leaned forward and took it. Silently, he sounded his way through it. "I'll be damned. Your folks' farm seems to grow and grow." He looked up at Simon and handed the letter back.

"And now yours. Have you opened it?"

"Not yet. I'm always scared it's bad news." He reached for the opener.

Buell read the hand-printed, single-page letter. His eyes blinked rapidly as he finished. "Good for Pa. No shit, Simon, I'm gonna have a ma," he said as he handed the letter across. He turned his head away and pinched his lips together, swallowing hard as he reached down and stroked Spud's head.

Simon quickly read the short letter. "Good news, huh?" he said smiling. "Your pa and my auntie Ruth will make a splendid pair."

"I'm thinkin' maybe I'll go home for the wedding. How 'bout you?"

"Don't think so, Buell. I'm not ready. And that's a long ride in October. You might get stuck."

"We could go to Cheyenne and ride the train. Hell, that's less than a hundred miles. It'd be easy. Think about it."

"I don't think so, Buell."

"Looks like John Lindstrom and Judge Kingsley went into law together. Who'da thought that five years ago? The town drunk and the best citizen Carlisle has, pardners." Buell slumped back and looked at Simon. "Any word abo—"

"Don't say it, Buell. I asked ya once, and you promised." Simon's eyes sparked.

"Sorry."

"I've got a lot of money coming from Grandfather Steele's estate. I was eligible for it when I turned twenty."

"Can I ask how much?"

"Sure. Almost forty-one hundred dollars."

"Holy shit, Simon, you're rich."

"I don't have to take it now. I can wait until I need it and let Uncle . . . er, Mister Lindstrom continue to manage it until then. All the grandkids got a share."

"David?"

"I suppose."

"Oh."

"What 'oh'? You're thinking something, I can tell."

"It answers some questions I had before we left, that's all. Nothing important."

"Anyway, I don't need it now, and I'll send John a letter telling him so. I have to take it all when I do though. And I don't want to go home now, Buell. Everybody is doing fine, and so am I. We'll leave it at that for now."

Buell patted the dog's head once more and stood. "About time to get up on my perch. I'll see ya later."

Simon watched Buell close the door and then unfolded the first page of the letter.

★ ★ ★ ★ ★

Judge Kingsley and I went into practice together when he decided to become fully involved in Nebraska politics. With Sarah gone, he and Missus Kingsley are much more free to travel to Omaha, and I needed something more to do.

Thoughts swarmed Simon's mind. Sarah. Gone? How? Surely not—I can't even think it. Maybe just back East to see her relatives. Why do I care? God, can't I ever leave that behind?

He crumpled the letter in his hand and put his head on it. The black ink dissolved as tears dropped on the words.

Chapter 9

Simon attached the last reflector on the last lamp, and stood down from the step stool.

"Got to admit, Simon, I had no idea what you had in mind when you started, but this is beautiful." Amos admired the highly polished, bright, nickel-plated stove and plum-colored carpet. The walnut-colored tables and matching purple-brocade-upholstered chairs invited a person to sit down and relax.

"I've let everyone I can think of know we're ready for tonight. I hope we've aroused enough interest to at least eat that delicious-smelling roast of beef Lori's been watching all afternoon." Simon picked up the stool, and took it into the main part of the saloon. Lori had two tables set up with a service for four at each. Two women were listening as Lori explained how to lift a plate over the customer's left shoulder. She'd been training them a couple of hours a day for the last week.

"You can't just walk up and surprise them with it. You'll eventually wind up with a plateful dumped right in the middle of the table, or worse. Let them know you're there."

"How?" the frumpy-looking older woman asked.

"It's best if you can walk toward them so they see you coming. If you have to come from behind, stop well short and say something. Like, excuse me, ma'am, or clear your throat lightly. Anything to let them know."

"You ladies going to be ready?" Simon asked.

"Never had to be so careful when I fed my husband," the

older woman said.

"But he had no place else to go, did he?" Simon joked.

"I reckon not, though sometimes I wished he would have."

"Everything ready, Lori?"

"I think so. These two are gonna do fine. I can't imagine both rooms being needed, so they won't have any trouble keeping up."

Three hours later the red bell over the icebox tinkled. Simon's heart started to race as he looked at Lori and her two assistants, and then up at the bell again.

"I was out in front of the saloon not thirty seconds ago. Where did they come from?" Simon asked.

"We'll soon find out. Go take their order, Melissa," Lori said.

Five minutes later she was back.

"They'll have the roast dinner. And a bottle of wine," Melissa said, excitement in her voice. "My first order."

"Our first order," Simon said smiling. "Who is it, do you know them?"

"Of course, it's Mister McCaffrey and Miss Pritchin."

"What! Oh, shit. I mean . . . oh—" Simon rushed out of the kitchen.

In the saloon, he caught Twiggs's attention. "Max, did you know Amos was going to have May for dinner?" he asked quietly.

"Yeah, why?" Twiggs said.

"Why? Oh, hell, we're cooked now. Shit!"

"What?"

"That's the reason for setting the rooms off. Our ladies are not supposed to be apparent, much less occupying one of the tables. And especially May."

Simon walked across the saloon and entered the dining room.

"Good evening, May, Amos," he greeted from behind May.

"Oh, Simon, what a lovely job you've done." She turned in her chair and faced him.

May wore a long-sleeved, dove-gray dress, buttoned to her throat. She had her hair combed back from her almost-rouge-free face and kept in place with tortoiseshell combs. The cameo figure on the brooch at her neck glowed amber and cream in the lamplight. May looked stunning.

"I'm pleased to welcome you as our first dinner guests," Simon lied.

"Thought it only appropriate to show our support," Amos said with a sly smile.

"I appreciate that. And Miss Pritchin, you look beautiful tonight."

"Why, thank you, Simon."

"Max will be by shortly with your wine. Enjoy your meal," he said and went back into the saloon.

"What's with the big grin?" Twiggs asked.

"Have you seen May?"

"This morning, why?"

"Take them a bottle of wine. You're in for a surprise."

"Did they have the beef or the trout?"

"The beef." Simon went back into the kitchen.

Melissa was scooping butter-flavored potato pieces onto a plate, and Lori had two generous slices of roast beef laid on the cutting board.

"Looks wonderful and smells even better," Simon said.

Tinkle tinkle. Simon's head snapped up to see the red bell moving.

"Another one?"

The stream of customers continued until the blue bell rang, and Simon was pressed into service as Lori's kitchen assistant, the two waitresses attending to a room each. They were down to three trout and about five servings of beef when the last customer arrived at nine o'clock.

"Well, there goes tomorrow's dinner menu. I planned on at least half of that roast being left over," Lori said as she wiped an arm across her sweaty brow. "That was as busy as I've seen my father's place, and he's been there for twenty-five years. I think you've got a business going here."

"If we judge by the compliments to the cook that kept coming back," Simon said. "What did you put in that beef to make it taste like that?"

"Wasn't in the beef. It's in the sauce and I ain't gonna tell you or anyone else what it is."

Twiggs's gleaming eyes showed his pleasure. The dining rooms had closed a little before ten. In the two and a half hours they'd been open, he'd sold two hundred sixty-six dollars' worth of wine, of which nearly sixteen dollars was his. "This is going to make the summer months as good as the winter, Simon. You're a genius."

"First we have to see how many come back," Amos said. "I'll admit, I'll eat in there regular. That's as good as anything you can get in Saint Louis or Denver."

"That's exactly what I need, a nonpaying regular," Simon teased. "Hope others feel the same."

"Sure kept it quiet in here," Buell said. "The usual bunch couldn't hardly wait to see who showed up out front."

"I see Rosie's still around, and Saint Louis Bob. Want to play a little poker, Buell?" Amos asked.

"Why not? I like takin' your money. Ain't no use in askin', but I'll be polite. How 'bout you, Simon?"

"Nope, I've had enough. All you had to do was snooze on your chair. I worked my butt off in the kitchen. I'm gonna get my dog and go home." Simon opened the door to his office. "C'mon, Spud, let's go get some sleep. Good night, you guys."

★ ★ ★ ★ ★

The bright moonlight cast distinct shadows, and Spud took advantage of it. He raced around the end of the stable before Simon made it halfway across the street. He barked twice as he headed into the open. The night air, warm and almost liquid, wrapped him in nature's essence. Trapped close to the ground, the aroma of the river and the dry dusty scent of sage blended with the sweet-sour smell of the corrals. Free of the overused air in the saloon, Simon strolled past the cabin and continued walking into the low brush and patchy grass, pausing occasionally to listen for his dog. After he'd walked about half a mile, he retraced his steps to the porch of the cabin, and once more paused to listen for Spud.

"Guess you'll be waiting for Buell when he comes home." He turned to open the door.

A shadow flicked to life on the porch, and Simon's eyes followed naturally. In a heartbeat, a form passed the corner of the cabin, and moved across the porch toward him, following the shadow. Simon spun around to catch the moonlight glint on a knife blade. It cut an arc out and then in, aimed for his belly. Sucking in his breath, he arched his back and blade's tip plucked at his shirt. Scrambling, Simon retreated, his arms flailing for balance.

The porch ended a foot shy of his last step, and he fell heavily to the ground. Searing pain shot through his shoulder as it took the brunt of his fall, followed by a bright flash of light when his head bounced off the hard dirt. He was vaguely aware of a hand shoving his face to one side. Then, suddenly and acutely, he remembered the flashing knife, and knew his throat was being exposed for a reason. Terror fueled the strength he found in his injured arm as he balled his fist and punched out. A grunt signaled a hit somewhere and the hand came off his face. He caught the glint of steel again, and his arm rose to fend it off.

A black form streaked from nowhere, ghostly silent. Spud struck the attacker, who let loose an anguished scream as the attacking dog tore into his flesh. Both fell across Simon and rolled away. Still dazed, he managed to sit up in time to see the man get to his feet, and run out of sight behind the cabin. The deep growling snarl of the determined dog was followed immediately by its pained howl, and then the beat of hooves as a horse surged into a gallop. The sound faded away toward the north.

Buell spilled his chair as Simon carried the dog into the saloon. "What in hell?"

"He's been cut, Buell. Can you take a look?" Simon's face twisted with concern. He knelt and laid the squirming dog on the floor. Spud tried to get up.

"Hold his head," Buell said as he got down on the floor. "You guys get outta the light." He took hold of the dog's leg and pushed on the right-front paw. Spud pushed back. "Doesn't look bad." He worked the leg a couple of times. "That works fine. Somebody go get a dish towel from the kitchen."

Amos hurried away and back. Buell wiped the blood away, and gently spread the sides of the cut, inspecting closely. Spud whined, and looked at Simon with fearful eyes. Buell tore a strip off the towel and folded it into a pad. He pressed it against the wound, and wrapped the remainder of the cloth around the dog's leg.

"That'll stop the bleeding. He's got a little cut in the muscle but it's not deep. If we can get him to leave that on for a couple hours, I think it'll be to the point where he can take care of it himself. Pa always said if a dog can get at it, he'll keep it clean."

Spud turned to get his teeth in the bandage. "No!" Simon

pushed the dog's head away.

"How did this happen?" Amos asked.

"I took a little walk, and when I come back home, he was waiting in the shadow by the house. He had me down and was about to . . . God, he could have killed me so easy."

"Who had you down? Did you see 'im?" Buell asked.

"No. I saw a shadow, and then he was across the porch and on me."

"Real quiet like?" Buell asked.

Simon paused for a minute with his eyes closed. "Not a sound." His eyes locked with Buell's. "Just like by the river."

"We'll take a look in the morning," Amos said. "Was he just lookin' to cut ya, or do you think you caught him trying to rob your house?"

"Oh, shit," Buell said. "The son of a bitch. I'll be right back." He raced out of the saloon.

The bleeding had stopped as Buell predicted, and Spud lay by the door and licked diligently at the cut leg. Buell sat in the easy chair, face stern and hard-looking.

Simon was exasperated. "We should have known not to leave our money lying around like that."

"It weren't lying around. It was in saddlebags, in a cabinet, in our house. That should be safe enough. I'm gonna get it back."

"You don't even know who did it."

"You know damn well who did it. Knife. And I'm gonna settle with him once and for all. I should've gone to Scott's Bluff when I heard he was there."

"You can't go after a man just because he leaves moccasin tracks. Other Indians do too, and so do some white people."

"For once in your life, can't you wake up and see what's real? That bastard tried to kill you. From what you said, if Spud hadn't saw you down, you'd have a knife stuck in your neck.

Doesn't that bother you one bit, for chrissakes?"

Simon looked at his friend for nearly a minute while Buell, his jaw muscles working furiously, stared back. "You're right. Knife did it. No one else would wait after a robbery to attack me. He knows we're looking for him, and saw an opportunity to fix one of us. He's going to get what he earned."

"Finally, you see the light. I'm gonna go see Walks Fast. He knows about Knife, and who's doing what everywhere. Sometimes I think he's a ghost." Buell got up, and put on his gun belt and coat. "Tell Amos I'll be back late afternoon."

"We'll tell him. I'm goin' with you."

They walked their horses across the street, and Simon waited while Buell went into the saloon. His mind played back a half dozen of the lessons he had been taught him about fairness and integrity. Was it Lacey who told us that an innocent man's death is no less permanent than a guilty one's? God, I hope Buell doesn't find Knife. Not till we're sure.

An hour later they rode up to the tepee, and as they climbed off their horses, the flap opened and Walks Fast stepped out. He nodded at Buell.

"I expected my friend to visit." His gaze then shifted. "You are Simon." He smiled a welcome, and stepped to one side of the entrance.

Simon had never been in a tepee before, and its spaciousness surprised him. Expecting smoky air, the freshness was even more apparent. Two women sat on the floor against the outside wall and opposite the entrance, working on something he couldn't make out.

Walks Fast pointed at a pile of hides. "Sit," he said and then spoke quietly to the women.

One got up and took three cups from a hide basket. She filled them with coffee from a pot that set next to the low fire in the center of the floor.

"I learned to like coffee. The women think that as strange as you do," Walks Fast said as Buell looked at his cup and then at the pot. "Many say I'm a little strange."

"I admit, didn't expect a cup of coffee," Buell said.

Simon sipped some of his and watched Walks Fast fix Buell with a concentrated stare.

"You look for Knife, yes?" Walks Fast made it sound more like a statement than a question.

Buell choked on his drink and put his cup down.

The two women snickered and Walks Fast said something sharply. He then nodded at Buell. "Not that hard to see. Simon was attacked in the night, and the tracks say it was an Indian. You think the Indian was Knife. I say it isn't."

"How'n hell can you know all that? It only happened last night."

"Is Walks Fast wrong?"

"Well, no."

"Then it doesn't matter how I know. You are looking for your possessions?" He spoke to the women again, and the same one got up and pulled two saddlebags from under a bearskin. She dropped them between Simon and Buell.

"That's mine," Buell exclaimed. "Where'd you get it?"

"It is yours. Now you have it back. The People take care of the People's troubles. I am sorry for Simon's Shadow Dog. The man who attacked you is punished. He has left here and will go to Wind River. He will not come back. His family is much ashamed."

"And it wasn't Knife?" Simon asked.

"Walks Fast says it is not Knife. Drink your coffee, it is good." The old man settled back and sipped his cup as he watched confusion cloud Buell's face.

Relief made Simon's chest feel light. Then he felt slightly angry. "But Buell could have shot Knife for this. Doesn't that bother you?"

"Knife did not get shot. I am more afraid for the man who shoots too fast. It is best to follow a trail close and make sure it is the right man who dies. The wrong man stays dead just the same."

Simon stared at the Indian in amazement.

"You question that?"

"Not really a question. I heard someone else say exactly the same thing, a white man."

"You believe the white man is the only one who thinks?" Walks Fast sighed and gave him a sad smile. "Simon is not the only one who thinks that."

The three of them sat sipping the coffee for a few minutes, and then they heard a pair of horses stop outside the tepee. Walks Fast slowly drank the last of his cup, and waited until Simon and Buell had drained theirs.

"Here is a present for Simon. The punished man left a horse, a very good horse. We will go see it."

He got up and pushed open the flap. They followed him out. An Indian man stood in front of the tepee, head down. His extended hand held a halter rope made of braided horsehair. Tied to it was the strangest-looking horse Simon had ever seen. Pale gray in the front quarters, the coloration changed toward the rear. It looked like nature had splattered black paint on its haunch. The long, flowing, black tail had streaks of white through it, and the horse's hooves were light colored with dark stripes. He looked at the man holding the horse, and then at Walks Fast.

"This is the man's brother. The family is very ashamed. You take the horse. It is yours to sell, trade, or keep. It will make them feel better."

Simon took the braided rope. The man raised his head and leveled a cool, steady gaze at him for a moment, then turned and got on his horse. Walks Fast said something, and the man kicked the animal into motion.

"Walks Fast thanks Simon. Family can now sit with their face to the fire."

"I don't know what to say."

"Say nothing. You gave honor back to the family."

"We're goin' back to the ranch," Buell said. "Thanks for gettin' our stuff back. I'll see you again soon."

"Welcome when you come. Walks Fast welcomes Simon too." He turned and went into the tepee.

Several days later, Buell, his back and one heel against the stable wall, shook his head in frustration as Simon walked around the horse for the third time.

"I'm not really that good at judging them, but he looks sound," Simon said.

"That's not what I meant when I asked what you thought of him." Buell snorted. "How do you like his looks?"

"You mean his color. Frankly, he looks like a mistake."

"A mistake! That has to be the most beautiful horse I've ever seen. And run. It's hard to stay on him when he turns. You should've rode him a little harder."

"I've got a good horse, Buell. You like him so much, you keep him."

"You serious?"

"Sure. Walks Fast said it was mine to sell, trade, or keep. I'll presume that means I can give him away as well. You can have him."

"Let me pay you for it. We have our money back."

"There's something about the way I got him that makes me not want to take any money. No, you like him, he's yours." Simon stroked the shoulder of the spotted horse and grinned at Buell. "Enjoy him."

"Thanks, Simon. This's the nicest present I've ever got." He put his hand on the velvet-covered muzzle. "Walks Fast says that it takes the shadows with it. And he's right. It looks like his butt is in a spotty shade and his front is in the sun."

"So, what are you going to name him?" Simon asked.

"That's easy, Shadow Walker. I've been thinkin' about it all week. Not that he was mine, but that would make a good name for him no matter what. I like the way Indians name things, and that's what I think when I look at him."

"So now we have Shadow Walker and Shadow Dog. I'll stick with Spot and Spud," teased Simon.

"You laugh. I'm gonna ride over and see Tay. Wanna come along?" Buell asked.

"Yeah, I've got something I need to ask him."

Simon went into the stable and a few minutes later joined Buell. They were even with the saloon when, almost simultaneously, they kicked their mounts, and in three strides were headed down the road at a full gallop.

Amos nodded as he approached T. P. at the counter.

"Mornin', Amos," the sutler said. "Unusual to see you out this early in the morning."

"Simon and Lori are workin' on something, so he asked me to check on a couple things they need. Spices, extracts, and such."

"We can see. Anything you need that I don't have, I can order."

"Here's what they want." He handed T. P. a piece of paper.

"Got it all," he said after he'd scanned the list. "Couple of things I'm gonna have to look for a bit, but I know I have 'em. I thought I'd keep the cardamom forever."

"Well, whatever those two need, I'm gonna try to find. That's the second idea he's come up with that does nothin' but make me money."

"That reminds me of something." T. P. glanced at a woman who had entered after Amos. "Let me help her, then we can talk."

"Thank you, ma'am," T. P. said a few minutes later. The customer nodded as she left and the sutler came back to Amos. "I've been out to your place four times in a month, and I gotta tell ya, the food and drinks and service . . . well, everything about it is first-class."

"Why, thanks, T. P. I'll pass that on to Simon and Lori. Good of you to say so."

"But that ain't what I had to say. Well, it is, but it's not what I had on my mind."

Amos nodded his head and waited, curious.

"What I mean to say is, the wife, that is Missus Triffet . . . uh . . . well, she'd like to go, but doesn't want to."

"Now that don't make no sense at all, T. P. Listen to what you just said."

"It's them women upstairs," T. P. blurted. "The missus and several other ladies on the post can't abide the thought of eating downstairs when . . . well you know." He jabbed his thumb in the air three or four times. "Goes on upstairs."

"Well, I'll be damned. I'll be double damned. Who do they think the customers are?"

"I'm not gonna argue the point, Amos. I'm just suggestin' if you was to make your place just a saloon and restaurant without no whores, you could make even more money. I've seen how people like havin' a nice place to go." T. P. shrugged. "If you was to clean . . . I mean, not have the girls there, folks would come by three or four times as much, and bring the wives too. Think about it. Even though the men are goin' for the cards and the food, the wives don't like the thought of available girls just upstairs. See what I mean?"

"Well, you said your piece, for sure. And I can see your point. I'll think on it."

"Figgered we was friends enough that I could say that. No hard feelings?"

"No, not at all. Let me have the stuff on that list, and I'll go talk with my young manager and see what he thinks."

Chapter 10

Tay Prescott sat in front of his dugout, half asleep in the morning sun. The staccato two-two beat of a running horse invaded his daydream. He opened his eyes to see a pinto horse lay over at a sharp angle as it rounded the point of hillside leading into the meadow. Its long flowing tail streamed in the rushing wind.

"My gawd, that horse can run." He stood up and peered to recognize the rider. "Buell."

The horse and rider thundered past, then slammed to a stiff-legged skidding stop, turned in the horse's length, and pranced back to the dugout.

"In a hurry and change your mind, or just showin' off?" Tay chuckled.

"Ever seen a horse stop and turn like that, Tay?" Buell swung down, and tied the horse to the post by the woodpile.

"Can't say that I have. That's one of them Palouse horses ain't it?"

"Don't know what ya call it. Walks Fast gave it to Simon and he give it to me."

"Give it to 'im?"

"Yeah. Walks Fast found out who jumped Simon, and I guess the family made him give Simon the horse for punishment. And Simon likes the horse he has so he gave this'n to me. Ain't he purdy?"

"I don't think I've seen more than one or two of those in my life. Indians way north and west of here raise 'em and don't part with 'em lightly."

"I love 'im. He will run flat out for five miles, then be ready to come back just as fast. I can't wear 'im down. Want to ride 'im?"

Tay looked at the horse and smiled. "My bowels move reg'lar and I can still make water, Buell. At my age, I ain't lookin' for a fast horse." He looked toward the south again. "That another horse comin?"

"Yup, that's Simon. We come together and he started a race. I can't wait to see his face. I beat him by a half a mile."

Simon came into view, coat flying as he leaned over his horse's neck. Slowing to a stop, he pulled up beside Buell's horse, and got off.

"Damn, that horse can run. Is he as smooth to ride as it looks?" Simon asked.

"Ever bit. Sorry ya give him up, huh?" Buell punched Simon on the arm.

"Nah, you look good on him, and I got here didn't I?"

"Sure, a day late."

"How you doing, Tay?" Simon asked.

"Fine. Sittin' in the sun when this damn fool near run my camp over."

"Weren't goin' all that fast," Buell said. He cast an admiring look at his horse.

"So, just sitting out, enjoying the morning?"

"We got a good storm comin', and that first one can last till April. You'll learn to sit in the sun ever chance ya git."

"How kin ya tell?" Buell asked.

"Nothin' special," Tay said as he shrugged his shoulders and studied the clouds. "The air feels a little slow somehow, and them high wispy clouds looks like they's attached to somethin' heavier there in the northwest. 'Sides that, my hip hurts. Took an arrow in it in forty-four and it'll tell me if the weather's gonna change . . . rain, snow, wind, or hot."

"When you going to come visit the new place?" Simon asked.

"I ain't. No offense, but the only diff'rence 'tween you boilin' a spud or fryin' a piece a meat, and cookin' it my ownself, is I git my poke shook fer the priv'lege. No thanks, I'll keep my cash."

"I can see your point, but you could relax and let us take care of you. Doesn't that sound good for a change?"

"I s'pose that's all right when yer young, Simon, but after ya been shot at a few times, and slept wet fer a week or two, you'll re'lize gettin' it done yerself is a habit ya want ta git into."

"And that's why you stay here by yerself?"

"That and I git along with me more'n most other folks."

Simon squinted his eyes and cocked his head sideways.

Tay chuckled. "That'n hit yer brain sideways, didn't it?"

"Sounds like some of those Greek writers I used to read. They always had more than one meaning to what they said. Do you old-timers do that on purpose?"

"It's our job to make you young'ens think. Anyways, I'm pleased yer plans're workin' out. I've heard some good talk about what yer doin' out there."

"Got some good help, and a little luck don't hurt."

"Speakin' a luck, glad that Injun didn't stick ya. A good dog can be better than a man at times. And ya made the right choice about the horse."

"Huh?" Buell asked, and snorted. "Why's that?"

"Fast horse's like a fast woman. Sometimes they'll get ya there before you're ready. Simon strikes me as a feller who likes ta take things a little slower."

Buell looked at Simon for help.

"Like I said, old-timers talk like that," Simon said. "There's a French word for it, double something, I can't remember exactly, but I think you just got insulted, Buell." He laughed.

Buell took a playful jab at his shoulder.

Simon dodged, then looked at Tay. "Where could I find a good source for some standing dead timber?"

"You mean stuff the bugs've got into?"

"Yeah, I guess so. I want to make some lumber, and I might not have time to wait for it to cure."

"How much ya need?"

"Enough for eight sixteen-by-twenty-foot cabins."

"Oh, hell, you ain't lookin' for much. Right up the creek here about sixteen miles there's a whole hillside that's over a third dead. Been that way for over ten years and still dyin' in spots."

Simon looked up at the rising hills. "Was last year fairly typical for snow?"

"Fairly. You'll get three feet, more or less, where I'm talkin' about. Thinkin' 'bout cuttin' this winter?"

"Maybe. Depends on how an idea is received."

"Workin' on Amos again?"

"A little." Simon smiled at the older man. "If it comes about, would ya like to sign on?"

"Ya know, I jist might. I've been gettin' soft, and I completely skipped a year in the Dakotas. Let me know. You fellers drink a cup of coffee? Got some left over from breakfast."

"Sure. That sun feels good, and we don't have anything else to do, do we, Buell?"

Tay entered the dugout and rounded up two more cups.

Sergeant Barrschott tapped on Lieutenant Maupin's door, waited a heartbeat, and entered. The officer jerked forward from his semi-reclined position and looked up, his eyes overly open.

"Yes, Sergeant?" His voice had a snap to it.

"You told Trooper Twining you needed to see me."

"But can't you kno . . . can't you wait until I bid you enter?"

"Thought I heard you say so . . . sir."

"I've decided I want you back on the supply detail. You'll take a contingent of eleven wagons and leave for Fort McPherson Monday morning. See the quartermaster for a list of requirements. That will be all." He looked down at his desk and picked up a sheet of paper he studied intently. Barrschott smiled at the top of the lieutenant's head for a second, then turned and left.

The dark confines of the supply building smelled of cowhides, kerosene and damp wool. Barrschott found Sergeant Lemming in the back, playing cards with four other men. "Fuzznuts sent me to get the roster for Monday. I appreciate you puttin' in the word with the major, Lem," Barrschott said and pulled up a wooden box to sit on.

"You weren't worried about it, were you?" the quartermaster asked. "When I told the major the lieutenant wanted to lead it, he laughed out loud. Hear Fuzzy ain't happy about it though. We may have to be extra careful this trip."

"How much of it have you put on a Form Forty?"

"All the stuff you wanted, and a couple things for me. The rest are in as regular requisitions. Nothin' to worry about, we just have to be sure nobody checks till we get it all unloaded."

"We gonna come in at night again?"

"Yeah, that works best. I think the sixth will be good. Fuzzy likes his sleep. Let's go get the lists." He laid his cards down with a pointed look at the younger men. "I'll be right back."

The two sergeants walked toward the front of the supply building.

Amos entered Simon's small office and sat down in a soft chair. Spud raised his eyebrows in greeting and dozed off again. "Got something I want to talk to you about."

"Okay." Simon leaned back in his chair.

"I've been thinking. The dining-room idea has worked out well, real well, but I noticed something." He paused a few seconds, eyebrows raised.

Simon waited.

Amos continued, "I noticed that about nine out of ten of our customers are men, and the women that come in don't seem to come back." He paused again.

And again Simon waited him out.

"So what I think is happenin' is the ladies might be offended by our ladies, see what I mean?"

"Our ladies? From the dining rooms they don't even see the saloon, much less our ladies."

"But they know they're here, upstairs, uh . . . doin' what they do."

"So what's your solution?"

"Well, I ain't got one. I just come in to tell ya what I thought. Figgered maybe you could come up with somethin'."

"Like build six or eight cabins across from the stable?"

Amos sat upright in the chair and stared at Simon.

"And let each girl have one to decorate like they want, pay you rent on it and, as you put it, do what she does right there. Probably never have to set foot in the saloon again, unless she wants to."

"I might have known." Amos sagged back into the chair, shaking his head.

Simon opened his desk drawer and took out a twenty-inch square sheet of paper. He handed it to Amos. "Here's what they'll look like. I think we can support eight. We have three girls now, but Saint Louis or Omaha can supply five more soon as we tell May." Simon waited a minute as Amos studied the drawing, and then handed him a smaller sheet. "That's a detailed list of materials, down to the nails. How they are furnished will be up to the lady who lives there. We'll subsidize the furnishing fifty percent, and lend them the other fifty. I think you can get your money back in less than two years."

Amos studied the list carefully and then asked, "You really think you can build them for three hundred fifty each? Freighting that much wood in can't be cheap."

"You're right, costs us a dollar per hundred pounds per hundred miles. Nearest mill would cost us over seventy dollars a thousand."

"Then according to this, you can't build them for three fifty."

"I could if I get the lumber for a fifth of that." Simon leaned back in his chair. "And I can."

"Mister Tapola, your sawyer friend?"

"Right. Tay Prescott wants to help, and I've asked Daggett to go along."

"Daggett?" Amos scoffed. "He won't last three days without a bottle."

"Something I saw when I was a kid tells me he will. We don't need to go into detail. Anyway, the three of them can cut all winter. Zahn says they can throw up a log hut in ten days. Say the word and we're in the building business again."

"Green lumber makes a drafty wall after one summer."

"We'll cut only dead stuff, dried and standing for five or ten years. Tay knows where there's a hundred times what we need. They can be very selective."

"Just how long you been thinkin' about this?" Amos tilted his head forward, his brow furrowed.

"Since we started the dining rooms."

Amos laughed out loud. "I'm sure glad I hired you when I had the chance, Simon. You're an amazing young man. Sure, let's do it. I've always been ready to put money back."

"I'm glad you hired me too. You're a good man to work for. Got a request though."

"What? Uh-oh, the catch."

"Not at all. I'd like to put some of my own money into it."

"How much?"

"I want to finance the little houses. At the end of three years, you have the option to buy them from me for what I put in them, plus a flat twenty percent of the difference between what a girl made for you on average over the three years before, and what she makes you in the three years after she moves into a house."

Amos wrinkled his brow in thought for a minute. "You have the money?"

"I will have, come the twenty-fifth. My grandfather left it in trust."

"Then let's do it." Amos got out of his chair and extended his hand. "Partner."

Buell faced Simon across the table as they waited for Lori to bring them breakfast. The first signs of morning light shone through the windows of the saloon.

"Sure would like to have the company. I can wait a couple more days," Buell said.

"I know, but I'm not ready to go back yet. I've committed myself to this deal, and I better stay here and see it goes right."

"Nothin' gonna go wrong. Ya can't even start till March at the earliest. C'mon, we'd have some fun. Get to see Jake."

"Nah, I'm gonna stay here. But I want to ask you a favor."

"Anything."

Simon picked up an envelope that lay on the table and handed it to him. "That's what's called a Power of Attorney. Give it to John Lindstrom. He'll give you what I have coming from that trust fund I told you about. Bring it back with you."

"Sure, I kin do that."

Lori served their food about five minutes later, and half an hour after that Buell left the saloon and rode south toward Cheyenne.

Zahn and Daggett stopped by the carpenter shop at the fort and loaded the stack of boards, two small boxes of nails, and four rolls of tarred paper that Simon said would be waiting. Along with the logging tools, household things, a table and two benches, a sheet-iron stove with ten feet of stovepipe, and food supplies for both men and mules, the load had to be thoroughly lashed down on the flat wagon. Just as the sun crested the hill on the far side of the meadow, they arrived at Tay's to find him waiting. By three that afternoon, they were stopped on a wide, flat meadow, surrounded by tall pine trees.

"First thing is to fix us a place to sleep for a week or so," Zahn said. He drew his ax from the foot box. "I'll go cut some poles to set up the tent. Plato, you unharness the mules, and string a rope corral for them and Tay's horse. Tay, you kin start throwin' the stuff off the wagon." He turned, and his long easy stride soon carried him out of sight in the trees.

"Gawd, I ain't slept outside since I was a kid," Daggett said. "Kinda lookin' forward to it."

"I'll be happy when we have something solid around us. These tents have a way of headin' downwind at the damnedest times," Tay grumped.

It was nearly dark by the time they'd lashed together a rough frame and draped the canvas across it. Tay had a hot bed of coals going, and the sliced spuds were about half done in the eighteen-inch, cast-iron skillet. He stood by the rough table slicing thick steaks off a twenty-five-pound ham.

"I've marked the trees we'll need for the cabin," Zahn said. "Two of us on a crosscut and one swampin', we'll down what we need in a day. Then, another day buckin' the sticks into eighteen-foot lengths and we're well on our way to having a home for Christmas." He sat on the ground with a short piece of log between his knees, his double-bitted ax stuck in it. He slowly drew his stone in smooth sweeping strokes across the gleaming edge. "A little work tonight will save a lot of work tomorrow," he said to Daggett. "I needn't tell you what happens if this thing gets away from you." For emphasis, he tested the steel with his thumb.

Simon walked through the propped-open door of the kitchen to get another cup of coffee. Lori stood at the table, white flour a third of the way up her arms, kneading a six-loaf-lump of bread dough. The muscles in her forearms rippled under her summer-brown skin. She puffed at a strand of light-brown hair that had escaped from her scarf. After a minute, she stopped to straighten her back, and her gingham dress stretched across her bosom as she flexed her shoulders.

"Oh! I didn't hear you come in," she said when she finally noticed him. She looked at the cup in his hand and smiled. "Pour me one too. I'll set this to rise and have one with you."

A rush of heat flashed towards the top of Simon's head and he hurried to the stove. With his back to her, he deliberately poured the two cups full.

"Go on out to a table and I'll bring the cups," he said, still facing the stove.

"That's all right, I'll get it." She picked up the dough and dropped it in a large pan.

"No! I mean . . . go ahead, I'll bring them."

He glanced over his shoulder just as she covered the dusty white lump with a cotton dish towel. Then, she walked into the saloon. Simon waited as long as he dared, then followed.

"That will taste good," she said as Simon came from the kitchen.

"You work hard, I'll tell anyone that. But your bread is so much better than what I can get at the post bakery, I'm not going to discourage you." Simon fiddled with his cup.

"You couldn't. I'm used to working, and don't know what I'd do if I weren't busy. I'm very pleased you offered me this job."

"You earn what we pay you and more," he mumbled.

"How long did you stand in the door and watch me?"

Simon felt the familiar rush. "I'm sorry. You reminded me of S—something my ma used to do. Guess you caught me staring." He blushed, and unable to meet her eyes, stared at his cup.

"I'm a married woman, Simon. I know from experience that what we have here could cause both of us trouble."

"But I wouldn't—"

"Not on purpose you wouldn't, but most people who get hurt in a situation like this are not hurt on purpose. Just the opposite, the reasons are so filled with good that they fail to see the bee in the blossom."

"But—"

"Please listen to me, Simon. I dearly want to be your friend, even your best girlfriend, but I am truly happy with Zahn. So don't let yourself create reasons to think otherwise. A smile from me is a smile because I like you. There can be nothing else."

"I don't know what to say."

"There is nothing you need to say. A fine-looking man like you, smart and hardworking, must have attracted someone. I can only guess that something went wrong. I don't know you well enough to offer my shoulder, but I do understand."

"Thank you, Lori. You not only make bread like my ma, you are as straightforward as she is. Friends, then?" He picked up his cup and with a half smile, saluted her.

"Friends."

Chapter 11

Buell let his horse pick its way along the trail, easy to see and follow in the bright moonlight. Eager to get back and unable to sleep, he'd saddled up Shadow Walker at midnight, and continued his journey from Cheyenne. Fort Laramie was only another couple of miles farther. Expecting to see the lights of the fort as he crested a ridge, a wagon train moving from the east surprised him. He stopped and watched as someone from the front rode toward the rear of the column. Soon, two wagons swung away from the road and headed toward the hills to the north. The rider rejoined the head of the train.

"Just like when I was a kid, Shadow. Used to watch goin's on like this back home. Think we ought to go see?" The horse pricked his ears, turning one back to listen.

Buell waited until the main column moved out of sight, then rode in the direction the two stragglers had gone. They were fording the shallow water of the river when he caught them. He followed them upstream as they passed a half mile north of the post. An hour later, they crossed the river again, drove straight toward McCaffrey's ranch, and into the open rear doors of the stable. The doors swung shut.

Buell swung his leg over his saddle and had just planted a foot on the ground when the door to the house opened and Spud bounded out, tail wagging furiously.

"Hey, dog." Buell reached down and stroked his head. "Heard 'em comin didn't ya?" He looked at Simon's shadowed face.

"And looks like you were expectin' 'em too."

"Guess some things are meant to be. What in hell are you doin' up at this time of night?" Simon asked, chuckling. "Old habits die hard I guess."

The front door of the stable opened and two men walked toward the house.

"Who's that with you, Steele?" a voice asked.

"Rankin. And Pettit," muttered Buell half under his breath.

"I ain't lookin' for trouble, Buell," Rankin said when he recognized him. He edged warily toward Simon. "He in on this?"

"I guess he is now." Simon looked at Buell, his eyebrows raised in question.

Buell shrugged.

"Fine," Rankin said. "This was my last trip. I'm discharged next week."

"I'll get Twiggs," Simon said and headed toward the saloon. "You go with them, Buell."

When he entered the barn Buell saw two men pulling the canvas covers off the loaded wagon. They stopped when they saw Buell.

"It's all right," Rankin assured them. "Get that uncovered. Pettit, help me with this one." Rankin climbed the wheel and waited for him to undo the ropes on the sides. Soon both wagons were uncovered.

"Everything goes against that wall," Simon said as he walked in.

Twiggs was right behind him. "Hello, Buell. Simon said we were found out. Have a good trip?"

"Yeah. Am I understandin' this?"

"I think so," Twiggs said. "Want to help us get this off? They have to get back downriver. The rest of the train is waiting for them a half mile east of the post."

"And they arrive, unload, and everything the army ordered is marked off the list?" Buell smiled. "And McCaffrey gets his coffee and sugar for cheap."

"McCaffrey doesn't have a lot to do with it," Twiggs replied. "He knows, but right now he's hard asleep—on purpose like."

"Give us a hand, Twiggs. You'd think someone would find a way to put handles on a barrel." Simon rim rolled a thirty-gallon cask toward the end of the wagon. "Ham-Smoked" was burned in the wood.

Buell and Twiggs manhandled it off the wagon, and Buell rolled it toward the wall.

An hour later the empty wagons left, and the three men formed a wall of bundled meadow grass, the contraband completely hidden. With a gaping yawn, Twiggs headed for the saloon. "I'll see you guys later this morning. I've gotta get some sleep."

Simon followed Spud into the house where Simon sank onto the couch and the dog curled up in front of the door. About five minutes later, Buell came in carrying his saddlebags and slumped into the easy chair. Simon avoided Buell's eyes for as long as he could. "Well, go ahead and say it," he finally blurted.

"I'm havin' a hard time findin' the words. This is exactly what Gus at the store back home was doin', and it's what damn near got you thrown in jail. I remember the holy hell you raised about how you couldn't trust anyone anywhere. Well, now you know why."

"Are you condemning me?" Simon pulled himself to the edge of the sofa. His face had started to heat up.

"Hell, no—I'm gonna go celebrate. Simon has finally come down here where most of us live. Now you see what it's like to take care of yourself."

"I'm not just takin' care of myself. I have a business to run, and people who depend on me. There are over twenty soldiers who will get a few extra dollars for this. And Twiggs and Barrschott are just that much closer to getting what they need. So it isn't just for me."

"Horseshit. You still won't admit it. Simon did this for Simon. Take a look. You got muck all over ya. Everybody can see it, but nobody minds cuz they got it on them too. This is what it's like down here, Simon. You'll learn to live with it. I've been here all my life."

Simon threw his hands in the air. "I'm having a hard enough time with this without you preaching to me, Buell."

"Preachin'? I'm not sayin' a thing. You're the one who's lookin' around for reasons to feel better about somethin' most of us have to do jist to get along. I really don't care what you do, and care even less about why. I just don't want ya lookin' down yer nose at the rest of us while ya do it." Buell's eyes glinted in the lamplight.

Simon's mouth worked itself open and shut a few times, then he swallowed hard. "I guess I'm trying to have it both ways. I apologize."

"Fer what? I told ya I don't care."

"I apologize for the deception. Somehow it made it easier if you didn't know. Maybe I was dreading to hear you say, 'I told you so.' I expected you to gloat. I had no reason to think that. You walked in on me stealing—outright thievery."

Buell's face wore a faint smile and he returned Simon's gaze.

Simon looked down at the floor. "And while you were gone, I watched Lori in the kitchen one morning, and I imagined her naked. To make things worse, she caught me looking." Simon felt miserable.

"Is this that confessin' thing at church that Jake used to tell us about? So what, ya didn't do nothin' did ya?"

Simon raised his eyes. "She's married, Buell. I know better

than to lust after her."

Buell looked at him, his face neutral. After a moment he picked up the saddlebags beside the chair, opened a flap, and took out two canvas sacks.

"Oooff," Simon said as he caught one of the bags in the stomach. He hefted the other one. "You got it all in gold?"

"Yep. And there's a letter from Mister Lindstrom." He poked around in the bag and took out a crumpled envelope. "Sorry," he said as he tried to smooth the creases.

"It's okay." Simon opened the envelope and stared at the letter for several seconds. He took a deep breath and looked at Buell. "And now I'm going to take an inheritance my grandfather left me and use it to buy a whorehouse." He shook his head. "He must be turning in his grave."

"I'm done arguing with ya, Simon. You do what you need to do."

"You're right. To hell with it." The bags thudded to the floor. Spud raised his head and looked at them.

"So how's your pa? And your new ma?" Simon forced a smile.

"I've never seen him so happy. Reason I'm back so soon, they took off the next day for Saint Louis for two weeks." Buell's face spread with a grin.

"Did ya see my folks? Of course you did. How are they?"

"Yer pa give 'em the house as a weddin' present."

"That's good. That's really good. What do Axel and Abe and the rest of them look like? Has the town gotten bigger?"

Buell held up his hand. "All right, all right, I'll get to it."

He dug his tobacco out and rolled a smoke. The flaring match gleamed in his eyes as he leaned back in the chair. Then they talked for the next two hours, the stillness of the night split by laughter as they relived many moments of their boyhood in Carlisle.

★ ★ ★ ★ ★

The stillness of the cold air amplified the squeak of leather as Simon rode through the light snow cover. Twin blasts of steamy breath blew out the horse's nostrils as it followed Spud north through the wide valley. The stream meandering down from the heights had not yet frozen over, and to the dog's delight, ducks, spooked from the beaver ponds, pounded into the air with quacking protests.

"Shouldn't be long now, boys," Simon said to his animals. The horse snorted in reply and Spud paused briefly, head cocked to receive his orders. Hearing none, he bounded off in search of more ducks.

They traveled another two miles when Spud stopped and turned to look at Simon. Halting his horse, Simon listened and heard the faint "throck" sound as an ax bit onto cold wood. He smiled. "Go find 'em, Spud." The dog took off at a dead run.

A squat, square log hut sat amongst the tall trees. One side was stacked front to back, and ground to eaves, with split wood. The black barrel of the stovepipe pointed into the sky, breathless for the moment. Simon rode past as he followed the sound of the ax, and then he heard the rhythmic stroke and retrieve sound of a saw ripping through wood. He found them, Zahn standing on top of a log that lay in a frame, with Daggett underneath in the pit. An eight-foot-long whipsaw worked the length of the log, cutting half an inch with each stroke, twenty-four strokes a minute. He watched for five minutes before Spud went close enough for Zahn to see him.

"Hold up," Zahn hollered at Daggett and let the saw stay down at the bottom of the stroke. "Looks like we got company, Plato."

Simon swung off his horse and walked toward the pit. Plato emerged from the end, and Spud started barking furiously. The man was covered with sawdust; only his face under the bill of his cap remained clear of the debris. He shook, and a half a bushel of chips and dust fell away. Spud's hackles bristled.

"It's all right, Spud. That's Plato," Simon said.

Daggett took off his hat. With a woof, Spud charged across the distance, tail wagging furiously, and nearly knocked the man over.

"What brings ya up here, Simon?" Zahn asked, tugging his gloves off and extending his hand. "How's Lori?"

"She's fine. Never met a harder-working woman. She'd keep up with my mother. Actually, I came up out of curiosity. Like to see how this is done. How long did it take you guys to make that frame and dig this hole?" Simon peered into the cutout hillside. The smell of pine resin permeated the air.

"For a couple of fellas who say they're out of shape, Tay and Plato damn near beat me to death. We dug the hole in a day, and built the frame in two more. Never seen it done that fast. And the cabin—we normally roll the wall logs into place, these guys just lift 'em. I'm careful not to irritate either one of 'em."

"Where'd you get the material to stuff the cracks?"

"Weren't hardly no cracks," Daggett said. "This feller kin ax a line down a log like it was run from a mill. We got mud down at the creek and stuffed some in."

"There really wasn't much need to shape," Zahn said. "With all the trees we had to choose from, nearly all the logs were about the same size. Wished we had a piece of glass though. Dark as the inside of your dog when the door's closed. I know from experience that will crawl into ya after a couple of months."

Spud heard the word "dog" and looked up at Zahn. Then his ears pricked, and he rumbled deep in his chest.

"What do you hear?" Simon followed the dog's gaze. A moment later Tay came striding out of the trees.

"Thought it went too quiet down here. Leave these two alone

for five minutes and they sit down. Drive an old man crazy. How ya doin', Simon?" He strode up and stuck his hand out.

"Wanted to see how this was done. It's all very interesting, and looks like hard work."

"I started out with Plato swamping the trees and Tay in the pit," Zahn said. "Tay's too impatient. Ya gotta wait for the saw to be pulled up. He was always pushing. So he went to swamping and bucking the logs into lengths. He can go as fast as he wants out there. Turns out Plato is perfect for this. If I didn't know it was a man down there, I'd swear it was a machine."

"So how fast you can produce lumber?"

"Plato and I can make twenty-four sixteen-foot planks a day, that's two twenty-four-inch logs. We can lay down in a day enough to keep us busy for a week. And Tay chews 'em off for length 'bout as fast as we cut 'em. We make a hell of a crew."

"We gonna call it a day, Zahn?" Tay asked.

"I think we can. You go get the mule, and we'll meet ya at the cabin. Plato, go pull the wedge on that last cut and we'll leave the saw there."

Simon and Zahn started for the cabin.

Even with the door wide open, the inside of the cabin was gloomy, the front corners completely hidden. The sawyer lit one lamp, then the second, to reveal the orderly interior. Four low box-like affairs stood hard against two walls, eight feet long and about two and a half feet wide. Three were filled with pine boughs. A black stove sat angled in the corner with lengths of firewood stacked on either side. A simple split-plank table with four legs was bounded on two sides by equally stout split-log benches. A stack of shelves stood along half the width of the back wall, four fifteen-inch-wide planks separated vertically by short lengths of squared-off log. A more conventional table stood alongside with a washbasin and water pail on top. About two inches of sawdust covered the dirt floor.

"Does it get warm in here?" Simon glanced at the stove.

"It will. With another twenty inches of snow on top and some more drifted against the front, you'd survive without any heat if you could stay in bed."

Simon inspected the cabin construction carefully. The notching of the corners was nearly perfect. The only light showing through was around the door. Zahn noticed him looking.

"A couple moose hides lapped over the door, and you'd never feel a draft. We used moose a lot at home. They're plentiful and stupid." He grinned. "The stupid part is important."

"Is everybody getting along up . . . uh . . . no other way to say it. How's Daggett's drinking coming along?" Simon asked.

Zahn smiled. "It's not. He come up here without a thing. I thought for sure he'd put something away, but he didn't. He had several bad nights and even worse days, but I think he was going to prove something, and he has. We haven't talked about it, but I can see he's proud of gettin' through it."

"I was hoping that would happen. I'm really pleased. Plato is a good worker and a genuinely good man. Odd, now I think about it, but when I was in school I had a teacher who encouraged me to read the Greek philosophers. One of them was Plato. He said, 'In the world of knowledge, the idea of good appears last of all, and is seen only with an effort.' I thought then, and I told her so, that none of what they wrote could have much to do with how we live today. And now I see Plato proving Plato."

The door opened and Tay and Daggett came in, followed by Spud. The dog did a survey of the place and lay down by the door.

"Didn't hear you guys come up," Simon said. "Thought I would have heard the mule."

"Nope, it's a real snug place," Tay said. "The wind gets to blowin' hard you'll know it, but, otherwise, you can't hear a thing. So how's things at the ranch?"

"Nothing much to say. Lori more or less runs the dining rooms and kitchen, and Twiggs the saloon. Doesn't leave much for me to do. Been playin' cards more."

"Did you see anyone at my place when you rode by?"

"Nope. Looked closed up to me. I didn't even think to check. Should I?"

"Not really. I asked Walks Fast to stop by every once in a while just to chase the critters out. Thought maybe he mighta been there."

"We better get you something to sleep on while we still got light," Zahn said. He pointed at the empty box. "Tay had the notion you'd come up for a look. C'mon." He opened the door and went out.

About twenty minutes later they came back, arms loaded with pine boughs. They stuffed them into the spare box.

"Go get your horse blanket, and we'll find something for ya to sleep under. Don't need much, Tay keeps the stove goin' all night."

The evening passed quickly as Tay impressed them with stories of his scouting days in Kansas and Oklahoma. Daggett, it turned out, had been a stagecoach driver for the Overland Stage and had been robbed three times. And the three prairie dwellers were fascinated by Zahn's account of cities with five and six thousand residents, five-story buildings and streets with lights that stayed on all night. It was nearly midnight before the last man came back in from one final trip outside.

Simon woke to someone shaking his shoulder. His eyes fluttered open to see Tay standing over him.

"What?" Simon mumbled as he freed his arms from the heavy buffalo coat that lay on top of him. He gripped the edge of the box and sat upright.

"We got us a storm comin' and I think you got a decision ta

make." Tay moved over to the stove and fed it another short piece of wood.

Simon struggled to get his legs over the edge of the bed. "Is it snowing?"

"Not yet, but the wind shifted during the night and now it's still as death. Might be an hour or might be half a day, but it's comin'." He rubbed his leg. "Guaranteed."

"What time is it?" Zahn asked as he sat up and stretched.

"Figger six hours since we all finally shut up and went to sleep," Tay said. He filled the black coffeepot with water from the bucket and set it on the stove.

Simon sat on the bench and tied his shoes. "You hear what he said about the weather, Zahn?"

"Yeah. I don't have any experience with mountain storms."

"Well, yer gonna get some," Tay said. "Soon's it's light I kin tell a little more. I'm gonna go string a line to the mules." He opened the door and left.

"String a line?" Zahn asked.

"Sometimes it snows so hard you can't see two feet," Simon said. "I remember one time at home my father had to dig us out of our house. We were completely covered. First time I was ever scared in spite of being with my folks."

Simon and Zahn were dressed when Tay returned. They left as he came in. The air outside didn't feel as cold as when they had gone to bed, and the air stood calm. Spud disappeared into the morning gloom. Finished with their morning call, they went back into the cabin. Daggett sat on the edge of his bunk scratching at his beard. Tay stood, beating a batch of pancake batter into shape.

"See what ya mean by calm. It's almost . . . I dunno, ghostly," Zahn said.

"That'll change," Tay said. "First it'll start to snow, big flakes, then the wind will pick up and the flakes git smaller. Ya feel that hard, gritty stuff hittin' yer face, look for a place to hunker down." He grinned at the discomfort showing on the flatlanders' faces.

Steam swirled off the coffeepot. Tay shook out two hands full of ground beans into the boiling water. The aroma filled the cabin in the time it took for Tay to settle the foaming coffee. Two cast-iron skillets came off the shelf, and he unhooked a ham hanging from a rafter above the back wall. Soon, several large slices were sizzling. Scratching at the front door gained the dog entrance, and he padded through the sawdust to sit by the stove.

Tay stacked the hot ham steaks on a tin plate, salvaging the grease in a used milk can. The first pancake came off the stove about three minutes later, and for the next half hour a steady stream of batter poured into the smoking skillets transformed into the golden disks that the men subconsciously urged out of the pan. Satisfied, the three men, elbows set on the table, breathed the coffee smell off the cups they held.

"That was wonderful, Tay," Simon said. "You ever need a job, you got one in my kitchen."

"T'ain't likely." Tay cooked five more cakes and lay the skillet on the woodpile to cool. Picking up a full serving of ham, he put the slice between two pancakes and laid the improvised sandwich on the overturned kindling box. Zahn's eyebrows went up in surprise as Tay smooched Spud away from the door, and pointed at the food. "There ya go." He met Zahn's surprised expression with a chuckle. "Ya don't think he ain't hungry too?"

"Just never seen a dog fed in the house, I guess."

"Out here a dog is more'n a dog, he's a partner. Person who don't see it that way shouldn't have one. Personally, I find 'em a nuisance, but this'n is special. He's earned his keep."

Tay poured molasses over his own pancakes and ate standing up. When he was finished, Daggett gathered up the dishes, put them in a beat-up pan and grabbed the water bucket. Tay followed him out the door.

"Sure glad he agreed to come along," Zahn said. "I'm a terrible cook, and Plato can't even get out of bed unless he smells coffee. Tay had all the groceries boxed and ready when we picked him up. Half the stuff I would have never have thought of."

"Buell and I spent some time with him when we first came to Fort Laramie. He's an amazing man, full of talents you'd never dream he had. You ought to hear him whistle. He can actually warble like a bird. He grumps and huffs a lot, but he's as good as they come."

Tay came back in and shut the door. "You kin almost touch the clouds out there. Setting right on the treetops. I wouldn't want to make your decision."

"What would you do?" Simon asked.

Tay's eyebrows shot up. "What'd I just say? If it were me, I'd sit, but then I ain't never in a hurry to get anywhere."

"I really should get back. Monday's are usually slow, but I have things that need attending to." Simon grimaced. "Hate getting caught in a storm though."

"Ya got tracks to follow out so you kin move right along. If ya really hustle, you kin be out of the high stuff in a couple hours. Ain't no way o' knowin' how long it'll last, but I don't need ta tell you that. Wish I could figger which way it was a comin'."

"I'm gonna go." Simon put his hat and coat on, and was just headed out the door when Daggett pushed through it, sloshing water from the full bucket.

"Starting to drop right now. Straight down. If we didn't have to work in it, it would be beautiful to watch." He set the bucket on the washstand. "You gonna go?"

"Yeah. We can hurry, even lope for quite a bit. We'll be all right."

"I'll help ya saddle up." Tay put on his coat and followed Simon out to the pole corral.

A few minutes later Simon was mounted. "If it looks like you could make it, come on down for Thanksgiving. If we don't see you then, I'll try to be back up the end of December."

"Give Lori a squeeze for me, Simon," Zahn said.

"I can do that, Zahn. She sent her love." Simon wheeled his horse and rode off.

With two-inch-wide flakes falling softly but steadily, Simon lost sight of the cabin after traveling only a hundred yards. Spud barked with excitement as he jumped and bit at the huge pieces of fluff. Finding his tracks from the day before yesterday, Simon urged his horse into an easy canter, and Spud, sensing the urgency, charged out ahead of the horse. The rocking rhythm of the horse as it followed the dog soon put Simon at ease, and he relaxed in the saddle.

Soon, snow plastered his chest and steam formed on the neck and shoulders of the loping horse. An hour of riding passed, and lost in thought, he was not aware that the snow no longer fell straight down, instead, it moved before a slight breeze. Body in synchronization with the horse, he was shaken from his reverie when the horse slowed to a walk.

Simon squinted his eyes against the snow to see Spud, stopped in the trail. He reined the horse to a halt and looked up at the treetops. The sky was a mass of swirling white and gray. The wind, no longer a breeze, picked up snow from the branches and whipped it off to the northeast. The dog had stopped a ways down the valley. A wall of white, boiling and breaking, tumbled over the ground. The storm hit with a fury that turned the horse. Simon let him have his head, and kicked hard against his sides. The frightened animal bolted for the trees two hundred yards away.

"C'mon, Spud!" Simon screamed above the howling wind. "Run."

Streaking toward the trees at a full gallop, the horse had no time to jump as a deadfall loomed out of the swirling snow. The panicked horse locked both forelegs and slid. Simon heard the vicious crack as a leg went under the log and snapped. Pitched over the animal's head, the agonized scream of the horse assaulted his ears. He fetched up hard against a tree, his yet unhealed shoulder bursting anew with pain. Then the sounds and feeling ceased to matter as a grinding collision with the frozen ground knocked him senseless.

Walks Fast, lost in dreams, sat motionless by the low fire. The sides of the tepee breathed in and out with the wind as the storm gathered strength. His wife and sister-in-law lay asleep in their robes. The vision that hovered in the center of his dream was of a horse in flight. It disappeared in and out of a storm as it ran without sense of direction, flying above the ground. He slowed his breathing and willed his heart to beat softly. A sense of euphoria flooded him, leaving no room for self-consciousness.

Then, he saw the rider clearly: Simon, bent over the horse's neck, trusting the animal to carry him to safety. The ghostly beat of the hooves slowed, and the horse and rider floated effortlessly away from the melee. And then another form appeared, Shadow Dog, tail streaming as he raced to catch the horse. Cold sweat flushed Walks Fast's body as an unseen danger made its presence felt.

He searched frantically for the source, but saw nothing but swirling white. Then, a piercing scream undulated with the waves of fear that pounded his brain, ripping him from his lofty realm, and flinging him back towards earth. One last fleeting glimpse of Simon, wheeling through the air, and a flash of bright red, brought Walks Fast back to his tepee. Eyes wide open, his fingers clutched the robe around his shoulders, and he stood. The lone figure left the sanctuary of the tepee, and walked away, into the storm, and toward the mountains.

The gentle touch of his mother's hand on his forehead pulled Simon back from the depths. He felt the cold around his feet and wanted to move closer to the fire, but his body would not respond to his commands. Frustrated, he submitted to her soothing touch and drifted back to sleep. Spud continued to lick at the wound on Simon's head and whine softly until finally he laid his head over Simon's and closed his eyes to wait.

The strength of the storm continued unabated, snow drifting and sifting over the still forms lying under the trees at the edge of the meadow. Soon they were only round humps, still and blended into obscurity. Then, the smaller mound moved, barely perceptibly at first, but suddenly exploding into the shape of a man sitting up.

Simon looked around confused, pushing at the form struggling beside him. And then he recognized the dog. "Spud." He choked the word out, and his hand went to the dog's head, clutching at the fur for assurance. "I came off the horse," he said and squinted through the blowing snow for any sign of the animal. He spotted the still lump. Shaking his head in despair, he rolled to his hands and knees, to finally stand unsteadily, one hand on the tree beside him. The dog shook the snow from its body and nuzzled Simon's other hand. Wind tousled Simon's hair and his hand instinctively went to check for his hat. He grunted, then gingerly felt the painful lump before inspecting his fingertips for blood. He saw a little.

"Took a whack, but it doesn't seem to be bleeding much. Where's my hat?" He kicked at the snow until the hat appeared. He slapped it against the tree. Nearly free of snow, he settled it back on his head, careful of the wound. "Let's look at the horse." He moved to the log that blocked his view.

Climbing over, he stooped and pushed his hand through the snow to the animal's ear. Cold as the snow, it didn't move. As he made his way around the head and stepped toward the saddle, his boots left tracks that showed bright red in the bottom. And then he remembered the sound of breaking bone.

"Oh, God, you poor thing, you lay there and bled to death. I hope it was quick."

The dead horse had one hind leg extended awkwardly forward, under its belly. It held the horse off the ground just enough to enable Simon to retrieve his rifle from the scabbard. He unbuckled one saddlebag where he found a length of leather strap and another pair of gloves.

"Now what do we do, Spud?" He looked out across the meadow. He could see about fifty yards. The ground away from the trees hadn't drifted nearly as much as where he stood. "How far have we come? Must have been ten miles, at least. Maybe twelve. That would leave us about five or so." He looked at the dog for his acceptance. Spud wagged his tail and gave him a quiet woof.

"We stay here, we could freeze. We take off walking, we could get stuck in deep snow and freeze. Hobson's choice. Come here." The dog stepped closer and sat. Simon tied a loop in the end of the strap, and put it around Spud's head. The other end he tied around his wrist. "That'll keep us together, boy. Let's go."

The shelter of the trees tempered the force of the wind, and Simon's breath was cut short by the first full blast of cold air. The snow stung his face and he shuddered. Head down, he and the dog walked side by side, suffering the choice of either walking in drifted snow in the shelter of the trees, or forcing their way against the wind on the clearer ground in the middle of the valley. Both proved exhausting work. Simon plodded ahead for nearly two miles to where the valley turned more to the west. Here, they were met with a wind unhindered by hill or trees. Hard-driven snow blasted into every crevice and crease of his clothes and blinded him with icy pellets. It had stopped snowing, but at ground level he couldn't see more than a few feet in front. Every few paces he had to half step to keep from falling, and his arms became heavier. His mind, blank to anything except the next step, was suddenly overwhelmed by the terrifying memory of being lost in the snow. The vision struck him with such force that he stopped, then slowly sank to his knees. Spud sat down upwind of him and buried his nose in Simon's coat, whimpering.

Walks Fast strode up to Tay's dugout, the wind pushing him as it had done all the way from the fort. He unlashed the door, and went inside. Several small animals scurried for cover. The lamp chimney came off, and he transferred the flame of a sulfur match to the wick. With the wick soon trimmed, a warm glow drove the darkness from the small shelter.

He busied himself at the stove until another match set light to the tinder in the firebox. With the fire going, and several pieces of wood laid on, he turned to face the door and sat down. Eyes closed, he let his breath out slowly to start a low hum in his throat. He tuned it to resonate until the vibration swept from his chest into the bones of his skull. Taking slow deep breaths, the hum continued until he could sense it even as he inhaled. The gossamer gates of his dream world opened, and he started his search for Simon. And soon found him.

Spud growled deep in his chest, and the hair on his neck stood up. He turned his head and tried to catch the scent of the intruder, only to be assaulted by the icy wind and driving snow.

He barked out loud in frustration.

Simon's head jerked erect at the sound. "What! Why are we stopped, Spud?" He looked down at his hands, folded between his bent knees. Leaning forward, he slowly pushed himself off the ground and stood.

Spud barked again, several times, and tugged at the strap around his neck. Simon did not look up as he shuffled after the dog, trusting the animal to find the way. Lost in a daze of confused thoughts, he had no sense of time or space, but simply responded to the tug on his hand. Countless times, he struggled back to his feet, up from a fall he didn't remember taking. Through the driving blizzard, Spud followed his nose, and Simon followed Spud. Then, the dog stopped, and Simon, no longer feeling the strap's tension, quit moving. Not feeling the wind or deadly cold, Simon stood still and waited.

Walks Fast saw the dog lift his head, and breathed a breath of warm air into its face. He smiled to himself as the dog reacted, barking furiously at something it knew was there, but could not see. Walks Fast turned and drifted easily back toward the dugout, sure the dog would follow. Slowly the bright light of the other side dimmed, and the Indian felt the heat of the stove on his back. He opened his eyes and rose to his feet to open the door. Outside, a white apparition stood as a statue, tied to an equally immobile dog, now on its belly, peering intently at the open door. Spud's tail wagged once in recognition and then went still.

Simon took another swig of the steaming brew and leaned closer to the stove. His bare feet sat immersed in the water bucket, the cold water felt warm. Walks Fast studied him intently as Simon quietly drank his herb tea, and watched Spud tug at the ice balls on his feet. The Indian got up, went to the wood box, and picked out the largest piece. He set it by the water bucket. "Take your feet out of the bucket now. Put them behind the wood."

Simon did as he was told and protected his red feet from the direct heat. Even then, he could feel the pain start to rise. "Have I froze them?"

"I don't think so, but they will hurt plenty. Soon we'll cover them with stockings."

"I'm sure glad you were here. I don't remember finding the dugout."

"Shadow Dog brought you. I was here to help Taylor."

Spud stopped worrying the ice for a moment and looked up.

"Yeah. He's a good one." Simon leaned over and ruffled the soft ears. "I'm not sure I could have made it to the fort."

Outside the wind continued to blast up the valley, piling drift on top of drift. Anything with warm blood sought shelter where they could, and waited until nature had sated her anger.

Chapter 12

The storm shut down the area for nearly a week. Buell had started for the logging site, but stopped when he saw smoke coming from Tay's dugout. The spotted horse again proved its mettle by carrying both Simon and Buell back to McCaffrey's ranch. Slowly Simon's feet stopped itching, and then started to peel. He'd narrowly avoided frostbite.

The evening diners, the first in a week, had gone home, and with the restaurant closed, Simon joined Amos at his table for some cards. Rosie and Saint Louis Bob sat in their regular places. Rosie owned the freight business near the fort, and, with hauling all manner of goods and equipment for both the army and anyone else who needed the service, he was not a poor man. Rosie had an addiction for gambling and, as is often the case, lacked the skill to counter the affliction. And to make matters worse, he was terribly unlucky. His round, florid face always gleamed with a sweaty sheen and could be counted on to betray the worth of every card he was dealt.

Saint Louis Bob was a professional gambler and whiskey salesman and he probably should have avoided both. He made it his nightly goal not to lose so badly that he couldn't play the next. That made him an overly cautious player, and one prone to flashes of anger when his nerve failed to support his intuition and card sense. The ever-present bottle of Saint Louis Best whiskey, Bob's mainstay brand, worked steadily to degrade both.

Those two, along with Amos, Simon and Buell, made up the group that played cards well into the morning, every morning. Tonight, Sergeant Barrschott made the sixth player.

A banjo picker joined the usual weekend piano player that Amos hired. Both were troopers from the fort. After being weathered in for a week, the crowd, large and noisy, kept Twiggs busy. The wide smile on his face grew wider as the cash box filled.

Amos was being his usual circumspect self, peering from under his hat brim at the card spots. He grunted as Saint Louis Bob called his one-dollar bet. Sergeant Barrschott passed, threw his cards down, and leaned back in his chair.

Rosie, as he always did, opened and closed his hand like a fan. Close . . . then edging one card at a time onto view, until all five became visible, then closing the hand again. He seemed to think the process would change the spots somehow. This irritated everybody to no end, and Simon thought that was exactly why he did it. Finally, Rosie flicked a five-dollar gold piece with his thumb; spinning and flashing its worth, it landed neatly in the middle of the pot. "Raise ya four."

Buell, sitting next, met the five-dollar bet and raised twenty.

Simon looked closely at Buell's impassive face. Buell hadn't looked at his cards—he was dealing—and had just bet twenty-five dollars. It was pure audacity, and he did the same thing at least once or twice in every session. The fact that he managed, just occasionally, to make the rest of the players pay dearly tended to make them leery. That Buell might be a cheat never entered into Simon's mind as he watched, fascinated. "Just can't be," Simon grumbled as he folded with a pair of eights.

Amos, face completely hidden, shifted slightly in his chair, hands folded across his cards. You never knew what Amos was going to do. He was the smart one and, using ciphering and such, actually knew how the game worked. He pushed his cards into the pot. "Fold," he said quietly.

Bob had already stacked his coins, and pushed the twenty-four dollars across the green felt. "Call, and I'll take one card." He sailed his discard toward Buell.

Open . . . close. Open . . . close. Open . . . Rosie's Adam's apple made a quick trip up and down . . . close. He sailed two cards towards the pot and then hesitated, studying Buell's blank face. "Well, you ain't buyin' it," Rosie said. "Bob's keeping you honest." He threw his remaining three cards onto the pot with disgust. The smirk that appeared on Buell's face only enhanced the irritated look on Rosie's face.

"I'll play these," Buell said and still made no move to look at the five cards lying in front of him. Bob's card came off the deck and floated from Buell's fingertips. It landed with one corner tucked under the four that lay on the table. "Your bet."

Everybody looked at Bob as he stared bleakly, first at his cards, and then the gold pieces lying in the middle of the table. Simon could see the poker player's perennial question as it stormed around in Bob's head: was the hand good enough?

Buell simply bored a hole through Bob's head with his blank stare, the irritating smirk fixed like it was painted on. Bob forced himself to turn the edge of his final card up to take a look. His face clouded with disappointment. He might just as well have been shouting the card's worth out loud.

"Your bet, big fella," Buell said.

"Yeah, right." Bob's voice sounded dry and raspy. "I'll check."

"Betcha another twenty." Twin gold pieces clinked into the pile.

"Fold," Bob said, his defeat palpable. He flicked over the ace. "Only when I don't need the damn thing do I get it. How in hell did you know I didn't have four of a kind?"

"I didn't," Buell said, "I was a lot more worried about the trips Rosie had."

"You what? How can you know that for sure?" Rosie looked incredulous.

"Wasn't sure, till just now," Buell said, pulling the pile of gold towards his poke. "Some people shouldn't play cards, and that includes you two guys. Amos and Simon sit and think about the odds and that works. Barrschott plays for the fun of it, and that works too. I just sit here and watch you two, and you just learned how that works." Buell chuckled and started shuffling the cards. "Five-card draw, jacks."

The dealing had gone on well into the morning as Bob's whiskey thwarted his efforts to get his money back, and Rosie spent about fifteen dollars an hour on poker-face lessons, the money completely wasted.

Zahn's mules huffed pillow-sized clouds of frosty breath into the frigid air. Simon had not made it to the lumber camp as planned, so Tay, Plato and Zahn had left camp early one brittle morning in the third week of December. Daggett, wrapped in two blankets, sat beside Zahn in the driver's box. He was comfortable in his north-woods wool clothes and high-top boots. Tay, wrapped in his shaggy buffalo robe, tagged along behind on his horse. They pulled to a stop in front of Amos's place.

"I ain't never gonna thaw out," grumped Daggett as he gingerly dropped to the ground. He winced as his feet struck the frozen earth.

Tay climbed off his horse. "Hell, that weren't nothin. Ya coulda been walkin' with half a dozen Injuns doggin' yer trail." The grimace on his face betrayed his discomfort.

Zahn joined the two of them, and they pushed open the door of the saloon.

"Who are these bearded ruffians?" Twiggs asked, his voice teasing. He hustled around the bar and across the room.

"How're you doing, Plato? You look like hell, but somehow fit as a draft horse."

"I need a bath, a shave and something, anything to eat that Tay ain't had his hands on." Daggett sidestepped a perfunctory kick from the prospector.

"Ya don't have no trouble eatin' yer share, I noticed," Tay said.

"Where's Lori?" Zahn headed for the kitchen.

"You're headed in the right direction," Twiggs said. "Bang on the door when you go by Simon's office."

Zahn knocked once on the office door as he passed and then went into the kitchen.

Simon's head snapped around at the squeal of delight he heard as he walked out of his room. "What in hell?" he half shouted. Then he saw Tay and Daggett. "Hello, fellas. I'm really glad to see you. I gather Zahn has found Lori?" He nodded at the kitchen door and grinned as he headed toward the three men.

"Found we were not going to make it another month on the food," Daggett said. "Tay didn't figger on feeding lumbermen. We eat a lot."

"You can say that agin," Tay said. "I ain't never seen folks eat the way those two do. I've shot two deer since you left, and we've eat every scrap."

Zahn and Lori came out of the kitchen, Lori's face radiating the happiness that showed in her step. "What a wonderful Christmas present," she said.

"Everybody take a chair at Amos's table, and I'll get us something special to drink," Twiggs offered. He started back to the bar.

"Better not count on me," Daggett said.

Twiggs stopped and turned back. "Nothing?"

"Nope. Had my last drink the night before we pulled out in

September."

Twiggs exchanged a knowing smile with Simon and continued on to the bar. When he returned, he had a decanter of French brandy and a bottle of sarsaparilla in one hand, and six stacked glasses in the other. Set up, he poured five glasses full.

"Here's to our friends, home safe and sound, and to the empty glass that shall remain empty ever more. Congratulations, Plato." Twiggs raised his glass, and the others followed.

"Congratulations. Welcome home. To a warm welcome." The salutes all melded into one chorus as the group drank the warm liquid.

The front door opened and Buell stepped in. "Hey, where's mine?" he asked when he saw the fancy bottle.

"You can use my empty glass, Buell," Plato said. "I ain't needin' one."

"Ya quit? Well, I'll be damned." Buell looked at Twiggs, and some private message silently passed between them. Buell then poured himself a glass of Amos's expensive brandy and tossed the shot back. "Damn, that is good stuff." He wiped his lips with the back of his hand. "Amos is about half an hour behind me. I saw him at the tradin' store."

"How was yer trip back in October, Simon?" Tay asked. "I was worried as hell after ya left. That storm pounced on us like a polecat on a prairie chicken. I was hopin' you'd hustled on out ahead of it."

"Caught me. My horse broke a leg running for cover, and Spud more or less dragged me to your place. Lucky for me, Walks Fast just happened to be there. My toes still itch when they get too warm."

"I knew that dog was special. Ya say Walks Fast was waitin'?"

"Yep. Opened the door and there I stood."

Tay's eyebrows shot up for an instant, and he stared at Simon's face for a moment. "I see," he said. "Lucky for you."

The look on the older man's face puzzled Simon, and he resolved to ask him about it later. "How's it going up there, Zahn?"

Zahn didn't answer. He held Lori's hand and stared placidly at her face.

"Zahn?" Simon pressed.

Lori nodded her head toward Simon and made a face at her husband.

"What?" He looked at Simon.

"I said, how's it going with the timber cutting?"

"Oh, real good. We have everything we need down and stacked by the pit. The three of us are just sawing now. I think we'll have it done in another month if the weather holds. So far, the snow has helped. Makes the skidding easy."

"That's good to hear. The sooner you guys are back down here, the better I'll feel. I've seen firsthand how easy it is to get in trouble."

"I'll agree with him, my husband. I don't like it with you in the mountains."

"Did it at home. What's the difference?"

"How 'bout forty men compared to three."

"Well, you're right there. Like I said, if the weather holds off, we'll be back in a month."

"Okay, I've got work to do," Simon said. "You folks take it easy for a while and get warmed up. Tay and Plato, you're welcome to free rooms upstairs until you go back."

"I ain't gonna turn down a clean bed," Tay said.

"Me either." Daggett's face lit in a smile. "I want a hot bath. I've been standin' in sawdust for two months, and I can feel it startin' to stick permanent."

Simon left the group just as Twiggs poured another drink for everybody. The barkeep winked at Buell and mouthed, "You lose," holding up five fingers and nodding toward Daggett.

★ ★ ★ ★ ★

As expected, Zahn, Daggett and Tay were back at the ranch the middle of February, all the lumber they needed sawed, stacked and covered with side slabs to keep the snow off. Tay returned to his dugout to spend his time visiting with Walks Fast. Daggett went back to his job at the saloon, now with new responsibilities and an increase in pay. Zahn found work cutting firewood for the inevitable few around the fort who had not lain in sufficient wood for the winter. Simon completed the plans for the little houses, and with time on his hands, spent nearly every evening playing cards and drinking with the regular players. Last night had been such a night, and this morning Simon was paying the piper.

Six inches of oozing mud mixed with horse dung made a quagmire of the street in front of the saloon. The simple act of walking from the house to the saloon had Simon splattered with muck to his knees, and in a mood to quit the area forever. He banged open the door and stormed in. "Lori, bring me a cup of coffee!" he shouted at the closed kitchen door. He wiped his feet as best he could on a couple of feed sacks, then walked across the floor to his office and went in.

A minute later, Lori set the cup on his desk. "Aren't we in a fine mood this morning?"

"Don't start. I've got a headache, my boots are ruined, and we're about to run out of flour, in case you haven't noticed." He picked up his cup and scowled at the brew. "This fresh?"

"Probably not after you've looked at it."

Simon glared at her. She gazed back, hands on her hips, her head cocked slightly. "Oh, all right," he said, "I'm sorry. These late nights are killing me, and I'm at fault for not keeping track of the supplies."

"That's better. I've got three hundred pounds of cake flour coming from Mister Ward. It'll be here tomorrow. The bad head is your problem." She smiled at him and left, closing the door.

Simon looked at the door and remembered another time. If she was any more like Ma, I'd be looking around for Pa. He picked up his cup and rocked back in his chair. He was deep in thought, chasing memories of home around in his head when Buell pushed open the door and came in, followed by Spud.

"Mornin'." He sat down in the easy chair and looked at his boots. "Ain't this the shits?"

"What's got you up this morning? I left you sound asleep, and Spud took one look at the road and went back to bed." Spud stopped his nest circling for a moment to look at Simon.

"Got something botherin' me. Did you notice that cattle buyer won last night and pretty good?"

"Yeah. So?"

"This is the third time in as many weeks that some stranger has come in and done that."

"Cheating?" Simon leaned forward in his chair.

"I've been watchin', and I can't see it." Buell shook his head. "I'm not the most experienced player in Wyoming, but even I can see bottom dealing, or something comin' out of a sleeve or pocket."

"I really haven't paid much attention I guess."

"And another thing. Bob's been playin' all three times, and he either won a little or broke even. That ain't like Bob."

"So what do you want to do?"

"I want to look at the deck we were using last light. Twiggs has it locked in that little box he keeps the cards and dice in. Only I don't want Twiggs to know. Do you have a key?"

"Yeah, right here." Simon opened his desk drawer and took out a set. "I hate to go behind his back though."

"Would you mind if I got in that drawer when you weren't here?"

"No, you're more or less the law here. But now I know why

you want to, it's the same as me—" The look on Buell's face stopped Simon in midsentence. "No, I don't care." He dropped the keys back in their place and shut the drawer.

"Okay, and I'll keep it to myself." Buell stood, looked with disgust at his boots, and left.

With the snow gone and the mud dried up, Simon and Buell rode out to see Tay. They found him in front arranging his pack. He stepped to the doorway as he greeted them. "Climb down and I'll git ya a cup of coffee." He disappeared into the dugout without waiting for a response.

The men dismounted and were tying their horses up when Walks Fast came out of the hut.

"Good to see you, Simon. And Buell. You come to see Taylor go to Dakota?"

"Guess we are," Simon said. "Only heard yesterday when I was at the trading post. T. P. said Tay was leaving, but he didn't say this soon."

Tay come out of the dugout gingerly handling four cups, steam lifting from them.

"Git aholt of one of these, they're hotter'n hell." His face screwed up in discomfort as he quickstepped toward them.

"Smart man knows where to throw a skunk before he picks it up." Walks Fast chuckled as he slowly relieved Tay of one of the cups.

"Well, gawdammit, ya took yer time." Tay shook his hand in the air and scowled at the Indian. "Come on. Sit down and tell me what's goin' on."

"Not a lot," Simon said. "We're going to go get the lumber you guys sawed last winter. Think all the snow will be gone up there?"

"How'n hell would I know? Reckon you'll see when ya git

there." Tay noisily slurped from his cup; his eyes sparkled as he teased.

"Well, yer the mountain man," Buell said. "Yer s'posed to know stuff like that."

"Says who? Ask Walks Fast. He's probably already been up there."

Simon looked at the Indian, color rising in his face. "I'm sorry, Walks Fast. I've done it again. Have you been up there yet?"

Walks Fast smiled. "Yes, two times. Your saddle is in bad shape. Pine pigs have eaten much of it. I left it to them. The snow is gone. I stayed in the cabin. The man who made it knew how. Your wood is covered and dry."

"That's good to hear. We're ready to start building the little houses. Exactly when are you leaving, Tay?"

"Anytime. I've got my pack made up, and I've loaded the mule once already. Sonuvabitch sure hates it in the spring. I always let him kick and bite down here where he's easy to catch. He knows what he's doin', and he knows I know. Little game 'tween us." Tay looked over at his shoulder at the animal. The rangy mule's ears were both turned toward them as he listened intently. Tay chuckled. "Sonuvabitch knows his name."

"Where exactly are ya go—oops." Buell's hand went to his mouth. "I don't mean exactly. Are ya still goin' to the Dakota Territory?"

"Reckon so. I found a spot in sixty-eight that was just startin' to pan good. Weather set in and I damn near got caught. I'll let ya know this fall."

"Were you going to leave without saying anything?" Simon asked.

"I was gonna leave. Do ya mean was I gonna go all the way out ta McCaffrey's jist to tell you wouldn't find me here if ya come visitin'? Now that don't make a lot of sense does it?"

Simon looked at Buell and then back at Tay. "You have a way of squaring things off, I'll give you that. But you're right. Eventually we would have come by and discovered the place shut up."

"Right, and me sayin' my good-byes wouldn't a changed a thing. I'd still be gone. Only difference is, you made that trip 'stead o' me."

"Well, I'm glad we got to see you before you left. That's the way I like it. Will your place here be all right?"

"Oh, yeah. Walks Fast will stop by once in a while, usually when his women start to stick in his craw. But if ya happen to come by and see anything goin' on, I'd 'preciate it if ya'd stop a minute and look."

"We can do that."

The four men sat and drank the first cup of coffee. Then they had another as their sun-deprived bodies soaked up the heat of the early afternoon, reluctant to let go of the good feeling of friends being friends.

Chapter 13

Tay had been gone a week when Simon rode to the Indian camp to see Walks Fast. For several months sleep had not come easily to Simon, and he sensed in the Indian a person he could trust to at least listen. He dismounted and waited the customary minute or two for someone inside the tepee to come out and greet him. Walks Fast's wife soon appeared, and when she recognized Simon, she smiled, her short work-worn teeth exaggerating the width of her grin.

"Walks Fast gone. Taylor," she said as she pointed north.

"Thank you, Missus Walks . . . Uh, thank you," Simon stuttered over something that had never occurred to him: what is an Indian missus called?

He got back on his horse and set off at an easy canter toward the low hills.

Walks Fast sat on the split-log bench in front of the dugout as Simon rode up. "My woman told you I was here? Wondered if she would."

"Only four words, but I understood what she meant." Simon secured his horse to a post, then sat beside the old man.

"New horse maybe run off?"

"Yeah. He's not as smart as the old one, or he's smarter. I haven't decided which."

The two men went silent, and the pause lasted over five minutes as they studied the creek bottom and gazed at the rising slopes on the other side of the grassy valley.

"Your mind is full of clouds."

Simon heard it as a statement and when he turned to face the Indian, he saw Walks Fast had his eyes closed.

"I get confused sometimes . . . about things I do." The ease with which he'd voiced his admission surprised Simon.

"Your father worked hard to teach you, and your mother has you in her heart now. Many people think much of Simon and wonder why you left. Your family wants you to be safe."

"I decided it was time to leave home and see something else."

Walks Fast turned to look at him, his brow creased. "I'd say you ran away. I'd say you let dirt eaters make you feel the same as they do. One day, you will go back and see why you left."

"I know why I left. People were laughing at me and didn't respect me."

"That is the reason you carry in your head. It is not same as reason you have in your heart."

Simon stared at the lined face, now relaxed and tranquil. The slightest hint of a smile lay on the edge of the Indian's mouth. "Why do you say that?"

"Confusion comes when the head and heart won't agree. Your heart can only ask, your head will tell your feet what to do."

"But I tried to do what was right. I did what my parents taught me. And it didn't come out like they said it would."

"So you blame your parents?" The Indian now held Simon in a fixed gaze, eyes clear and intent.

"No, they're good people. But others, even some I trusted, wouldn't see I was right."

"So you blame others?" Walks Fast pressed.

"Sure I do. I was accused of stealing. I would never st—I didn't steal. But the sheriff believed I did, and so did the town."

"Your heart knows, but your legs carried you away. You need a stronger heart." Sadness crept into the Indian's eyes.

"But even if I know I'm right, and I stay where people don't want me, what then?" Frustration jammed Simon's words together. "A person can only take so much."

A slow smile spread over Walks Fast's face, erasing the troubled look. The Indian's eyes seemed to shift out of focus, and then closed for a few seconds. "When one strong heart is not enough, you must have two. I know you once shared your heart with another person. Walks Fast knows it is the same today."

Simon's heart sped up and a flush of apprehension prickled his skin. Unable to meet the Indian's eyes, he studied the ground between his feet.

"That is good place to look for an answer," Walks Fast said as Simon's discomfort grew. "The answer you get from there will be good one. The Earth does not have a reason to hide the truth."

"I don't understand what you're saying."

"You have trouble in your heart, and you don't know the question to ask. Maybe I'll tell you of a place to go and find the question. And maybe the answer will come from Earth there."

Simon was silent again, and the Indian closed his eyes once more. A striped chipmunk scurried from the corral to the corner of the dugout, and sat back on its haunches. As Simon watched, lost in thought, and not completely aware of it, the little animal went to all fours and walked deliberately to the two men and sat again.

"Good sign," Walks Fast said.

"Wh—what?"

"Small creatures know many secrets. The chipmunk knows your heart is good."

Walks Fast stood to face Simon. The chipmunk scolded him and scampered away. "I go now," he said. "Soon we will talk more. Talk to the spirits who visit in the night. They know your heart too."

Before Simon could answer, the Indian turned, and with long, steady strides, soon passed out of sight around the bend in the valley. Simon leaned back against the rough logs of the hut, and the warmth of the sun felt better than it had in a long time.

The spring shipment from Fort McPherson brought several bags of cement, army-ordered but delivered, courtesy of Sergeant Barrschott, to McCaffrey's ranch. Along with the cement, came paint, window glass, eight doors, and eight small coal stoves. Simon stood in the barn and surveyed the stolen property. "Where were these stoves going to go?" Simon asked Barrschott.

"If someone asked, we were going to put them in Old Bedlam. Some of the rooms don't have any heat at all."

"Old Bedlam?"

"Officer's mess and social place. Got rooms for people visiting and such."

"And how about all the glass?"

"Easier yet. They're constantly adding rooms on to buildings they got, or adding windows and repairing broken ones. Quit worrying. Ya ain't gettin' cold feet, are ya?"

"No. Just nags at me a little, sometimes. Here, help me cover it up."

The cement foundations for the eight little houses were all laid, and Zahn, Daggett and a carpenter from the fort were laying out floor joists for the first one. May Pritchin and two of her girls, Agnes and Flo, stood beside the building site and watched the work, but mostly they watched Zahn.

"Morning, ladies," Simon said as he joined them. "So what

do you think?"

"I can't wait," Agnes said. "I've always wanted a place of my own, and even if it really belongs to Mister Amos, it's still mine."

"Me too." Flo batted her dark eyes at Simon. "One of the reasons I left home was cuz I shared everything with six sisters, including our father."

"Ahem." May raised her eyebrows at Flo. "There are some things that need not be shared, Florence."

Simon pretended he hadn't heard. "This one is yours, May. Zahn says they can have it ready for paint and paper in a month. You ready to decorate?"

"Oh, yes. I didn't think much of the idea when Amos talked to me, but I can see now it's going to be nice."

"Have you heard anything from your inquiries in Saint Louis?"

"Matter of fact, I have. Two sisters want to come out, and I've found a Creole girl from New Orleans. A couple more have written, but one was thirty-nine and the other forty-two. I'm not running a rest home."

"When do they want to come out?"

"Soon's we have a place."

"Well, I can always find another carpenter to speed things along. Tell 'em to come on. We'll be ready for them by the middle of June." Simon touched the brim of his hat and walked over to talk with Zahn.

The seven-note trill of a meadowlark wafted into Simon's slumber. Half awake for over an hour, he'd about worked out what he needed on the next supply run to Fort McPherson. He'd have to get with Twiggs and Barrschott in the next day or so. New customers continued to visit the new hotel and restaurant, and every improvement had increased the numbers. He was considering a new bar with a back mirror. A new saloon in Denver had burned down before the bar could be installed, and the bar was going cheap. The owner would get it to Cheyenne by rail, and Simon needed to talk to Rosie about freighting it up from there.

The four new girls were due in two weeks, so he'd need to check with Zahn and make sure the last three houses were on schedule. Five were finished, with four occupied, the ladies adding curtains, lamps and rugs as fast as they came in to the trading post. Already the profits showed on the books. May demanded a premium for the privacy of the detached bungalows, and the option to spend all night with the girls cost even more. There were several soldiers who went out on patrol but spent the first night at McCaffrey's. Suddenly, Simon sensed a presence, and opened his eyes to look directly into the warm brown gaze of his dog. "Mornin'. Need to go out?"

The dog thumped the floor with his tail, and looked toward the parlor door. Simon swung his legs over the edge of the bed, and Spud padded to the door in anticipation. Simon smiled at him, and reached for his pants. Minutes later, he stood in the doorway and listened to the songbirds greet the morning. The dog disappeared toward the river. Simon stretched hard, and then went back in to get ready for the day.

Twenty minutes later, Simon and Spud walked into the saloon. Twiggs and Lori sat at a table, Twiggs working on a plateful of creamed beef and biscuits. Lori sat nursing a cup of tea.

"Mornin', Simon," she said. "Coffee?"

"Yes, please. Got any of that left?" He pointed at Twiggs's meal.

"Sure. Sit and I'll get it."

Simon took a seat, and Spud trotted toward Simon's office and disappeared.

He watched Twiggs take another bite. "You expecting Barrschott today?"

Twiggs chewed for a moment and swallowed. "Said he was comin', but today's Monday. He'll be busy at the fort till late afternoon. Wonderin' about the next supply run?"

"Yeah. I've got a list, and I need to know how much we can, uh . . . appropriate, and how much I need to order out of Cheyenne."

"Here ya go." Lori set a plate of steaming biscuits and gravy on the table along with a cup of coffee.

"My, that looks good," Simon said. He forked a chunk of biscuit into his mouth and smiled at her.

"I hear we're getting four more girls," she said.

Simon swallowed. "Yep, couple more weeks, and we'll have a full stable."

Lori looked at her cup.

Simon heard her sigh.

"What's that for?"

Lori looked up. "Got to thinkin' about them last night. First time I've done that."

"And?" Simon put his fork down.

"Is it right that someone makes money on what they do?"

"Uh-oh," Twiggs said. "I've had this discussion before, and if you'll excuse me, I'll go tend to something I know about. No offense." He picked up his plate and coffee cup, and headed for the far end of the bar.

"I asked myself the same question about a year ago," Simon said. "We need someone who's capable of enforcing order, maybe even shooting someone. Buell does that. And nobody wants to swamp a saloon on a Sunday morning, but it has to be done, and Daggett does it. And we need women, and we have May and her girls. They all do what they're doing of their own free choice, and Amos pays what he thinks they're worth."

"But, do you understand that maybe they don't have free

choice? The girls, I mean?"

"How so?"

"I was talking to Flo last night, actually early this morning. Her home life was a living hell. She had six—"

"I know. Six sisters and a lecherous father."

Lori's eyes sparked. "He should be hanged for what he did."

"I thought as much, but didn't want to hear it," Simon said. "I've talked to May. Most of the girls are from less-than-desirable homes or had no homes at all. Some get into it for the excitement, and then find it's not so easy to quit. I had a hard time with it, too, but I'm convinced that if a girl wanted to quit, May and Amos would help her. Least that's what I try to believe. Maybe it's just me trying to justify what I do."

"That helps, Simon. Thanks."

"You're welcome. Now, I'm going to finish this, and then let's talk about what you need for your kitchen."

Lori relaxed in the round-backed chair and watched him finish his breakfast. Then they went into the office to work on the supply list.

Sergeant Barrschott walked to the end of the long barracks room and found Rankin lying in his bunk. "Get up and come with me."

"I just got off duty, Sarge. I'm tir—"

Barrschott jerked the bony private off his bed, one hand full of collar and the other ahold of his belt. Suspended thus at arm's length, Rankin twisted like a falling cat when the burly sergeant let go. The crack of a skinny elbow on the wood floor was followed instantly by a howl of pain.

"Gawdammit, Sarge, that hurt." Rankin scrambled to his feet and rubbed his elbow.

"S'posed to. When I say move, move. Now come with me."

Together, they walked across the parade ground and into the

dim confines of the supply warehouse. Barrschott led Rankin to the back and then turned. "Okay, Rankin, tell me who you been talking to about our little deals?"

"I ain't be—" A punch to the sternum made Rankin gasp. Clutching his chest, he sucked in tiny breaths of air as he tried to cope with the excruciating pain under his clasped hands.

Barrschott smiled. "I talked to someone who knows what you did. Lie again, and they'll find your body in that barrel of vinegar over there." He waited until Rankin managed to get a full breath and halfway straightened up. "Now, what did you tell him?"

"I said, uhh . . ." He winced in pain with every breath. "I said I could get him . . . a case of rifles . . . for three hundred dollars."

"And where did you say you could come up with this case of rifles?"

"I didn't tell him." Rankin's hands went up defensively. "Don't! I can't take another hit."

Barrschott dropped his fist and waited.

"I said we were going to McPherson in June or July, and I would get them there."

"Who was *we*?"

"We. Us guys. The supply detail."

"You mean me?" The sergeant moved half a step closer.

"I didn't mean to get you in trouble, Sarge. I just wanted to—"

"You didn't. Your customer won't be needin' those rifles, or anything else, for that matter. He had an accident. And you're going to have one too if you're around here next month. Your enlistment is up in two weeks, and I want you gone. Understand?"

"But Sarge, I don't have any place to go."

"Should have thought about that. You heard what I said. Two weeks."

Barrschott strode out of the building and into the late-afternoon sun. He surveyed the compound. The quartermaster lounged against the wall of the building opposite, and Barrschott headed for him. "I think you need to do a little records cleanup," he said when he got there. "Maybe some of those old requisition forms could get burned. You know . . . army efficiency."

The quartermaster touched his hat and smiled. "I'll get right on it, Adolph."

The warm spring day made it hard for Simon to concentrate, and he was relieved when he looked up from his work to see Rosie enter his office. "Afternoon. Appreciate you dropping by, Rosie. Sit down."

The teamster settled into the leather chair and scratched the dog's head that suddenly appeared. "Hey, Spud." The dog stood for a moment, and then, duly acknowledged, he lay down again. "What can I do for you, Simon?"

"I need a new bar. With clear mirrors behind and lots of fancy wood."

"And a polished counter and brass foot rail?"

"Exactly. There's one in Denver I can have shipped to Cheyenne. Could you arrange a wagon or two?"

"One wagon or two? Big difference."

"The man who has it says it weighs about two and a half tons. It's in thirteen crates."

"The weight's no problem. Can ya find out how big the crates are? I have a four-horse dray that will take twelve feet in length."

"There are eight big crates, each fourteen feet long. Two feet sticking out be okay?"

"No problem, but we better put the rest on another wagon."

"When could we go get it?"

"We? You goin' along?"

"If you don't mind. I haven't been out of Fort Laramie for going on three years."

"Sure, pleased for the company."

"Good. I'll let you know real soon. I've got to work on Amos a little."

Rosie got out of the chair and stooped to ruffle Spud's ears before he walked out.

The two wagons, Rosie in front and Daggett following, rattled past the front of the house, and turned around in front of the barn. Simon stepped out on the porch as they came to a stop. Spud sat beside him.

"You're gonna get a look at the big town, and not wanna come back," Buell said. He leaned against the doorjamb, his arms folded.

"I doubt that. Can't be much more than we have here."

"You're in fer a surprise. Have a good time, and we'll see ya in about a week." He reached inside the door and brought out Simon's rifle.

Simon threw his valise up to Rosie and climbed the wheel to the seat. Buell handed him the Winchester and stepped back on the porch.

Rosie kicked the brake loose and smacked his lips as he loosely slapped the horses with the reins. All four horses leaned forward, then stepped off at a fast walk. Simon waved at Buell, and absorbed the first jolt as they hit a rut in the road. They drove past the saloon, and continued on toward the fort for about a mile when Rosie swung the team toward the Laramie River.

"I thought we would have continued east to the fort," Simon said.

"Naw. I want to get across the Laramie here, and then climb up. There's a fair trail that heads almost due west. We drive that to Chugwater Creek and then follow it south. Hang on. It's gonna be a little rough till we get on top."

By the time they were above the river and on the plain, Simon was wondering if this had been such a good idea. Already his back hurt and his arms ached from hanging on. A succession of rolling hills met them, one running into the next for as far as he could see. Five hours later, they reached the creek and stopped on a large patch of green by the stream.

Simon climbed stiffly down from the wagon. "Want a fire?" he asked hopefully.

"Actually, we usually don't even stop, but I don't think I can take another hour of watching you wince every time we hit a hole." Rosie clapped Simon on the shoulder. "Go ahead. I could use a hot cup of coffee."

The next two days were a repeat of the first as they followed the stream southwest and then south, leaving it completely on the third day. Simon alternated sitting alongside Rosie and standing in the back.

He was standing when they topped a low rise above Cheyenne. "Judas Priest," he said, his jaw dropping.

Spread below lie a settlement ten times the size of Fort Laramie. The rail line disappeared east and west of the town, and set track-side near the center stood a two-story building that looked like a hotel. Alongside, a huge windmill turned slowly in the light breeze.

"Big, huh?" Rosie looked at Simon and grinned.

"How many people?"

"Well over five thousand."

Daggett pulled his wagon alongside. "We gonna stay at a livery, or we gonna camp down Crow Creek like last time?"

"What do you think, Simon?" Rosie asked. "We usually camp

out, saves us a few dollars."

"Is that a hotel there by the tracks?"

"Yep, that's the Union Pacific Hotel. Nice place."

"I think I'll stay there. I've about had enough of hard riding and rough sleeping."

Rosie nodded his head. "Okay. Plato, you head out and find us a spot. I'll drop Simon off and meet ya there after I swing by and get a sack of oats for the horses."

Daggett gave Simon a high sign and spoke to his team. He angled to the east as Rosie headed straight for the imposing building by the tracks.

Simon counted eighteen windows, evenly spaced across the front of the second story. Boardwalks ran along the front and down both sides; the one bordering the street was covered. People moved to and fro in a steady stream: women in beautiful long dresses, carrying parasols and wearing hats near as big as their bustles, and men in shiny shoes and striped coats.

Simon felt like a bumpkin as he stepped up to the counter in the lobby and set his valise on the floor.

"How can I be of service?" The short clerk wore a smile as artificial as his hair.

"I'd like a room."

The clerk looked at Simon, obviously measuring his worth. "Will you be staying with us long?"

"Probably tonight and tomorrow." Simon was acutely conscious of his filthy clothes and dusty face. "Can I get a bath here?"

The clerk's eyebrows rose. "We are a first-class hotel. Do you want a bath in your room?"

"Well, yeah, that would be fine. Right in my room?" He mentally chastised himself. Bumpkin indeed.

The clerk cleared his throat. "We offer a laundry service as well."

"No, I've got a change or two in my valise, and I'll be back on the trail day after tomorrow."

"Very well." The clerk turned his ledger around, handed Simon a pen, then watched Simon stroke his name and "Fort Laramie" in bold longhand. "Fort Laramie," he said as he turned the book around. "Businessman?"

"I manage a restaurant and roadhouse just outside. Not nearly as nice as this, but—"

"I'm sure. Will you need help with that?" He looked at Simon's rough bag with disdain.

"No, I'll manage, thank you."

"One thirty-eight. See the maid in the first room at the top of the stairs about your bath. The dining room opens at six." He handed Simon a brass key and turned away.

The room would have held two beds easily. All the wood in the room was dark, polished and carved, the seating upholstered. Best of all was the hot bath. Ten minutes after he'd asked for it, two women had a five-foot-long copper tub filled with water, and the biggest towel he'd ever seen hung across the privacy screen next to the bath. He soaked until the water cooled, then shaved and dressed in clean clothes. After damp mopping the dust off his hat, he felt ready to see the sights.

He stopped halfway down the stairs to survey the dining room. Big enough to easily seat two hundred fifty or more, most of the tables were full. He decided to have a look at the town, and continued down and out onto the boardwalk. The street, nearly wide enough to turn a freight wagon around in, flooded with a sea of people and horses. One particularly well-lit saloon, across and down the street, caught his eye and he headed for it, dodging shays, surreys and horses all the way.

The noise inside was as loud as McCaffrey's at its best. He jostled his way to the bar, and waited for a bartender to catch his eye.

"What'll ya have?" the harried man asked.

"Rye." Simon turned to survey the room. The scene was familiar, except the customers were a lot better dressed, and there was gambling other than cards. He watched a man spin a three-foot gambling wheel, and a dozen men crowded around it immediately start to shout.

"That's a dollar," he heard the barkeep say.

Simon turned back, laid an eagle on the bar and reached for his drink.

"You old enough to be in here, boy?"

The hair on his neck bristled as tension seized his body. And then he recognized the voice. "Lacey!" Simon turned to see the Texan, his hands on his hips, grinning widely. "I'll be double damned."

"Howdy, Simon. I couldn't hardly b'lieve my eyes when I saw ya walk across the floor. What'n hell ya doin' here?"

"I live up north, Fort Laramie. I . . . ah . . . boy you're . . . damn."

"Still jest as unflustered as ever, I see." Lacey chuckled. "We'll try agin. What ya doin' in Cheyenne?"

"Came here to pick up a bar for my saloon."

"Yer saloon? Ya own a saloon?"

"I manage one. Buell works there too."

"How is thet boy? Got hisself shot yet?"

"Dang near, but no, he's fine. What're you doing here?"

"Rode a herd up from Texas on the Goodnight. I'm stayin' 'bout five miles down Crow Creek. Work fer a fella named Iliff." He studied Simon for a moment. "Damn, it's good ta see ya. How's yer folks?"

"They're fine. Near's I can tell, Pa's done real well since you and Mister Greene brought up that first herd of cows. He's bought quite a bit of land and grows grain. I haven't been back since sixty-eight."

"What about that sweet young gal you was sparkin'?"

"Didn't work out." Simon looked directly at Lacey, his eyes unblinking.

"Oh." A moment of awkward silence passed. "Well . . . how's Mace?"

"Let's go find a table, Lacey. There's lots to tell you."

Two hours later, the Texan leaned back in his chair, and fixed Simon with a steady gaze. "I figgered Buell might get a little wild, but yer somethin' of a su'prise. Hell far, ya can't let people thet don't count more'n a grasshopper fart run ya off."

"Well, I'm where I am, and I kinda like it."

"Yep, I kin tell," Lacey said sarcastically. "I'm 'bout done with the spring calvin'. I jist might ride up and see what yer doin'."

"That would be grand. Buell will be real glad to see you."

"Let's go over to the railroad hotel and I'll buy ya supper. Damn, can't say how good it is ta see ya agin."

CHAPTER 14

The trip back to Fort Laramie seemed endless. The scenery, monotonous at best, was even more so because Simon had already seen it once. He'd vowed never again to ride a wagon for more than a few hours. It was about four o'clock when Rosie hauled the tired horses to a stop behind Amos's saloon. Simon groaned when his feet hit the ground.

"Gawdamn, Simon, that's one hell of a load. What'n hell did you buy?" Amos stood on the back step.

"Just the bar and the mirrors. There has to be half a wagonload of sawdust and shavings packed around that glass. Anybody in there that can give us a hand unloading?"

"Yeah, there's four or five."

"Good, 'cause I'm about beat to hell."

"Well, see if you kin get 'em out here, Amos," Rosie said. "I'd like to get home before dark."

An hour later, they'd stacked the crates next to the back wall, and Rosie and Daggett headed for the fort. Simon slumped into a chair, and Twiggs brought him a beer.

"Glad to see you back. How was the big city?"

"Lot bigger than I would have thought. The dining room in the hotel where I stayed would seat near three hundred people. And they were full till after eleven o'clock. Food ain't as good as Lori's though. Where's Buell?"

"Went to see Berggren. Should be back pretty soon."

"I'm gonna go clean up. I feel like I've been rolled in the

dirt." Simon took another long pull on his beer and got up. "I'll be back in an hour or so." He headed for the door.

Simon sat relaxing on the couch when Buell pushed open the door. "Well, I see ya came back."

"Missed your ugly mug."

"Sure ya did. How was Cheyenne? Big, huh?"

"Yep. And that ain't all." Simon looked at Buell, a half smile on his face.

"Well?"

"I saw Pat Lacey. Had supper with him."

"Sumbitch. Lacey? How is he? How'd he look?"

"You'll see for yourself. He's gonna ride up in a week or so, and have a visit."

"A week? What's he doin'? Boy, I can't wait." Buell sat.

Getting back to the saloon was forgotten as they spent the next hour remembering their summers spent with Nathan Greene and Pat Lacey in Nebraska, living rough on the prairie and learning how to be cowboys—and how not to be.

The next week saw a flurry of activity as three of the best carpenters Amos could find uncrated and installed the new bar. Solid mahogany wood with carved panels and spiral-turned posts surrounded the heavy plate-glass mirrors of the back bar. The countertop of the service bar measured fifty-two feet of French-polished beauty, thirty inches wide. Twiggs had three beer-pumping stations instead of two, and real cash drawers built into the back counter. He looked like the captain of a new sailing ship.

Just one day after the last house was finished, three very dusty women arrived in a covered surrey. May and her girls were up to greet them, and ushered them into the new houses with squeals of delight and a stream of chatter. Word of their arrival spread rapidly, as did news about the remodeling, and curious patrons packed the saloon nearly every night. More and more, people were making their way to McCaffrey's ranch for the accommodations and the gambling. Adventurers, gamblers, hunters, and Europeans out to see the West, came and went without a letup.

Buell, from his perch at the end of the saloon, watched every face that came through the doors. Simon had been back nearly a month and Lacey had yet to show up. Buell had more or less decided his shooting mentor had finished his job and gone back to Texas. And then one morning, a horse stopped outside at the livery, and someone knocked on the door of their little house.

"Sumbitch, Lacey! Been expectin' ya fer two weeks. Come on in." Buell stepped back.

"Got tied up a little. How ya doin', Buell?" Lacey offered his hand.

Buell clutched Lacey's hand with both of his, and shook it vigorously. "Real good. Ya been to the saloon yet?"

"Nope. Simon said you fellas lived next to the livery. Only place I could see, so I stopped."

"Let's go see Simon, and I'll introduce ya to the rest of the crew." Buell grabbed his hat and followed Lacey out the door.

It was still early so there weren't many people in the place, and Buell led the way to Simon's office. "Look who's here."

"Hey, Lacey, we about gave up on you." Simon got up and stepped around his desk, hand extended. "Good to see you again."

"Same here." He shook Simon's hand. "Nice place ya got. I'm su'prised to see somethin' this fancy out here in the middle of nowheres."

"Well, we've improved it a lot since we arrived." Simon

headed out the door. "C'mon, I'll buy ya a drink."

Outside the office, Simon caught the barkeep's attention. "Twiggs, pull me a beer." He turned to Lacey. "What'll you have?"

"I think a beer would be good," Lacey said to Twiggs. "Little early fer the firewater."

"Let's sit down," Simon said.

A minute later Twiggs brought them their drinks.

"Max, I'd like ya to meet Pat Lacey. Lacey, this is Maxwell Twiggs, late of Pennsylvania."

"Pleased to meet you, Mister Lacey. Buell has told me some about you, mostly because he took your name."

"He what?" Lacey looked at Buell.

"I said my name was Buell Lacey when we first came here. Amos, the guy that owns this place, he found out real quick, but I never changed. Everybody knows me as Buell Lacey."

"Be damned. Ya ain't got a sprout runnin' around do ya . . . or shoot someone important?" Lacey grinned.

"Naw. Used that short wagon spoke ya told me about. Since then, most folks keep one eye on me when they get to feelin' frisky."

"Actually, it was a rifle butt," Twiggs said. "And then he faced down the biggest man in Wyoming Territory. Things stay pretty even when Buell's on his perch." He nodded at the high chair by the stairs as he headed back to the bar.

"I noticed thet fancy Remington," Lacey said. "Where'd ya get it?"

Simon told him the story about the river bottom ambush.

"Gawdamn, I hate bushwhackers," Lacey said. "You fellas coulda been kilt."

The screen door opened and Lori came in. She walked directly to the table. "Mornin'."

"Lori, I'd like you to meet Pat Lacey. Lori is our chef, Lacey.

We wouldn't be in business if she hadn't come along."

Lacey stood and gave a slight bow. "Ma'am, pleased to meetcha."

"Likewise, I'm sure. Simon's told me a lot about you and Mister Greene. You going to be staying a while?"

"Naw, got to get back. Maybe a coupla days."

"Well, enjoy your stay here. Nice to meet you." She disappeared into the kitchen.

"Nothin' shy about her," Lacey said.

"No, sir. She's a bear cat, that one," Buell said. "But she'll do anything for her friends."

"So, Buell," Lacey said. "Let's go out and you kin show me how yer shootin's gettin' on. I ain't kicked up no dust in a long time."

"Sure. I got a place down by the river. Simon, you comin'?" Buell was already heading for the door.

"No. You guys go ahead. I talked his leg off in Cheyenne."

"Okay. We'll be back in a couple of hours." They headed out the front door.

Twiggs came around the bar again and over to the table. "So that's the fella that taught Buell how to shoot?"

"Yup, actually the whole crew did, but we used Lacey's gun."

"He don't look like no hard case."

"He's not. One of the mellowest guys you could meet. But I wouldn't want to back him into a corner. All them Texans were like that."

Simon picked up his half-empty glass, and headed for his office. "Nice to see someone from home, kind of."

The fact three quarters of the tables were occupied on a Thursday evening surprised Lacey. Twiggs had two helpers at the bar, and Lori and her kitchen staff had been running full tilt all evening. Now, with the dining rooms closed and the more genteel customers gone home, the saloon was left to the gamblers, skirt chasers, and drinkers.

Lacey and Simon joined Amos and three others at Amos's table: two regulars, a teamster named Rosie and a whiskey drummer called Saint Louis Bob, plus a man from Kansas City named Quinn. Buell sat in his chair by the stairs, vigilant.

It was Quinn's turn to deal again. Over the course of the last three hours, he had won a dozen hard-fought hands, draining Rosie and Bob's finances considerably. He had lost only one seriously contested hand, his kings-over-fives full house to Rosie's aces-over-threes.

"Straight five-card draw." Quinn dealt the cards for the next hand expertly, then laid the deck on the table. "Openers?" He looked around the table.

"Check," Simon said.

Lacey looked at the two aces in his hand. "Check." A frown shadowed Quinn's brow for the briefest moment.

Amos shook his head. "Check."

Rosie pushed his bet into the middle. "I'll open for two dollars."

"Call," Bob said.

Quinn dropped two dollars in the pile. "Cards."

Simon shook his head, and tossed his cards onto the table.

Lacey stared at Quinn for a bit, then pushed two dollars into the pile. "I'll take three."

"Fold," Amos said and threw his cards toward the center.

Rosie slowly fanned his cards open and closed. "Give me three."

"I'll take one," Bob said. He flashed a smile at the rest of the players.

"Dealer takes two." Quinn dealt himself. "Your bet." He looked at Rosie.

"Five." Rosie pushed a gold piece forward.

"And ten," Bob said, the smile now fixed on his face.

"And ten more." Quinn looked at Lacey. "That's twenty-five to you, cowboy."

Lacey glanced at Rosie, but couldn't catch his eye. Then at Bob, who was now grinning from ear to ear. His gaze settled on Quinn's impassive face for several seconds, then he looked down at his three aces. "I'll fold." He laid his cards facedown on the table.

Rosie spread his cards in his hand, looked at them for a moment, and then closed them. His face gleamed with sweat. "Call." He pushed the twenty dollars across the table.

"See your ten and raise ya twenty." Bob chuckled and glanced around the table proudly as the rest of the players gasped.

"And twenty," Quinn said quietly, and pushed the money out. He looked at Rosie.

"Gawdammit!" Rosie slapped his cards down and glared at Bob.

Bob's smile had disappeared, and he studied his cards intently while Quinn leaned back in his chair and half closed his eyes. Bob glanced at Amos, and then settled his gaze on Simon's face. Lacey could see the desperation. There was complete silence from the other players as Bob nervously turned the twenty-dollar gold piece over the backs of his fingers. "Call." He flipped the coin into the pile.

Quinn shrugged his shoulders. "Four kings." He turned his cards face up.

Bob slumped back in his chair and flipped his hand over, a six, seven, eight, nine of hearts—and a five of diamonds. "Beautiful," he said, then slowly got up, gathered his meager stack of coins and walked out of the saloon.

"He came close." Quinn chuckled.

"I've had enough," Rosie said as he turned his hand over. "When ya ain't got the balls to bet this, it's time to quit."

Lacey looked at the ten-over-jacks full house and then at Quinn. Quinn's return gaze exuded pure arrogance.

"Reckon I've had enough too," Lacey said. "Had a long ride today. Maybe tomorrow."

Twiggs came over from the bar. "All done?"

"I think so," Amos said as he got up.

Twiggs gathered the cards up and squared the deck. "I'll put these away."

"Another one tomorrow, then?" Quinn asked.

"I suppose so," Simon said.

"Right. I'll see you all then." Quinn got up and headed for the stairs.

"You don't look happy," Buell said as he came over to the table.

"I ain't," Lacey said. "We jist got cheated, and I don't know how he did it. I had aces and he knew it. I think Bob almost lucked into beatin' him but Quinn knew Rosie's hand too. Sumbitch is slick, I'll give ya that."

Simon's brow furrowed in thought. "But he lost a big hand to Ros—he meant to, right?"

"Ya got it. That last hand was worth over one hunert and fifty dollars and that was what he was waitin' for."

"But Twiggs keeps the cards, and he wouldn't cheat us," Simon said.

Buell shook his head. "I looked at the cards, Simon. They ain't marked. I studied 'em close." He glanced toward Twiggs. "I better not catch anyone at it."

"Well, we got cheated. I'm goin' ta bed." Lacey got up and stretched. "I'll figure it out. See you two in the morning." He turned and went up the steps.

Lacey came downstairs about nine o'clock the next morning and found Twiggs idly staring at a cup of cold coffee. "Mind if I join ya?" Lacey smiled at the bartender.

"No, not at all. It's always too quiet in the morning. I like the action in the evening better."

"Some action. Did you happen ta catch that last hand at Mister McCaffrey's table last night?"

"Some of it. I saw Rosie get excited, but he always does, win or lose."

"Mind if I ask ya a couple questions about the cards?"

Twiggs looked at Lacey for a moment, then sat up straighter in his chair. "I don't suppose so."

"I noticed you picked up the deck when we were done last night. D'ya always do that?"

"Sure. Amos doesn't let the customers use their own cards or dice. Makes sense."

"And that deck we used last night, do ya still have it?"

"Well, actually, no. When they get worn, and that one was, I burn 'em. That deck went in the stove this morning, with breakfast."

"Was it the same deck as the one you gave us to start?" Lacey raised one eyebrow as he studied Twiggs.

"What are you driving at? I'm not sure I like what you're inferring."

"Ain't inferrin' nothin', Mister Twiggs. Simon says yer honest, and that's good enough for me. But we got cheated last night, and I'd like to know how he did it. I've watched double-dealin', palmin', corner nickin', you name it, and I didn't see that happenin' last night . . . none of it. I'm thinkin' he switched decks on ya."

Twiggs sat silent for a few seconds, his lips pursed, apparently thinking. "That deck was fresh two nights ago. I took it out of the pack myself."

"Have ya seen that Quinn feller before?"

"Yeah. He's been here four or five times. Stays about a week."

"Does he win?"

"Now that you mention it, I believe he does."

"And usually one big hand toward the end of the game, right?"

"Right again." Twiggs frowned. "But he's not always dealing when he wins."

"Ya might want to take a good look at the cards tonight when they're done. He's got somethin' goin'."

"I'll do that. And I'll tell Amos as well."

"I 'preciate ya lettin' me be nosy. Now, where kin I get a cup of that coffee and somethin' to eat. Simon says the vittles here are first-class."

Lacey, Simon and Buell spent most of the day lounging around the little house, talking and smoking. About three, Simon went to the saloon to do some paperwork, and Buell and Lacey found themselves alone on the porch watching the road in front of the saloon. Three soldiers rode up and went inside, and a few minutes later a drummer—pots, pans and pails hanging from every available spot outside the wagon—clattered to a halt and went in.

"Reminds me of that wagon yer pa built fer us when we was herding them cows in Nebraska."

"Kinda does, don't it?" Buell said.

"J'know there's an outfit makin' one jist like that fer sale. Company called Studebaker. Yer pa shoulda got a patent on it." Lacey pulled his tobacco out and started building another cigarette. Buell watched silently while Lacey finished and lit it up.

"What went on in that card game last night?" Buell asked.

"Cheatin'."

"That Quinn feller?"

"Yep. I knew someone was, and finally figgered it was him.

Sussed him jist in time ta save myself a pile of money. Sumbitch fed me three aces and then grinned at me."

"Why didn't ya bust 'im? By damn, I woulda."

"Same old Buell, I see." Lacey chuckled. "Ya gotta be sure 'fore ya jump a feller."

"But ya said it was him." Buell frowned. "I suspected Bob once. Checked the deck and everything. Couldn't see a thing. What did you find?"

"That deck is gone, burned, so I can't prove a thing."

"Ya gonna play again tonight?"

Lacey grimaced. "Hate to play with a cheat."

"Well, I'm gonna, then."

"Kin ya play and keep an eye on things? Especially Friday."

"Yeah, maybe not Saturday, but Fridays usually ain't so bad."

"Look, Buell, I know ya. And I know if ya git yer teeth set in somethin', ya have a hard time lettin' go. This guy is slick, and I'd bet he has a hideout in his vest or coat pocket. Ya start somethin', he ain't gonna jist sit there."

"I'm just gonna watch close."

"Okay, and I'm gonna watch ya watch. I'll play."

Buell was right—the crowd was noisy and large, but not overly boisterous. Buell had stood up once to give a drunken freighter the evil eye, and the table in question had quieted down immediately. After the beating Bob had taken the night before, he was absent, but the rest were there. Lacey noted that Buell had made it a point to sit opposite Quinn. Lacey chose the seat immediately to Quinn's left.

"I feel like a Yankee in Charleston," Quinn said as he looked at the five serious faces. "My name's Quinn," he said to Buell.

"Call me Buell." He ignored the hand offered across the table.

"I got lucky last night. No hard feelings, huh?" Quinn gave

them all a smile.

"Deal me a couple hands like my last one yesterday and I'll forgive anything," Rosie said, finally cracking a smile.

Amos broke the blue-and-yellow seal on the package and shook the fresh deck out on the table. Expertly he flipped them faceup and extracted the two jokers. Then, he shuffled the deck several times. "You can start, Rosie." He put the deck in front of him.

Rosie gave the deck another shuffle and let Quinn cut the cards. "Five stud," Rosie said, and dealt the hole cards, followed by the face-up mates.

Quinn showed the high card, a queen, and bet a dollar.

As the night wore into early morning, Lacey found himself the winner by some forty dollars, followed by Rosie with about twenty-five. Buell, Amos and Simon were all down, and Quinn was about even. Quinn took the cards.

"Five stud." He dealt the cards, himself a four.

Lacey got a ten and a peek at his hole card showed a pair.

Simon had a jack showing. Amos, a king. Amos bet two dollars. Rosie, showing a two, folded, as did Buell, with an eight. Lacey and the others called, then Lacey watched Buell watch Quinn deal the third card. Lacey drew a six, Simon a seven, Amos a five and Quinn drew an ace.

"Ace bets five," Quinn said.

Lacey felt a chill as Buell's eyes narrowed.

"Call," Lacey said.

Simon turned his cards facedown and shook his head in disgust. "Not my night."

"Call." Amos had not raised his head since the first card.

Quinn dealt the fourth card. He paired his fours, gave Lacey another ten and Amos a queen. "Tens bet."

"Five," Lacey said as he dropped the gold piece in the pot.

Amos looked up and studied the two faces across from him. Both looked back impassively. He glanced again at his cards and pushed out his bet. "Call."

"Call," Quinn said immediately, and dropped his five in the middle.

The fifth card floated into Lacey's hand and Amos's skimmed across the table to stop against his coin stack. Quinn snapped his last card off the deck and put the remainder between himself and Rosie. "Tens bet."

Lacey tipped the corner of his last card up and saw a two. "Five." He dropped the coin in the pot.

Amos pushed two small gold pieces forward. "And five."

"Fold." Quinn turned his cards facedown and leaned back. He smiled at Lacey.

"Gotta beat three kings, do I?" Lacey watched Amos's face closely. "Or two pair?" Amos showed him nothing. "Call." Lacey pushed his money into the pot.

Amos turned over his down cards—a pair of kings to match the one showing.

Lacey snorted. "That pulled me off the pile. Trip tens." He turned his cards over. "What was keepin' you, Quinn?"

"Sucker aces." He flipped his cards over. "And a pair of fours. Ace in the hole will be my downfall one day."

"That's it for me," Amos said. "That about puts me even."

"I'm done too," Simon said. "But you guys played on my money tonight."

"Been good," Quinn said as he got up. "I'm off tomorrow, so I won't see you again till next time through. Mister Lacey, a pleasure to meet you." He put out his hand.

"Likewise," Lacey said, a little surprised. "Where ya headed?" He shook hands.

"Back to Omaha, and then Kansas City."

"I'm goin' to Cheyenne tomorrow. Want ta ride together?"

"Like to have the company, but I'm going straight east. Got business along the way." He pushed his chair back against the table. "Early up, gentlemen. Been a pleasure." He left up the stairs.

"Let me buy ya a drink, Rosie," Amos said, and they went to the bar. He handed Twiggs the deck of cards.

"Well, that proved nothin'," Buell said.

"You're right," Lacey agreed. "He knew we was watchin'. Crazy part is, he's good enough he don't have to cheat."

"Were you serious about leavin' tomorrow?" Simon asked.

"Yep, better git back and make sure the waddies ain't let ever'thing wander off."

"Shit," Buell said.

"Now that I run into you boys agin, we ought to try to keep in touch. You kin always reach me in Uvalde, Texas. Got a few acres there, and if ya send a telegram, I'll get it eventually."

"Good to know. It's been a lot of fun seeing you," Simon said.

"Yep, has been. I'm gonna have coffee and a biscuit at about seven or so. See ya then?"

"Not me, I hate good-byes." Buell stuck his hand out. "Real good to see ya Lacey. I count ya as one of my two friends."

Lacey took his hand. "I take thet as a compliment. Take care of yerself." He turned to Simon. "How 'bout you?"

"I'll be here."

"Good. See ya then." With a wave to Twiggs, Lacey headed for his room upstairs.

It had been broad daylight for over an hour when Simon and Spud walked across the dusty road to the saloon. Lacey's mount stood tied to the rail in front, and the dog sniffed the horse's leg as they walked by.

"Mornin'," Lacey said as Simon pulled the screen door open

and walked in.

"Good morning yourself. I see Lori's taking good care of you."

"Coffee? As if I need to ask." Lori spoke from the kitchen door.

"Yes, please, and good morning." Simon pulled out a chair and sat.

"Looks like I got a fine day to ride." Lacey picked up a biscuit and halved it.

"One of the things I like about this place, the spring," Simon said.

"So, ya think this is what you're gonna do with your life?"

"Wasn't when I got here, but it's turning out quite good. Amos has let me put some money into the business, and that's paying off. Nice folks here. So, yeah, probably so."

"Here ya go," Lori said. She put the steaming cup of coffee down, and looked at Simon expectantly.

He looked at Lacey's plate and nodded toward it. "I think I'll have biscuits and honey."

"Okay. Be right back."

"Are ya keepin' in touch with yer folks?" Lacey asked.

"Yeah, they're doing real well. I write two or three times a year."

"That's important, Simon. Real important. Lost both my folks and I didn't know they was gone fer over three years. It's like m' roots was tore up."

"I can see that. No, I'll stay in touch. Matter of fact, I was thinking of going back next year or the year after."

"That'd be a good thing. Buell said he went back last year, and had a good visit. He also told me about the family troubles. Sorry." Lacey paused. "But ever'body else is doin' fine, and that's what's important." Lacey paused again, his eyes fixed on Simon.

Simon's jaw took on a hard set. "Only because you're a good friend."

"What?"

"I know what you're asking, Lacey. I don't know what happened to Sarah." Simon let out a long sigh and looked into his coffee cup. "She suddenly turned away from me." His throat convulsed and started to ache.

"Pains me ta see ya fret, Simon, truly does. I watched you two and I kin tell ya somethin' for true. Her reason was good enough to take a lot of pain on her ownself. Think on that, and try not to be bitter, it'll sour yer soul."

"I try. But mostly, I try not to think about her at all."

"Tain't possible. Like I said, I watched her and you. I ain't smart 'nuff to tell ya what to do, but I will tell ya, she's hurtin' too."

Simon could not trust himself to speak, and continued to look at his cup. They sat quiet for several minutes. Lori came to the kitchen door, looked for a moment, and went back in.

"Well then, I reckon I'll be ridin'," Lacey finally said. He pushed back his chair and got up.

Simon did the same. "Sure was good to see ya, Lacey."

"Yeah, it was." Simon followed Lacey outside where the Texan mounted up.

"Take good care of yourself, *compadre.*" Lacey leaned down and extended his hand. "And tell Buell *adios* fer me."

Simon squeezed hard on Lacey's hand. "I will, and if you see Nathan, tell him we think of him often."

"Oh, I'll see 'im, and I'll tell 'im." Lacey turned his horse and headed east, the animal high stepping with eagerness to get going. With one final wave over his shoulder, he let the horse have its head, and they soon disappeared at an easy run.

Simon felt the same emptiness he had experienced sitting on the ridge overlooking Carlisle. That seemed like such a long time ago.

CHAPTER 15

Simon sat with his elbows resting on his desk, his head cradled in both hands, lost in thought.

"Could I talk to ya a minute, Simon?"

Plato Daggett stood in the doorway, his hand on Spud's head.

"Of course, come on in and sit down."

Plato made no move to sit. "Got somethin' to tell ya."

"Something wrong?" Simon got up from his chair and walked around the desk.

"No. I'm leaving. Gonna go with the supply wagons next week, and take a job in Omaha."

"I don't know what to say, Plato. Is there a reason? I mean, is there something I've done to make you want to leave?"

"That's what I wanted talk to you about. I never thought a young whippersnapper could ever teach me a thing, but you have. I—"

"You don't—"

"Let me finish." Daggett crushed the crown of his felt hat in his calloused hands. "I'll never forget the first day I saw ya. Ya looked me in the eye like I was a man. Nobody'd done that in a long time. Folks mostly avoided me. And damned if ya didn't set me down ta breakfast with yer friends an—"

"I don't remember that, but—"

"Course ya don't. T'wern't unusual for you. That's the way you are. And then ya trusted me to go do a job that had to get done, knowin' I had a bad problem with the whiskey. I couldn't let ya down, and stickin' to that job got me ta see I could make it, without bein' fallin' down drunk most of the time. So I wanted ta thank ya. I owe ya a lot." Tears welled up in his eyes, and he smiled at Simon, his lips trembling.

"Damn, Plato. I don't know what to say. You're sure welcome to stay."

"I heard from an old pardner. He needs some help with his freightin' business, and somehow got word I'd dried up. He and I always got on real good. 'Sides that, I got some nephews and nieces there I ain't never seen."

"Sounds like you're going home."

"Reckon I am." Daggett clapped the floppy hat on his head and wiped his eyes with the back of his left hand. "I appreciate your friendship, youngster." He extended his right toward Simon. "I'll be seein' ya some 'fore I leave."

Slightly numb, Simon watched Daggett and Spud walk across the saloon, the dog's tail wagging slowly. Daggett pushed through the door, and the dog sat down to watch him go.

"Feels good, huh?"

Simon started, then turned to see Lori just inside the kitchen.

"Couldn't help but overhear, both doors were open," she said.

"I didn't think I did anything unusual. Obviously he does." Simon walked over to her.

"What you did for him was special, Simon. And the beautiful part is, you don't see it. I'd sure like to meet your folks."

"My folks?"

"Yeah. Now get out of here, I've got a batch of bread to take care of." She turned around and took the towel off the bulging dough.

The quarter moon cast scant light over the quiet stable yard. Simon sat on the porch in the cool of the night, Spud beside him. The last of the rowdy soldiers had either gone back to the fort or bedded down in one of the little houses across the road. And now Simon waited for the supply wagons to arrive. A half dozen coyotes keened to each other across the still air, and Spud grumbled his annoyance. Perched in the top of an old cottonwood snag by the river, a screech owl did his best to unnerve some rodent below. The unearthly sound caused gooseflesh to ripple across Simon's arms.

Then the tenor of Spud's semi-indifferent protest changed to a low, warning growl. Simon laid his hand on the dog's head. A couple of minutes later he heard the sound of hooves. He got up from the chair and headed for the barn to open the back doors. He was halfway there when the unmistakable sight of Buell's spotted horse ghosted out of the dim light and stopped in front of the building.

He swung his leg over the saddle and got down. "Don't bother with the doors, they ain't comin'."

A chill charged his body. "Indians?"

"Worse. Lieutenant Maupin. He rode out this afternoon to where they was camped, waitin' for dark. Barrschott told him the horses needed restin', and that seemed to satisfy him. But when we set out a couple hours ago, there was the lieutenant, waitin' by the river. Escorted Barrschott to the guardhouse."

"The guardhouse? They put him in jail?"

"Near as I could tell. The wagons went to the warehouse and three riders went to the guardhouse by the river. I expect that was Barrschott."

"Damn. What got him to poking around?"

"Rankin. I'd bet on it. Barrschott sent him packin' a couple weeks ago. Seems he was makin' side deals and talking outta turn."

Simon glanced at the barn, his lips pursed. "Do you think he'll tell about us?"

Buell snorted. "I guess we'll find out."

"Well, this causes some problems, even if we stay clear. Shit!"

"Let me put Shadow up. I'll be right in." Buell led his horse into the stable and Simon walked back to the house.

Quiet reigned over breakfast the next morning. Simon, Amos and Buell were the only people in the saloon other than Twiggs. The bartender stood at a table absently polishing lamp mirrors, another reminder of how much Daggett had done around the place. Simon fiddled nervously with his coffee cup, unsure about how much to tell Amos. Buell sat quietly demolishing three oversized, gravy-smothered biscuits. Simon felt certain Amos knew about the supplies, but they'd never discussed it openly. "Sergeant Barrschott was put in the guardhouse last night." Simon broke the silence.

Amos shot him a sharp look over the lip of his cup. "Do you know why?"

"I think so. Misappropriation of army property would be my guess."

"And why would you guess that?"

"Because some of it came here." Simon bit the inside of his lip.

Amos didn't blink an eye. "And if they prove he was . . . misappropriating, as you call it, can they prove any of it came here?"

"Not unless someone involved comes forward and says so."

"And do you think Adolph, Sergeant Barrschott, will say anything?"

"Not a chance," Twiggs said.

Amos turned in his chair. "You sound pretty sure."

"I am." Twiggs came over to the table. "Adolph won't tell. No reason for him to, and every reason not."

"Maybe you better tell me what I don't understand."

"I can't. For the same reason Adolph won't. He and I had a business deal, with mutual assurances. He tells, he loses everything he's saved for the last seven years. His retirement fund is forfeit, and I don't mean that pittance the army will pay him in three years."

"And you hold the key?"

"Like I said, I can't discuss it."

"You mean you won't?"

"Same thing, Amos." Twiggs met Amos's cold stare, unblinking.

"So now what?" Amos tried to swallow, and reached for his coffee cup.

"So nothing," Simon said. "Max told me from the start that you didn't want to know anything about it. Therefore, you don't. Your accounts are clean . . . I guarantee it. A good bookkeeper, which I am, keeps accurate books, crooked or otherwise. If anyone has to pay for this, I will."

"You saying they can't prove I knew anything about this?"

"That's what I'm saying."

"And you're willing to take the rope? They *are* going to want to hang someone, you know?"

"It won't be you." Simon stood.

"You're sure?"

"I'm sure. Now I need to talk to Twiggs and Buell." Simon nodded toward his office, and Buell and Twiggs followed him into it.

"All right, Max, I have to know as much as you can tell me." Simon leaned against his desk, facing Buell and Twiggs, seated in the two chairs. Simon felt ready to collapse.

"Barrschott thought this was coming," Twiggs said. "He's taken care of the requisition forms from past shipments. Don't ask me how. There was somebody sneakin' around, and he took care of that too. We think Rankin sold us out, but can't be sure."

"But they're going to get Barrschott on this last shipment. They caught him red-handed."

"Did they? The requisitions are filled out properly, always have been. The supplies are still in army control. Maupin's promotion to first lieutenant didn't make him any smarter." Twiggs snorted. "He jumped too soon. All they have is suspicions and circumstance."

"Damn, yer right. We didn't steal nothin'." Buell grinned. "Ol' Fuzznuts got an empty tote sack." He chuckled out loud. "The dumb ass."

"That's about it," Twiggs said. "We don't have to say a thing. If the provost asks, we can tell him that anything dropped here by an army wagon is accounted for, right and proper."

"That's good," Buell said. "I wasn't lookin' forward to high-tailin' it outta here. I'm gonna go have a nap. I'm beat." He got up and left, closing the door.

"That had me worried," Simon said. His face felt clammy and his voice not quite under control.

"I can see that," Twiggs said. "Comes from not knowing the whole story."

"Speaking of such, can you tell me what kind of arrangement you have with Barrschott?" Simon walked around his desk and wearily slumped into his chair.

"Ten minutes ago I would've never considered telling you anything. But what you said to Amos makes me think otherwise."

"I was telling him the truth."

"Not that. You'd take the blame, when you could easily turn it on us."

"I wouldn't do that."

"I know that . . . now, and just between you and me, I'm not sure the reciprocal would be true." Twiggs looked away for a few seconds, his brow furrowed. "I'd like to think so, but really,

I'm not sure."

"I'm responsible for what I do. I knew appro—stealing that stuff was wrong. And I figured if I got caught, I'd pay some sort of a price."

"You're not what I'm used to, Simon, put it that way. Now, about Adolph and me. We grew up together, two streets apart. He was married to my sister, Meighan."

"Was?"

Twiggs leaned forward in his chair, his brow creased. "She's gone now, diphtheria. But their home is still there, in Philadelphia. And their two children are still alive, and live with their aunt and uncle. They refuse to let Adolph even write to them. They accused him of doing what they thought every nasty German did after losing a wife, consorting with prostitutes. The judge, a Philadelphia bluenose and friend of the family, saw what they wanted him to see." His lips set in a straight line as he clenched his teeth. "He lost the children and the house. Adolph has two more years to retirement, and then he wants his girls and his good name back. And no, the irony of the situation is not lost on me. But he needs a good lawyer and he wants to educate his girls. Both cost money. So that's Barrschott's story."

"And yours?"

Twiggs snorted. "Different, much different. I'm a black sheep. My father fought for and won me an appointment to West Point. I went and got caught up in a cheating scandal my second year. Being from a family that lived too close to the river, I took the lash for another man whose royal blood couldn't possibly condone cheating. I was ejected in disgrace. My family, except for Meighan, rejected me as well. That scoundrel is now a congressman, and I intend to see him done. That's Maxwell Twiggs's story."

Simon stared past Twiggs, seeing nothing. "A rush to conclusion risks missing a better outcome."

"I haven't heard that one."

"A lawyer friend back home. Damn, he was smart. And he'd be so disappoi—" Twiggs came back into focus. "Anyway, you said Barrschott is all right financially?"

"Oh, indeed. He arrived here at Fort Laramie, and saw what was happening with the supplies. He wrote me and I came out. We've worked the system ever since. He's worth thousands, all secure."

"It looks like the cost of doing business is going to go up here." Simon slumped back in his chair.

"Looks that way. It was nice while it lasted."

"I'm going to get few a few hours of sleep." Simon stood up. "What a night."

The provost's deputy and three troopers showed up four days later, and asked politely if the deputy could take a look at the inventory for the roadhouse. Simon, just as politely, gave them full run of the saloon and restaurant. Three hours later they left. Lori asked several questions that Simon satisfied with blatant lies.

Sergeant Adolph Barrschott and two corporals on the supply train were each fined one month's pay for malingering—the specific charge, halting a column to avoid duty. A forfeiture of two months' pay was assessed the quartermaster for malfeasance. The charges were several, and included poor record keeping, and not properly securing government equipment. The other soldiers on the detail were covertly encouraged to visit Evans's place if they felt they had to leave the fort for recreation. The availability of the sutler's store was pointed out, inflated prices notwithstanding.

Rosie made a hastily arranged supply run to Cheyenne, back in eight days with everything they had not received courtesy of the US Army. Simon could not accurately calculate the impact on his profit margin as yet, but he expected to see something less than ten percent, easily made up with some selective and modest price increases. It was now the end of July, and business had returned to normal, the stream of customers steady and spending freely.

Amos stretched his arms over his head and flexed his neck muscles. He looked around the nearly empty saloon. "I've about had enough." He yawned, then opened his purse and scooped the small stack of coins into it. The few bills he had, he folded and stuffed in his vest pocket.

Saint Louis Bob had left over two hours before, again losing more than he could afford, and the table had grown progressively less animated.

"I hate playing with less than five," Zahn said. He slid his chair back and stood. "I'm gonna go out and breathe some unused air, and then I'm goin' to bed."

"Just about the time I start feelin' lucky, you guys wanna quit," Rosie groused.

"We're doing you a favor, Rosie," Buell said with a grin. He dropped the deck on the table.

Amos picked it up. "I'll see Twiggs gets these in the morning." He gave the group a nod and headed for the stairs.

"C'mon Spud, let's go," Simon said.

The dog uncurled and stood, back legs extended in a stretch so hard his belly nearly touched the floor. He gave his coat a good shaking and padded across the floor for the open door.

Outside the four men stood for a moment on the boardwalk, the air still and pleasantly warm.

"I love this time of year," Simon said.

A low grumble started in the dog's throat, and he pointed his nose at the stables, the hackles on his back standing. He let out a quiet woof sound.

"What do ya hear, boy?" Buell said as he followed the dog's stare.

The four men looked toward the stables. "Somebody's got a light in there," Buell said. "Wait right here a minute." He went into the saloon and returned immediately with his Sharps carbine. "Let's go see who's visitin'."

"Be quiet, Spud," Simon said as he touched the dog's head.

The rumbling sound quit, and the dog's ears came erect again. They hustled to the barn. The front of the stable had a smaller front entrance door, and the four men stopped at it and listened.

"Someone's moving around in there," Simon whispered.

Buell put his head closer to the door for a moment, and then they all stepped back a little. "I can hear two of them," he said. "I'm gonna go around to the west side, and come in through one of the manure holes. Give me about two minutes, then all three of you come in through here. Okay?"

"Two minutes," Simon whispered.

Buell nodded and hurried around the corner. Moving around the side of the barn, he came to the first opening. It was clear of manure. He silently thanked his luck and stooped to climb through and into an empty stall. The pungent smell of pounded earth mixed with dung, sweat and urine rose to meet him. He moved slowly toward the front of the cubicle, the layer of fine dirt over the hard-packed floor silencing his footsteps. A kerosene lamp hung on a pillar.

The yellow glow cast an unsure light over the two men standing in the middle of the room—Rankin and an Indian. Heads together, they carried on a whispered conversation. Rankin held a bridle in his left hand. The Indian pointed at the Appaloosa, Rankin nodded his head, and then started toward the horse. Buell moved closer to the front of the stalls, leveled his carbine and waited.

The front door burst open and Simon burst into the room, followed by Zahn and Rosie. Rankin's hand dropped to his holstered pistol.

"Touch it and I'll cut ya in half," Buell said quietly but distinctly.

The words punched the air out of Rankin's scrawny chest. Slowly, he turned around and his gaze dropped to the Sharps carbine.

The rifle crackled to full cock. "Kinda hopin' it was you," Buell said. His words carried the cold, emotionless resolve he felt. "Always lookin' for the narrow angle, aren't ya?"

Rankin glanced at his partner, who stood two steps away to the right, and then he looked back at the shadows.

Buell could see him calculating his chances.

"We weren't doin' nothin'," Rankin said. His tongue sought moisture in his mouth, and the pink tip tried to wet his lips. "Jist lookin' for a place to put our horses." His eyes blinked rapidly.

"Prob'ly been a good idea ta bring 'em in then, wouldn't ya think?" Buell kept his voice steady, almost conversational. Slowly, he stepped out of the shadows and pointed the heavy rifle at Rankin's chest. The ex-trooper's body reacted to the called bluff, eyes open wide, a slight jerk of his head.

Rankin started to breathe more quickly.

"I want ya to drop the bridle. It's mine," Buell demanded, his voice now sharper.

Silence ensued, so total the air felt brittle. Rankin froze in place, his eyes blinking rapidly. The Sharps remained centered on his chest. Buell glanced at the Indian. "Finally get ta see my work, Injun."

He took another step forward, and a flash of surprise winked into Knife's eyes as he caught Buell studying the mangled hand.

"Yeah, I'm the guy that messed that up. The one ya didn't see in the dark by the river." Buell glanced at Rosie, standing closest to the Indian. He pointed the carbine at the sheathed blade hanging by the Indian's side. "Hand that knife to him." He indicated Rosie with a nod.

Rankin swallowed hard, his Adam's apple working up and down his neck. His eyes followed the movement of the Sharps toward the Indian. He glanced at the door.

"Give it up," Buell said, his voice a warning hiss. His jaw muscles worked furiously as he eyed the Indian.

Rosie moved forward slightly to take the blade. Knife's eyes followed like a cornered fox, darting to Simon, then to Zahn and then back to Rosie. Buell, his jaw now set in a rigid line, followed the Indian's every move.

Simon could feel the animus radiating from Buell. His heart sped up, and he realized he'd stopped breathing. Spud, rigid with anticipation, leaned against his leg and Simon glanced down. Don't do it, Buell, he silently prayed. He'd no sooner finished the thought than Knife's blade flashed from the sheath, the point aimed for Rosie's huge belly. The Indian's arm shot out, like a snake striking a gopher. Buell's Sharps blurted fire and powder in a ferocious gout, and the minié ball ripped into Knife's arm halfway down from the shoulder. The streaking gray bullet smashed through, ripping bone, muscle and nerves as it went into his chest, leaving a horribly mangled wound where his elbow had been. Knife shrieked, and spun half around, already dead as he fell against a saddle rack. The terror-stricken horses in their stalls slammed against the rails.

The blast of the fifty-caliber rifle made Rankin turn his head, and Simon saw the black powder pepper his face and neck. Half hidden by the cloud of smoke, Rankin clawed at his pistol and found the grip. Buell dropped the Sharps, and drew his pistol in the space of a heartbeat. The revolver spit fire, and a bullet hit Rankin just below the ear. His eyes bulged out like a stomped frog's, one making it back into his head, the other not. Without a sound, he slumped to the ground, the braided bridle still clutched in his hand.

In two strides, Buell stood over Knife. "You're owed this, ya filthy bastard." The cocked pistol steadied on the dead man's head and exploded in a blast of smoke and sparks.

"Buell, don't!" Simon shouted and he started forward.

Zahn caught his arm in a vise-like grip. "Stay away." His whispered warning carried both fear and revulsion.

The Remington roared again, and again, three more times, as Buell emptied the pistol into the Indian's head. Then, he stepped away from the shattered body, and calmly returned his gun to the holster.

"Jesus," whispered Rosie as he stared at the gory sight. He sat on the ground, legs splayed, and rubbed the sides of his head. "What'n hell happened? I can't hear." He dug his thumbs into his ears.

Buell walked over to him. "That'll clear in a day or two."

"What's this?" shouted Rosie as he saw blood on his shirt. "Oh shit, I'm cut." He tugged frantically at the buttons, finally ripping the bottom three loose.

"Just nicked ya. You'll be all right." Buell turned to face Simon and Zahn.

Spud, ears laid back, flashed his teeth once and started a low warning growl.

"Spud, quit it." Simon bumped the dog in the side with his knee.

"What the hell's wrong with him?" Buell looked at the tense dog.

"What's wrong with you?" Simon nearly shouted. "My God, Buell, you didn't have ta do that. I saw he was dead before he hit the ground. Wasn't any call to . . . to mutilate him."

"We made a promise, remember? And now it's done."

Buell picked up the bridle and hung it by his horse's stall. The spotted animal looked around and announced its tension with a lip-fluttering snort. Walking back toward the door, Buell glanced at Rosie, still on the ground, glassy eyed and rubbing his ears. A little trickle of blood seeped out of the right one and ran onto his collar.

"Might be more than a day or two before they stop ringin'," Buell said matter-of-factly. He pushed past Simon and was nearly run over by Amos who came rushing through the door.

"What'n hell's go—Holy Mother." He stared at the grisly mess to his left, and then hurried over to Rankin's prone body. His head jerked back forcefully when he saw the man's face. He looked at Buell. "Oh. My. God. What happened?"

"They were stealin' horses. The Injun there stuck Rosie, and Rankin went for his gun. I shot 'em both."

"I'd say." Amos turned to Simon and Zahn, his ashen face asking a question he couldn't manage to speak.

"Happened the way he says," Zahn said. "So quick, I never saw his pistol come out."

Amos wiped the back of his hand across his mouth. "Well, we better get 'em out a here." He nodded at the two dead men. "These horses ain't gonna stand for much more of this. Stick 'em in the buckboard, and see if we can keep the night critters off 'em. We'll have to report this to the fort provost." He puffed a long sigh. "What a mess."

Simon and Zahn wrapped the dead men's heads in feed sacks, and then laid the bodies side by side in the wagon outside the stable. Buell had announced his intention to go to bed and left.

The Fort Laramie provost marshal was a West Point graduate, newly arrived from Virginia. Unlike the young lieutenant who had investigated the supply-pilfering charges, Captain Van Dyke was not polite, and certainly not friendly. Simon, Zahn, Rosie and Buell stood next to four chairs lined up along their side of a long table. The captain and a sergeant sat on the other side.

"This inquest will determine if capital murder was committed at McCaffrey's stable on July twenty-second. Toward that end, I am going to compel each of you to testify, under oath, to what you witnessed. You will answer the questions I pose, forthrightly and to the point. I will brook no interference. The sergeant will record my questions, and your answers. You will not be accorded the services of a lawyer, as this is not a civil proceeding. State your full name and occupation when asked by the sergeant, and then be seated."

The sergeant took all four names, beginning with Simon, and when he was finished, Captain Van Dyke started the questioning. Simon told of the event in detail, starting with the light they saw in the stable. He was telling about Knife's assault on Rosie and Buell's reaction, when Captain Van Dyke stood and leaned across the table.

"Did the Indian threaten Mister Mace with the knife you describe?"

"No, but he—"

"Was Mister Mace in danger of being attacked with the knife?"

Simon glanced sideways at the other three. Buell smiled slightly, and Zahn shrugged in resignation. Rosie looked irritated.

"Answer the question, Mister Steele."

"Yes, he was."

The captain looked surprised, and then annoyed. "How so?"

"The Indian had the knife and knew how to—"

"The question, Mister—"

"I'm answering. And knew how to use it, as evidenced by

him being able to wound Rosie, even while under Buell's gun."

The captain's face started to color and the pitch of his voice rose. "Mister McFarland's wounding has not been established as yet."

"What?" Rosie nearly shouted his protest. "I got stuck, Captain."

"You were not asked—"

"What'n hell you drivin' at? We been sittin' here thirty minutes, and I'll be damned if I couldn't tell you the whole thing in five."

"I was questioning Mister Steele."

"Like hell ya were. You were pokin' around, lookin' for something that ain't there."

"You will answer when a question is directed at you. Your unsolicited comments will be stricken." The captain looked at the sergeant, who nodded and made a notation on the page.

Rosie glared at him a moment, and then leaned back in his chair.

"You are obviously well educated, Mister Steele. And as such, you can understand the need for order here on the frontier. But I can see that you people have a peculiar sense of justice, and your own way of expressing it. The same goes for your opinions." He looked pointedly at Rosie. "That said, I want you to continue, being as succinct as possible. You may proceed." He sat back down.

Simon described the way Knife had gone for his blade, and how, when Rankin had taken advantage of the commotion and went for his pistol, Buell had shot him. Then, he described Buell's continued attack on the Indian. Finished, he sat back.

The captain cleared his throat. "Mister Mace asked the Indian to surrender?"

"Yes," Simon answered.

"He didn't provoke him?"

"No."

"Did he provoke Mister Rankin?"

"No."

The captain leaned back in his chair with a sigh and looked directly at Rosie and then Zahn. "Is there anything either of you two want to add to that?"

Both men shook their heads.

"Please answer yes or no."

"No," they answered in unison.

"Very well, Mister Mace. The surgeon's report says the Indian's heart was shredded, literally. Why did you see it necessary to shoot the man four more times . . . in the face?"

"I wanted him dead." Buell's cold stare met the captain's.

"You wanted him dead." The captain shook his head slowly. "You actually saw him as a threat? Prone and bleeding profusely. He *was* dead, Mister Mace."

"And rightly so."

"I think you're a dangerous man."

Buell continued to meet his eye, his face passive.

The captain couldn't hold eye contact and looked at the others. "Very well. I'll report my findings to Colonel Masters. Should there be charges, you will be notified. This hearing is concluded. You are dis—you may go." He picked up his leather binder and left, followed by the sergeant.

"Never saw such a pile of horseshit in all my life," Rosie said. "He was lookin' to hang Buell, pure and simple."

"I think he was doing his job as he saw it," Zahn said.

"What! You takin' his side?"

"Eventually, people like Knife and Rankin will be handled by the law. But no, I'm not takin' his side. I'm simply saying, I can understand why he did this."

"You might think diff'rent if it was you, and Lori had got jumped in the night," Buell said, staring at Zahn.

"You're probably right, but—"

"No buts about it. Unless—" Buell stopped in mid sentence, his eyes narrowed in a look of disdain.

"Unless what?" Zahn said. He glared at Buell.

"We're done here," Simon said. "Let's go back to the saloon."

Buell sniffed, then scooted his chair back. "I'm gonna go get some tobacco. I'll see ya later." He snatched his hat off the table and left.

"What was he gettin' at?" Zahn asked, irritated.

"Let it go, Zahn," Simon said. The incident by the river came flooding back, and he knew what Buell had in mind to say: unless you couldn't do it yourself. "Let's get back to the ranch."

The three men rode back to McCaffrey's in silence.

The bad taste of the provost marshal's interrogation still lingered after four days. Unable to concentrate, Simon sat in the still, suffocating air of his office, doing absolutely nothing. He had just resolved to leave when Buell stepped into the room and pulled the door shut.

"Bein' around you the last few days ain't been no fun," Buell said as he slumped into a chair. "You're like a badger with a bellyache. What'n hell's got up your ass?"

Simon couldn't meet his eyes. "I really don't want to talk about it, Buell."

"Well, I do. And I'm here." Buell eased to the edge of the chair. "Ya ain't never had any trouble before tellin' me how wrong I am."

"I'm having a hard time getting that night in the barn out of my head."

"And I'm havin' a hard time understandin' what yer problem is. What choice did I have?"

Simon was quiet, not wanting to say what he thought.

"Well, gawdammit, what choice did I have?"

"That's part of what's botherin' me, Buell. I get the feeling you didn't want a choice."

"Meanin' what?"

"I don't want to fight about this. Just let it go, and I'll sort it out."

"Same every time. You don't wanta face it."

"And that's the rest of the problem, Buell."

"What?"

"You said it. The same every time. You've killed four men Buell, and maimed one, and we're barely over twenty-one. That ain't natural." Simon's breath drew in sharply.

Buell's face darkened and he slowly stood. "Ain't natural? What're you sayin', Simon?" He stepped closer to the desk.

"I . . ." Simon's heart raced and his mouth went dry.

"Rankin wasn't goin' to shoot *me,* Simon. He was lookin' to get out the door. And guess who was standin' in his way?"

Simon's mind flashed back to the killing.

"Uh-huh. Ya remember now, don'tcha?" Buell leaned across the desk, his eyes ablaze. "So whose biscuit got saved from the dog? Again!" He turned, jerked open the door and stormed out.

Simon struggled to calm his emotions, his mind swirling around what he knew to be true and what he wanted to believe. He had to talk to someone.

An hour later Simon rode his horse up to Walks Fast's tepee. A moment later the old Indian's wife pushed back the flap and came out. She pointed toward the hills. "Taylor," she said and reentered the tepee.

Simon found the Indian sitting on the ground in the shade of the trees, his eyes closed, apparently asleep. His hands were folded in his lap, his legs crossed under him. Simon dismounted and tied his horse to a corral pole. As he approached, the Indian looked up, and with his hand to his mouth, indicated silence.

"Sit and listen," he whispered, then closed his eyes again.

Simon sat beside him and waited. The old man breathed slowly and deeply, his face relaxed. After several minutes he took a deep breath, and opened his eyes.

"Simon has trouble. I have gone with Simon's spirit on a truth search for many nights. You have a worry for what white men call soul. And the worry is not for your own."

"Somehow I knew you'd know."

"When trouble is big enough, every night walker sees it. It can't be a secret."

"Do you mean others can see what I dream about?" The thought made Simon uncomfortable for some reason.

"Not see, like see with our eyes. We see like we are in the dream with you."

"Do you understand what I see in my dreams?"

"No. Your dreams belong to you, but my spirit can talk to your spirit."

"Then how do you know I'm worried about Buell?"

"Because I worry about him too."

Both men sat silent for a few minutes as Simon thought about what he had just heard. "Does he want to kill people?" Simon finally asked. He hated the question as much as he feared the answer and bowed his head.

"We are born with all kinds of spirits inside. When a man grows, a good family will push out the bad ones. Buell didn't have a whole family. Is this true?"

"His mother died when he was born."

"The spirit of the Devil Bear is strong in him. Devil Bear is a crazy spirit. Sometimes he will bite his own leg in anger."

"What's a Devil Bear? A grizzly?"

"No. It's a small animal, but very strong, and it smells very bad. It does not know fear and lives alone in the mountains."

Simon recalled the times Buell had confronted others older

and bigger than himself, apparently unafraid and cocksure. "How can he get away from this thing?"

"That might not happen."

"Then he'll always look for a fight?"

"He does not look for a fight, but he will not turn his face away either. Devil Bear fights without seeing. Buell fights like the Devil Bear."

"Do you mean he doesn't really know what he's doing?"

Walks Fast didn't answer immediately, his expression one of a man in deep thought. Sadness shadowed his gaze when he looked at Simon. "I think maybe the Devil Bear closes Buell's eyes to many things."

Simon sensed that Walks Fast had said all he wanted to say but pressed on. "What can I do to help? He's more than my friend, he's like a brother."

"Then treat him like a brother." Again Walks Fast paused as though weighing something. "Trust him like a brother." He leaned forward slightly, his eyes narrowed.

"Can he ever be rid of this devil?"

"You must find his Devil Bear and kill it. Then its spirit will leave Buell."

"And how do we find it? How do we kill the thing?"

"Walks Fast does not know that." A look of pain strained the Indian's calm demeanor. "The Devil Bear does not like you, and I think it will find you one day." The Indian's eyes lost focus and then slowly closed.

Soon the old man was breathing slowly and deeply again. Simon sat for a minute or so, then got up and went to his horse. He looked back as he rode away and was startled to see a shaft of sunlight pierce the trees and bathe the Indian in bright light. For a moment the stoic figure seemed to float in the air.

CHAPTER 16

The air had a clarity that made the distances across the rolling hills shrink by half. Simon breathed deeply of the cool air as he stood on the porch. Spud, as usual, took off toward the river, his bounding gait soon carrying him out of sight. Simon could hear his harassing bark when he found something to chase. The oppressive heat of August had finally given way to this, the first cool morning in September, and the road in front of the saloon was deserted, something it hadn't been since midweek. And the last four days had been particularly chaotic.

Four English gentlemen, with their dogs, and an entourage of eleven handlers, helpers and assistants, had descended on McCaffrey's for a week of hunting. Up at the crack of dawn, the noisy group, oblivious to the desires and needs of the other guests, clamored to get out on the prairie and ride in pursuit of some unfortunate wolf. Returning late in the afternoon, they demanded baths, meals, and every imaginable special consideration. By the end of the third day, Lori, Twiggs, and the ladies had had their fill of them, despite the enormous sums of money the foreigners were willing to spend.

Then, relief came in a form that only nature and circumstance can provide. Simon could only guess at what really transpired based on the after-the-fact argument that ensued. Walks Fast explained that for the event to make sense, he had to understand two facts: dogs will pursue anything that runs, and a prairie coyote is the most intelligent animal living on the plains.

★ ★ ★ ★ ★

The hunting party was east of Fort Laramie in the vicinity of a cattle ranch owned by a Scotsman named Connery. Mister Connery's pride and joy was a small herd of shorthorn cattle, a breed not necessarily suited to the harsh winters of the area. But the determined Mister Connery pampered and coddled his herd, convinced they were the future of the Wyoming beef industry. And today, as was often the case, four armed cowboys rode protection over the cattle, shooting wolf, bear, rustler, or Indian as they were identified.

A pack of coursing hounds ranged well ahead of the mounted English hunters, the occasional deep booming bay of the lead dog kept the men, usually out of sight, in touch with the dogs. And then, the sound of the dog's voice changed to one long howl, and the entire group took up the chorus. The hunting dogs had their prey in sight.

Over a mile farther east, Mister Connery's cattle grazed. "What'n hell's that?" the first herder shouted across to the second.

"Them gawdamn huntin' dogs." The second puckered his lips and issued a long shrill whistle.

In a minute, two riders came charging over a low ridge and joined the first two.

"Ya hear that?" the first herder, obviously the boss, asked the newly arrived pair.

"Yep. Huntin' dogs. Heard 'em once before."

"They bother cows?" the boss asked.

"Don't rightly know."

"Well, we better be ready. I go back to the ranch and tell Mister Connery we us got a chewed-on cow, all hell will cut loose, right along with our jobs. Drag out them rifles."

★ ★ ★ ★ ★

As the cowboys were discussing what they'd heard, a hungry coyote, nearly half a mile away, scrounged around for something, anything, dead or alive, to eat. He flushed a small rodent from a tumbleweed heap and chased it into another one, twenty yards away. Nose down, having sniffed out the trail of his potential breakfast, he stood, staring intently at his meal. Suddenly, his hackles rose at the sound of the dogs. He turned to look just as the pack crested a ridge a quarter mile away. He, too, heard the long raying howl as the leader spotted him, and he knew he had a problem. He headed east.

As fast as a coyote is, he picks his route carefully, putting hill, tree, brush or whatever he can find, between himself and his pursuer, but always moving away. Unfortunately, compared to a coursing hound, a coyote is a small animal, and the gap between them was soon reduced to a couple hundred yards. But what he lacked in strength and size, nature had made up in intelligence. He turned sharply left, shot up the hill, in plain view of the pursuing hounds, and disappeared out of sight.

The effect on the hounds became instantly clear to everyone listening. The chorus of blood-curdling howls carried back to the hunters, who shouted and urged their horses forward.

The cowboys also heard it. "My gawd, they're comin' right at us," shouted the boss. "Git on the ground."

All four men scrambled off their fidgety mounts, and faced the unnerving sound of the unseen pack. Four levers, on four rifles, loaded four .44-caliber cartridges.

The coyote knew of the herd. He also knew men stood watch over them, and had deliberately stayed well away from them. But he needed a place to hide, and he needed it now. The milling mass of legs seemed just the place. Straight into the herd he ran.

Out of sight, but not out of scent, the lead dog followed the distinct airborne trail of the coyote. Over the crest of the hill and down he charged, howling like he was wounded, oblivious to everything but the smell of the coyote ahead of him.

The first rifle spit out the herder's objection, followed in an instant by three more. Three dogs, including the leader, piled up and lay still. Well-oiled machinery worked to carry four fresh rounds to the ready. Four more shots split the air in near unison and four more dogs died. The herders then watched as the two remaining animals slid to a stop in a tangle of heavy feet and taut haunches. Terrified by the sudden thunder of gunfire, and the agonized howl of their dying pack mates, they turned and bolted back the way they'd come.

"Good shootin' boys. Now mount up and git these cows settled down." Without a glance at the dead dogs, they hurried their horses to encircle the herd.

"Lookit that," the boss shouted, and pointed at the moving cattle. "Gawdamn coyote right in the middle of 'em. Jist ambling along with the herd. I'll be damned."

The hunters heard the first sharp crack of the rifle. The following seven shots, in the space of five seconds, snapped their heads around as they looked questions at each other. They urged their horses toward the sound and crested the ridge, just as the herders had gotten themselves positioned around the small herd.

The first rider leapt off his horse and knelt beside a large gray dog. "Bloody hell! It's been shot in the head." He stood up and spotted another one, and another. He ran to his horse, mounted and furiously charged across the shallow depression toward the cowboys.

Later that day, at Fort Laramie, the irate Englishman demanded justice from the Scottish cattleman. He received scant sympathy, nationalism aside, and the army sided with the Scotsman. The Englishmen had taken their two surviving dogs and departed.

Next week, a party of three Germans was expected, bear hunters, so Simon stood for a few more minutes, enjoying the quiet. He was about to go back in when Buell came out.

"Got up last night to take a leak. Knew this mornin' was gonna be a beauty." He stretched. "That Spud?" He pointed at a fleeting shape, racing belly down along the riverbank.

"Yup. Rabbit." Simon smiled as the dog suddenly changed direction and lunged at something on the ground. And then the dog stood stationary. "Looks like he got his breakfast."

"Well, let's go get ours." Buell stepped off the porch and headed across the road. Simon followed.

They were halfway through breakfast when Tay pushed the door open and came into the saloon.

"Look what crawled out of the hills," Simon said, getting out of his chair.

"Ain't no need ta git up, t'ain't royalty." The smile on Tay's face looked wide enough to hook on both ears.

"Good ta see ya, Tay," Buell said. He, too, got out of his chair.

"Got back a week ago and got tired a waitin' fer ya to come visit. Walks Fast was there, no su'prise. Tol' me 'bout yer English cust'mers gittin' their blue noses put outta joint. That were a good'n. Tol' me about the other stuff too." His brow furrowed for a moment, and then he smiled.

"Had yer breakfast?" Buell asked.

"Hell no, and ya owe me one, if I rec'lect," he said to Simon. He arched an eyebrow.

"Absolutely. Sit down. What do you want to eat?"

"Eggs. It's one o' them things ya can't have when yer roughin' it. I could eat a half dozen."

"I'll go tell Lori. Ham? We got some good ham."

"Sure, and some coffee. Got any o' that canned milk, and some white sugar?"

"Comin' right up." Simon went into the kitchen.

"How was the gold huntin'?" Buell asked after a minute.

"By jigger, I think I've found it." Tay's eyes gleamed. "Let's wait fer Simon so's I don't have to tell it twice."

"Tell what?" Simon asked from the door.

"Tay struck it rich."

"Didn't say that. I said I think I found it."

Simon set a cup of coffee in front of Tay, then unloaded his arm of the sugar bowl with spoon and a milk can. The old man dumped three heaping scoops of sugar into the cup, and poured in milk until the cup wouldn't hold any more. Carefully picking up the drink, he slurped three or four times and sighed. "That's good." He settled back in his chair.

"Well, start tellin'," Buell said eagerly.

"Still snow when I got there this spring, and I took my time goin' in. Saw Sioux several times and had to cold camp fer four days once. I don't think they were lookin' fer me, jist movin' around."

"So how do ya hide?" Buell asked.

"Ya stay outta sight. Troublin' part is keepin' the damn animals from fussin'. Stick 'em together if ya can. Anyhow, I fin'ly got to the creek I was at in sixty-eight without gittin' spotted and set up my camp."

"Meanin'?" Buell looked at Tay intently.

"Meanin' I pitched my tent back in the trees, and found a

place to put the horse and mule."

"The trees so ya won't get seen? Right?"

"Exactly. Ya sure are in'erested, Buell. Figger on goin'?"

"Might. And yer right, it's interesting."

"Well, ya put yer tent in the trees, and cover it with pine branches. Don't use the brush, 'cause it'll turn yellow on ya in a week and stick out like a wart."

"So you've got your camp all set. Go ahead," Simon said to Tay. He frowned at Buell.

"Like I said, I was up in sixty-eight and found some good color in that creek, but never had the chance ta foller it up. This year, I had water aplenty, and I panned upstream fer over a mile 'fore I found where the gold was comin' from. In one spot, I was pickin' three or four nice nuggets in every hole. Then the next move upstream, nothin'. In between there was a draw with no water runnin' out and I went up 'er. Where she leveled out a bit, I dug a couple dozen holes. Then I hit a spot where I could fill one pan'yer, haul it down to the creek and pan half an ounce. I'd found it."

"So what did ya do with it?" Buell asked, his eyes glittering.

"Whatcha mean, what'd I do with it? I brought it out."

"Well, ya got any with ya?"

Tay chuckled. "Sure do." He stretched back in his chair, and pulled a pouch from his pocket. It made a decided thump when he dropped it dramatically on the table. "Open 'er up." He pushed it toward Buell.

It took a minute for Buell to untie the knot in the leather thong. Finally, he got it unwound and the bag open, then shook some of the contents into the palm of his hand. "Oh." He uttered the single word as he stared at the bright yellow pieces in his hand.

"Impressive, ain't it?"

"It's beautiful," Simon said. He reached over and picked a

nugget out of Buell's hand.

"Got near a hundred ounces of that. And the good Lord knows how much more is left up there. I was still diggin' in gravel, no bedrock to be seen." Tay could not hide his excitement.

"Why'd ya quit?" Buell asked.

"Water run out. Ya only got a few weeks 'fore the creek dries up. Can't be packin' it too far or you're gonna git caught. Wish'ta hell the Indians'd let us in there. But that ain't likely. Them hills're sacred to 'em."

"The newspaper says there's a lot of agitating by settlers to be allowed in," Simon said. "And the politicians in Washington are talkin' about letting them."

"Not without a fight, and we've seen how them Sioux kin fight," Tay said.

Lori came out of the kitchen with a serving tray. She set a plate of eggs in front of Tay, then unloaded a plate full of ham and fried bread. A dish of fresh butter and a honey crock followed. She spied the gold as she laid his knife and fork down. "Good Lord, look at that." Her eyes fixed on the dazzling chunks lying beside the pouch.

Tay's equally intense gaze was directed at the food. "Service like thet's gotta be rewarded, pretty lady." He reached over and picked up the biggest nugget in the pile and handed it to her. "There ya go, that'n is yers."

"I've never seen it natural before. This one is shaped like a footprint. I love it. Thank you very much." She leaned over, lifted Tay's hat, and kissed the top of his head.

"Oh, pshaw, yer welcome. Meant to be spent, and I kin see this is gonna be worth it." He picked up his fork and slid a ten-inch-wide ham steak onto his plate. Then he speared a piece of bread.

Lori smiled as he fit one whole egg in his mouth and chewed, cheeks bulging. She went back into the kitchen, admiring the nugget.

Simon and Buell examined the gold as Tay demolished everything Lori had brought him. Finished, he leaned back in his chair and patted his taut belly. "Damn, that was wonderful. What'n hell's she put on them eggs?"

"Don't ask me. I just know she's a fine cook," Simon said.

"So, ya think you've found a place where ya could make enough for life?" Buell asked.

"That's the funny part about gold huntin', Buell, ya never know. I may have got it all, and then again, I may have just scratched it. Ya dig till it's gone."

"How did ya know where to look?"

"Ya look at the rocks. Gold is around quartz. Copper says there might be gold, too, and copper's green, easy ta see. Quartz, ya gotta git yer nose right into the stuff. Knock chunks offa outcrops and take a good look. Or you'll see bits a quartz in the gravel. Ya see it, pan some, and see if ya find black sand, that's a good sign. Then ya pan upstream till it gits better. Keep at it till ya run out of water or time. That's if'n the Indians don't run ya off first."

"And nobody knows where ya were?"

"I'm countin' on that, Buell. Gold does funny things ta men." Tay looked at him closely. "Turns good men bad and bad ones worse. Kin make one friend bushwhack another."

"Doesn't seem to have hurt you any," Simon said.

"I ain't never had a partner, and never will." Tay watched Buell's reaction. "I kin see thet don't make ya happy. If I was to take on a partner, and I won't, I couldn't 'magine a better one than either you or Simon. But it's jist cuz I like ya both that I wouldn't. I'll be plumb tickled to show ya how ta look, teach ya what I know, but I can't take ya with me."

"Makes sense, I s'pose," Buell said, the disappointment plain on his face.

"That's the way it's gotta be."

"Is there any around here?" Simon asked.

"Sure. Matter a fact, there's gold on the creek where I hole up. Not enough to make it worth chasin', but there's some there all right."

"Maybe you can show me and Buell how to pan. What do ya say, Buell?"

"I dunno, if there's not enough to really find something."

"Be glad ta show ya anytime. Come out early one mornin' and I'll fix ya breakfast. And then we'll go poke around."

"Aren't ya gonna work with the army?" Buell asked.

"I got enough now I ain't gonna even tell the army I'm back. Gonna be a real relaxed winter fer ol' Tay. And I think I'll be back here fer the 'casional breakfast."

"I want to learn how," Simon said. "Seeing it there on the table makes me want to find some for myself."

"I know the feelin', Simon. Ya been bit. I'll offer my 'pologies later. Now, what's chances a gittin' 'nuther cup a coffee?" He held his cup out.

Simon returned with a fresh cup, and the two young men listened to Tay for another hour, fascinated, as he described the Black Hills country.

A week passed before Simon found the time to visit Tay. When Simon asked if Buell wanted to go, he'd mumbled something about the damn dog and a bad night, then rolled over.

The cool air, almost cold, felt good as Simon gazed in appreciation at the golden display of fall colors. Spud kicked up a forty-bird flock of ducks, overnighting in a beaver pond. Three deer sprinted from the creek bottom to the shelter of the trees when he rounded the point below Tay's place. Tay's horse whinnied a greeting as Simon rode up to the dugout.

The old man poked his head out the door. " 'Mornin'. Git in here and help me eat these taters."

"Stay there, Spud." Simon pointed to a spot outside the door. The dog's ears drooped and he lay down with a sigh.

"Mutt kin come in," Tay said.

"Nope. He ate something rotten last night and his farts'll crack your teeth. Best he stays right there."

"Yer dog. Grab a plate and help yerself. I always make too much spuds. There's bacon too."

The two men sat down and tucked into their breakfast, not talking a lot until the plates were clear and the second cup of coffee had been poured.

"So Buell decided he weren't gonna do it."

"Naw. He was up two or three times last night. Some nights he doesn't sleep two hours."

"That's what Walks Fast says. Do you believe that old man can see yer dreams?"

"I'm not sure what I believe. I've read some about it, and there's some stuff in the Bible too. I know when I was lost in the snowstorm, I wound up right out in front of here and Walks Fast was waiting for me. I was dead where I stood. That was strange."

"D'ya mind talkin' about Buell a little?"

"No. Matter of fact, I've wanted to ask you a couple questions and never had the chance."

"Walks Fast says he's watched Buell in his dreams and thinks maybe Buell ain't quite right."

"Buell has . . . he's been a . . . I've never completely understood Buell. We've been best friends since we started school. And I've seen him do stuff that I know he don't remember doing. When I've asked him about it, he seems confused, and then he either gets mad at me or simply won't talk about it."

"What happened in Amos's barn?"

"That was awful. The look on his face when he was shooting that Indian was . . . I don't know. Inhuman isn't the right word, but that's close."

"But it wasn't Buell?"

"No. Buell isn't the most friendly guy you can meet, but he's really quite mellow, ya know. Quiet. There in the barn he was frenzied, like—" Simon shook his head.

"Like an animal?"

"Worse. I've never seen anything like it."

"Walks Fast says it's a demon, a bad spirit, he calls it."

"And I don't want to think that of him, he's never . . . I mean I've never felt—" Simon lowered his gaze to the table.

"But ya have, haven't ya? Felt scared of him."

"Yeah," Simon said, his voice hushed. "After the barn. He looked at me like I've never seen him do. It only lasted for a moment, but I damn near peed my pants."

"I've been movin' 'round fer well over fifty years, and I've seen one other feller like him. Lived alone, cuz nobody could stand to be around him. Most of the time he was fine, but once in a while he'd change ta somethin' else completely. Went out one night and kilt his horse with an ax. Couldn't 'member a thing, but he was covered with blood, so weren't no doubt it was him that done it. Buell ever done somethin' like that?"

Simon shook his head. "I've tried to remember. Nothing as strange as that, but little things. I was gettin' the tar beat out of me one day, and he just watched. I thought I was gonna get killed."

"Well, obv'ously ya didn't. What happened?"

"He finally kicked the boy on top of me and knocked him off. I don't remember him doin' it, but he told me later that's what he did. When I asked him why he waited so long to help, his answer didn't make any sense at all."

Tay grunted and took a sip of coffee. "So sometimes he does change?"

"I guess so."

"Ain't no guessin', Simon. It's jist hard fer ya to admit it, him bein' yer friend."

"You're probably right." Simon took a deep breath. "Did your friend get better?"

"He weren't my friend. I jist knowed 'im. One day he up and left. His cabin was straight, bed made up, clothes all there, even his rifle. But he was gone. Never did hear what happened to 'im."

"Buell isn't like that. Most of the time . . . I mean it's only rarely that he seems to drift off like that." Simon paused for a moment. "The only time he looks a little crazy is when he gets threatened."

"Like in the barn?"

"Yeah, and once when we were in a saloon back home."

"I like Buell, Simon, don't git me wrong. I think he's as good a friend as you could have. But I want ya to think about something. Don't you ever threaten him."

"I'd never do that."

Tay held up a hand. "Ya ain't understandin' my meanin'. Don't cross him on somethin' he thinks is important."

"Do you think he might . . . he wouldn't shoot me. Would he?"

"Buell might not. But that devil in 'im? That's a mule ya ain't rode yet."

Simon stared at his long-cold cup of coffee. His thoughts went back to Nebraska and all the good times he and Buell had spent together. The sense of loss that started to well up in his chest made his heartbeat feel unsteady.

"Ain't exactly what ya came fer t'day, is it?"

"No, sir."

"Sometimes yer love fer someone will blind ya to truths thet ya have to know. I'm glad we had this talk, Simon."

"Me too." Simon sighed deeply, and closed his eyes for a moment. "Think we could put my gold-huntin' lesson off till another day?"

"Sure thing. Ya come back when ya want. I ain't goin' no'ers."

The trip back to McCaffrey's was over the same ground, but Simon didn't see the beauty of the changing trees or the grace of the high wispy clouds in the milky blue of the autumn sky.

Zahn had joined Simon and Amos for breakfast, and Lori had just cleared the table.

"I've got a problem that I need some help with, Amos," Zahn said.

"Shoot."

"I have a chance to make some real good money, but I have to leave here to do it."

"I don't like the sound of that." Amos frowned. "You mean, you'd have to leave Fort Laramie? You and Lori?"

"That's the problem. I would, but I can't take Lori."

"What kind of a job is it?" Simon asked.

"Makin' railroad ties."

"Oh, you talked to those railroad people who were here two weeks ago."

"Yep. They need more ties than they can get their hands on. They're branching off the main line faster than the supply will keep up."

"Can't ya find work here?" Amos asked.

"I can, but I need something that will put my team to work as well. These folks are eager to hire me *and* the team. I can make twenty dollars a day in a tie hacker camp."

"And you're worried about Lori? I can see your concern, but you needn't have any," Simon said. "We couldn't be happier with her, right Amos?"

"That's for sure. Matter of fact, I'm glad ya ain't takin' her off. Now, how's that fer selfish?"

Zahn gave him a wan smile.

"She'd be safe here, Zahn. I guarantee it," Simon said. "Everybody knows her, and she's around people she can trust. It's not like she was living in a cabin somewhere."

"Then she can stay where she is?"

"Can stay? I'd insist," Amos said. "Was that what was worryin' ya?"

"I wasn't sure, and we didn't want to take advantage." Zahn forced a sheepish smile.

"Well, consider it done, for hell sakes. She's part of this place." Amos reached over and slapped Zahn on the arm. "Tell her she's welcome."

"Thanks, Amos. You, too, Simon," Lori said from the doorway. "I've been listening, couldn't help myself."

"Well, you're sure welcome. Damn, the things folks worry about," Amos said with a chuckle. "So, when ya gotta leave?"

"Tomorrow. I'll drive the team to Cheyenne, and catch a supply train to the tie yard. It's about fifty miles west. The ties are cut in the mountains a little to the south."

"And you been stewin' about this for two weeks?" Amos rolled his eyes.

"We're an independent couple," Lori said.

"Well, I am too, but what's friends for? No, we're glad to have ya. And we'll take good care of her while yer gone, Zahn. You can count on it."

Zahn left McCaffrey's ranch early the next morning. Breakfast was a quiet affair.

Chapter 17

Simon lay still, listening to the morning. Memories of lying awake in the quiet of the sod house back home drifted in and out of his consciousness. Recalling the simpler time of his youth made what he was doing now seem so complicated.

This morning was like several he had spent over the past week or so, awake for no reason, and tired. Buell had not completely gotten over their last argument, and the demands of the business continued to grow. More and more hunters, gamblers, and people just seeking the excitement of the West visited the ranch, and the mental stress of keeping everyone satisfied had started to take its toll.

He heard the saloon doors open and shut, then the sound of several people moving around the stable, presumably getting horses ready for an early-morning excursion. Probably the party from New York City. Arrogant and demanding, they were due to leave Monday, three days hence. Wide awake now, Simon heard the group mount up and leave.

He swung his legs over the edge of the bed and sat up. Buell was a mound of blankets in the bed across the room; not even his head showed. Simon could hear his quiet snoring. Spud raised his head, then got to his feet, and stretched. The dog watched, his gaze steady, anticipation in his eyes as Simon got up and dressed.

Stepping out onto the porch, Simon looked east and judged the sun had another half hour or so before rising. He walked around the side of the house and toward the barn. The crests of the low hills to the northeast were tinged with gold as the sun lit them. Suddenly, he felt a powerful urge to walk into the mountains. He strode quickly to the end of the barn and stood, heart pounding, to stare off into the distance. The presence he felt was almost palpable, the hair on the back of his neck rose, and his nostrils flared as he brought every sense to bear on the strange feeling. Whatever it was, it now held him spellbound. He had no sense of how long he stood immobile, watching.

"What'n hell ya doin'?"

Buell's sudden appearance startled Simon, and his sharp intake of breath snapped his eyes into focus. His body relaxed so suddenly, he felt weak.

"You okay? I've been standin' here for over a minute and you weren't breathin'."

"I . . . I don't know. I came out to take a leak, and felt something pulling me out there." Simon pointed a shaky finger toward the hills. His hand came back, and covered his mouth.

"I heard ya go out."

"That was really an odd feeling. I mean, I almost took off walking."

"Don't get too upset about it," Buell said. He sounded reassuring. "I've done that dozens a times."

"Ya have?" Simon smiled weakly.

"Sure. Ain't never told nobody, but it's what made me go out and sit in the prairie back home. Woke up on the riverbank once, and it was mornin'. I remember leaving the livery, but that's all. Scared the hell outta me the first time I did that."

"What is it?"

"Don't know. I think it's like a dream, only in these kind, you move around."

"Like walking in your sleep?"

"Not really. It comes on me when I'm awake, and then I just

drift away. Sometimes . . . I don't know . . . it's like daydreaming, ya know, just thinkin' about stuff. But then something seems to take over. I quit worryin' 'bout it."

"I don't like it." Simon shook his head, and then he shuddered.

"Don't blame ya. But ain't much ya kin do about it, I don't think. Let's go get some breakfast."

They walked around the front of the barn and crossed the road to the saloon. The place was still quiet.

The following Monday, Simon made a trip to the fort. After he'd finished his business at the sutler's store and picked up some mail, he decided to see if Walks Fast was home. He sat his horse until the old Indian emerged from the tepee.

"Come in." Walks Fast held the flap open and waited.

After they were seated and had waited the customary minute or two, Simon spoke. "I've had a strange . . . can't call it a dream, but I felt something wanted me to see, or hear some . . . I can't describe it." Simon shook his head in frustration. "It happened three days ago."

"Were you lifted from sleep?"

"If you mean, was I sleeping, no. I was outside."

"Not all spirits work when we sleep. We have day spirits too. Day spirits tell a man when he is wrong. Day spirit is gentle and doesn't make much noise. You had a night spirit visit in the daytime."

"You mean I was daydreaming?"

"Not the same. Daydreams are lazy, and come when you're not worried. Night spirits come when a man has many problems. It comes to help the day spirit."

"Why did I feel I needed to walk into the hills?"

"Night spirit is strongest when a man is still. Your night spirits want you to go to a quiet place, and take the truth."

"But it almost felt like something had hold of me."

"Spirits are very strong. They can stop a storm, and heal a broken body. It is easy for a spirit to carry you into the mountains."

Walks Fast looked at Simon, and the gentleness in his face made Simon feel warm. "But I didn't hear anything. I felt like going, but that's all. I have a hard time saying this, but shouldn't I hear something?"

"When a night spirit works in the day, it, too, is quiet like the day spirit. Simon must listen close to hear. You should go to the mountains. Soon. Go alone and listen. A strong spirit waits for you."

"Where?"

"It will show you." The old man nodded his head and smiled.

As Simon started to get up, Walks Fast reached over, and put his palm on Simon's chest. He held the brown, wrinkled hand hard against his body for a moment, then nodded again. "Very strong. Heart of mother," he said and dropped his hand to his lap.

Amos laughed out loud when he heard about Walks Fast's advice of the day before. "You're an educated man, Simon. This spirit talk is bullshit."

"I know what I felt, Amos."

"Everybody goes through that once in a while. Same as knowin' something bad's gonna happen. It never does. Phooey. But hell, ya want to take off fer a few days and chase an elk or deer, go right ahead. Lord knows ya earned it. Don't think mucha you goin' alone though."

"Neither do I," Buell said.

"It's not that I don't want you along. Walks Fast said I should go alone."

"Well, at least take Spud," Buell said.

"All right. I'll take the dog. Now I'm gonna go."

They left the saloon and walked across to the barn. Simon's horse stood ready, saddlebags bulging, his Winchester rifle riding in the scabbard. Simon climbed on the horse, and with a whistle to the dog, rode past the saloon. McCaffrey's ranch was soon out of sight.

Without thinking about it, he followed the river toward the fort, then, when he came to the creek that ran past Tay's dugout, he turned toward the mountains. The old prospector's horse was gone, and the cabin looked vacant, so he rode on by, and was soon three miles up the valley. The creek forked and the horse went right. Simon remembered the canyon to the left was where Zahn and the men had cut the timber for the little houses. He remembered, too, his walk out of the canyon after his horse had been killed.

"Wonder if I could find that place again?" he said out loud.

The sound of his own voice made him aware that he had no idea where he was and could not remember anything about the ride, except for the quick once-over of Tay's cabin. He stopped the horse and looked around. The willows along the creek had the look of something prepared to meet the coming cold. Their bright summer lushness had given way to a dull gray-green look of hardiness, the result of the first frost over a month ago.

The aspens looked scruffy. Blotches of dulled red and orange still spotted the hillside, with the occasional defiant splash of brilliant color from a sheltered copse. The dark green of the timber higher up had a forbidding appearance, a warning to stay in the shelter of the lowlands. His horse edged toward the creek, and Simon let him drink. The water was clear as the air. Simon got off and knelt beside the stream, cupped hands lifting the sweet, ice-cold refreshment to his lips.

Simon continued climbing slowly, and after passing several low outcrops of rock, he came to an abrupt narrows, impassable, the creek cutting through the naked rock. Again, he let his horse have his head, and they climbed above the creek to the left, into the trees. An hour or so later, they emerged into a two-hundred-acre oval-shaped meadow. Near the far end, a rock slide had created a small lake of about two acres in size. To his left a stream, barely a foot wide, sprang out of the hillside from under a hundred-foot-high sheer rock outcrop. The gentle hiss of the breeze in the treetops rose to a peaceful sigh for a moment, then subsided to a silence so complete, Simon could hear the horse's heartbeat. An overwhelming sense of tranquility settled on him that took his breath.

Then anxiety seized him, and the stillness turned frightening. He looked around for the dog and couldn't see him. Turning in the saddle to search behind, the trees leaned over him, threatening to cut off the sky. He kicked his horse in the flanks and bolted into the sunlight, the sound of squeaking leather and hooves in the dirt reassuring. After a hundred yards he stopped and looked back. Spud trotted out of the trees and sat. Simon looked at the gently panting dog, content to sit in the shade, and wait for his master to show him what to do. Simon felt like an irrational fool and with a sheepish chuckle called, "C'mon, Spud, let's find a place to spend the night."

After looking the meadow over, Simon decided to camp next to the rock outcrop. The rest of the meadow, though beautiful to look at, turned out to be damp and soggy. He left his unsaddled horse to roam, hobbles slowing his gait to ungainly half hops. With his hatchet in hand, Simon cut short pine boughs for a bed and dragged some deadwood out of the trees. He felt well prepared for the night that fell suddenly, and for the solitude he knew this place offered.

The dusk of evening turned into darkness. The firmament, a cathedral with the ultimate vaulted ceiling, soared from the buttresses of the mountainsides to arch through infinity and back again. Even though perforated countless times by points of light, the mystery of darkness still dominated the awesome depths of the black sky. Simon scanned the heavens, and his gaze settled on the reassuring "W" of Cassiopeia. At that moment he felt at home, and at peace.

Slowly, Simon's unconscious self took leave of the nether places. He pushed through the gauze his mind had spent the night weaving, his dreams reluctant to fade. He became aware of a rhythmic whisper somewhere near his head. That'd be Spud, his breathing even and sonorous, nose burrowed in the warmth of his own belly. The creek carried on the same soothing conversation that had put him to sleep. It murmured as it broke around the rocks strewn in the streambed, the cadence perfectly even and steady. He lay still for a few more minutes, then opened his eyes. The eastern horizon was ablaze, the mountaintops stretching to their fullest height to protect their shadows from the morning sun's exuberance.

He threw back the blankets, and stood. Goose pimples proudly formed ranks as he gazed across the frosted meadow. The cold, calm air of the magnificent mountain morning condensed his breath. Absorbing the sheer serenity of the scene, he thought of a church without walls, a sanctuary, passive, begging to be left in peace. Simon realized he had slept all night, undisturbed by dreams, the first such night in a long time. He reached down and rubbed Spud's ears; the dog's tail wagged a message of pleasure.

Simon fussed over the dead fire for a few minutes and brought it back to life. If he could gauge by the fringe of ice nature had applied along the creek side, the temperature had dropped to about twenty-five degrees. After filling his coffee pan, Simon sat cross-legged by the fire, and waited for the water to boil.

With a flare, the sun cracked a peek over the far mountain, and Simon watched in wonder as it slipped free of the horizon and beamed in triumph on its reclaimed realm. He closed his eyes, and held his face up to the sun. A subtle but unmistakable change flashed through his body. His chest felt full, his skin charged with sensitivity. A diaphanous veil filled his vision. It radiated white light, tinged with gold, undulating like a wheat field in a breeze.

His parents' faces appeared in the shimmering mist, side by side, silent, but approving. A barely perceptible humming sound moved around in his head. Then, in quick succession, images flashed through his mind: his brother Abel, Miss Everett, Sheriff Staker, and all the good people he had known. Each scene brought with it the faint smell of rain-dampened earth, and each one left his heart lighter. Sarah! A fleeting glimpse, the wisp of a smile, and then gone again.

The warmth of the sun matched the heat of his emotions as he felt a purging of his heart, the blackness changing to brilliant light. At last, he felt complete again, and tears welled up to overflowing. At that instant, Simon understood what the old Indian had tried to tell him. His spirit, alive and waiting, had simply needed to be fed. He drank fully of the glorious power that flowed from the radiance around him. His cheeks now wet, Simon leaned forward, bowed his head in submission, and wept without shame.

The experience unsettled him, but not in a negative sense, and the tears he shed were those of relief and release. After a while, Spud, whining his concern, poked his muzzle under Simon's arm, and forced him to raise his head. The sun, now higher, had cleared all signs of frost from the meadow, and he and the dog had breakfast. Basking in the warmth of the sun, he spent the rest of the morning reading.

During the summer, he had received a book of poetry by a

man named Wordsworth. It was from Carlisle, but there had been no indication of who'd sent it. Simon absorbed *The Prelude* and was astonished by the poem's appropriateness. After reading it four times, he lay down on his blankets, now hot from the sun, and slept the sleep of the sated.

Simon explored the fringes of the meadow in the afternoon and saw fresh elk and deer sign. He located his horse, settled in on the far side of the meadow. He checked the hobbles. A leisurely meal, eaten as the sun had set, finished the day, and darkness had again turned the trees black against the sky. The fire burned low, and the Milky Way stretched its band of cosmic confusion across the heavens, and the stars drew near as he looked, settling, to hover just out of reach.

He put another piece of pine on the shimmering embers, and yellow tongues of fire licked hungrily at the feast of dry wood. Staring vacantly, images, real and surreal, formed and transformed while he watched, mesmerized. Peace and tranquility surrounded him as he sat with the dog, until, feeling sleepy, he banked the fire, took off his boots and lay down.

"The calm existence that is mine when I am worthy of myself." The seeds that were the poet's words, rode the wafting currents of twilight sleep, swept back and forth across the fields of Simon's subconscious, searching for a suitable place to land and take root. Sleep took him.

An unearthly sound, a nerve-shattering scream, jerked Simon awake. Eyes wide open before his brain was ready, the blackness he faced struck him rigid with fear for an instant. Then, Spud stood, and a low rumble warned of a dog ready to fight. The keening screech came again, and this time he knew what it was, a night-hunting owl.

"It's okay, Spud," he murmured, relief slowing his heart. "Just a screech owl looking for something to eat."

The dog circled in his nest a few times, grumbled once, and

lay down. The owl tested the nerves of the ground dwellers again, and a few seconds later, Simon caught a glimpse of the bird's dark shape against the stars as it descended on silent wings. A high-pitched squeal ended abruptly as an unwary rodent died. Silence reigned once more, and he drifted back to sleep.

After breakfast the next morning, he was of two minds. It felt wonderful to face a day with nothing more important to do than gather enough wood for the campfire. But, he knew there were things at home that needed doing, changes that had to be made, and he was eager to get back. As he cleaned his coffee pan in the tiny stream, he scanned the secluded meadow for the hundredth time, basking in the quiet.

"We can always come back, can't we, Spud?" he said, his decision made.

The dog raised his eyebrows in acknowledgment, and sleepily dozed off again. Simon smiled and stood. It only took a few minutes to pack his saddlebags, and he soon had the horse standing by the dead fire ring.

They slowly picked their way along the game trails as they descended into the valley. With the sun cut off by the big trees, the air remained chilly, and Simon was ready to get out of the shade. Spud had disappeared again, searching dark, secluded places, catching scents he'd never smelled. Soon, more and more low bushes and aspen trees appeared, and Simon knew they were nearing the edge of the dense forest. Still, the transition from dark to light occurred abruptly.

The horse snorted his pleasure as they stepped into the sun, some two hundred yards from the creek bed below. Simon looked upstream, and saw the narrow defile that had prompted his climb two days before. He looked around for the dog and couldn't spot him, then urged the horse toward the creek.

On nearly level ground again, he turned downstream. Ahead loomed the first of several outcrops of rock that partially blocked their way. Simon carefully maneuvered the horse over the rock-strewn ground. The head-high wall of mountain granite on his right made him nervous. As they approached a wider section of the trail, he caught a glimpse of something moving.

"Spud?" He glanced uphill, and then toward the creek. Nothing.

Simon halted his horse, and looked up at the horse-sized boulders on the hillside. Nothing moved, but the feeling of a presence was strong, and the back of his head tingled with fear of the unseen. He tugged the rifle loose in the scabbard, and reset it, the feel of the cold steel reassuring. As he straightened in the saddle, his horse snorted, and a tremor coursed through the animal. He cast about for the cause of the horse's agitation. The sight of a mountain lion, crouched in the trail fifty feet ahead, snatched his breath away. The yellow eyes, unblinking and steady, were fixed on Simon's own, and the tip of the incredibly long tail twitched back and forth like a metronome.

He rapidly sorted through his options: turn and run, charge straight at the cat, or shoot it. He didn't want to expose his back, and a charge might be met with a countercharge. Simon reached behind his leg to grasp the stock of the Winchester, thankful he had eased it loose only moments before. The long barrel slid clear of the scabbard, and Simon swung the rifle to his shoulder. He pressured the horse with his left knee as he levered a round into the chamber.

The horse wouldn't turn toward the rock wall, and snorted anxiously. Simon realized that the twitch of the cat's tail had stopped, and the belly of the animal lifted off the ground with a fearful ripple of bunched muscle. Panic rode hard over his common sense, and standing up in his stirrups, he aimed over the horse's head, struggling to center the front blade on the cat.

He took a heavy blow on his right shoulder a fraction of a second after the sights settled and the trigger released the hammer. The Winchester recoiled with the crash of the shot, and the horse reared back as the concussion slapped the top of its head. Simon, the Winchester still in hand, was bowled off the horse by the weight of a second mountain lion.

He landed flat on his back in the willows, his mind gathering information frantically, trying to work out what was happening. The second cat splashed into the creek, and the first cat let loose an ungodly howl as the heavy bullet poured fire into its lungs. The sound of his horse bolting up the trail was nearly lost on him.

Simon scrambled to get up, and had barely reached his knees when the second cat turned to catch sight of him. The deadly concentration in the golden eyes matched the ferocity of the hissing cough as it bared yellow-brown teeth. Simon could not get the rifle unsnarled from the willows, and could only watch as the cat dug its claws into the bank, and lunged at him.

Spud sank his teeth into the cat's cheek as he flashed by. Ninety pounds of enraged canine twisted in the air as his clamped jaws ripped the cat's upper lip back. The dog tumbled into the willows. Growling ferociously, he scrambled to his feet, seized the cat's tail and furiously twisted his head back and forth. Tawny hair flew in every direction as the lion defensively blew its fur, and with a screaming snarl, jerked loose of the dog's grip. In two twenty-foot leaps, it disappeared over the outcrop.

Spud rolled the fist-sized patch of hair and skin out of his mouth, and shook his head. Breathing heavily, he looked at Simon for a moment, and then in the direction the lion had gone. He growled nervously, walked over to Simon, and sat down, shivering. Man and dog sat silently, touching each other for reassurance.

The horse had not run very far, and its limited brain was concentrated on the lush grass by the creek, the smell of the cat long gone, and therefore no longer a threat. Simon mounted, and after some coaxing, rode the horse past the dead feline, and out into the widening valley. Several hours later, Simon smiled in anticipation at the familiar sight of Tay's dugout, and the blue-gray tendril of wood smoke winding into the sky.

Tay stepped out of the dwelling as Simon whipped his reins around the hitching post.

"Thought it might be you. Sit yerself down there and I'll be right out." He ducked back into the dugout.

Simon sat on the log bench by the door, and leaned against the warm wood. He could hear Tay fussing around inside, and a couple of minutes later he came out.

"So, heard ya took a little trip." He handed a tin cup to Simon and sat down.

"Spent the strangest two days I've ever lived," Simon said. "I saw things I'm not sure were real."

"Walks Fast said ya would. I cain't get too worked up 'bout that stuff, but I know what ya mean." He grunted as he settled back against the wall. "It's the bein' alone, the emptiness of the place thet gits ya. Ain't nothin' to in'erfere with yer thoughts. I love it."

"Then you do know what I saw?"

"Didn't say I didn't. I jist don't set no store in the spir't'chul part."

"I was raised kinda religious. Pa always read to us from the Bible on Sunday evenings, and I heard Ma and Pa pray when things weren't goin' right. I listened, but I never did seem to get the same feeling they had. I felt kinda guilty about it then."

"Like ya shoulda felt like they did?"

"Yeah. Sometimes, I could see their faces light up when they were done prayin'. Like they had seen something I hadn't. Up there in the mountains, I think I saw a little of what they did."

"See, thet's the spir't'chul part I'm talkin' 'bout. I know exactly what yer sayin, but yer puttin' into it what ya want. Yer lookin' fer somethin'. Be damn careful t' remember what the question was when ya think see the answer." The old man's eyes glinted in the afternoon sun and Simon couldn't tell if it was a smile of mischief or satisfaction.

Simon nodded his head, and gazed across the meadow toward the creek. The distinct smell of autumn permeated the air, and made the coffee taste that much better. The two men were silent for several minutes. Then Simon put his cup down on the bench. "Do you think that maybe we lose track of where we were going when we stop moving?" He continued to gaze across the valley.

"I git the sense yer gonna ask me something I can't answer."

"I left home 'cause I was disappointed. Nothing turned out like I'd expected it to. And since I've been here, things have gone real good. I mean, I've got money and a good job. I like the people here, and you and Walks Fast have been like my folks."

"But?"

"Yeah, but." Simon shook his head sadly. "But, somehow I think I'm missin' something."

"I want ya to think about this, Simon, and I kin talk cuz I been exactly where you are now. I ain't been this old all my life, ya know." Tay turned sideways on the bench and looked Simon full in the face, a half smile flitting across his lined features. Then, his expression turned serious. "When the things thet matter the most to ya are pushed aside by things that should matter the least, it's time t' change where yer beddin' down the mule."

Simon started to speak, and Tay put up his hand. "Think on that, boy. Don't worry on it, jist think. Now git outta here. All this philosophizin' makes my head ache." He softened the order with a warm smile.

"Okay. Thanks for the coffee, Tay . . . and the talk. Maybe I'll see ya Sunday for breakfast."

"Maybe so."

Just before he rounded the first bluff, Simon turned to see Tay, still sitting in the sun in front of his dugout. He wished he felt the peace that the image offered.

It was nearly a week before Simon could find the time to go see Walks Fast. The day turned out blustery and cool. Smoke made tentative dashes for freedom past the wind flap in the tepee top, only to be snatched and torn apart by the vigilant wind. Simon had not stopped completely when Walks Fast stepped out and held the flap back.

"Come in out of the wind." The welcome in the Indian's face gave Simon a warm rush.

He climbed off his horse, and looped the reins around a pole driven in the ground by the entrance. Holding his hat on his head with one hand, he stooped, and entered the warm, earthy-smelling interior. He could see no one else. His nostrils flared as he breathed the unusual smell. Boiled meat, wood smoke, body sweat and tanned hides blended to produce a sense of being, he thought, almost primeval. It felt both alien, but at the same time, on some more primitive level, familiar.

"Sit. The women are gone." Walks Fast took a seat by the low fire, and waited for Simon to speak.

"I went to the mountains as you suggested," Simon said.

"And now you want to tell Walks Fast what you saw?"

"Yeah, I talked to Tay about it a little, but he wasn't very empathetic." Simon watched the Indian's face to see if the fancy word had registered.

"It is because he does not want to say what he knows is true.

Some men deny what they see because it is hard to tell others. Words come out wrong and make a man look foolish. Tay is empathetic, but he is wise man too."

The smile on Walks Fast's face told Simon he had just been caught looking. A bit chagrined, he fussed with the robe under him, then realized what he was doing and folded his hands in his lap. "I saw my folks, just as clear as though they were there. And several other people. I thought my chest was going to blow up, it felt so full."

Walks Fast's face softened. "That is a good thing. Their spirits were with you, and they will know in their dreams that they were there. Their hearts feel full too, and they wonder why."

"What was I supposed to learn? You said I would learn up there."

"I said the spirits would show you the truth. Spirits can only open your eyes. You see what you know."

Simon sat quiet, not really understanding what the old man was saying, but not wanting to ask. I see what I know? Then, he said, "I had to kill a catamount."

"I know. Bad spirits will make your path a hard one. The mountain cat did not want you to come back here. Bad spirits were in the cat."

"There were two of them."

The old man reacted as though he had been hit from behind. His eyes went wide, and he mumbled something unintelligible. Walks Fast shut his eyes and took several long, slow breaths. "I must rest now." He looked at Simon. "I must think. I'll see you soon." And he shut his eyes again.

Simon stood, looked at the stoic face, and left the tepee, very confused, and a little scared.

Chapter 18

Weeks later, the stinging bite of the driven snow banished every thought from his head but one—get out of the weather. Simon pushed down on the top of his hat, and hunched his shoulders against the cold. "Gawdamn wind," he muttered as Spud hunkered down by the saloon door, anxiously waiting for Simon to cross from the house. He stomped his feet on the porch, and then pushed open the door. "All right there," he said as the dog rushed past, and headed for the horse blanket by the stove. He hurriedly shut the door, then took off his hat and slapped it against his leg.

"How long is this going to last?" Lori asked rhetorically. She sat at their table, hands wrapped around a porcelain cup.

"I'm beginning to think we're doomed to never see another person." Simon walked to the stove, and turned his back to it. The wind drew air up the chimney and fanned the fire inside the stove, producing a fierce heat. He turned and reached for the poker leaning against the stack of wood.

"I just filled it," Lori said. "Come and sit down. I'll get you a cup of coffee."

Simon shrugged out of his coat and walked to the hooks by his office to hang it up. He had just sat down when Lori returned, and put the coffee in front of him.

"I hate the wind," she said as she reclaimed her seat and fidgeted with a spoon.

"Me too." He picked up his cup and looked at her. "Don't

worry. He's safe in a camp."

"It's that obvious, is it?"

"Yep."

"Well, I can't help it. I've never seen it last this long."

"When I was a boy, we had a storm like this, and it covered our house. We were stuck in there for days. Pa had to dig a tunnel to get to the chickens. Froze most of 'em. I'll never forget that."

"But this is so late. Good grief, it's February."

"Could be worse. We've got enough wood and plenty of food. Zahn will be the same."

"Where's Buell?"

"Sleepin'. That's his solution, sleep through it. You'd think he was part bear."

"Same with Amos and Twiggs. Haven't heard a sound."

Simon leaned back in his chair and studied her for a moment. "Do you ever have second thoughts about working here?"

Her lips pursed, and her jaw worked slowly back and forth as she pondered the question. "You mean because of the . . . what do we call it . . . sinful nature of the place? Are we part of it?"

"I guess that's what I mean. And I don't mean you're . . . well, you know, I—"

"We've talked about this before, Simon. We all have to do what we think best. I've never told anyone here, but I'm a divorced woman."

Simon's jaw dropped and he blinked rapidly as he faced her. "You're what?"

"You heard me. Zahn is my second husband. It's why we left home. We had to."

"I . . . uh—"

"Can't help but change the way you look at me, can it?"

"No! It's not . . . I mean, I don't care—"

"But it does, Simon, and you do care. And that's my point.

Since you had your experience out there in the wilds, you've been bothered about being here. We are the same people as we were before you went up there."

"I know that. And I've thought a lot about what happened. I went to see Walks Fast, and something I said upset him. I've been back twice since then, but he's gone. When I ask where, his wife just says, 'Mountain.' A person can't live up there this time of the year. Anyway, it's becoming less and less clear what that trip of mine meant."

"Sometimes, Simon, where we are is what we are. We adapt to our circumstances. Do we become sinners if we live with the sinful? I suppose we do, a little. And how much can we change before we are no longer ourselves? I don't know. That old Indian has experienced a lot. Maybe something you said reminded him of his younger days. I'm sure you'll figure it out."

"You could, Lori, but that's my problem: I'm not. I sometimes wake up at night wondering if I'm lost. And then, two or three brandies with some friends the next evening, and I feel fine. Is that normal?"

"I think so. But you give me too much credit. I'm only thirty years old, Simon. Seems more like a hundred and thirty sometimes, but in those years I've learned we don't always have the luxury of satisfaction. Sometimes we just have to make do."

"Sounds like I've missed the best part," Amos said from halfway down the stairs.

"No, just waitin' for the wind to change," Lori said. She winked at Simon. "Come and sit down, Amos. I'll get your coffee."

The February blizzard was as bad as anyone could remember. It snowed and blowed for almost two weeks, then cleared out and got almost warm. Folks spent March waiting for mud holes to dry out, and getting wagons unstuck from those that hadn't.

By April, the first signs of spring were welcomed universally by both man and critter. May brought the first influx of hunters, treasure seekers, and all the other people, out to experience something different in their boring lives. They descended on McCaffrey's ranch, drawn like bears to a honey tree.

Zahn was sitting at the appointed breakfast table when Simon and Buell came in. They hadn't even sat down before Lori brought their coffee. She stood close to Zahn as she poured two cups. He wrapped his arm around her hips and pulled her close, tucking his head into her side. "Sure missed ya, hon," he said.

"We can tell," Buell said with a grin.

"I would have been here a month earlier, but they needed me to see the ties downriver. I've never done that before, so it was interesting."

"Ya mean they float those things to where they need 'em?" Buell asked.

"Yep. I stacked thousands of ties above the river. When the ice was gone, we knocked the supports loose and the whole mess went flyin' down the hillside. Hell of a sight."

"Did ya go with the ties?"

"No. I understand they catch 'em downstream at wide spots in the river, then carry 'em on wagons to the yard by the rail line. I coulda done some of the haulin', but I wanted to come home."

"Home?" Lori looked at her husband's face. "First time I've heard you call this place home."

"It's where you are. That makes it home."

"So what are you going to do now?" Simon asked.

"I've been offered a job at the sawmill. They're putting in a steam engine and another saw. I made good money at the tie camp, but that's a miserable place. Wet and cold for five months, and the cook was not a Lori."

"That's good news, Zahn," Simon said. "I've been thinkin' about maybe showing Lori more about the business end of this place. Amos thinks it would be a good idea too. What do you two think?"

"Ya know, I thought about a lot of things up there. When we came here, it was just a stop on the way west. And we were looking for a place to maybe settle. I'm a sawyer and I've been offered a sawyer's job. Does it matter if it's here or in Oregon?" Zahn looked up at his wife and Simon saw a flicker of relief cross her face. "Lori and I haven't talked about this specifically, but I think generally, she agrees."

"I sure do," she said. "I love this job, and the girls I work with. I'll go wherever Zahn does, but I'd like to stay here."

"Good. We'll talk a little later about what I have in mind. Now, what's for breakfast?"

Lori gave her husband a touch on the cheek and went to the kitchen.

"Amos said we have a huntin' party comin' in next week. Germans," Buell said.

"Yeah, they've been here before," muttered Simon. "Leastwise, the one that wrote Amos has been." He couldn't hide his distaste.

"Looks like you aren't looking forward to their visit," Zahn said.

"Got a hard spot where Germans are concerned. I know it's not rational to condemn the lot because of one bad experience, but there's something about their air of superiority that grates on my nerves. And Count Rindfleisch is as superior as they come."

"I like the way they gamble," Buell said. "Get one to thinkin' ya got him outsmarted, and he'll lose a lot of money provin' ya wrong."

"Well, there is that." Simon smiled. "But still, I'd just as soon entertain a . . . I don't know, anything but a German count."

Thursday, on schedule, and replete with an arsenal that would have supplied a well-equipped army platoon, the Germans, far more than the three expected, descended on McCaffrey's. They took every available room. Eager to show his guests the experience he'd boasted about for a year, the count led his party off into the hills early the next morning. The first excursion was to be an overnight affair, so the saloon stayed relatively quiet Friday night with only the regular customers to attend to. That peaceful scene changed radically Saturday afternoon as the hunters returned, tired, hungry, and disappointed. They had not seen one animal that they considered worthy of shooting.

With everyone demanding baths, the kitchen staff was dragooned, along with Lori, to help the two upstairs women. A hectic couple of hours were spent attending to the overbearing group. About six thirty, the count came downstairs, followed shortly by the rest. They filled one entire dining room.

Half an hour later Lori stepped into Simon's office and stood, hands on hips, a disgusted look on her face. "If this isn't going to be a repeat of last year, Simon, I want you to go in there right now, and tell them this is not Berlin or New York City, and we do not have fine crystal and porcelain, and our wine list is very limited." The tenor of her voice had risen with every word.

"What now?" He knew what, but was anxious to delay the inevitable.

"I agreed to stay late and help because you asked me to. I did not agree to be insulted and groped."

"Groped? Who?" Simon stood and came around his desk.

"Not groped, just brushed—accidentally. You know what I mean."

"All right." Simon sighed. "I heard them come down.

Sounded like a herd of buffalo. I'll go talk to them." He left the office and headed for the dining room.

Buell caught his eye as he walked past and grinned. "Temper, temper."

Already the noise was as bad as a bunch of drunken skinners, the hard-edged sound of spoken German shouted across the small room. At the doorway, Simon looked around until he saw the count. He had his back to Simon, his boots planted on the seat of one of the upholstered chairs. Simon's pulse increased as he strode across the room and around the table to face the man.

"Good evening, Herr Rindfleisch," Simon said as he pointedly looked as the German's shiny boots.

"Ah, the landlord," the German replied in perfect English. He looked at his feet as well, and then back to Simon's face.

Simon's his jaw muscles tightened. "As most of your friends are new to us, I'd like you to tell them what kind of service they can expect." He paused and forced a smile. "And equally important, what they may not expect."

"You may go on," the count said, but before Simon could continue, said something in German to the noisy crowd. The whole room burst into laughter.

Simon felt the color rise in his face. "Our wine selection is limited, and exotic foods are simply not available. No *pâté de foie gras* or *fromage Camembert.*"

The count's nostrils flared as he took his feet off the chair and stood. "Ah, yes, I forgot. The educated one." His five-foot-six height forced him to look up to meet Simon's eyes. "That we would have any interest in fancy French cheese or liver *pâté* is doubtful, and I take their mention as an insult."

The room had quieted when he stood, and the tone of his voice had silenced the group. Simon could see the anger build in the little German's body, but could not suppress the twitch in his eyebrows that he knew confirmed the German's accusation. "Those were two that came to mind," he said as politely as he could. "There was nothing intentional."

"Nor was there when my friends asked for something as simple as a good German wine."

"We, on occasion, have German wine. But this early in the hunting season, we are out of wine, and not just German wine."

"You Americans. Rustics. No wonder you fight amongst yourselves."

Simon felt the color rise in his face. "Please explain to your friends, Mister Rindfleisch, that we will do what we can to make their stay here as pleasant as possible. And remind them that the ladies who serve their meals are exactly that, ladies. I trust you understand my meaning."

Simon abruptly stepped around the little man, and was almost through the doorway when the count said something, again in German, and the room burst into laughter. Heat climbed the back of Simon's neck as stalked across the salon toward his office.

"Whoa, what'n hell went on out there?" Buell asked as Simon rushed past.

"Arrogant bastard. I damn near punched him in the mouth." Simon came back to Buell's station. "They were giving Lori and the girls a hard time about what we had available to drink. And sounds like someone a*ccidentally* touched Lori."

"And you let 'em get away with it?"

"They're what makes this place pay. I told them Lori and the other servers are out of bounds. It's my business to be civil."

"Yeah, but ya gotta be a man too."

"They'll be gone in a week. I can live with it." Simon puffed his cheeks and sighed. "They'll be your problem in an hour or so—after they're done eating. Don't get a hot head."

"They'll get the same treatment as everybody else. They know the rules." Buell settled back in his tall chair. "And they know I'll enforce 'em."

Two hours later, the German visitors came out of the dining room, and into the saloon. The first nice week of spring had just passed, so the saloon was full of people: soldiers, civilians from around the fort, and the usual number of itinerant travelers. They all wanted a good time, and all vied for the same attention. Twiggs and his two helpers set glass after glass on the bar as the customers consumed amazing quantities of whiskey, brandy, and beer.

Four card games going on simultaneously made open tables scarce. The Germans spotted one with only two men sitting at it, and some of them headed for it. Simon saw Buell track them like a cat watching a mouse. Five Germans arrived at the table, and the count said something to the two men. One of them nodded his head, and the Germans located two more chairs at other tables and the five sat down. The four remaining Germans headed for the bar. Simon breathed a long sigh of relief, and caught Buell's eye.

"I'll be in here," he mouthed and pointed at his office door. Buell nodded, and went back to his surveillance.

Lori was beat. She usually made breakfast for anyone who wanted it, and then relaxed until early afternoon. From about two thirty to six, she prepared for the evening meal, and after seeing the service well-finished, put up her apron about nine thirty. It made for a long day, but she enjoyed what she did, and found meeting all the new people exhilarating.

Today had been different. Simon asked her to serve the German hunters, which took her out of her kitchen domain. She'd made innumerable trips from there and the bar, to the dining room. Her feet and arms ached and she needed some fresh air. She stepped out of the heat of the kitchen, and into the saloon.

Walking behind the bar, she stopped at the first beer pump.

"I need a beer, Max."

"Sure." He grabbed a glass and filled it slowly with the straw-colored brew. "There ya go."

"Thanks." She shuffled back into the kitchen, across the room, and out the back door.

The cool night air embraced her, and she turned left toward the wood stack on the eastern end of the building. She found a section of log standing on end and up against the stack. With a sigh of relief she sat, her back against the rough wood. After taking a sip of her beer, she looked around in the dim light for a place to set the glass down. Finding it, she leaned her head back and looked into the night.

A soft glow from the rising moon turned the scruffy cottonwoods by the river into near perfect specimens, the dead branches and bare spots hidden in the uncertain light. She located the Big Dipper, dumping its magical contents into the spring sky. Following the alignment of the end stars in the cup, she repeated the perceived distance between them until she located Polaris. She remembered when Zahn had first shown her how to do that. They had been completely alone on the endless prairie, and the memory of what had happened later in the vast privacy of the plains made her giggle softly.

The back door opened, and a shadowy figure weaved his way to the outhouse. A few minutes later he returned, the kitchen door banged shut, and once more, the privacy of the evening belonged to her. She missed Zahn, gone again into the mountains, this time to find a good stand of timber for the mill. As her body relaxed, she leaned her shoulders against the top of the woodpile and closed her eyes.

The arm that passed around her neck and encircled her throat scared her so badly, she stopped breathing. Before she could gather enough air to scream, a hand clapped across her mouth.

Fingers dug into her flesh on either side of her jaw. The man jerked her to her feet, and shoved her away from the hotel. They headed toward the brush by the river, his arm still tight around her neck, moving six or seven paces before Lori could react. She reached behind her head and her fingers found skin. She dug in with all her strength and scratched.

A barely audible grunt came from the man, and his grip loosened slightly. She ducked forward and turned around at the same time, freeing herself from his grasp. His fist shot out and struck her in the breast. The flash of pain blinded her for a moment, and she let go a high, ear-splitting scream. Another blow cut it off a mere second after it started, and her legs began to fail her. Fighting to remain conscious, Lori slumped to her knees, both hands on the ground for support. The man grabbed her by the hair, and tried to pull her to her feet. She resisted and her scalp began to tear. With what she knew would be her last effort, she turned her head and sank her teeth into the man's thigh. She bit so hard her head shook.

"Gott!" the man cried, and Lori gasped as he slammed several blows into her back. One punch looped around and caught her in the side and she cried out. As searing pain shot through her ribs; she nearly let go.

And then she heard Buell. "You son of a bitch!"

Dimly, Lori heard a sodden blow and a man crying out in pain. Her hair came free and the earth tipped sideways under her body. She slipped off the edge to slowly drift down into complete darkness.

Simon had been sitting in his office, staring into space when Spud stood, the hair on his shoulders bristling. Then, with a low growl, the dog lunged through the door. Simon got out of his chair just in time to see Buell rush past, and a second later the back door crashed open. He nearly fell over his desk getting around it, then ran out of his office, through the kitchen and into the night.

A man shouted, and he turned in the direction of the voice. Dimly, he could see two men, one with a rifle. The glint of moonlight on steel winked once, and Simon heard Buell swear. Then came the sound of a body being struck—hard. He rushed toward the two and found Buell, the Sharps carbine in both hands, flailing away at a prone figure whose foot was being savaged by the dog. Screams of pain came from the man, blended with snarls of rage from the animal and unintelligible swearing from Buell.

And then Simon saw Lori, lying still and flat on her back. His frantic mind was torn between stopping the assault on the man, and getting to her. "Buell, stop it. You're killin' him." The heavy rifle rose and fell again, this time bringing the sharp crack of a breaking bone. Another unearthly scream came from the man on the ground, and then he fell silent. Buell raised the weapon again, and Simon grabbed it. "Stop!" He held fast to the barrel as Buell tried to wrest it free. "Quit, Buell. He's not moving. Spud! Spud! Let go. Come here!"

Buell stopped pulling at the carbine. "Okay, I'm done. The son of a bitch."

Simon let go and knelt beside Lori. He put his fingers to the side of her neck.

"She all right?" Buell asked.

"What the hell happened?" Twiggs said, as he rushed toward them carrying a lantern. Several other people followed him from the saloon.

"Who's that?" Twiggs stepped over to the man, facedown on the ground. He stooped to look at his face. "It's that German count, what's his name, Rheingold?"

"Rindfleisch?" Buell asked.

"Vas iss?" a man in the crowd said, and pushed his way through. A torrent of German spilled as he shouted back toward

the crowd, and three more men came forward. They picked up the unconscious count and hurried into the saloon.

"Lori, can you hear me?" Simon said.

She muttered something, and then reached out and grabbed his arm.

"Lori?" He took her hand and she squeezed his. "You hear me?"

"Yes. Yes, I'm okay. Help me up."

Buell moved to her other side, and together they tried to sit her up.

"Oh! It hurts something awful on my right side. Be careful."

They eased her back to the ground.

She reached her left hand around, and felt her side. "It's a rib." She winced again.

"You've cut your head," Simon said as he ran his thumb over his fingertips. "That's blood." He held out his hand to Buell and Twiggs moved the light to it.

She put her hand to her head and felt about until she winced. "On top. Not much. Help me stand up."

Both men held out their arms, she got her legs under her and stood, groaning. "That feels better. Let's get inside."

Twiggs cleared a path through the crowd, and they all went into the saloon. Inside, a deafening din met them as details, real and imagined, circulated through an angry crowd. The sound of German being shouted reverberated from upstairs. They made their way to the stairwell.

"Get the hell outta the way," Buell demanded. The crowd on the stairs scrambled to stay clear of the thrusting barrel of his rifle. They helped Lori into her apartment where May took control. She had them seat Lori in a straight-back chair, and then herded the two men out into the hall. Simon felt the cold stares from the contingent of Germans crowding around the door at the end of the hall. He and Buell went downstairs and headed for Simon's office.

"She gonna be okay?" Twiggs asked. He stood at the end of the bar, concern furrowing his brow.

"May has her. She has some hurt ribs and she lost some hair on top of her head. I think she'll be all right."

"We gonna let that bastard stay here?"

"Soon's they get their stuff together, they're leavin'." Buell looked at Simon. "Right?"

"If not sooner," Simon said, his voice tight with anger. "He can't be here when Zahn gets back."

They walked into the office, and shut the door. Spud sat between the two chairs opposite Simon's desk. His thick body trembled as he looked at the closed door, and a low rumble came from his chest.

"Ya did a good job, Spud," Buell said as he stroked the dog's head.

"Is that how you knew Lori was in trouble?"

"Yeah. I saw her go out carryin' a beer. Figgered she was just gonna have a breather. And then I saw Spud come tearin' outta here like he'd been shot at. I knew it must be somethin' wrong with Lori. She must've hollered and ol' Spud heard her."

Simon sank into his chair. "We got a mess. That bunch upstairs ain't takin' this lightly."

"I don't give a damn if they do or not. Ain't no doubt the army will stick their nose in, but there's forty witnesses who can tell them what happened. Piss on 'em."

"I'm getting tired of this, Buell. Ya know that?" Simon leaned back in his chair and shut his eyes. The picture of the high mountain meadow flooded in for a moment, only to be replaced by the image of Buell whaling away at the German, and Lori lying unconscious on the ground. He wanted desperately to just go to sleep and wake in the morning with all his trouble taken care of.

★ ★ ★ ★ ★

Amos, Simon and Buell sat across from the scowling provost marshal, who sat behind a desk reading a paper. Finished, he looked up. "I once said you were dangerous, Mister Mace. I can now add sadistic to that," Captain Van Dyke said. He glared at Buell, his distaste obvious. "And on top of that, you have created an incident with a foreign government. Do you have anything to say?"

"Nope." Buell glared back.

"I thought the fiasco with the English dogs was messy. This will prove to be a hundred times that. And the fact that it happened outside your saloon, as you are quick to point out, Mister McCaffrey, does not exonerate you. That man was a guest at your establishment. And you, Mister Steele, as manager, are also culpable."

The three men sat silent.

"Well, is anyone going to say anything?"

"Like what, Captain?" Amos said. "We're sorry? Didn't mean to interrupt his rape of Missus Tapola?" He leaned across the desk, his face getting red. "Whatcha want me to say? If we was another hundred miles away, his stinkin' carcass would be swingin' from a cottonwood right now. He's gawdamn lucky Zahn ain't back yet."

"Might be a good idea to get that sumbitch outta here before he is," Buell said.

"Meaning what? Are you threatening him again?" The captain looked directly at Buell.

"Not me ya have to worry about. I give 'im best I could and didn't kill him. Zahn might be another story."

"What do you mean, best you could?"

"Just that. I couldn't see well enough to get past his arms, and the dog kept jerkin' him around."

Van Dyke half rose from his chair. "You were deliberately trying to kill him?"

"Buell!" Simon turned to confront him. "Better not say any more. Ya hear me?"

"I asked him a direct question, Mister Steele. I'll thank you not to interrupt. Go on, Mister Mace."

Buell looked at Simon, then Amos, and Amos shook his head. "I've said what happened," Buell continued. "It's in that paper you have in your hands. All of it."

"How do you know what's in this?" He waved the two sheets.

"We know you've tried to paint Missus Tapola in a less-than-favorable light," Simon said. "We also know T. P. Triffet and your commander have told you different. We also know that unless you can find premeditation on somebody's part, you have to cope with the 'mess,' as you call it."

Rage boiled up in the captain's face, the veins in his forehead pulsing. "You nearly beat a man to death, Mister Mace. You could have just as easily restrained him and brought him here for justice."

"Didn't see that as a choice," Buell said. "The bastard was abusin' a lady and my friend. The fact that you're willin' to defend him puts you down there with 'im." Buell's tone was low and steady, his eyes fixed on the enraged officer.

"Are you threatening me?" Van Dyke shouted.

"Seems you think so."

The door burst open and a sergeant came in, his pistol at the ready.

"Get out!" Van Dyke screamed at him. The sergeant blinked once, and scrambled out.

"And you get out . . . all of you." He was standing now, spittle in the corners of his mouth. "You're rabble of the lowest order. You give the United States a black name. Get out!"

The three men rose from their chairs and started toward the door.

"If I had my way, those places you and Evans run would be burned to the ground."

Amos jerked to a halt and turned around. "And if you had your way, the German bastard would have gotten away clean. So much fer yer army justice, Captain."

They walked out, leaving the captain red-faced and trembling.

Zahn pushed the door shut with exaggerated care and stepped to Simon's desk. Simon knew he had just visited Lori upstairs, and he hadn't been looking forward to seeing him. "I'm sorry, Zahn. Really sorry. How is she?"

"I don't know what to do to you, Simon." Zahn's hands clenched and unclenched.

"And I don't know what to tell you, Zahn. I feel responsible for—"

"You are responsible! Let's get that straight right now. I *hold* you responsible." His eyes blinked rapidly and his hands shook.

"And I accept that. I had no idea she was outside."

"When I came here, I thought you were one of the most honest fellas I had ever met. And decent. I felt perfectly safe leaving my wife alone with you in this place."

"I appreciate that. I thought we were taking care of her."

"By making her work sixteen hours, and serving a bunch of foreigners who you knew she didn't like? Who you knew were making things difficult for her. That's taking care of her?"

Simon could not meet his friend's eyes. He watched the rapid rise and fall of Zahn's chest as he struggled.

"If I had my way, she wouldn't be upstairs now," Zahn continued. "But you know as well as I do, she's as stubborn as they come, and she takes the blame for this."

"She shouldn't and—"

"I know that! You put makin' an extra dollar ahead of her, Simon, and I ain't never gonna forgive ya for that." Zahn walked to the door, and jerked it open, then turned around. "And she still trusts you, Simon, damn your soul."

Simon sat in stunned silence, looking at the empty doorway, as Zahn's words burned into his conscience.

Chapter 19

Simon was standing at the bar talking to Twiggs when the screen door banged shut. He glanced up at the back-bar mirror and recognized the man wearing a long, light-colored duster and a brown hat. Quinn. Simon turned around.

"Hello, Mister Steele. Mister Twiggs." Quinn sauntered across the floor toward them.

"Mister Quinn," Simon said. "I apologize, but I don't remember your first name."

"Farrel. As in wild, only spelled with an 'a.' " He stuck out his hand.

"Good to see you again." Simon hoped the lie wasn't too obvious. "Come to visit, or on your way?" He recoiled mentally at the gambler's feminine handshake.

"Thought I'd stay a week or so, and see if I could take some more of your money." He chuckled, then looked at Twiggs. "How're ya doing, Max?"

"Fine. Well into the summer now, so everybody's ready to come out and play." He shook the extended hand. "How're things back East?"

"Don't know, spent the winter in New Orleans. I like that place. Ya still got that Creole gal here?"

"Yeah, she's here, in number four."

"I see ya got those little houses finished. This is really nice." He swept his arm toward the long mirrored back bar.

"Picked it up cheap," Simon said. "I've got work to do, but

let me buy you your first drink."

"Okay. Think I'll have a beer. Still got the games going at night?"

"Yeah, there's always one or two Friday and Saturday. Depends on who's around."

A few seconds later, Twiggs set the glass of beer on the bar.

"Thanks, Max." Quinn picked it up and quaffed about a third of it. Putting it down, he winked at Twiggs. "That's good."

Simon headed for his office.

"I'll see ya later, then," Quinn said.

That evening, the saloon filled with loud and boisterous men who apparently thought the more noise they made, the more fun they'd have. The smoke, almost a living thing, hovered about seven feet off the floor. Periodically, it fled out the front door and into the night as a bladder-plagued patron went out the back. The air was warm and thick, heavy with the smell of coal oil, sweat, liquor, and bad breath. Buell felt the dull throb of an impending headache. He had intended to join Amos at the table for some cards, but, as he looked over the milling crowd, he decided he had best sit tight. He caught Twiggs's eye and brought his empty beer glass to his lips, signaling. Twiggs pointed at the pump handle and Buell nodded.

The game he'd wanted to join was going on only a few feet away, and Buell could see Amos's cards all the time and catch occasional glimpses of Saint Louis Bob's. Farrel Quinn and another gambler, whom he didn't know, were playing, as were Rosie and Kent Berggren. The play had been fairly even, with Rosie up a little at the moment. Quinn had just dealt a new hand. Rosie fanned his cards open slowly, and Amos leaned back to give Buell a clear view of three nines. Amos needlessly sorted his cards, then closed the hand and waited.

At that moment, Twiggs walked up and handed Buell his

beer. "Gawd, it's noisy tonight. You'd think these fools hadn't been out of the barn for months."

"Yeah, and smoky. I'm gettin' a real skull-splitter. Maybe this'll help." Buell took a pull on his beer.

"Need another, just holler." Twiggs started to leave.

"Do you know that new feller sittin' at Amos's table?" Buell asked.

Twiggs stopped. "Says his name's Weston. Come up from Cheyenne." His eyebrows shot up in anticipation of another question.

"Okay. Didn't recognize him. Thanks fer the beer."

Twiggs nodded and made his way back to the bar.

Buell scanned the pulsing mob, then went back to watching the card game. Weston appeared to be a young man, early twenties. Unlike everyone else at the table, he didn't wear a hat, and his friendly, open face invited trust. He caught Buell looking at him, and beamed a big smile in his direction. Buell nodded back, feeling neither friendly nor trusting. He was truly grateful there was no piano player for the instrument standing against the wall only five feet away.

Apparently, Rosie had opened because Bob threw five dollars in the pot. Amos raised him ten, and Kent folded. Weston and Quinn made eye contact for an instant, and then Weston looked at Amos. "Raise ya twenty," Weston said. The gold coins hit the table. Quinn folded his hand and looked to his left.

Rosie peeked at his cards, exposing one corner at a time as though sneaking up on the pips might change them. Then he closed the fan. "Crap." He threw down his hand and slumped back in his chair.

Bob breathed a long sigh, and slid his cards slowly toward the pot. "Fold," he said glumly.

Amos picked up two twenty-dollar gold pieces and dropped them in the pot. Then, he laid his hand down on the table and leaned back. "Cost ya twenty more."

Buell watched Weston's face closely. There wasn't a sign of apprehension or concern on his face, and he shoved two double eagles across the table and into the pot. "And twenty."

Amos picked another coin off his stack and dropped it in the middle of the table. "Four of 'em," he said with a smile and turned over his nines.

"Lookee here," Rosie said with a chuckle. He smiled across the table at Weston.

Weston, not a ripple of emotion showing, laid his hand out on the table. Four kings!

"Gawdammit!" Amos said as Weston pulled the money toward his cache.

Quinn's face started to color. "Kings are a killer," he said loudly and cleared his throat. "I'm glad it's your deal, Rosie, if I can't do any better for myself than that." He gathered the cards, squared the deck, and dropped it in front of the scowling teamster.

"Not me. I lose every time I deal." Rosie passed the deck to Bob.

"Let me buy ya a drink," Weston said with a smile. He stacked his coins neatly, then raised his hand and waved at Twiggs.

Twiggs hailed one of the women moving about the saloon. She soon stood by the table. The six players ordered their drinks and she went to the bar.

"I gotta take a leak," Amos said. He stood and headed for the back door.

Buell followed him. When they got to Simon's office door, Buell stepped inside.

"We got a card cheat, Simon. New guy that's playing at Amos's table."

"You sure? I'm sorry," he added quickly as Buell flushed. "What did ya see?"

"Amos had three pat nines and drew another. Weston, the new guy, had four kings dealt. And he knew it."

"How so?" Simon asked.

"He just did, dammit. I've been watching players for more nights than I can remember, and nobody gets dealt four kings and just sits there like nothin' happened."

"But it does happen."

Buell blew out a puff of air. "And Quinn and him were in it together. They were lookin' at each other."

"Ya can't *not* look." Simon held his hand up, palm out. "Now wait a minute, I can see your temper comin' up. What you're sayin' is that Quinn knew what Weston and Amos had."

"That's right."

"Well . . . how?"

"I don't know. Lacey said they can mark a deck. I'm going to get that one and look at it."

"What's goin' on?" Amos asked from the door.

"Buell says you just got skinned."

"Bullshit. That's just cards. I had a bettin' hand, and so did that new guy."

"You don't think he's cheating?" Simon asked.

"Hell, no. How would he know what I had? That was a new deck."

"Well, I'm gonna look at it anyway." Buell stepped back into the saloon and went over to the bar.

"Max, I want a new deck at Amos's table."

"Just did that. Bob asked for it when they got their whiskey."

"Dammit. Where's the old one?"

"Right here." Twiggs reached under the bar and handed Buell the pack.

"You sure this is the same one?"

"Yeah. The other two games are still using the same decks. Why ya asking?"

"I don't like the way that last hand went."

"Neither did Amos," Twiggs said with a chuckle.

"I mean, I think someone is cheating. I'm serious."

"Well, all right. I guess you can keep that deck and look at it if ya want. Just let Amos know you have it."

"He knows, and so does Simon."

Buell put the deck in his vest pocket and went back to his stool. The six players sat studying their cards.

"Fold," Rosie said and he slapped his cards down on the table. "You can't deal any better than me." He glowered at Bob.

Saturday night was a repeat of Friday, with Quinn and Weston again at Amos's table. The same people played with the exception of Kent Berggren, his place taken by an army trooper. Buell had studied the deck Twiggs had given him the night before for over an hour. He paid particular attention to the nines and kings but had been unable to detect anything wrong. The game had been going on for over four hours. Amos and the soldier were the winners, Amos doing the best. Then it happened again. This time the heavy betting came from the soldier, with Weston calling and raising. And, as Buell expected, Weston won over a hundred and fifty dollars with four queens against four sevens.

"That does me," the trooper said. "Thought I had ya."

"Ya bet 'em when ya see," Weston said. "It's what I like about the game."

"Do you do this for a livin'?" Rosie asked.

"Nope. I work for a cattle buyer in Cheyenne. Heard about yer place and decided to come up for a week. Glad I did." He flashed his bright smile at the soldier. "Can I buy ya a drink?"

"Sure," replied the trooper. "No hard feelings."

"I gotta go outside for a minute." Weston stood. "Come on, I'll get ya that whiskey."

"Ya gonna keep playing?" Saint Louis Bob asked, speaking up for the first time.

"Not me. I'm busted," the trooper said.

"I'll be back," Weston said as he slid his winnings into a leather bag. "I just gotta get rid of a couple beers."

They walked up to the bar, and when Weston headed out the back way, Buell got off his high chair and followed.

Outside, Buell, moving as quietly as he could, hurried to catch up with Weston. Just as they reached the privy, Buell poked his pistol between the man's shoulder blades. "Keep right on walkin'." Weston's back stiffened and he stopped. Buell applied a little pressure. "Go on down by the river."

Weston didn't move. "What do you want? I left my money on the table."

"I know that ain't true. But I'm not after yer money." He jabbed the narrow back again. "Git."

They arrived at the river's edge, and Buell stepped back.

Weston turned around slowly. "What do you want?" His voice was even, with no sign of panic or fear.

"I want to know how a man can be dealt four of a kind two nights in a row."

"I wasn't dealing."

"I don't need you to tell me that." Buell could feel his anger rising.

"Look, Mister Lacey, I don't look for trouble, and I don't want any here."

"Look or not, you got it. I see cheatin' at the table, and you're the one comin' out with the heavy poke. You tell me what I should think."

Weston stood silent, staring at Buell in the dim light. His gaze dropped to Buell's pistol. "I needed the money."

Buell sniffed derisively. "I damn well knew it. You son of a bitch. I knew it."

"So what're you going to do about it?" Weston's voice was not quite steady.

"How are ya doin' it?"

Weston glanced toward the back of the saloon. "I'm not." He licked his lips.

The metallic crackle as Buell cocked the Remington widened Weston's eyes. "I'll ask ya one more time. How?"

"Quinn's doin' it." Weston blurted the admission.

"Quinn?"

"Uh-huh." The reply came quickly. "He came by the place I play at in Cheyenne. Took me for over five hundred dollars. He was taking my paper since I didn't have the cash. Afterward, he told me I could get it all back and then some if I'd agree to come up here and give him a hand."

"Do you split with him?"

"Not yet. So far he's got it all. I'm supposed to see him tomorrow morning sometime. He gets it then."

"And how does he do it?"

"I don't know, honest. He must mark the cards or something."

Buell shook his head. "Bullshit. I looked at the deck from last night. There's not a mark on 'em. 'Sides that, those are our cards, fresh packs every night."

"He said to wait for three or four face cards to come, and then call and raise. That's what I did."

Another long pause ensued while Buell stared at Weston, and Weston stared at the cocked pistol.

Finally, Buell lowered the hammer and jammed the weapon back in his holster. "You don't want to think about touchin' the Smith you got tucked in your belt."

"I wasn't going to," Weston said, his voice almost a whisper. He swallowed hard. "So, now what?"

"Ain't you I want to settle," Buell said. He took half a step toward Weston. "But you're no longer welcome here. I want you to go back inside, play a few hands, and then leave. When you do, let 'em know you need another trip to the privy, then go find your horse and ride out . . . quietly."

"And that's it?"

"Not quite. You know that little house by the stables?"

"Yeah."

"That's where I live."

"And?"

"That's where I want you to leave the money you stole from that soldier. Throw the poke under the porch. I'll find it."

"Okay."

"You know I'll come lookin' fer ya. Right?"

"I've heard. I'll leave it. And . . . thanks."

"Jist remember, you're not welcome. Now finish your business, and go back inside." Buell turned abruptly and walked quickly toward the saloon.

The next day Buell stood at the bar and waited for Quinn to appear. It was Sunday, usually the quietest day of the week for the saloon. Lori had opened only one dining room, and left the day's business up to the other women. She still suffered from sore ribs, and lifting anything caused her pain. Twiggs had not opened the bar yet, so Buell stood behind it, having served himself a beer. He didn't have to wait long. Quinn came down the stairs, peering anxiously around the room as he did.

"Mornin', Mister Lacey."

"That it is."

"Quiet as a tomb."

"Usual for Sunday. There'll be more here this afternoon and tonight, but the morning is nice. I get tired of the noise."

"I hear that." Quinn glanced at the dining-room entrance. "They open?"

"Just did."

"So, nobody in there yet?"

"Nope. Help yerself. They'll find ya." Buell nodded as one of the women hustled by, a small tray of dishes in her hand.

"Ya haven't seen that youngster we played cards with have ya?"

"Ya mean Weston?"

"Yeah. Was that his name?"

"He's gone."

"Gone!" Quinn said, surprise in his voice. "Hmm, I understood he was gonna be here for at least a week." His tone now seemed to be carefully controlled.

"Nope. Saw him early this morning at the stable," Buell lied. "Said he enjoyed the stay, but had to get back."

"Oh. Too bad. I enjoyed playin' with him. One lucky fella, I can say that."

"Real lucky," Buell said. "Real lucky."

Simon woke Monday morning to Buell getting dressed, unusual for Buell, who rarely got up before nine or so. "Where you off to?" Simon swung his feet out of bed.

"I want to see if Quinn is still here."

"I noticed he didn't play last night. You let Spud out?"

"Yeah, he's off chasin'." Buell sat down on his bed and pulled a boot on.

"And that young fellow from Cheyenne. He was gone too."

"I told him he wasn't welcome." Buell stood.

"You what? Told him? How . . . Buell?"

"I saw 'em cheatin' again Saturday light. When he went out to take a leak, I followed and kinda encouraged him to tell me how they were doin' it."

"It was Weston?"

"This time, yeah. Last year Quinn had another partner. It's Quinn that actually does the cheatin'. He doesn't necessarily have to win. Him and Weston were gonna split what they stole."

A sinking sensation settled in Simon's stomach. "Were?"

"I made Weston give me what he had before he left."

"He rode off, didn't he?"

"He rode off, Simon. Damn! What'd ya think?"

"I've seen ya riled, Buell."

"I want to catch Quinn. Weston kinda got dragged into it."

"Like how?"

"Not important." Buell stood and shook his pants cuff down. "He's gone, and I don't expect we'll see him again."

"So what are you going to do about Quinn? Ya can't just accuse him based on what another cheat says."

"I'm gonna catch him at it. But damn it, I still don't know exactly how he does it. That's why I want to see if he's still here."

"I don't think he's gonna tell you, Buell."

"I know that." Buell snorted in exasperation. "But if I can watch enough, I'll figger it out. He doesn't know I know." Buell grabbed his hat off the dresser and left.

Twiggs glanced up as Buell came through the door. "Mornin', Buell."

"Max." Buell nodded. "Have you seen Quinn?"

"About an hour ago. Didn't even stop for breakfast." Twiggs leaned on the bar.

"Stop? He was leavin'?"

"Yep. Said he needed to get to Cheyenne."

"Did he say he was comin' back?"

"Nope. But I didn't ask either. Did you want to see him for something?"

"He's a card cheat, and I'm gonna catch him at it." Buell's jaw muscles worked furiously.

Twiggs's breath caught in his throat, his gaze fixed on Buell's pistol.

Chapter 20

Wednesday morning, Simon saddled his horse and headed for the fort. He had written a short letter to his folks, and knew he had to get it mailed before he changed his mind. That had happened many times in the past, and today he needed to finish the job. Since Quinn had left, Buell's mood had been stranger than usual. He'd been staying late at the saloon or leaving in the middle of the night and not returning until after Simon had gone to work. And he sensed a change in Lori as well. She didn't seem as friendly and open as before, but the signs were so subtle, he thought he might be imagining them. Feeling a little isolated, Simon had responded to the urge to reach out to home again.

The letter mailed, he tied his horse at the store and went in.

"Hello, Simon," T. P. greeted him from the back of the room.

"Good morning. Lori asked me to get this." Simon sauntered over to counter, and handed him a slip of paper.

The sutler looked at it for a moment. "Yep, I keep that. She's got a dozen women around here cookin' with these strange ingredients, so I have 'em in stock. So, how's things goin' for ya?" He walked over to a cabinet and rummaged through several things inside.

"All right, I guess. Never thought I'd say it, but sometimes I feel—oh, never mind."

T. P. stopped digging around and looked at him. "Feel what?"

"Useless."

"Aw, hell." T. P. chuckled out loud. "Thought it was something serious." He reached deeper into the cabinet. "There they are." He held up two small tins. "That it?"

Simon nodded and reached for his purse.

As Simon stepped out of the store, he nearly ran into Sergeant Barrschott. "Sorry," he said automatically and without looking up.

The man stepped back to allow him past. "Hello, Simon."

"Hello, Adolph. Head in the clouds I guess."

"What brings you to the fort?"

"Matter of fact, you. And some spices for Lori. Got the spices." He held up the fist-sized package.

"And you run into me." The sergeant grinned at him. "What kin I do for ya?"

Simon dug a money pouch out of his pants pocket. "Give this to Private Blaise."

"Ooookay." Barrschott took the pouch, and weighed it in his hand. His eyebrows asked the question.

"Blaise got cheated the other night. Buell got this back for him."

"Uh-ooh."

"No. The guy gave it back, peaceably. We try to run an honest place out there."

"Strange that you should say that." The sergeant looked as his feet, a broad smile on his face.

"What?"

"Might get even more honest. I'm retirin'. My replacement is here, and I've kinda felt around the edges of his, how do I say it . . . tolerance for misplaced supplies."

"And?"

"Appears he has none."

A surge of panic gripped Simon for a second, and then another emotion surfaced that he couldn't quite identify. "So we start payin' full price?"

"Looks like it. I talked to the quartermaster, and he says if he can't count on the new guy, he ain't gonna risk it. I can see his point. That last episode nearly cost me my pension."

"We'll get along." The odd feeling persisted, and so did its mystery. "What made you decide to leave? Thought you were going to stay on for another hitch."

"I've saved the money I need to do what I want to do. Twiggs said he told you about my little problem back East. I want to go sort that out before I'm too old to enjoy it."

The crooked smile on Barrschott's face told Simon the giant looked forward to the fight. "Yeah, I understand. When's your retirement date?"

"Got a little over five weeks. Don't worry. I'll be seein' ya plenty. Best way for a new man to learn the job is to do it, so I'm lettin' 'im."

"Good for you. Come on out anytime."

"I will. I'll give this to Blaise." He shook the pouch. "It's real good of you guys to do that. Most wouldn't."

The sergeant offered Simon a mock salute and went into the store.

It wasn't even mid morning when Simon had finished his business at the fort, and almost automatically turned his horse into Tay's canyon. He rounded the point and immediately felt better when he saw the telltale tinge of blue-gray smoke lingering in the treetops. He urged his horse forward.

"Been a spell, stranger." Tay stood in the doorway, holding a cup.

"I know it. I keep meaning to come over, but—" Simon swung off his horse and whipped the reins around the post. He ducked under the horse's neck and approached the old man. "Got a few minutes to talk?"

"Cow got tits?" Tay grinned at him and nodded at the wood bench.

"Thanks." Simon sighed as he sat.

"So tell me, how ya been. Heard 'bout Lori. That coulda been bad."

"Yeah. I'm really surprised the German bastard survived at all. Buell was madder'n hell."

"For Buell's sake, I'm glad he lived. The US Army ain't somethin' to fool with. They git it in fer ya, there ain't no place ta hide."

"I think they're satisfied. T. P. helped a lot."

"He's a good sort. If'n ya don't have ta buy stuff from 'im, that is."

"Yeah, I was just over there. Got a package in my saddlebags that can't have cost him over a dollar. Cost me four."

"If ya need something bad, you'll go where it is and pay what it costs. Life in gen'ral works like that." Tay winked at him.

Simon shook his head. "How come it is that you seem to know when I'm chewin' on something?"

"Well, ya sure as hell don't come jist ta see me. Easy to figger ya must need somethin'." Tay's soft eyes soothed the sting. "And it ain't my cookin'."

Simon paused for a moment, the words he wanted eluding him. "I come 'cause when I leave here I feel better."

"Man could take that either way, but damned if that ain't one of the nicest things anybody ever told me. Still gonna make ya pay though." Another easy smile softened the rough ground Simon was plowing.

"I felt like I knew where I was goin' when I came back from my mountain trip. Everything seemed so clear. I had a goal."

"And now it's not so clear."

"Exactly."

"Let me tell ya sumpthin'. From a distance a mountaintop is

clear as the dickens, but the closer ya git to it, the harder it is to keep it in sight. That don't mean it ain't still there."

"I don't think I'm any closer than I was last winter."

"I think ya are."

"But the hotel and the headaches that come with it keep getting bigger."

"Last time I looked it was exactly the same size."

"That's not what I—"

"I know what ya mean, son, and I ain't tryin' to make ya seem smaller. I'm jist sayin' ya got ta keep yer perspective. And that's all that's changed. So what ya seein' that I ain't?"

"For one, Lori's different."

"Well, hell yes, she's diff'rent. What'n tarnation did ya expect?"

The same sensation he'd felt when Barrschott had told him the cheap supplies were a thing of the past returned. This time he recognized it immediately—shame. Its weight pushed his head down. "Oh, damn, Tay."

"Yeah, now ya see it. She's dealin' with her own devils 'bout what coulda been. She's the kind of person that can usually put that second to her consideration fer others. Well, this time she can't—too much to deal with."

"And I've been mopin' around 'cause she doesn't want to hear about my problems. Right now I feel like a pile of horseshit."

"Ya ought to." Tay took a sip of coffee and waited.

"Buell's got a burr under his saddle too."

"I'm not sure I kin say much 'bout that. Buell is hard to figger."

"Ya got that right. He caught a man cheatin', and the feller even confessed to it. All he did was make the guy give the money back and leave the ranch. That ain't Buell."

"It is, and it ain't. My guess is the feller didn't challenge him, and Buell got what he wanted."

"I don't know. I wasn't there. Buell told me about it. But, he's been real—I don't know—edgy since then. There's another gambler involved, but he took off."

Tay huffed and put his cup on the bench. "That's the problem. For Buell, anyhow. He feels owed. Same as the Indian thing."

"Ya mean he's after the second man?"

"He's after whoever pissed in the campfire. Buell feels real protective about some people, and some things. I saw right off that he sees that saloon as his home, and he feels real strong about pertectin' it." The old man nodded sagely. "Yep. That's it."

Simon thought about it for a few seconds, then recalled Rankin's abuse of one of the girls. "Of course. Quinn took advantage of what Buell sees as his hospitality."

"That's the way I see it. I could be dead wrong."

"No. I know Buell. He's always been that way. You didn't mess with where he lived, or with his pa. And the fight with Rankin and Barrschott right after we got here. Same thing. They were disrespecting his home. Damn, Tay, it makes so much more sense now."

"If he didn't have such a short fuse, that wouldn't be no problem. But seems he goes off like a busted beaver trap."

"I know he's waitin' for that gambler." Simon bit the inside of his lip. "I just hope nobody else sets him off, and pays for not knowin' that."

"Not a damn thing ya kin do 'bout it. From what you've told me, he doesn't exactly control what he does."

"And that really scares me."

Tay didn't say anything for several seconds, then: "Have ya thought about leavin'?"

"Here?"

"Sure. Jist pack up a few things, and go som'ers else."

"Well . . ." Simon paused as the thought sank in. "No. I haven't."

"Then ya ought'a. Ya don't need much. A mule, a shovel and an ax. Plenty have started with exactly that."

"Naw, I'll work out what's botherin' me. I still like it here."

A smile worked its way across Tay's face. "That's what I want to hear. Man shouldn't be where he ain't happy. They's jist too many other places where he can be."

"Ya got me to thinking, though. Where would you go if you decided to leave here?"

"That's easy, Idaho Territory, or Sitka, Alaska."

"Alaska?"

"Yep. Somethin' about gold that gits me goin'. Never met a man that could look at a nugget in the bottom of a pan, and not want to touch it."

"But you've done that, in the Black Hills."

"Yeah, but I been there. Never been to Alaska."

"And Idaho Territory?" A page from one of his school geography books came to mind. The territory covered a huge expanse, a lot of it mountainous.

"Ain't nobody there yet. I've heard folks talk about the Oregon Trail from jist west of South Pass to Boise City. Plumb awful country. Folks take a look at that, and keep on goin'."

"So why would you want to go there?"

"Cuz Walks Fast says if ya go jist a little north of the Snake River and them lava beds, it's the most beautiful country ya kin imagine. He tells of a patch of mountains that the Indians call the White Clouds, cuz that's what the tops look like. Sounds like my kinda country."

"But I get the sense you're gonna stay here."

"Yep. Got too old, too quick." Sadness flickered across his

eyes. "Don't let that happen to you. Now, I wanna hear 'bout what thet provost had to say to ya."

Lori stepped through the office door and smiled at Simon when he looked up.

"Oh, good," he said. "Let me go get a chair so you can sit beside me." He went into the saloon. "Sit in mine," he offered when he returned.

"Another lesson?" Lori moved around the desk and sat.

"Yep." He lifted the chair over the desk and set it down on Lori's left. "I want to go over this list of suppliers with you, and tell you what you need to know about them. Some you can trust completely, and some you have to watch a little. There aren't any who are actually dishonest. They just won't save you from yourself." Reaching past her, he picked up a folder. The scent he caught made him falter, and he glanced at her to see if she had detected it. She had. "I'm sorry," he muttered nervously. "Didn't mean to reach."

"Simon?" Her arched eyebrow left no options.

"Lavender. It brings back some strong memories."

"Zahn bought it for me. Did your mother wear it?"

Simon didn't answer, but could feel his old nemesis start to color his face.

"Your girlfriend? The one you won't talk about."

"The one I *can't* talk about."

"I guess that's the same thing as far as you're concerned."

"It is."

"Simon, I love you like a brother, and anytime you want to talk about her, I'd be a good listener. I've got my problem settled now, if that's what's stopping you."

"No. I'm best when she's gone, and most of the time she is. Thanks."

"If that's what you want."

"Okay," Simon said and picked up the first sheet of paper. "Alstroms in Cheyenne. He supplies coal oil. He's completely honest and appreciates our ordering regularly. I've never seen his price to be out of line."

Simon reached for the next sheet.

The house he was in appeared huge, and had so many lamps it hurt his wide-open eyes. Sarah must have just been in the room, because her delicate lavender scent floated in the air. He looked around the room to see if she was there and saw that the parlor opened up onto the riverbank—no wall, just open air. There was Sarah, spreading a blanket on the grass. She smiled at him and sat down. Simon closed the book he'd been reading, got out of his chair and went to the shelf to put it away. For the life of him, he couldn't find the place he had taken it from. The bookshelves were now filled with cans, boxes, bags and jars of every description, and it was his task to write all the names down. And Mr. Swartz was watching his every move, making notes on his little ciphering pad.

Suddenly a soldier came in and demanded that all the goods be returned, and for Simon to pay for them immediately. Simon's heart competed with his rapid breathing. He knew all the items were stolen. And then the room filled with smirking faces, accusing eyes and pointing fingers. He looked around frantically for someone to explain his situation to, and saw his mother. She stood at a table, smiling gently, kneading a large batch of dough. Simon felt better as he pulled a chair out and sat, the smell of fresh bread so soothing. She reached over and stroked his sweating brow.

And then he realized he was late for the picnic. With a glance at his mother, he rushed from the sod house and into the prairie. There was no river in sight. Where had it gone? He knew it was at the end of the pasture, but that was gone too. Into the prairie he ran, only to be confronted by large bushes with grasping thorns that caught at his clothes. He fought them savagely, but they finally entangled him so tightly he couldn't move. He collapsed, exhausted. Then came the scent of lavender again, and Sarah called his name. "Simon, help me. Please, help me. Simon, I need you." The desperate sound of her voice ripped at his heart, but fight as he might, he couldn't move. His frustrated rage escaped in a long full-throated scream. "Saaarrrrahhhh!"

"My gawd, Simon. Wake up!" Buell jostled him, and Spud's front paws bore down on his legs. "Yer having a bad dream. Simon?"

The air felt cold on Simon's wet flesh, and he stared dumbly at Buell.

"You all right? Ya scared the hell outta me."

"I—I was caught. Couldn't get out of the brambles. Sarah called."

"Just a dream, Simon." Buell stood and Simon heard the scratch of a match.

In the light, Simon could see his torn-up bed, the blankets mostly piled around his shoulders. He shrugged them off and got to his feet.

"Looks like a boar's nest," Buell said.

"Damn, I haven't had one of those in a long time. Dreamt ol' Swartz was watchin' me count cans again."

"Want to sit up for a bit and talk?"

"Naw. I'll be all right. Let me put this bed back together." Simon started to untangle the blankets.

"Okay. You get the light." Buell climbed back into bed, and turned to face the wall.

Simon made up his bed and sat on it. Spud's concerned eyes mellowed as Simon petted him, and after a couple of minutes both felt the therapy take effect. Man and dog sought sleep again.

★ ★ ★ ★ ★

After breakfast the next morning, Simon went into the kitchen. Lori stood washing dishes, and turned her head as he came in. "You've been quiet this morning."

"Offer still open?"

"About what?" Lori turned around.

"Talkin'."

"Of course."

"You can finish what you're doing. I can wait."

"I'll never finish what I'm doing, Simon." She reached for a towel. "And you came in, so you don't want to wait. Sit down." She pointed at one of the chairs by the table, then sat on another.

"I had a really bad dream last night. So bad it woke Buell up."

"About what?"

Simon looked into her clear gray eyes for several moments, and he bit his trembling lower lip into submission. "Sarah," he said, his voice barely a whisper.

"Ah. The girl." Lori reached across the table, and laid her hand on the back of his.

Simon nodded. The ache in his throat was actually painful, and he swallowed hard to compensate.

"What's her name again?"

"Sarah."

Lori waited while Simon gathered himself.

"I dreamed we were in a fine house, like my aunt Ruth's place back home, and Sarah was outside waiting with a picnic by the river. I could smell her." He paused as the dream started to repeat itself, then swallowed hard and told her the rest. His heart raced as he finished.

Lori squeezed his hand. "I'm sorry, Simon. Those helpless dreams are horrible."

"Do you believe dreams have meaning, Lori?"

"I do. My grandma told me dreams will say things we don't dare."

"I miss her. Oh, how I miss her." He could not stop the misery that ran from the corners of his eyes.

"What happened, Simon? Why are you here and she's somewhere else?"

"I don't know. We were together from the time we started school. Then, one day I was goaded into finally asking her if she'd marry me. I'd tried several times before, but could never get the words to come out."

"Sometimes that's difficult for a man. You fear being turned down. It's something we ladies have to help you overcome." She smiled at him and he appreciated the reassuring warmth of her hand.

"I know that now. But when I asked her, she said no. She just said we were never in love. And I know as sure as there's a God, that she loved me. And I know I loved her."

"Simon, look at me."

He looked up from his hands and into her steady gaze.

"Did you ever go beyond just spoonin'?" The way she tilted her head down asked the real question.

"No," he said, amazed that he felt no embarrassment.

"And neither of you courted anyone else?"

"No."

"And she never gave you a reason other than that?"

"I really don't remember. That afternoon is a complete tangle. I can't see anything but her standing there, seeming to get farther and farther away, yet not moving her feet. Buell and I decided to leave that very day."

Lori wrinkled her brow and leaned forward. "Haven't you written to her?"

"No. And I told my family I didn't want to hear about her. And I haven't, except a reference to her by a friend."

"That's terrible, Simon." She puffed her cheeks. "You have to write. There's more to this."

"What do you mean?"

"I'll be blunt. Could it be she was seeing someone else you didn't know about?"

"Not in a town that size. Everybody knows everything."

"Then, is it possible a man paid her some unwelcome attention?"

"You mean . . . raped her?" Simon whispered the last word.

"I've seen it happen. If it's true, and I pray it's not, she's taking all the blame. She might have seen herself unfit for you."

Simon sat in stunned silence. It might just be, he thought. The memory of her seclusion, even from her own mother, made his head swim. But who?

"I think she's left Carlisle," he finally said. "Our family lawyer mentioned that her father and mother had time for politics now that she was gone. He didn't say anything else, and I don't think he even realized he'd said as much as he had."

"Buell went home. What did he say?"

"I told him to say nothing. So he hasn't."

"Why not? Surely, you realize you need to know. Your dream should tell you that."

Simon groaned. "I don't think I could take another day like that."

"Your dreams will tell you things you don't dare admit, remember?"

"And that's what has me worried, Lori. The dream wasn't just about Sarah."

Chapter 21

Waves of noise rolled off the walls and struck Buell with near physical force. Sergeant Barrschott and nearly thirty soldiers had arrived about three hours before to fill the saloon as full as Buell had ever seen it. So far, there had only been one minor scuffle, taken care of almost immediately by Barrschott. The contingent of soldiers split into two distinct groups, about fifteen clustered around three tables with Barrschott, celebrating the sergeant's upcoming retirement, while the rest sat across the room with a wiry corporal. The corporal's group wore the yellow stripes of the cavalry. Barrschott raised his glass, and tried to attract the attention of one of the harried barmaids. She finally saw him, and headed toward the table.

As she swept past the cavalry corporal, he grabbed her arm. "Get us some more drinks here," he ordered.

She deftly twisted out of his grasp and continued on her way. "I'll get to ya when I'm done there." She indicated Barrschott's table.

"Slut!" The word cut through the hubbub like a fart at a funeral.

Buell had been watching someone near the bar, and he snapped his head around to see who had shouted.

The lanky corporal stood, and waved his empty whiskey glass. "You serve the real troopers before ya serve those rear-echelon sumbitches."

Barrschott's head came up, then he stood and turned around.

A hush settled over the saloon, and Buell glanced at his Sharps, then over at Twiggs. Max hurried toward the center of the bar.

"I hope ya wasn't talkin' 'bout us, Landers," Barrschott said quietly. The sergeant's companions murmured their assent.

"Well, matter a fact, I was." The corporal stood unsteadily, eyes blinking slowly. "Fort sitters are 'sposed t' wait for the fightin' men to git theirs first." His gaze shifted to the barmaid. "So git yer scrawny ass back over here."

"You!" Buell shouted across the room.

Every head in the saloon turned in his direction, and twenty men cleared a path across the floor as though an invisible plow had been pulled through the room.

"Don't start any trouble, corp'ral," Buell said.

The tall soldier looked around at his friends, who were now eyeing Barrschott's table.

Barrschott smiled. "He ain't gonna, Buell. I suspect that yellow stripe on his leg runs up his back."

The whiskey glass flashed through the air, narrowly missing Barrschott's head. The crash as it carried across the room and into the stack of glasses on the back bar brought a gasp from the room. Barrschott crossed the distance to the trooper in four long strides, and tackled him, carrying both onto the table. It collapsed on three seated cavalrymen. A shout came up from Barrschott's men, and they charged headlong into the horse soldiers. The front door banged open and several civilians escaped into the night.

Simon appeared in his office door. "What in hell?"

"Better stay out of it," Buell shouted. "They're drunker'n pigs."

He climbed off his stool, retrieved his Sharps from the steps, and headed into the milling crowd. Simon followed.

Fists flew in every direction, and the grunts of pain and shouts of anger combined to drown out Buell's shouted order to stop fighting. A short, wide-shouldered trooper had hold of a civilian's shirtfront. He had his fist cocked back, ready to slam it into the grimacing face. Buell drove the butt of the carbine hard into the stocky man's kidneys. He collapsed with a groan, dragging the other man down with him.

"Buell, look out!" Simon hollered, and Buell turned to find him.

A man with an insane grin on his face swung a piece of splintered tabletop at Buell's head. Buell ducked, and jammed the muzzle of the carbine deep into the man's ample belly. The civilian's eyes went wide, and a gust of foul-smelling breath whooshed out. Clutching his stomach, he fell to the floor, retching. Buell looked up to find Simon again. He spotted him just as a man landed a balled fist on the side of Simon's head. He collapsed without a sound, and two wrestling men fell over him.

Buell rushed forward and kicked at the two brawlers until they let loose of one another and got off Simon. He glanced around the room. Twiggs stood at the bar with his shotgun resting on top of it, cocked, and leveled at the crowd. Every man in the room fought someone, one-on-one, two-on-one, four men in a heap on the floor, flailing away blindly. Buell cocked his Sharps and pointed it down. The thundering shot had little effect save blasting some splinters into a man's thigh.

Buell reached down and grabbed Simon by his collar. He struggled to drag him to the office in the far corner, stopping twice to beat a person away. He looked at Twiggs again, and saw the grim determination on his face. "Useless," the bartender mouthed, shaking his head. "Go."

The sound of a dog's bark drew his attention, and Buell spotted Spud standing in the office doorway, hackles up, and ears back. Picking his way through smashed furniture, he dragged his unconscious friend into the office, and hiked him into one of the soft chairs. Simon groaned, and his eyes fluttered open for a moment, and then shut again.

"You stay here, Spud. Stay." Buell pointed at the floor, and then walked out, pulling the door closed behind.

He cussed himself for not having another cartridge for his Sharps, and looked toward his high chair. A dozen men blocked the way to his extra ammunition. He sidestepped two, furiously pummeling each other, and went behind the bar. Twiggs stood toward the center, and his two helpers were at the far end, each with a bung mallet in their hands. Buell continued down the bar to Twiggs.

"You check to see if that thing is loaded?" Buell asked, indicating the double-barreled Greener shotgun.

"It's always loaded," Twiggs said grimly.

"That shot in the floor didn't even turn a head."

"It won't either. All we can do is stay behind the bar, and keep them on the other side." Twiggs looked at his helpers. "I told them to smash flat anything that touches the bar."

"So what do we do?"

"They'll run out of steam. But, it's going to be expensive."

A tremendous crash at the right end of the room turned Buell's head just in time to see the stove tip off its perch, and dump cast-iron parts all over the floor. Slowly, as though reluctant to make a mess, the stovepipe came loose from the ceiling, first one joint at the bottom, then two more, and finally the remaining four or five came crashing down. Fluffy soot flew everywhere. One man took the full brunt of a section that hit him on the shoulder and turned him black as a coal lump. The flying particles of chimney filth started to slow the melee. A pair of fist-fighting civilians near the fallen stove suddenly stopped, pointed at each other, and started to laugh. The effect was contagious. Like a cloud's shadow on a still summer day, the calm spread slowly from one side of the room to the other. Men stopped punches in mid swing, and looked around. Those on the floor either stood or sat up, and everybody looked around at the destruction.

Of the ninety-plus chairs that once stood on four legs around the twenty-odd tables, it was hard to find a dozen that would still support a person. Not one table remained standing. Miraculously, not a single coal-oil lamp had been broken, but half the glassware on the back bar lie below on the floor, shattered.

"Adolph!" Twiggs shouted.

Barrschott trudged across the room, a half grin on his face. "I know the drill," he said. "Blaise, Wilkins, you two get the front door. Peterson, Lancaster, you get the back. Move!"

The four soldiers hurried to their assigned posts, and stood facing the crowd.

"All right, you've had your fun," shouted Twiggs. "And now Amos is going to get his furniture back. All you civilians get to the right side of the room. I want you to file past me. You all owe me ten dollars each. Those I recognize and don't have it, can owe me personally. Those of you that I don't know, pay me ten dollars now, cash, or kind. Sergeant Barrschott will deal with you soldiers."

Reluctantly, the brawlers moved to the sooty end of the bar, and formed a rough queue. As they passed the grim bartender, they paid their fine, which Twiggs put in an empty cash box, or in the case of two or three, signed or made their mark on a piece of paper, which he then put in his pocket. Two cowboys had to give up their pistols in lieu of cash. With their restitution made, most walked past the guards at the door and left. A few stayed.

"The saloon is closed," Twiggs said when he had dealt with the last man. "And from the looks of things, it will be for a couple of days."

The rest of the patrons shuffled out the door, including most of the soldiers.

"I'd say the army owes us about three hundred dollars, Adolph," Twiggs said.

The four guards looked at Barrschott.

"You can go," Barrschott said to the troopers. "Tell the rest they better be comin' up with ten dollars each. We don't want the old man knowing about this, or it'll be off limits for a while." He turned to Twiggs. "You'll get it." Barrschott chuckled. "Some party though, don't ya think?"

Simon stood in the office doorway, leaning against the jamb.

Buell saw him. "You gonna be all right?"

"Yeah. Can't hear anything in this ear." He grasped his left one with thumb and forefinger and shook it vigorously.

"I saw the punch," Twiggs said. "You dropped like a sack of spuds."

"Who was it?"

"Doesn't matter, does it?" Buell said.

"No, I guess not." Simon slowly panned the room. "Damn, what a mess. Amos is gonna be mad as hell."

"Not really," Twiggs said. "Happens every few years. Remember that fight you had with them skinners, Adolph?"

"That was a battle. I was stiff for six weeks. Took out both stoves that year . . . and they were lit. Damn lucky we didn't burn the place down." Barrschott laughed, then stopped, and grabbed the side of his jaw. "Ouch, that hurts." He reached into his mouth with two fingers and tugged at a tooth in back. His fingers came out bloody. "They're all still there, but it's gonna be sore."

"Well, I don't like it," Simon said. "And Lori's gonna be furious."

"Lori is furious." The voice came from the stairs. "You're going to help me clean this up." Her arms, folded tightly in indignation and anger, held her long dressing gown snug around her body. "Did they get into the dining rooms?"

"Uh-oh. I haven't looked," Twiggs said. "They're locked aren't they?"

Buell strode around the end of the bar and to the left dining-room door. "Locked. This wall is a little pushed over, but that's all." He jiggled the partition.

Barrschott had walked to the other end, and checked the other room. "Same here."

"Well, you can thank heaven for that. I can't believe you men sometimes." Lori let out an exasperated snort and went back upstairs.

"Don't suppose we could talk ya out of a drink?" Barrschott grinned at Twiggs.

"Why not?" The barkeep turned to survey the wreck on the back bar. "Let's see if I can find an unbroken glass or two in this mess."

Simon looked across the table as Buell finished up the last bite of scrambled eggs. They were in the kitchen, sitting at Lori's worktable, the saloon still a shambles. Amos had returned the next afternoon, and he was, as Twiggs predicted, mildly irritated, but fatalistic. Some of the replacement furniture was already on its way from Cheyenne and Denver, and two carpenters were busy at work salvaging some of the less-battered remains.

"What're you going to do this morning?" Simon asked Buell.

"Thought I'd go target practice a little, then maybe go see Tay fer an hour or so. Why?"

Simon glanced at Lori, who stood quietly by the open back door, looking outside.

"I want to ask you about . . . let's talk some more about your trip home."

Buell tilted his chair back and studied Simon's face. "We already did that."

"I wanna talk to ya 'bout Sarah." Simon's words rushed out.

The chair thumped back to all four legs. "Sarah?"

Simon looked past Buell, and Buell turned to see what drew his attention. Lori gazed steadily back, her eyebrows raised slightly. She nodded.

"Okay. I'm done here," Buell said. "Let's go." He got up, and Simon followed him out through the saloon.

Buell had a place by the river where a bend formed a natural backstop, shaded by trees and shielded from the breezes. The two men tied up their horses and pulled the saddlebags off. Simon hauled his rifle out of the scabbard, and they moved over to a forty-inch downed cottonwood that served as a table for the ammunition. Wide boards stood in the ground at several distances. Each displayed the charcoal outline of a man. The closer one, riddled with bullet holes, portrayed only the head and shoulders. Buell laid out a tin of caps, a powder flask and a pouch of balls for his pistol. Simon did the same with three boxes of cartridges for his rifle.

Buell leaned against the downed tree and gazed upriver. "So, why the change of heart?"

"After my dream the other night, I had a talk with Lori. She made me think about something I've never considered. Maybe between you and me, we can figure it out."

"Are you sure you wanna do this? Sometimes it's better to just let things go."

"That's what I thought, Buell. But if Lori's right, I've done a terrible thing."

Buell shook his head. "So if Lori knows, why ya askin' me? I'll help, sure, but I'm not very good at this woman stuff. You know that."

"Lori doesn't know how we lived. How close our town was. But she sure has a way of figuring things out."

"Well. You gonna ride around it all day, or rope it?" Buell looked down at the ground.

"Lori thinks maybe Sarah was raped."

Buell's head snapped up, and he stared at his friend. "You sure you wanna weed that row?"

"If you know something, Buell, you have to tell me. I know what I said before about you not mentioning her, and I know I've repeated it since. But now it's different."

Buell let a long sigh escape, and he looked past Simon again. A full minute passed with nothing but the sound of flies winging to nowhere, and the soft lap of water at the river's edge. "I'm going to take a real chance here. My horse sense says to keep my mouth shut, but another kinda sense says I owe it to ya."

"I don't understand. What are you chancing?"

"If I tell ya something, I jist know yer gonna hate me." Buell looked directly at him.

Confusion and fear clouded the usual clear gray of Buell's eyes. And there was something else, something he couldn't put his finger on for a moment. And then it struck him—longing. Buell wanted to do this, really wanted to. Then, uncharacteristically, Buell dropped his gaze again.

"I can't imagine that. Me, hate you?"

"I'm counting on that, Simon. But it still scares the shit outta me."

Simon reached his hand out, and grabbed hold of Buell's upper arm. The muscle tensed with the contact. "You're my brother, same as. And I think we ought to talk about whatever you've been holding."

Buell swallowed hard, and then looked up. The gray eyes now held only fear. "I shot David."

The flies fell silent, and the flowing river paused, as the enormity of the admission hit Simon like a giant fist. He jerked his hand back and stared. "You? Mace is married to his mother . . . your mother now. Why? My God, Buell, why?"

"See. I knew it."

The fear in Buell's eyes turned to misery, and Simon saw him shrink, his head drooping. "Good Lord, Buell, why?"

Buell simply stood and shook his head.

"There's gotta be a reason. What is it? How'd ya shoot David?"

Buell turned his back, and stood silent for a bit, then, after taking a deep breath, he turned around. "I waited for him on the Kendrick Road. I was going to tell him to leave Pa alone or else, and to leave your aunt Ruth alone too. I told him we was leaving, but I'd come back if I had to. I guess he thought he could tackle me, cuz he tried, and I whacked him with my pistol . . . twice. He was madder'n hell and went crazy."

"Did he have a gun?"

Silence.

"Well, did he?" Simon shouted.

"No." Now Buell had his head up and he looked at Simon defiantly. "No, he didn't have a gun."

"Gawdammit, Buell. Do you always have to go to extremes? Ya can't shoot a man just 'cause he argues. And you shot him in the back. That's crazy!" Simon found himself rigid with anger.

"Crazy, Simon? Crazy! He raped Sarah. That's why I shot the sonuvabitch! He raped yer girl."

Silence fell on the sandy gallery like a sodden horse blanket, and Simon's legs failed him. He slumped to the ground.

"There, ya satisfied?" Buell's voice hissed in the air.

The anger in it cut through the horror that stormed around in Simon's head. Raped, raped, raped . . . raped Sarah. "Tell me," Simon muttered, his voice hollow in his head.

"When David was on his knees, he was threatening everybody. Pa and me . . . and Sarah."

"Sarah? Threatening? Why? I don't understand."

"He hated her, always had, and said he'd get another look at the red mark on her . . . butt."

"What!" Simon eyes went wide, and then came the sting of tears. With one deep sob, his sorrow turned to fury and he scrambled to his feet. "Noooo!" The scream of outrage filled the quiet grove, and spilled across the water. "The rotten son of a bitch. The dirty bastard. Oh, no." He looked at Buell and saw his grimness. "Did ya kill him good, Buell? Did the filthy beast suffer? Did he feel it?" Simon lashed out at his rifle, leaned against downed tree. He kicked it savagely, and it crashed into the sand. Then, he swept his arm along the top of the log, scattering cartridges everywhere. One more kick at the rifle, and he stopped. With his head down, he put both hands on the big cottonwood log, desperately needing to hang on to something. "Filthy bastard," he muttered. His head swung from side to side, denying what he knew. "You should have told me."

"Ya didn't leave me much room on that, Simon."

Both men stood absorbed in the moment, the quiet belying the turbulence that tore at their souls, each man's storm from a different kind of cloud.

"Did you see her when you were home?" Simon broke the silence.

"She was gone. Went to Philadelphia to teacher's school. Pa said she slowly come back to the regular Sarah, and then she left. Yer aunt Ruth . . . my ma, said she would be gone three, maybe four years. She said Missus Kingsley told her Sarah was doin' real good there, and was staying with cousins."

"Did David actually say he did it?"

"Let it go, Simon. I said enough."

"I have to know, Buell."

Buell returned his adamant stare. "I saw the look on his face, Simon. I know that look."

Simon winced. "I have to ask ya, Buell." He looked directly into his friend's face. "Did you keep it a secret 'cause I asked or 'cause you knew I might stay had I known?"

At first, Simon could not understand the look on Buell's face. Anger flashed to disbelief and back to anger. Simon glanced down at Buell's clenched fists, and then he looked back at his face. Buell's mouth was now set in a grim line, and his eyes conveyed a more familiar emotion. Buell was angry.

"Thanks, Simon," he said with a sneer, and grabbed his saddlebags.

"I'm sorry, Buell, that wasn't fair."

Buell climbed on his horse, and roughly sawed the reins across the Appaloosa's neck. Without another word, he charged up the slope of the bank and was gone.

As though she had been expecting him, Lori plopped the last lump of dough into a bread pan and dusted her hands on her apron. "Let's go where it's a little cooler. Those have to rise for a while," she said, touching the last pan.

Outside, they seated themselves on sections of upsplit logs by the woodpile. The smell of summer, with its soft scent of blossoms and fresh leaves, hung in the still air. Unseen insects hummed with satisfaction as they hurried about their day. The serenity did not extend to Simon.

"I can tell from the look on your face, Buell told you something you didn't know."

"And something I'd never have dreamed about in my worst nightmare. You were right about Sarah." Simon gripped both knees and hung his head.

"Someone forced her?" The question came soft and gentle.

"My cousin . . . David." Simon saw an image of the hulking bully, and he shuddered.

"I'm sorry, Simon." Lori reached across and put her hand on

his shoulder. "At least now you know why she turned from you."

"Do you really think that's the reason?"

"I can't say for sure, of course, but I think maybe she made a great sacrifice."

"But why? I would've understood."

"Would you have? Really? You can't say that, because it didn't happen that way."

"But—"

"She felt she wasn't good enough anymore."

"But she is. She's better than I am . . . she's still Sarah, she's . . ."

"She needs to know, Simon. Those are the things you have to tell *her*, not me. You need to go home. Go home and tell her."

"But she's not there. She's gone to school in Pennsylvania."

"Then write. Tell her in a letter what you feel. And then do what she wants you to do."

"You think?"

"I'm sure. I think it's best for both of you. But this may reopen a terrible wound that has started to heal, so please understand something." Her eyes fixed on his, understanding and sympathetic. "You may not hear what you want."

"Then maybe I shouldn't. I don't want to hurt her."

"She was thinking the same thing, Simon. Don't you see that? And what has it done to you?" Lori's concern furrowed her brow, and she squeezed his arm. "No, she deserves to know. Then you can both go forward with the truth, painful as it is."

Simon sat at his desk, staring at yet another blank sheet of paper, three aborted attempts, crumpled and cast aside, mocked him for his ineptness. Shutting his eyes tight, he concentrated on the words and began again.

Dear Mrs. Kingsley,

I take pen in hand to beg a favor of you . . .

Simon dropped his letter off and considered the trading post for a moment, then thought about Berggren's shop. Mentally, he knew he was in no mood to make good casual company, so he turned his horse across the bridge. Tay's mule brayed his arrival at the hillside dwelling about twenty minutes later.

"Ya home?" he shouted as he dismounted.

No answer came but the rough door was open so Simon poked his head inside. The smell of coffee, old bacon grease, and tobacco smoke soothed his jangled nerves. The place was empty, and he turned to leave. A piercing whistle, sounding much like a mountain marmot, turned his head toward the creek. He spotted Tay, water bucket in hand, trudging up the worn path.

"Hello, friend. Jist in time to do m' dishes."

The familiar grin and warm smile brought a surge of warmth. "Ain't doing anybody's dishes, 'specially yours." He followed Tay into the dugout.

"Well, let's jist leave 'em, then, and see if they somehow get done by their selves." The old man set the tin bucket on a bench.

"Don't suppose ya got a cup of coffee ready?" Simon eyed the speckled pot on the stove.

"Will a Cheyenne buck steal a horse?" Tay picked up his half-empty cup and pitched the cold remains out the door. "Inside or out?" Tay refilled his cup.

"Let's sit outside."

Tay filled another cup, handed it to Simon, then followed him out the door.

"So what's been goin' on with you lately? Ever'thing all right?"

"Pretty good. Got in a scrap with Buell again."

"So, what's new?"

"This time it looks like he's gonna stay mad for a while. He won't hardly look at me."

"Let's hear it." Tay leaned back, and put his cup down.

"Starts with Lori, actually. I had a talk with her about my girl back home."

"Ah, the mystery girl."

"I had a strange dream and needed to talk to someone, and Lori's as good a listener as you are. Sarah, that's her name, she kinda rejected me. Just outta nowhere, she said we weren't gonna be a pair and wouldn't give a reason. Lori said it might have been 'cause she was . . . raped. I made Buell tell me what he knew about it, and turns out it was a whole lot. My cousin David raped Sarah."

"I'm sorry to hear that, Simon, truly sorry. Most terrible thing a man kin do short of killin' kids."

"I wrote Sarah a letter, mailed it just today. I told her I knew David had attacked her, and that it doesn't make any difference to me. If she'll have me, I'm gonna go home."

"Two quick days to Cheyenne, and less than a day east and yer home. Why wait? Sooner ya git something like this settled in yer craw, the sooner you kin crow again."

"She ain't home. She's in school back East."

"Ah, I see. So, ya wait. And this's what's chappin' Buell's ass?"

"No, it's a lot more'n that, I'm afraid. I said something I shouldn't have. Something I felt but didn't stop to think about."

"Sometimes that ain't all bad. What'd ya say?"

"I didn't actually ask Buell about Sarah. David was killed and robbed just before we left home. Shot in the back, and left by the road. Buell admitted he did it. It really took me by surprise. I know it was Buell protectin' himself, but I could see him goadin' David too. Buell's like that. He won't back down, not for an instant. And I told him he was crazy."

"That's a mistake."

"Yeah, I know. That's when he said why he did it . . . David admitted forcing Sarah."

"Still don't see the fork in the trail. Why's Buell got his back up? Ya backed off didn't ya?"

"Not till I said one more stupid thing. I asked him if the only reason he didn't tell me about Sarah was to make sure I left Nebraska with him."

"Damn, Simon, I kin sure see his point. That was plumb sideways."

"Soon's I said it I knew I was wrong. I said so, but he was madder'n hell."

"Ya tol' me a lot 'bout you two growin' up, and knowin' that, it's hard to see how's you could ask such a thing. Mind ya, I wasn't there, but damn, them's some gritty fritters you's expectin' him ta swallow."

"I know it, Tay. And I haven't slept much since then. When I think on one thing, something else comes up. And every time I see a way through, the way gets cut off."

"Well, a gate that don't open is jist more damned fence, Simon. Tell me 'bout this stuff that comes up and maybe we kin see a way out."

"He needed to get out of town. He'd killed a man, and the sheriff was lookin' at him. Doesn't make any difference if it was justified or not. Buell didn't have the best reputation, and I know from experience, he might have been found guilty of plain and simple murder."

"I know, you told me about yer storekeeper and all. Anything else?"

"I think he took a lot of money off my cousin."

"Robbed him?"

"There ya go, I don't know. Did he shoot him for money, or

get the money after, or did he get the money at all? David inherited the same money as I did from our grandpa. His ma said he carried it with him. And I saw Buell take that man's pouch after he shot him by the river on our way here. Can an honest man do that? Do ya see what I mean?"

"I see more than ya think, Simon. Yer wondering if what he might have done is any worse than what you yerself have done since ya got here. Yer wonderin' if maybe you ain't become jist like him."

"Wha—whatcha sayin'?" Simon sputtered, his voice rising.

"Sumpin ya don't want ta hear, seems like. Ya run a whorehouse, Simon. Ya stacked yer storeroom with army supplies. Ya sold watered whiskey, and ya know that Quinn feller is a cheat. Yet ya keep at it."

"I ain't killed nobody." Simon was completely taken aback by Tay's accusations.

"And I don't think ya would. But, yer gittin' uncomfortable in your own skin, and it's causin' you to see things that ain't there. Hellfire, man, Buell's yer friend. Accept that and be damn thankful ya got one like 'im."

Simon didn't answer for quite a while, his mind trying make order of the confusion Tay's words had sown. Tay sat quietly. "Ain't no doubt I owe him an apology," Simon said finally.

"That's the very least. But I don't think I'd say anything jist yet. You have so much as told him the only thing he could really count on, yer friendship, is gittin' shaky. He's feelin' a little exposed right now. Let 'im cool off a little."

"Okay. I was feeling a little surrounded is all. I don't need to do this anymore. The little houses at the ranch have paid me back a lot of money. I'm rich by many standards. You told me once, that if a man gets unhappy, he oughta move on. I can see that now."

"Didn't mean ya should jist run off. There's a big difference.

Leavin' has to be a choice, not a condition. Any other way and you won't think much of yerself later."

Simon shook his head. "Did ya ever think about writing some of that stuff down. You know, like in a journal."

"Naw, ain't nothin' but common sense. If a mule could talk, he'd put us all to shame."

"I don't know, Tay. You sure have a way of putting it all in a neat little bundle."

"And whatcha think makes that bundle neat, Simon? Ya don't put nothin' in there ya don't need. Folks have a habit of packin' too much stuff. And that's what yer startin' to do. Don't pack around the clutter, Simon."

Relaxed for the first time in a week, Simon spent the next hour or so talking with Tay about the country west, the vastness, the purity and the loneliness of the high country.

CHAPTER 22

Buell walked into the office and pushed the door shut. Startled, Simon looked at the scowl on Buell's face and put his pen down. Buell had not ventured into the office since the incident by the river, nearly a month before. Even as contrary as his friend looked, Simon was glad to see him standing there. "Mornin' Buell. Devil after ya?" Simon tried to make his voice sound light and easy.

"I just saw Quinn." Buell folded his lanky body into a chair, his scowl intact.

"So. He's a customer. Not the first time he's been here."

"You know damn well what I mean." Buell's temper flared.

Simon sighed. "I know. Please try to keep a hold of your—"

"The sonuvabitch is a cheat. And I hate cheats."

Simon leaned back in his chair, tired with disappointment. "I don't want to preach, but—"

"Then don't!" Buell sat up straight in his chair and glared.

"But we aren't exactly snow white ourselves," Simon continued. "If Barrschott was still here, we'd be taking everything we could from the army."

"Gawdammit, Simon, it's not the same. He stealin' from us."

"That doesn't make sense, Buell."

"I'm not here to make sense. I'm here to tell you I'm going to play one of these nights, and if I catch the sumbitch cheatin', I'm gonna make him wish he'd stayed in Cheyenne, or wherever the hell he come from this time."

"Don't start something that'll get the army in here, again." Simon regretted the challenge as soon as he made it.

"Don't tell me what to start or not start." Buell stood up. "I don't work for you."

"Amos is going to see it my way."

Buell stared, his eyebrows raised in amazement. "You'd go to Amos?"

"If you're thinkin' what I think you are, yes."

Buell leaned over the desk. "I'm askin' ya not to. Fella like Quinn needs to be taught a lesson."

Simon saw another gate that wouldn't open. "Not your kind, Buell. There's nothin' left to talk about after one of your lessons."

"I'm playin'. You do what you want."

Before he could respond, Buell jerked the door open, and without a backward glance, stormed into the saloon.

Since Buell's threat two days before, work had been drudgery. So far, Quinn had sat in on three games, one in the mid afternoon, and two in the evening. Buell had watched, but not played. Sitting in the office waiting for the sounds of an altercation had frayed Simon's nerves to breaking, so when Amos had stuck his head in the office just before suppertime and invited him to sit in on a game, he'd agreed just for something to do.

It was nearly nine thirty, and Simon shut the ledger he'd been working in, and pulled open the desk drawer. The blue-black Smith and Wesson pistol lying there immediately confused his intentions. After staring at it for a few seconds, he sighed and picked it up. He broke the barrel back to expose five dull-gray .32-caliber bullets. After locking the barrel in place, he dropped the small pistol into the inside breast pocket of his coat. Simon placed the ledger in the drawer, stood, and left his office.

He spotted Twiggs, busy, well down the saloon. Lifting the countertop, he went behind the bar and walked toward the bartender.

Twiggs nodded his head. "Had enough book work for the night?"

"Yeah. Amos asked me to join him for his game. Figgered why not. Been busy?"

"About normal. Lori's just shutting down the dining rooms. That usually slows things up a bit. Is Quinn gonna play with you guys?" Twiggs scanned the saloon. He looked nervous.

"Don't know. Buell's been meaning to sit in one of these nights."

"Buell?" Twiggs glanced toward the tall chair by the stairs.

Simon's gaze followed, and he met eye to eye with the vigilant enforcer. Buell's look was suspicious and cool. Simon nodded and smiled. Buell gave his head a barely perceptible dip and resumed looking over the customers.

"He don't trust Quinn much, does he?"

"Not really. He's convinced he's cheating somehow. I hope to hell he's wrong."

"He wouldn't do anything rash, would he?"

"With Buell, you can almost count on it." Simon spotted Amos coming down the stairs. "There's the boss. Have Molly keep an extra-sharp eye on the table will ya?"

"Okay. And . . . good luck." Twiggs took one more careful look around the saloon before he acknowledged the waving hand of a persistent customer at the far end of the bar.

Just as Simon cleared the end of the bar, Rosie and Saint Louis Bob come through the front door. They steered a direct course to Amos's table.

"Hey, Simon," Rosie greeted. "Amos said you was gonna play tonight. Been a while since we took any of your money."

"And that'll be nice," Bob said, "cuz it'll keep ya from takin' it from me."

Simon looked at the two men, as different in demeanor as two people could be. Rosie, round face wreathed in a permanent smile compared to Bob, long slim face creased with worry lines and a look as serious as a snakebite. Simon felt himself relaxing.

"You in tonight, too, Buell?" Rosie walked around the table to his usual chair.

"Yep. Ain't played cards for weeks. Quinn is back in town, and I want everybody to get a shot at some payback. He got real lucky last time, and took off before anybody got a chance to get even."

"Well, c'mon, then," Amos said as he dragged out a chair. "Let's get 'er goin'."

"I hate shorthanded poker, Amos," Bob complained. "Ya know that. I ain't got no luck at all playin' with four."

"I don't think the number has a damn thing ta do with it, Bob," Rosie said. He pulled out his chair and settled down. "Yer just a lousy cardplayer."

"Who walked out of the last game over fifteen dollars ahead?" Bob scowled at Rosie.

"You did. And how many times a month do ya manage to do that?"

"Well, how many times have you won?"

"Yer dodgin' my question."

"Aw, sit down, Bob. I'm gonna skin ya both tonight," Simon said.

Amos turned in his chair and looked at Buell. "C'mon, ain't nothin' goin' on in here. Git yer tall self down here."

As Buell slid off his chair, Quinn pushed through the screen door and headed for the table.

"Now quit yer whining, Bob, we got six." Rosie punched his friend on the arm.

"Gents," Quinn said. "Looks like I'm the last one in."

"Just settlin' down," Amos said.

Quinn took a seat between Bob and Amos. Buell pulled out the last chair next to Simon.

"Everybody ready to lose?" Simon asked. He looked directly across the table at Quinn.

"Not my intention," the gambler said.

"Well, let's get something to drink before we start," Buell said.

Simon looked around the saloon for the nearest barmaid and spotted Molly, already on her way to the table.

"I see you're paying attention." Amos gave her a wide grin. "Knew you were the smartest of the bunch."

"Smart 'nuff to know who runs this place. What's yer pleasure?" Six orders, and she was on her way to the bar.

Amos picked up a fresh pack of cards and dragged his thumbnail across the seal. Buell's eyes narrowed as Amos extracted and discarded the two jokers from the deck.

"Regular five-card draw." Amos shuffled the cards several times, then put the squared deck in front of Quinn. "Cut?"

Quinn's manicured fingers lifted the top half of the deck and set it on the table. "That'll put what I need on top," he said. He flashed a smile around.

Simon glanced at Buell and saw his jaw muscles twitch. Amos put the bottom stack on top of Quinn's cut, then dealt everybody five cards.

Bob won the first hand, and declined the deal when Amos offered. To everyone's surprise, Bob won the second hand as well. Smiling for the first time since they all sat down, he winked broadly at Rosie. "Now that's how poker's played, ya fat old fart."

"Oh gawd, win two hands and now he's the expert," the teamster replied. "We gonna have to listen to this all night, Amos, or you gonna do us a favor, and kick his ass outta here?"

"Let 'im crow. We'll clip his wings soon enough. Wanna deal, Bob?"

"Hell no, you're doin' fine." Bob chuckled. "Keep 'em coming and I'll have all yer money."

"My gawd!" Buell half shouted. "Can we play cards, or are we gonna sit and jaw all night?"

Amos looked at him and wrinkled his nose. "What'n hell climbed up yer ass?"

"Well, we gonna play or not?" Buell's tone wasn't so sharp, but sounded almost contrite.

"Yeah, we'll play." Amos looked around the table at the silent men. "Keep yer hat pulled down, cuz I ain't gonna deal ya nothin' now." His face lit with a wide smile, eyes sparkling. "Sheesh."

The rest of the table responded in kind, pent-up breaths expelled and shoulders relaxed. Bob picked up half a dozen coins, and stacked them neatly as he leered at Rosie. Amos started dealing the next hand.

Simon's eye caught Buell's, and Simon saw the question. Buell's nod toward Amos was so slight, nobody but Simon would have seen it. Simon, too, glanced at Amos, and shook his head the least bit.

"Good." Buell mouthed the word, and for the first time since the altercation at the river, his eyes were friendly again.

Simon relaxed in his chair, pleased that he hadn't said anything to Amos. He picked up his five cards, and mentally selected two for discard. He won the hand.

The game went on, Bob still winning more than usual, and Buell watching Quinn's every move. Rosie was having a terrible streak of bad luck. Every time he had a half-decent hand, one of the others would edge him out by the slightest margin. He had three sevens, Simon had three nines; Quinn's queen-high straight beat Rosie's ten-high. Simon, feeling loose, started to enjoy the game, the company and the warm, mellow feeling brought on by the French brandy.

Quinn shuffled the cards, a blur, as he loosely held half the deck in one hand and chopped the other half into it. He did this four or five times, then Bob cut the deck. Quinn picked them up and started dealing.

Simon kept his eye on Buell's face through the whole sequence, and suddenly a sick feeling stormed the pit of his stomach. The comfortable ease of the evening vanished.

By the time Quinn had finished dealing, Buell's jaw was set in a hard clench. A couple of minutes later, Bob could hardly sit still. When Amos had failed to open, Buell had, Simon folded a handful of junk and Rosie, Bob and Quinn all called. Amos folded. Everybody got their cards, and Buell bet ten dollars, Rosie called. Bob did likewise and raised twenty-five. Everyone's eyes went to Quinn. He picked up his whiskey glass and took a sip, then called and raised fifty dollars.

Buell stared at Quinn's impassive face, then slowly pushed his cards toward the pot. "Fold," he muttered quietly.

"Sumbitch," Rosie said. "You bastards have done it to me once too often." He counted out seventy-five dollars and picked up the stack.

Simon caught his eye and gave a noncommittal shrug as Rosie's face asked the age-old question.

"Shit!" Rosie dropped the coins back into the small pile in front of him. "Fold," he declared, disgust in his voice.

Bob gave his beleaguered friend a superior smile, and dropped his bet, already counted out, into the pot. Then he picked up two large gold coins and dropped them after. "And forty more."

Simon shook his head. Bob looked as happy as he had ever seen him. Tonight must be the luckiest night of his entire life. Everyone watched Quinn.

"Must be good," the gambler said with a grin. "Forty more, huh?"

"Or you can fold," Bob replied. "I would if I was you." He leaned well back in his chair and laid his clasped hands across his belly.

"Naw, I gotta see 'em." Quinn nonchalantly tossed the two coins into the pot. "All right?"

Bob leaned forward and picked up his cards. Slowly, one at a time, he laid down his cards. "Four beautiful nines. Tonight has been my night." The breath Bob expelled was felt a third of the way around the table.

Simon had a hard time taking his eyes off Bob, but finally, along with everyone else, he turned his attention to Quinn.

The gambler, a ghost of a smile on his lips, picked up his cards.

"If those are four kings, you're a dead sumbitch!" Buell's tipped over chair clattered to the floor. He towered over the table, his face screwed tight in anger.

Simon's groin seized, his entire body reacting with a cold damp chill.

Quinn tried to swallow his emotion as his eyes fastened on Buell's gun hand. "You can't be accusin' me of cheating. I haven't won a decent hand in over four hours." His voice sounded steadier than his face suggested.

"And you ain't lost one either," Buell replied through clenched teeth. "You been waitin' for this one."

"Take it easy," Amos said quietly. He looked up at the angry gunman. "We can easy sort this out."

"Best move yerself, Amos," Buell said. His eyes never left Quinn's face.

"Now look, I ain't cheatin' nobody." Quinn's Adam's apple bobbed once. "But I'll step out of the game if that's what yer wantin'."

"I'm wantin' to see them cards." Buell's voice was now low and steady—and deadly.

"I ain't gonna die over a couple hundred dollars. I'm not gonna touch 'em."

"Then let yer partner do it." Buell's eyes glanced so briefly at Twiggs that Simon almost missed it.

"Partner?" Amos looked at Simon.

Quinn edged his chair back from the table, the legs squalling in protest. As he leaned forward to get his feet under him, his hand shot into his vest.

The flash and roar of Buell's pistol blended with the moan of total despair from Saint Louis Bob. "Aawwwwhhh." His chair went over backward, spilling him into the floor. In a continuing motion, he turned to get on all fours, and scrambled on hands and knees toward the front door. "Oohhhhh gawwwddddd," he wailed, his voice a tremolo of terror.

Rosie sat immobile and speechless, his mouth opening and closing like a fish out of water. Time slowed. Quinn clutched his chest as disbelief mixed with fear rippled across his face. He looked down at the rapidly spreading crimson on his white shirt. His hands tried to contain the edges of the stain, then he gulped as his lungs failed to function. Slowly, as though doing it quite deliberately, he sank back onto his chair. His breath now came as short, desperate gasps, and the color started to drain from his face. He looked again at his chest, now saturated with blood. One hand reached for the table's edge, missed, and he fell forward, smashing his shoulders and head into it. With one final attempt to breathe, a gurgle, he slumped to the floor, his feet tangled in the chair.

Dreamlike, Simon sought Buell's eyes. He was standing, but he couldn't remember getting to his feet. Slowly, Buell turned toward him. A look of finality filled his face, his leveled pistol went down and dropped into the holster. Amos, a puzzled expression on his face, gazed down at the fallen gambler.

Then Simon saw movement behind Buell. His brain slowly recognized Twiggs, moving quickly from the far end of the bar toward the center. He stopped at the beer pumps, and reached under the counter. And then Twiggs had his shotgun. The friendly bartender's easygoing features hardened with grim determination. As the scattergun came up, Simon heard first one hammer, then the other, make the unmistakable sound of being cocked.

Simon returned Twiggs's excited stare, both men looking down opposite ends of the twin barrels. The bartender's eyes blinked rapidly, and a twitch flicked across his face, sweat beads on his forehead betraying his fear. A slight shift, and Simon was once again looking at Buell. His friend's eyes now held a question. Simon answered when he reached into his coat pocket and drew his short pistol. The look on Buell's face changed to dismay, then to disbelief as Simon cocked the piece and pointed it at him. Buell turned his head away while Simon continued to swing past his face. Twiggs's frightened eyes appeared over the sights of the stubby Smith and Wesson. He vaguely heard Buell scream. "No, Simon. Nooooo!" Simon pulled the trigger.

A little tuft of hair flew straight into the air, and Twiggs's eyes went impossibly wide. The mirror behind him shattered as the deadly messenger, its task complete, came to rest in the back bar. Twiggs's eyes rolled up into his head, and he slumped forward, his shoulders caught between the two pump handles. The shotgun clattered to the floor on the other side of the bar, and Simon found himself looking into the dead eyes of the bartender. Twiggs's face remained held up for view by one folded arm, like a trophy animal. A thin trickle of bright blood flowed from the top of his head and down his face.

Simon looked over the saloon. Molly stood in the kitchen door, a white towel held to her face, eyes wide with fear. Half a dozen men peered over tabletops from their ridiculous hiding places. Amos, hands on hips in fatal resignation, stood away from Buell, shaking his head. Rosie, still transfixed and speechless, didn't even blink. The smoke from the two pistol shots hung in the air, mute testimony to mayhem.

"It wasn't loaded," Buell said, his voice leaden.

"What? What's not?" Simon heard Amos say. Buell's face came sharply into focus and Simon studied it. The clear eyes, now sad, looked back.

"I unloaded his shotgun, Simon. Last night. Ya didn't have to shoot."

Tay's words flashed through his head. "You run a whorehouse, Simon." And his own response. "But I ain't killed nobody."

Then the sight of Buell filled his consciousness—the acrid bite of burned gunpowder, odorless; Molly sniffling in her dish towel, unheard; the grotesque display of Twiggs's still body, unseen. Complete defeat twisted Buell's features. Simon felt his friend's soul reach out to him and felt his own recoil in revulsion. A shudder of disgust started in his head and rippled through his body. "I've become you," he said, his voice breaking with emotion. "I'm just like you." The pistol clunked to the floor and Simon slumped onto a chair.

"We're gonna have a hard time explaining this to the army," Amos said.

Buell looked at Amos and then at Simon. "I'll help ya out on that score." Buell said it as though he were simply offering to help unload some supplies.

Horrified, Simon watched Buell deliberately draw the long-barreled Remington, and coolly point it at the gray-white face of the dead bartender. Spellbound, and unable to avert his eyes, Simon watched Twiggs's head erupt just below the hairline. It came apart under the brute force of the .44-caliber slug, and pink and red spattered the broken mirror. Simon's brain did not register the roar of the heavy pistol.

"Aw, gawd," Rosie said. He bolted from his chair and ran for the front door, hand clamped over his mouth.

"Tell the provost I did it," Buell said. His voice carried no emotion. "He'll believe ya." He jammed his pistol into the holster, looked at Simon once, then slowly walked across the saloon and out into the night. Simon could do nothing, but stare at the jagged glass of the smashed mirror, the reflections as scrambled as his thoughts. He found himself marveling at the different colors, newly spread on his polished mahogany back bar.

Chapter 23

Simon felt a hand on his shoulder, then the sound of excited people penetrated the fog that held him spellbound.

"You all right now, Rosie?" he heard Amos say.

"Gawd, what a mess," Rosie replied. "What a terrible mess this is. How's Simon?"

"Ain't said nothin'. Just keeps starin' at the mirror. Ya see Bob?"

"Nope. His horse is gone. Expect he went home."

"Simon? Ya okay?" Amos asked.

Simon felt the hand shake him, and Amos's face drifted into focus, his brow furrowed. "Yeah, I'm okay. I shot Twiggs." He didn't recognize his own voice.

"No, Buell shot Twiggs, Simon," Amos said. "Buell did it. Only thing that makes sense."

"Here, Simon, drink some of this." Lori handed him a half-full glass of brandy. "It'll make you feel better."

Simon took a sip of the heady drink, then looked at the bar—the center of the bar. "Where's Max?"

"We laid him on the floor," Amos said.

Simon peered over the edge of the table and saw a pair of boots, toes-up. The legs disappeared at mid thigh under the green felt top. "He dead?" Simon asked, vacantly.

"Yup. Buell hit 'im right in the heart."

"How can this happen, Amos? I knew Buell was looking to get Quinn. I should have told you."

"I knew it too. Weren't no stoppin' Buell if Quinn decided to try it again. Not yer fault."

"How we gonna sort out that money?" It was Rosie.

"Money? Damn, Rosie." Amos sounded slightly shocked.

"Well, we gotta do somethin' with it. The army shows up, you know what'll happen."

"I suppose yer right. You remember how it went?"

"Yeah. If he was cheatin', everybody gets back to the ante. He *was* cheatin' wasn't he?"

"I ain't looked."

Amos reached across the table for the dead man's cards.

"Sumbitch, four kings and an ace." Amos laid the hand faceup on the table.

"How did Buell know?" Rosie asked. "I didn't see anything wrong."

"I really don't know. Simon? He say anything to you?"

"He thought a marked deck was getting into play. He just didn't know how. But Twiggs?"

"That's a little hard fer me to believe," Amos said. "He's been with me a long time."

"Well, he sure pulled down on Buell," Rosie said, "like he knew he was caught. That has to be the worsest sight a man can see, the nasty end of a twelve-gauge."

"Was Max's shotgun loaded?" Simon glanced towards the bar.

"Wasn't. It is now," replied Amos. "Thought it might be best for the army."

"I can't let this fall on Buell," Simon said. "Where is he?"

"Don't know. But what he said is best. The army is gonna want to know why these men are dead, and everybody but Bob has agreed to what we saw."

"But I shot Twiggs first."

"With what?"

"My pocket gun. It's right . . . where is it?"

"I don't know what yer talkin' about. Twiggs leveled his shotgun at the table. Had he pulled the triggers, he'd have killed more'n one or two. Buell shot him in self-defense. Same with Quinn. His pepperbox is still in his vest pocket, but it was plain as a runny nose he was goin' for it."

"Has the army been told?" Simon asked.

"They should know by now. I sent Fraser over to find Bob, and tell the provost that we've had a deal over here. They'll either tell 'em to wait till mornin, or they'll come right on out. I'm bettin' they'll come right out."

"I thought the shotgun was loaded, Amos. It was always loaded. Twiggs counted on it."

"I know he did, and ya did the right thing. Anybody would have done it. I've never seen Twiggs put it to his shoulder like that. He was serious gonna shoot us."

"But all of us? He would have hit all of us."

"That's what I'm sayin', Simon, ya did what anybody here would of done. Ain't no sense in givin' the army a reason to fix somethin' that can't be fixed. See what I mean?"

"But Buell shouldn't take the blame."

"He's gonna take it for Quinn," Rosie said. "He's already taken it for Rankin. One more ain't gonna hurt his reputation any. That's the cold hard fact of the matter."

"But we know he didn't kill Twiggs."

"And he knows it too. So who's to gain or lose?"

"I don't know if—"

"Ya can't fix Twiggs, Simon." Amos stood up. "Ya shot in self-defense. Ain't nobody here will dispute that. But you ain't never been involved in no shooting before, and ya don't need to be branded like a shooter. When Buell gets back, he'll tell you the same thing. I know what he said, and he's right. The army will believe he did it, and ain't no reason we should try to change their minds."

Lori walked up to the table.

"You can go upstairs again if ya want, Lori," Amos said. "You weren't here when any of this happened. Ain't no sense in the army botherin' you. I'm gonna go take a look in Twiggs's room, 'fore they get here."

"You'll find what you're lookin' for in the kitchen," Lori said.

"What I'm lookin' for?"

"Come on." Lori cocked her head and gave him a half frown.

"Yer right. I know he kept an account book of his take from the bar, and there has to be something about where he banked his money, too."

"He hid it in my kitchen. The sugar bin has a false bottom. Turn it around and . . . Never mind. I'll show you."

"How'd you know about it?"

"Only a man would try to hide something in a woman's kitchen or her bedroom."

Lori and Amos soon returned with two small books. Amos handed one to Simon. "Here, see if you can make sense of that."

Simon looked at the meticulous rows of entries filling the pages. Totals for bar receipts with a corresponding value representing six percent. Dollar amounts followed by names and dates. Larger amounts followed by the word "Deposit" and a date. All with running totals. Simon turned to the last entry.

56.00 Quinn July 9 488.75

"Look at this, Amos." Simon handed him the book. "He was taking money from gamblers."

Amos looked up and down the columns for several minutes. "He was making deposits to Taylor's Bank in Omaha every four or five months. Good Lord, Simon, he has thousands listed here."

"What's the other book?"

"A diary, this year. Wonder if this is the only one? Can't imagine so."

"You shouldn't read that," Lori said. "Really."

Amos studied her for a moment, then opened the first page. "Says here in the front, 'In case of my demise, please forward to Percival H. Paine, Attorney at Law, Philadelphia. Substantial reward offered for this kind service.' "

"You know anything about that, Simon?"

"A little. Did you know that he had gone to West Point?"

"Twiggs? I knew he was educated, but military? He don't . . . didn't have much use for the military."

"Yep, and there's a reason. Got railroaded out. He was looking to clear his name. I think that's what the lawyer's for."

"What do ya think's in here?" Amos waved the book.

"Hard to tell."

"It's private, Amos," Lori said quietly. "I know he wasn't exactly honest, but that is very personal."

"Might be something in here that could get us in hot water," Amos said.

"Then burn it," Lori said firmly. "And any others we find."

"What do ya think, Simon?"

"I'm not sure I should have an opinion on anything moral. You do what you want." Lori's look of disapproval stung.

"And what about his good name?" Amos looked at Lori.

"I'm afraid that's already been burned," she said.

An hour later, Captain Van Dyke strode stiffly across the floor, back so straight it must have been uncomfortable. "I warned you, McCaffrey." He barely glanced at the corpse of the gambler.

"We've left things pretty much as they were, Captain. Every witness is here except three, unless Fraser and Bob Pulver come back with you."

"They did. Who else is missing?"

"Buell Lacey or Mace."

"Which?"

"He uses both names."

"His kind usually do." He spoke now with a sneer. "I guess we can start with the obvious. Who shot these men?" He glanced around. "I was told there were two. Where's the other one?"

"Behind the bar. It's Twiggs, my barman."

"Again. Who . . . shot . . . them?" He bit off each word and spit it at Amos.

Amos flushed. "Buell, but—"

"As if there was any doubt." A look of sheer glee swarmed over Van Dyke's face.

"And where is Mister Mace Lacey?"

"Out." Amos said curtly.

"A little more precise if you please."

"He rode off," Simon said. "He does that. He'll be back."

"Ah, Mister Steele. My guess is, only if we drag him back."

"No reason for him to run. Twelve men witnessed what happened."

"Does that count Twiggs . . . and this one?" He pointed at Quinn.

Amos flushed again. "Now look here, Captain. It was self-defense. This gambler and Twiggs were in a cheatin' deal together. We caught 'em, and when they went fer their guns, Buell shot. That's what he was paid to do."

"And how many of these witnesses are what you might call 'regular' customers?" His double meaning came across clearly.

"Regular does not mean dishonest, Captain," Simon said.

"Your opinion, Mister Steele." Van Dyke turned to the door and shouted. "Sergeant!"

Simon recognized the soldier who came through the door.

"Yes, sir."

"Take the names of everyone in here, and also get a location where they can be found later should I see the need."

"Yes, sir."

"Do you know this man, McCaffrey?" The captain stepped over to Quinn.

"Only his name. He registered saying he was from Cheyenne. That was this time. He registered before as being from Omaha and New Orleans. He's a gambler; that's all I know."

"Have you searched his body?"

"I have not."

The captain knelt beside the dead man and quickly found his wallet and a purse, a pistol in a hideout holster under his vest, and another in a holster in his boot top, along with a dirk knife. Opening the wallet, he thumbed through what appeared to be several bills and various pieces of paper. The purse contained a considerable amount in gold and silver coins. "He was sitting where he fell?"

"Yup."

"And the money on the table is his?"

"All of it. Everybody else got theirs."

The captain started to say something, then shut his mouth. He took a linen bag out of his blouse pocket, and dropped the weapons and the money into it. "I'll see this is disposed of properly. You did know Twiggs well though, didn't you?"

"Yes. He's worked for me almost from the start. He's from Philadelphia. I even have an address of some of his kin."

Van Dyke walked around the end of the bar, then down it to where Twiggs lay stretched out on the floor. "Good Gawd," he gasped, and turned to look at Amos. "What was he shot with?"

"Buell shoots a Remington forty-four, and he's very good with it."

The captain stooped down, and almost immediately rose again. "There's nothing on his person. Because you know him,

I am going to charge you with burying him, and sending his effects to his family. Do you have any objections?"

"No. I can do that."

"Very well." The captain glanced down, and with a grimace, came around the end of the bar. "Make sure the sergeant gets your names on his list. I'll decide if an inquest is needed, and if so, you'll be called to attend. At the very least, I will want to see Mister Mace. You will inform him of such as soon as he makes his presence known. Am I clear on that?"

"I'll tell him, Captain," Amos said.

"Sergeant, put this man on the wagon and take him to the morgue. I'm leaving."

"Yes, sir."

With a final curt nod to Lori, he wheeled around and left.

CHAPTER 24

Buell did not return the next day or the next. Simon hired four women from the civilian community at the fort to clean the bar, and by noon of the second day, everything was more or less back in order. One of Twiggs's regular helpers, Seth Martindale, jumped at the chance to be head barman. Simon went into the saloon about two o'clock in the afternoon.

Amos came into the office a few minutes later. "Haven't heard a word from the army," he said, settling into a soft chair. "I was hopin' Van Dyke would see the obvious, and it looks like he has."

"They're not known for quick decisions," Simon said. "I still expect we'll have to face him."

"Buell showed yet?"

"Nope."

"Don't want to press, but have ya looked at his stuff?"

"Like his clothes and things?"

"Yeah. How about his saddlebags? Still there?"

"I haven't looked. I'm a little afraid to."

"Ya should. If he's gone, it's best if we know."

"I don't want to think he'd just leave."

"Me, either, but I think ya should look." Amos got out of the chair. "Just a suggestion." He left the office.

"You've missed him, too, haven't you, Spud? Should we go see?"

The dog stood up at the word "go" and wagged his tail. Simon headed out of the saloon.

Opening the wardrobe, Simon confirmed what he had hoped would not be true. Buell's two extra shirts and his slicker were missing. Simon opened the bottom drawer—empty. He checked the top drawer of the dresser for the half dozen letters that Buell kept there. All gone—like Buell.

A feeling of abysmal emptiness came over him and his chest felt light. An unfamiliar pulsing sensation surged through his head. In a daze, he went into the front room, and sat by the little table. Spud lay down and put his muzzle across Simon's foot. Simon fought in vain to contain the sobs that welled up out of his empty soul, and he cried like he hadn't since he was a boy, head down on his arms.

"He's gone, isn't he?" The words were spoken quietly and gently. Lori.

"I knew it that night." Simon could not bear to lift his head and face her. He sniffed his nose.

"I understand what you feel, Simon. I left my two sisters when I came here. I thought I would bust. Can you take comfort that he went because he thought it best?"

Simon raised his head and looked at her through blurry eyes. "I drove him away. I've never appreciated him for what he was until now. Tay must've told me that a dozen times, and I wouldn't listen. Now he's gone. Where?"

"I don't know, Simon. We don't know if he's gone for good either. He just may have needed to be alone for a while. Just like you were doing here."

"No. I've got a bad feeling. He's gone, and he isn't comin' back. He took the letters he got from his pa."

"I don't know what to say. I'm sorry."

Simon said nothing for several minutes, then: "Do you think

you could run this place for Amos?"

"You mean do your job?" Lori sounded surprised.

"Yeah. I've showed ya everything, and I've got good books set up."

"I suppose I could, but you don't have to leave. You still have lots of friends here, people who care what happens to you."

"No, Lori. It's a bad place now. I expect to hear about Sarah soon, and I just want to go back and live a normal life. I feel lost."

"If that's what you want, sure, we can talk to Amos. I'll do what I can." She put her hand on his and squeezed. "I never thought this would happen." She got out of the chair and quietly left.

Simon could not concentrate on work that evening, so as soon as it looked like Martindale had the bar under control, he went back to the loneliness of the little house. There he sat in the easy chair and did absolutely nothing. He was asleep in it the next morning when Amos banged on the door. Spud scrambled to his feet, hackles raised.

"Simon, you up?" He rattled the door again. "Simon!"

The dog barked once, then settled into a low menacing growl.

"Spud, be quiet." Simon winced as his crooked neck punished him. "Yeah, I'm here." He stood. "Come on in."

Amos rushed through the door. "Got a letter for ya, from Philadelphia." He could hardly contain his excitement as he offered the pale brown envelope.

Simon almost snatched the letter from his hand. "You go to the fort already this morning?"

"Yeah. Nothing else to do, so I thought I'd go check." The lie was blatant.

"Thanks, Amos. Uh . . . I'd like to—"

"Sure, I know. I'll see ya a little later for breakfast then."

Amos gave him another wide grin and left.

Simon sat back down. He stared at the buff envelope, Sarah's handwriting painfully familiar. His hand shook as he read his address, and then, turning the letter over, hers on the back. He dug his pocketknife out, carefully slit the top, and removed the single sheet of paper. He unfolded it and began to read.

July 14, 1872

Dear Simon,

I take pen in hand with some trepidation. I knew one day your letter would come, and I have thought often about what I would do. Even now, I can feel the panic. I am in school studying to be a teacher. It is so satisfying. I know now what Miss Everett felt. I so look forward to a room full of my own students. I have come to terms with what happened in the past, and I am much relieved that you know the truth. At times it seems so long ago and faded, yet at other times, some of the memories are very fresh and still very much alive. Please understand that I am happy, both with my life and with what I am doing. If you wish me happiness, wish me success here.

Sometimes I weep when I think of what could have been.

Simon could read no further. His eyes blurred with tears as a sob welled up suddenly and escaped. First Buell, and now this. He couldn't stand it.

Mental defenses charged to the fore, surging ahead to protect his innermost being. His mind screamed denial: forbid the light of truth a safe haven in which to shine, take that which you know to be real, and bend it to fit the form as you need it to be.

But truth is a resilient creature, and does not die easily. Back and forth, over the ravaged ground of his wounded soul, the keepers of his sanity stomped on the final flickering embers. With the indignation of the wronged appeased, a wave of self-pity swept clear the remains of verity vanquished. Simon wallowed in the soothing embrace of vindication.

"What's the use?" he muttered to himself, and raised the letter again.

> Sometimes I weep when I think of what could have been. The beauty of our time together comes clear in my dreams, and I wish for things that seem denied. For now, dear Simon, you must leave us as we are, knowing some things cannot be changed except with time. And knowing those things to be true, I pray you understand why I cry.
>
> Sarah

Simon refolded the letter, and carefully put it back in the envelope. He dropped it on the table, then grabbed his hat and headed for the stables.

Tay appeared in the doorway and stepped into the bright light of late morning. "Git down, son. I been expectin' ya."

Simon got off his horse, and Tay led the animal to the shade by the corral. Simon sat on the familiar bench and waited.

"From the look on yer face, I'd say yer biscuit landed jam-side down." Tay sat beside him.

"Sarah wrote."

"And ya didn't hear what ya wanted?"

"She wants to stay there, and says if I want to make her happy, to leave her alone."

"Them's the words?"

"More or less. Nothin's changed."

"I'm more used to workin' with mules and other fellers, so I haven't studied much on the ladies. What I do know fer some certain is, womenfolk have reasons that reason can't make no sense of. I want ya to think on that next time ya read that letter . . . and you will."

"Like I said, nothin' has changed for me and Sarah." Simon paused for a bit. "Do ya think Buell will come back?"

"Nope. Fairly certain of it."

"Why do you say that?"

"Cuz he said so."

"You seen him? Since?"

"He came by in the middle of the night. Told me what happened, and wanted to know a little bit about the Dakotas. Stayed about an hour, then he and that Appaloosa took off again. Tol' me he'd stay in touch."

"Where in the Dakotas?"

"Didn't say exactly. Big place."

"Did he say when he'd write or something?"

"Simon, he wanted to get lost. I figger he's done jist that."

"I want so bad to tell him I'm sorry."

"Don't know if he'd accept that or not. What ya said to 'im cut him deep. I'm not so sure what ya have ta say about it would make a diff'rence right now. He knows how ya felt. Said so. Said he could always hide behind something in his head, and you ain't got something like that. He said he wasn't sure who the lucky one was. I know that ain't what ya wanted to hear, but the truth will never choke ya to death like a lie will."

"You told me once that if I got to the place where I was unhappy, I should leave."

"Yep. Still think that."

"Then, I'm gonna. When I thought I was goin' home, I asked Lori if she would run the place for Amos. Only difference is, I'm going west instead of east."

"Idaho?"

"I think so. I'm gonna ask Walks Fast about those mountains you mentioned." Simon touched the rough log wall behind him. "I've looked over this place real good several times. I think I could build one like it."

"I'm sure ya could. I believe a man with a mule, an ax and a shovel kin purdy much land anywhere and make it. I'd add some more to that short list, but keep to the basics and you can move quick and quiet. Ya think you kin pack a mule like I showed ya?"

"I'm sure of it. Pack his back like someone was packing my own, right?"

"Ya got it. Nothin' as irritatin' as an unhappy mule. Make yer life sheer hell. But keep 'em fed and dry, and he'll outlast five horses."

"Will ya help me find what I need?"

"Nope. Best git where yer goin' as fast as ya can. That means takin' the railroad to Salt Lake. Buy yer mule there. And all the other stuff ya need, like a saw, and some candles and somethin' to cook with. I'll help ya make a list. Take a good look at Sonuvabitch over there. Find a mule like him. Short, straight back and good solid-lookin' chest. And look for the one that follows ya ever'where with his ears. Shows he cares what's goin' on. One like that will save yer hide one day." Tay stood up. "Come on in, Simon. We'll make that list fer ya, and we kin jaw a little more. Got a feelin' it'll have ta last me a while."

Simon did not miss the glassy sheen of the old man's eyes as he beckoned for Simon to follow.

A couple of hours later, Simon rode between the tepees of Walks Fast's small village. He noticed that the Indians turned their heads as he moved past. He stopped in front of Walks Fast's lodge, puzzled, and waited.

Soon the old Indian emerged, and held back the flap. "Welcome, Simon."

"Hello, Walks Fast," he said as he got off. He turned to look again at a couple of women in front of the next tepee. They looked away.

"They don't want the bad spirits you carry."

Simon turned to see Walks Fast looking at him.

"They know about the shooting?"

"Not the shooting they worry about. Village know Shoots Fast has gone. They know he feels pain, and they know Simon put the pain there. Come in. We'll talk."

Simon stepped through the opening and into an empty tepee. He waited until Walks Fast pointed to a spot before he sat. The old Shoshoni sat nearby, and both waited for a few minutes before Simon spoke. "I'm leaving here. I've decided to go into the mountains of your old home."

"Taylor told you of the White Cloud Mountains. I know of many reasons why you want to go, but I don't know which reason makes you go now."

"Buell isn't coming back."

"I know. I saw his spirit last night. He is safe."

"Do you know why he left?"

"I will miss Buell, and I will miss him if I know his reason or not. His spirit was not happy, and it's better for him if he is not here."

Simon took a deep breath. "I killed a man, and it wasn't necessary. And when I did it, I think I lost something I can never get back."

"I was told you saw danger." Walks Fast's brow furrowed. "It is bad that a man was killed, but he decided that, not you or Buell."

"Buell tried to stop me, but it was too late. In that moment I realized I was like him, and I said so. I insulted him. Real bad. I wish I could tell him I didn't mean to."

"Hard words are like the sting of a wasp. You can make him fly away, but the sting will not. Buell will know you did not mean to hurt, because he is your friend. But now he feels pain, and he needs time for the pain to go away. Why does Simon not go home?"

"I got a letter. The woman I want does not want me."

"Sarah."

Simon was taken aback. "You know her name. Did Buell tell you?"

The Indian smiled sadly. "Her spirit is strong, but now it is two. A heart can beat only for one, so now the two spirits fight for her heart. I don't know which one will win. One of the spirits wants Simon to be near."

"How do you see these things? I dream too, but none of it makes any sense."

"White man's talk made no sense to me when I heard it for the first time. I learned your ways by living your ways. It's the same with dream walking. A white man is in a hurry to leave the dream. Stay in the dream longer, and you will soon learn what it says."

Simon recalled the dream he'd had on his trip into the hills. What Walks Fast said almost made sense. But how can a person dream when interruptions disrupt them, or when one dream contradicts another? "Will you tell me where the White Clouds are?"

"I will make you a map. They are not hard to find. Good Indians live in the mountains there. They are sheep hunters, and are of my people a long time before. You won't find them, so don't look. They are in the high meadows in summer, and when the snows come, they move to the low valleys, to places that are hard to see. You would make friends if you leave a knife, or a hatchet for them. The Sheepeaters will find you."

Again the isolation of the mountains came to him, the exposure he'd be subject to. "Do you think I can live there?"

"It's not going to be easy. The map will show where the earth stays warm all winter. Hot water comes from the mountainside.

It smells bad, so your nose will find it for you. It's a good place for your horses. Build a strong house in case the big bears smell you. Be quiet there, and take time to listen. You can learn much."

"Am I doing the right thing?"

"You will know truth when you see it. That is all I know."

"Will you stay here?"

"This is where Walks Fast will die. I must tell you one more thing. Listen well. A bad spirit will go with you, maybe even get there before you. It will hunt you always, and one day you will kill it or it will take you. Fight hard and know you are strong. Now, Simon, go. Do not wait."

"You mean now, today?"

The Indian leaned forward, and placed the flat of his hand on Simon's chest. "Do not see night shadows here tomorrow. You must go now, or you will die here like me."

A surge of heat entered Simon's body and settled in his chest as he looked down at the wrinkled brown hand. When Walks Fast withdrew it, Simon looked into his eyes and saw what he thought was a look of deep satisfaction. Then Walks Fast closed his eyes, and started a low hum that grew in volume as Simon got up and left. Several Indians stood outside the tepee, watching and nodding their heads. A few wore friendly smiles as he mounted and rode away.

Amos and Lori watched as Simon undid the strap on his saddlebag. Amos handed him an envelope. "Here's a letter of credit for four thousand dollars, drawn on the Mercantile Bank in Cheyenne. They know me, so you won't have any trouble. I'd be more'n happy to give it all to ya."

"I don't need it, Amos." Simon pushed the letter into the bag and strapped it up again. "That's more than enough. I'll be back one day, and we can settle up. You know what to do if you hear something different."

"Yeah."

"Lori, enjoy your new house. I left it nice and clean for you and Zahn. Maybe when he gets back from the hills, he can find something here to keep him busy." Simon nodded at Amos. "Ya think?"

"Maybe so. We'll look at it."

"Will you try to keep in touch, Simon?" Lori asked. "I'm gonna miss you something terrible. I just know it."

"Can't promise. I've got a lot of soul-searching to do. You folks won't be forgotten, I can tell ya that." Simon stepped up on the porch. "Give me a hug, Lori." He wrapped his arms around her and held tight for a few seconds. "You're a real sweetheart, and I love you."

"I love you too, Simon. Be careful wherever you go. We'll wait to hear." With eyes brimming, she let her hand slide down his arm, and then raised it to cover her mouth before hurrying into the saloon.

Amos stuck out his hand. "You've been a real good partner. Best one I've ever had."

Simon took his hand and gripped it firmly. "I can say the same, Amos. I'll always appreciate you giving Buell and me a chance. So long."

He climbed on his horse and whistled. "C'mon, Spud."

"Ya take care now."

Simon kicked his horse into an easy lope and was soon across the river and making his way up the gentle slope to the ridge above Fort Laramie. Beyond lay the Chugwater and Cheyenne, Salt Lake City, Fort Hall, and the White Cloud Mountains. Simon could already taste the freedom.

ABOUT THE AUTHOR

Wallace J. Swenson was born and raised in a small rural town in southeast Idaho. From the very beginning, he lived a life of hard work supported by a strong family. He was taught by example the value of honesty and loyalty, and it is about such that he wrote. His family numbered ten, and though poor in a material sense, he considered himself blessed beyond measure in the spiritual. He resided with his wife of fifty-plus years, Jacquelyn, near where both were born, and close to all their children and grandchildren. He intended to live there the rest of his life and spend that time putting down on paper the dozens of stories that whirled around inside his head. He did just that. Wallace J. Swenson died suddenly in February of 2015. He left a literary legacy of which this book is a small part.